AROUND THE WORLD
IN EIGHTY DAYS

JULES VERNE was born in Nantes in 1828, the eldest of five children of a prosperous family claiming French, Breton, and Scottish ancestry. His early years were happy apart from an unfulfilled passion for his cousin Caroline. Literature always attracted him and while taking a law degree in Paris he wrote a number of plays. His first book, about a journey to Scotland, was not published during his lifetime. However, in 1862, *Five Weeks in a Balloon* was accepted by the publisher Hetzel, becoming an immediate success. It was followed by *Journey to the Centre of the Earth*, *Twenty Thousand Leagues under the Seas*, *Around the World in Eighty Days*, and sixty other novels, covering the whole world (and below and beyond). Verne himself travelled over three continents, before suddenly selling his yacht in 1886. Eight of the books appeared after his death in 1905—although they were in fact written partly by his son, Michel.

WILLIAM BUTCHER was formerly Head of the Language Centre at the Hong Kong Technical College. He has studied at Warwick, Lancaster, London, and the École Normale Supérieure, and has taught languages and pure mathematics in Malaysia, France, and Britain. His books include *Mississippi Madness* (1990), *Verne's Journey to the Centre of the Self* (1990), and critical editions of Verne's *Humbug* (1991), *Backwards to Britain* (1992), and *Journey to the Centre of the Earth* (1992) and *Twenty Thousand Leagues under the Seas* for Oxford World's Classics. Dr Butcher is at present working on a book on natural language processing.

OXFORD WORLD'S CLASSICS

*For almost 100 years Oxford World's Classics have brought
readers closer to the world's great literature. Now with over 700
titles—from the 4,000-year-old myths of Mesopotamia to the
twentieth century's greatest novels—the series makes available
lesser-known as well as celebrated writing.*

*The pocket-sized hardbacks of the early years contained
introductions by Virginia Woolf, T. S. Eliot, Graham Greene,
and other literary figures which enriched the experience of reading.
Today the series is recognized for its fine scholarship and
reliability in texts that span world literature, drama and poetry,
religion, philosophy and politics. Each edition includes perceptive
commentary and essential background information to meet the
changing needs of readers.*

OXFORD WORLD'S CLASSICS

JULES VERNE

The Extraordinary Journeys

Around the World in Eighty Days

Translated with an Introduction and Notes by
WILLIAM BUTCHER

OXFORD
UNIVERSITY PRESS

OXFORD
UNIVERSITY PRESS

Great Clarendon Street, Oxford OX2 6DP

Oxford University Press is a department of the University of Oxford.
It furthers the University's objective of excellence in research, scholarship,
and education by publishing worldwide in

Oxford New York

Athens Auckland Bangkok Bogotá Buenos Aires Calcutta
Cape Town Chennai Dar es Salaam Delhi Florence Hong Kong Istanbul
Karachi Kuala Lumpur Madrid Melbourne Mexico City Mumbai
Nairobi Paris São Paulo Singapore Taipei Tokyo Toronto Warsaw

with associated companies in Berlin Ibadan

Oxford is a registered trade mark of Oxford University Press
in the UK and in certain other countries

Published in the United States
by Oxford University Press Inc., New York

First published as a World's Classics paperback 1995
Reissued as an Oxford World's Classics paperback 1999

British Library Cataloguing in Publication Data

Data available

Library of Congress Cataloging in Publication Data
Verne, Jules, 1828–1905.
[Tour du monde en quatre-vingts jours. English.]
Around the world in eighty days: the extraordinary journeys /
Jules Verne; translated with an introduction and notes by William Butcher.
p. cm.—(Oxford world's classics)
Includes bibliographical references.
1. Voyages around the world—Fiction. I. Butcher, William, 1951.
II. Title. III. Title: Around the world in 80 days. IV. Series.
PQ2469.T7E5 1995 843'.8—dc20 94–18385

ISBN 0–19–283778–8

3 5 7 9 10 8 6 4

Printed in Great Britain by
Cox & Wyman Ltd.
Reading, Berkshire

CONTENTS

INTRODUCTION

'There are two beings inside us: me and the other'

(*The Green Ray*, 1882)

Around the World in Eighty Days occupies a key position in Jules Verne's series of *Extraordinary Journeys*. By 1872 his heroes have penetrated the heart of Africa, conquered the Pole, urgently plumbed the ocean's and Earth's depths, and even headed breezily for the moon. Now they have only one task left: that of summing up the whole travelling business, encompassing the entire globe in one last extravagant fling. Under its gay abandon, then, *Around the World* is streaked with the melancholy of transitoriness. Henceforth, there can be no virgin territory and no deflowering heroes—just glorified tourists.

Verne's reputation as a novelist is still under attack. What may appear at first sight as uncraftedness in *Journey to the Centre of the Earth*, *Twenty Thousand Leagues under the Seas*, or *From the Earth to the Moon* has been taken as almost childish naïvety by generations of readers. In Britain and America especially, the 'translations' have generally been atrocious, further fuelling the myth of Jules Verne as an un-novelist and often unperson. But his simple style conceals in reality considerable complexity and sophistication.

Nor is Verne's reputation for optimistic anticipation at all justified. *Around the World in Eighty Days* contains not a glimmer of science fiction; and very few of the other works contain any radically new technology. Even the early works display self-doubting and nihilistic tendencies; in the intermediate period, there appear opposing views on the characters' motives, the events reported, and even the narration itself; and these will eventually grow into mordant and distant pastiches that will attack the previous novels and undermine the series' whole being.

The transitional novel *Around the World* appears therefore all the more important. It has always been a favourite in the

English-speaking world, perhaps because of the nationality of the central figure. But its joyous tone and surface positivism are in reality subverted by a tendency for any authority to be mocked and for parts of the story to prove extremely unreliable. The work is also significant in its use of new conceptions of psychology.

Any explicit philosophizing is, however, abhorrent to Verne's pragmatic mind. There exists a distinctive Vernian metaphysic: the absence of metaphysics. Some critics have attempted to establish a coherent ideology or other theoretical construct from their readings of Verne's works. But these studies have generally been one-sided, for they have usually neglected the form for the content—consequently missing Verne's irony and ambivalence. Other commentators have claimed that real events do not impinge on the works, that the author only feels happy thousands of miles from reality, lost in some unmarked icefield or underwater labyrinth. The truth lies in fact somewhere in between: the amount of contemporary reference and implicit ideology in *Around the World*, especially, is quite staggering. But the real-world referents are merely an entry into the Vernian scheme of things. His abiding interest is man's position in the cosmos—making him one of the last of the universal humanists.

Again, Verne's technique is often amazing. The very idea that narrative devices might exist in the *Extraordinary Journeys Into the Known and Unknown Worlds* would initially meet with incomprehension and disbelief in many people. But their appeal to the most varied of audiences becomes more explicable when the texts are studied carefully. They are the product of a long and arduous literary apprenticeship, together with a visionary inspiration and an unparalleled amount of perspiration. Verne's works are full of pioneers and inventors who are ignored or misunderstood—perhaps standard fare. But his own technique involves radical innovations which themselves remained undiscovered for more than a century.

He omits, for instance, to use the two main past tenses over an entire novel (*The Chancellor*, 1873). Not only does this alter its structure and perspective—especially since there is only one present tense in French—but it even affects the free indirect style, for the present tense alone cannot indicate whether or not it is operating. It also transforms the tonality of the composition, like Nemo's eery effects using just the black keys. In the face of the loud silence from his readers that ensued, Verne then writes of a community that is so tone-deaf as not to have realized that its official music-maker has deleted two notes from the harmonic scale. Deafening silence again. He then publishes a second novel omitting the past tenses (*Propeller Island*, 1895), but written in the third person this time—an achievement again apparently unique in any European language. And still nobody commented. In sum, any view of Verne as the epitome of non-technique is based on ignorance of the texts themselves.

There must be technique for Verne's novels to be so different from each other. Understanding the mechanism of *The Adventures of Captain Hatteras* or *Twenty Thousand Leagues* proves in reality of limited use for interpreting *Five Weeks in a Balloon* or *Around the World*. Certainly, the *Journeys* are cross-linked by a whole network of intertextuality. Verne's method of work, involving five or six proofs and with more than one novel appearing each year, contributed to the over-lapping of the volumes. Common themes, *topoi*, and cross-references abound, constituting a Balzacian-style *œuvre* on a scale that is unique in literature. But each successive work is also designed in terms of its distinctive climax, often of a geographical nature. Where the heroes have to be at the end, in other words, determines how they must get there.

Around the World, in particular, is the only novel to depend on the theme of space and time, and this has important consequences on its whole structure.

> 'Did [he] find the world too small, because he had
> gone right round it?'
>
> (*Captain Hatteras*, 1864)

Around the World in Eighty Days was written in unsettling conditions. During the Franco-Prussian War of 1870–1, Verne had had to work as a coastguard. He was not paid royalties for his previous works, and his money difficulties even led him to consider taking up stockbroking again. His father died; and he was upset by attending a public execution. During this period he also moved to Amiens, abandoning the intellectual and Bohemian stimulation of the capital.

Despite everything, Verne wrote to his publisher Jules Hetzel that *Around the World* was amusing him: 'I have put aside worrying about the play, and . . . as regards the book, I often deviate from the plan drawn up by Cadol and myself.' The same outline served in fact for the writing of a play entitled *Around the World in 80 Days*. The book shows its influence, for it has what are called 'roles' and 'scenes', stage-like entrances and exits, extensive use of dialogue, Moliéresque master-and-servant relationships, and humorous reversals of situations.

The novel opens with a virtuoso presentation of one Phileas Fogg, about whom practically nothing is known. This gentleman hires an acrobatic servant called Passepartout, and then heads straight for his Club. The conversation there turns to the recent shrinking of the globe. Fogg bets that it can now be circumnavigated in 80 days; and, to prove it, he and Passepartout immediately set off via Calais and Suez. While crossing the Indian jungle, the travellers stumble upon the preparations for the suttee of a beautiful young widow called Aouda. Having rescued her, they travel on to Hong Kong, where Inspector Fix, on a mission from Scotland Yard, succeeds in separating Passepartout from Fogg and Aouda. The four meet up again, however, then cross the Pacific and catch the transcontinental railroad. During an attack by Indians, Passepartout is carried off, but Fogg manages to rescue him. Despite taking a land-yacht to Omaha, the travellers miss their ship in New York, so Fogg hires a boat and, when it runs out of fuel, has the vessel consume itself right down to the hull. But when he gets home, he is still five minutes late. He falls into deep despair and even plans suicide; Aouda proposes to him; we cut to the Reform Club at the moment of the deadline; and Fogg marches calmly in and wins the bet. The imperturbable gentleman had in fact gained a day in the Pacific, taking only 79 to go round the globe. The book closes with Fogg and Aouda happily married.

Ever since *Five Weeks in a Balloon*, Verne had playfully interwoven fact and fiction, using the most up-to-date sources and sometimes even adding material after going to press. Here he managed things so well that the closing date of the novel, 22 December 1872, was also that of its serial publication! His biographers report that as *Around the World* came out, British and American newspapers published excerpts from it. Some readers believed that the journey was actually taking place, bets were placed, and international liner and railway companies competed to appear in the book. The biographers are often wilfully inaccurate, but Verne's descriptions of the shipping and train lines must leave some suspicion that he was affected by the pressures.

Following Towle and d'Anvers's 1873 English translation, hundreds of publicity-seekers sought to reproduce or improve on Fogg's performance. Even today, journalists short of good copy often refer to Verne's idea. Recently Michael Palin has made a highly popular television series—and book—purloining Verne's title, but hardly acknowledging the literary debt.

The inevitable American film version was made in 1956. It starred Fernandel, David Niven, Noël Coward, John Gielgud, Marlene Dietrich, Frank Sinatra, and 70,000 extras. But it was little more than a spoof, deleting for instance the *tour de force* of the self-consuming vessel in favour of a balloon ride. Verne has the last laugh, however, for he comments ironically that a balloon crossing 'would have been highly risky and, in any case, impossible' (Ch. 32).

While the idea of circling the globe in a fixed time has become an indispensable part of modern mythology, remarkably little is generally known about the novel itself. Perhaps because of the many mistranslations, the best-selling work of probably the world's best-selling writer has rarely been studied in English-language schools or universities.

Surprisingly, no critical edition of *Around the World* has ever appeared to date. And yet half an hour with an encyclopedia or dictionary will reveal scores of insights into the work. Words like '*musth*', 'methodism', 'Obadiah', 'the *Alabama*', or 'Samuel Wilson' have been read by tens of millions of readers. But what seems never to have been recorded is that these phrases refer to massive and uncontrollable sexuality, to fascinating theories of human behaviour, and to major religious and international controversies.

Equally amazingly, there has been no systematic study of the manuscripts. Although large research grants are given to analysing commas in the laundry-slips of quite marginal literary figures, the handwritten pages where that archetypal modern hero Phileas Fogg makes his first faltering steps have never been transcribed. But a quick perusal of the first page reveals such fascinating elements as blatant anti-Semitism, a fourteen-year backdating, an explicit sexual allusion revealing Fogg's hidden motivation, and politically charged references to 'Hanover' and 'the Duke of Wellington'.

The manuscripts are even more revealing in showing the conception of the book. A miraculously preserved fragment mentions clubs, Britain, and 'Fog'—in that order. In other words, neither a journey, nor a circumnavigation, nor a time-limit exist at this stage. Instead, the functioning of col-lectivities appears central: Verne the anarchist is morbidly fascinated with how groups discard their intelligence to arrive at a mass opinion. Fogg then makes his entrance as the inter-section of social and national concerns: initially a mere cipher of British stuffiness, but taking on more complexity as the drafts pile up.

The idea of a trip around the world also has clear external origins. Verne's inspiration was stimulated by three distinct breakthroughs in 1869–70, changing the map of the world once and for all: the completion of railways across America and India and the opening of the Suez Canal. About half a dozen main written sources have also been suggested, including Edgar Allan Poe, Thomas Cook, newspaper and periodical articles, and books by a W. P. Fogg and a G. F. Train (see Appendix A for further details). But the idea of circling the globe had in any case already become a commonplace by the 1870s. Many of Verne's previous works had incorporated the idea, as indicated by even the titles of *Captain Grant's Children: A Voyage Round the World* (1865) and *Twenty Thousand Leagues under the Seas: A Submarine Trip Around the World* (1869). It may be more fruitful therefore to analyse the novel in terms of Verne's own trajectory.

'1858 ... Burgh'

(Verne's first jottings for MS1)

The main inspiration for *Around the World in Eighty Days* seems to have come from Verne's own travels. Much of the American section borrows from *A Floating City* (1871), a semi-fictional account of the author's 1867 visit to the United States. This includes details like the streets which intersect at right angles, stations without gates, a deadly duel, and proper names such as Blondin, Rothschild, the Hudson, Broadway, and Sandy Hook. But the narrator above all sardonically comments, as if he had advance information of Fogg's whirlwind itinerary: 'I have 192 hours to expend [*sic*] in America'; 'there are rabid tourists, "express-travellers", for whom this time would have probably been enough to see the whole of America'.

A record of exceptional value has in fact recently emerged, in the shape of the first completed book the novelist ever wrote, initially called *Journey to Scotland*, and then *Journey to England and Scotland*. This autobiographical account was written in about 1859, but was rejected by Hetzel and published only in 1989, under the incorrect title *Voyage à reculons en Angleterre et en Écosse* (translated as *Backwards to Britain* (1992)). Although it has received virtually no critical attention to date, this description of Verne's first foreign visit constitutes not only an important work of literature in its own right, but also an invaluable record of his stylistic and thematic development. In addition, many elements of *Around the World* are taken directly from it.

Thus both works feature Charing Cross, Haymarket as a place for debauchery, Regent Street repeatedly, and the all-important Greenwich meridian. Sydenham is a vital transition point in both books; and the Strand of 1859 serves to name Fogg's *alter ego*, James Strand, who will be arrested in Edinburgh, the sentimental heart of Verne's journey.

The Reform Club comes from the younger man's viewing of the clubs of Pall Mall, which he praises as 'veritable palaces [of the highest] distinction'. Other shared elements are the role of the Stock Exchange, the absence of retired soldiers at the

Bank of England, the *Morning Chronicle* and *The Times*, the 'great attraction' (in English) of a human pyramid advertised by sandwich-men, and even the lists of obscure learned societies. Similar descriptions of the Anglo-Saxon passion for mechanics appear in both. The Hong Kong ale and porter were first consumed in a rough Liverpool pub. An extended metaphor invented for Waverley Station serves to generate the American election meeting, for both systematically equate pulsating crowds and an angry sea. The 'ragged hat from which drooped a single bedraggled plume', worn by the barefoot beggar that Fogg encounters, is Liverpudlian. The marine terminology of the two ships, the cabins laid out in identical fashion, the blood-brother captains, a masochistic longing for seasickness, storms, and shipwreck—all are common to both works.

The trains, above all, whether fighting through the tiger-infested Asian jungles or snow-bound Rocky Mountain passes, are 'really' just crossing the Scottish hills. The poetry-in-motion of the Indian and American steam-engines, with the rhythm of their wheels reproduced in the long sentences, with their animal-like protuberances, their bellowing, whinnying, and bolting, their harmony with the curves of the land, their smoke, steam, and speed euphorically mixing in with the vegetation—all this is borrowed directly from the Caledonian visit which made such a lasting impression on the young writer.

The plots are even more revealing. Both works are full of the pressure of reaching Britain as soon as possible and the regret that, because of some uncultured businessmen, over three-quarters of the time is spent on a needlessly circuitous route. Although Verne and Fogg both want to sail to Liverpool, they are forced to head for Bordeaux instead. Writer and character both spend noisy and uncomfortable nights in Custom House Street in Liverpool. Both get involved in major punch-ups there. A Captain Speedy proves an invaluable help and a firm friend to each. Verne's visit to Madame Tussaud's, one and a half gruesome chapters long, emerges clearly in the repeated description of Fogg as an automaton and in Passepartout's instinctive waxwork comparison. The first fragment of *Around the World* even seems to bear the heading '1858': an astonishing indication of the importance of the 1859 trip.

In sum, the most British of the *Extraordinary Journeys* would have been impossible without the extensive borrowing from the author's own journey to Britain. Ironic thanks are due to Hetzel for his rejection of *Journey to England and Scotland.*

But the source of inspiration goes further, for *Journey to England and Scotland* is itself a major plagiarism. In *Around the World*, Verne acknowledges the influence of 'one of the acutest observers of British society', and reproduces an anecdote showing how easy it is to purloin gold ingots from the Bank of England. In the 1859 work, explicit mention is made of a 'book about Britain' by a Francis Wey. Previous researchers have shown that one or two details of the description of the Reform Club are indeed drawn from Wey's *Les Anglais chez eux: Esquisses de mœurs et de voyage* (1854). But it has never been shown before that in fact both of Verne's books transcribe entire sections of Wey wholesale.

Thus *all* the information about the Reform Club is drawn from Wey, down to his 'twenty Ionic columns of red porphyry' and the 'servants . . . in dress-coats and shoes soled with thick felt'. So is the terminology of 'colleague', 'fellow member', and '*circle*[s]', as is the aim of 'facilitat[ing] relations between people of the same opinion' (!) while at the same time permitting individual privacy. Other familiar traits include Wey's 'men transformed into walking advertisements', 'porter and ale', a dining companion announcing that he is leaving for Calcutta tomorrow, and the Crystal Palace exhibition as a 'summary of the entire world'. But all sorts of other information about London also comes from Wey. Shared place-names include 'Hay-Market', 'Charing-Cross', the Temple, Chancery, 'Lincoln's-Inn', the Ecclesiastical Court, Greenwich, and Sydenham, together with proper names like Minerva, John Bull, and Byron—repeatedly. Wey's explanations of the title 'Esq.' and the need for a Christian name between 'Sir' and the surname leave a plain mark on *Around the World.*

But it is above all on the British character that Wey is interesting. It consists of 'sobriety, self-interest . . . and silence', of 'looking without seeing', of 'independence', 'isolation', and 'permanent solitude', of 'the complete annihilation of the individual, the essence of non-being', of a tendency to suicide. These traits perfectly anticipate Fogg's personality, sometimes word for word.

In sum, London and the British character form the intersection of *Les Anglais chez eux*, *Journey to England and Scotland*, and *Around the World*. The reason why Hetzel refused *Journey to Scotland* may have been the extensive purloining; but it is surprising Wey did not complain about *Around the World*—had he himself perhaps taken the material from somewhere else? In any case, this discovery of blatant textual troilism has vital consequences for our understanding of both *Around the World* and *Journey to England and Scotland*— and must constitute a rich area for future research into the wellsprings of Verne's creativity.

'Do you want me?'
(MS1)

Clubs, Britain, Fogg: any reason for leaving—or for crossing India—has not been found at this stage. The blank automaton initially has no aim in life. Newtonian mechanics tells us that he will therefore remain stationary for ever or else on a fixed linear or circular course. The play emphasizes Fogg's inertia (and sexuality) when it compares him to 'a spring-driven watch needing to be wound up every morning'.

However, the imposing of the time-limit reduces the problem. Like Frankenstein's monster, Fogg can be sparked into some semblance of life by being made to iterate the algorithmic process of taking the quickest path between each two successive points. The rudderless personality and pointless journey thus gain some cohesion from the temporal aspect— the book was at one stage called simply *The Journey in Eighty Days*; and one of Verne's last letters to his father refers to his work on a 'journey carried out using the maximum of present-day speed'. The deadline also leads to the final *coup de théâtre*. This surprise ending allows Verne to correct the bland idea of travelling around the world in so many days; and it enables his anarchism to fight back against a world where everything seems totally organized and timetabled.

All the same, the gain of 24 hours can equally well be considered a waste of 79 days and 26,000 miles. Despite the brainwave, in other words, the *raison d'être* for the trip still remains problematic. A mere bet cannot be considered worthy of the successor of Hatteras, Lidenbrock, and Nemo. Too great a dependence on the idea of time is indeed dangerous, for Verne's seminal short story 'Master Zacharius' (1854) had already shown that time cannot substitute for a futile existence. The problem is that time has no tangible reality—and Verne instinctively avoids intangibles. In sum, Fogg's 80 days, with its bonus of a temporal shift, represents only a partial answer to the fundamental problem of motivation and meaning. It probably constitutes the least bad solution to an imperfect world where there are no metaphysical absolutes or transcendental journeys left.

As if to compensate for the unreliability of what modern critics call 'time as theme', the completed work displays great complexity in the 'time of the plot'. The purely linear trip as determined by the timetables represents in reality just the starting-point of a whole multiplicity of interlocking structures.

The narration starts off slowly, with leisurely parentheses and detailed social observations, but then accelerates from the Rockies onwards. The weaving back and forth between Hong Kong and Yokohama may cause many readers to forget where they are, but probably few even notice the narrative device that consists of remaining with Aouda and Fix while Fogg and Passepartout are away having adventures with the Indians. Above all, very few may realize that many sections of Fogg's journey are omitted, including the one from Sydenham to Suez! This jumping across the Channel, the Alps, the Mediterranean, and the Canal itself is achieved largely by means of concentrating on Fix's telegram instead—the nearest the nineteenth century got to instantaneous long-distance communication and hence ubiquity. Whereas critics have marvelled at novels of the period mirroring the *social* effects of technical innovations, apparently only poor Verne fully absorbs the changes into his *literary* technique. 'Poor' Verne, because it is so well done that nobody seems to have noticed the extent of the jump linking London directly to Suez.

However, the Hong Kong and Suez comings and goings pale beside the final crescendo, which is probably unique in the history of literature. Put simply, it is a flashback that does not exist! After Aouda's proposal, Chapter 26 presents itself as a flashback to the Reform Club—but then shows the astounding, divine appearance of Mr Fogg. The following chapter proceeds further back to show Fogg realizing what date it is, and then terminates this second flashback. And because of the 'missing' day, the flashback of Chapter 26 never needs closing.

Verne has here instituted an unparalleled time-machine, doing away with the tiresome need to resynchronize events afterwards. This unique temporal shifter produces the textual equivalent of a Klein bottle or a Möbius strip, for it flips you over but then smoothly brings you back to where you started from. Verne has often been presented as a past master at anticipation, and indeed he is. His anticipation is, however, almost never of the scientific sort but consistently and brilliantly of the literary variety.

If we examine the space of the novel, we find a similar originality. The route of Fogg's journey is 'overdetermined': simultaneously the quickest route, the one suggested by his colleagues, the one determined by *Bradshaw*, and the one that goes through the most British possessions. The trip is stripped down to the bare essentials: everything in the universe has been eliminated apart from the linear route itself. Fogg, Passepartout, and Fix can consequently never escape or get lost, but are destined merely to bump into each other indefinitely. Even the runaway engine has nowhere to go, and so must eventually reverse shamefacedly back.

But the one-dimensional route is rarely a *straight* line. There seems to be a hierarchy in the means of transport, from the most natural to the least, and correspondingly from the most direct to the least. The elephant and the land-yacht simply cut autocratically across the shortest route. The ocean crossings use a combination of sail and steam, and so represent intermediate-status 'loxodromies': lines that appear straight on the ocean but curved on the map projection. But the high-tech steam locomotives must temper their straight-line ravishing of the countryside by mixing in a degree of sinuosity; they must employ a roundabout approach to penetration. Their linearity has to be ecologically integrated with the rest of space. Tunnels are out.

Nor is orientation a simple matter. Why does Fogg head east, not west? Presumably so that Passepartout can see Paris again, so that the subplot of the bank-robber fleeing to America can be maintained for longer, so that the final day can be saved rather than lost, and because the *Morning Chronicle*'s schedule does. But no serious reason is ever given. Inspector Fix, on the other hand, perceives space as having a dual structure. Before Hong Kong he does everything to slow Fogg down; after, to speed him up again. His space is therefore equivalent to two distinct linear segments, both having the British colony as a pole of repulsion and London as a pole of attraction.

Even a straight line if continued far enough constitutes a circle. This does present some advantages: it avoids the narratorial catastrophe of having to cover terrain twice; it enables the hero to come back and reap the honours due; and it allows the book to come to a tidy conclusion. It also chimes in with a persistent psychological and narrative trait of the *Extraordinary Journeys*: the need to take the most circuitous route, the mingled attraction–repulsion of the object of desire. But the return of the wanderer, however much postponed, underlines the futility of leaving in the first place and the trite existence prevailing back home. Accordingly Verne originally abandoned Hatteras at the Pole, the astronauts circling the moon for ever, and Nemo permanently prowling the seas (although he was forced to recant in each case). Fogg's orbit then represents a once-in-a-lifetime solution to the conundrum: because the line becomes a circle, it gets him back to the Reform Club; because the circle remains a line, it satisfies his

penchant for forging ahead and the narrator's need to maxi-
mize contact with the new.

The collapsing of three-dimensional space to the linear
structure of Fogg's route corresponds, in sum, to the drastic
reduction in the modern opportunities for heroism. In this
strangely limited microcosm, the role of chance is radically
diminished, replaced by an iron necessity. The structure thus
pastiches the monomaniacal endeavours of Verne's previous
heroes, with their blindness to lateral movement and their
linear cries of 'Forward!' In a post-Romantic world, frostbite
and leeches have been replaced by fur coats and liners, freedom of movement by the narrowest of strait-jackets, and the
transcendental points of the globe by a transplanted Surrey
stockbroker belt—or by simply carrying on until one gets
home again. Verne pulls some surprising tricks out of Fogg's
one-way journey.

> 'Decidedly Phileas Fogg only had a heart when it was
> needed for behaving heroically, not tenderly'
>
> (Ch. 17)

Around the World represents a new departure for Verne in
terms of his exploration of the human mind. In the previous
works the quest had usually been as important as the questers,
but now one of the main centres of interest lies in Fogg
himself. Although he may seem a man without qualities,
we eventually come to observe his behaviour with bated
breath.

Much critical reaction to Phileas Fogg has been determined
by the opening chapters, which portray a psychological 'limit-
ing case', a tragi-comic living-dead creature. At the beginning he just plays whist and reads the newspapers, indulges in
clock-watching, and generally goes round in circles. He is
above all defined by his absences. We know nothing at all
about him except that he has 'probably' travelled, 'must have
been' a sailor—and writes with a leaden prose style. The
narrator comments freely, however: Fogg is highly punctual,
fixed in his ways, verging on the timeless; he is above all
monomaniacally single-minded. His essential problem ap-

pears to be social, for what distinguishes him is his isolation. He has no time for 'rubbing against people': neither social intercourse nor for that more intimate 'rubbing himself up against' people. Passepartout's first reaction is instructive. The Frenchman is seeking order and regularity, in reaction to the prevailing hedonism and self-indulgence; but even he seems shocked by the extremes his new master goes to.

In Verne's works, chronometric rigidity tends to destroy its own object. Some flexibility is necessary for all the things Fogg does not do—laugh, create, travel, and so on. Whether as a scientific theory or a mode of behaviour, then, what Verne calls the 'methodism' of mechanics constitutes its weakness in the face of the vagaries of the real world. Mechanics was of course a frequent model over much of the period 1850–80, the apogee of scientism. But Verne argues that it does not solve very much; and that time and space, especially, cannot be treated as mere physical variables. Fogg is thus at the beginning merely the intersection of several symbolisms, a sad mechanical shell, a frustrated figure waiting for an undefined Godot, a challenge for the narrator's inventiveness.

The portrait in the first manuscript is particularly unrelenting. Although Fogg is younger than the author, many of his traits resemble these of Verne's own father, who was obsessed with punctuality and ran the house like a monastery crossed with a prison. But once the paternal score has been settled, the portrait can then be progressively tempered. Passepartout comes to observe that Fogg is in fact quite tolerant and even shares his first-class compartment with his servant—if not his whist table.

Just as the servant is being won over, a second witness for the prosecution is wheeled on. The Indian Brigadier-General considers Fogg impossible to talk to, and his bet a selfish eccentricity serving no purpose whatsoever. Phileas has no reason for living, he is no use to anyone, not even himself. This view is corroborated by Passepartout's observation that Fogg has no curiosity, that he seems to listen without hearing and look without seeing. In a word, he is cold. Nearly everybody, down to the Royal Geographical Society, is thus ranged against him. Critics have echoed this opinion, arguing that

Fogg is, amongst other things, 'inadequate and ill-adapted . . . a dismal failure . . . as a human being'.

But the case for the defence is simultaneously being presented. Fogg invariably behaves generously; even his mechanical formality may be an ironic way of defending British law-abidingness; unpopularity is often a sign of originality in the *Journeys*. Fogg is efficient, polite, tenacious, fair-minded, truthful, intelligent, and inventive. He seeks rational solutions, sleeps perfectly, and never runs after trains or boats. Compared with his dreadful co-members, Fogg indeed represents the epitome of good sense.

He stops to rescue Aouda since he 'has the time'. But although this hard-headed, almost Thatcherian, self-description rings true, it is less than fair. He in fact risks his life, and has to be held back from 'a moment of selfless madness'. Later he saves Passepartout as well, risking his fortune 'through a sense of duty, without empty words'.

The sole remaining charge, then, is the buttoned-up aspect, the misogyny, the lack of spontaneity—his anti-Romanticism. The Brigadier-General's view is supported by Aouda, whose puzzlement persists almost to the end. So does Fogg's tendency to hermetic solipsism, as symbolized by the closed curtains of his return. The narrator himself joins in: 'The Fogg that had come back was exactly the same as the Fogg that had left.' And the closing words again echo the Brigadier-General's: 'But what was the point? . . . No[ne], agreed, were it not for a lovely wife, who—however unlikely it may seem—made him the happiest of men! | In truth, wouldn't one go round the world for less?'

Conventional happy endings were often forced on the novelist by Hetzel, more concerned with sales than art; and Verne admitted (or claimed?) that he was very bad at writing tender sentiments. The publisher may even have had a hand in the final chapters. If so, where would that leave Fogg?

My own view is that, although disguised by its three accompanying reservations, the conclusion is sincere, almost painfully so. The idea that Fogg might still be unfeeling had in fact been critically undermined in the Liverpool prison, where we perceive his inner being for the first time; and is then demolished by the proposal scene. Verne never fears simple language, and there seems no reason not to take the final assessment at approximately face value. His companions end up totally bowled over by Fogg. He is in fact revealed to be a hyper-sensitive being and a late developer whose emotions are not absent but simply concealed. Aouda (and the narrator) had been judging solely by appearances: fatal in Verne's world where most of the scenes are constructed from *trompe-l'œil* and whole books are traps. The price paid is undoubtedly the loss of Fogg's punctuality, logic, coolness, and self-sufficiency. Any claim that he remains unchanged by his experiences is therefore particularly wide of the mark.

It is also true that Fogg's interest in Aouda may be uncontrollable lust; that he may in the end have become just too much like the rest of us; that Aouda may not be happy married to someone over twice her age; and that Verne in any case opposes the idea of marriage. But, whatever Hetzel's role, and whatever traces of irony may be lurking in the background, the first manuscript demonstrates the primacy of the idea 'wife—happiest of men', and this survives untouched to the final version.

Verne often accepts contrary views—occasionally simultaneously—but he seems here to be adopting the position of the idealist. He adheres to the Stendhalian view that happiness, however elusive and short lived, should be aimed for—even if it means getting married. Fogg probably qualifies, then, on balance, for our approval. In later years, Verne always spoke favourably of his creation. Fogg is the ideal hero for the self-doubting and changeable modern age.

It will have been noticed that, in exploring Fogg's underlying nature, I have twice claimed that the narrator is mistaken about him. That we cannot trust the truth of Verne's text clearly represents a radical view. My claim does not, however, consist of the fairly common one in writing about nineteenth-century fiction, that the narrator is unreliable because of his limited knowledge. Nor is it even that he resembles twentieth-century narrators like Proust's, in being more and more unsure of everything in a process of indefinite regress. The hypothesis being proposed here is the stronger one that he is simply wrong—indeed actively mendacious.

The following are merely the most blatant examples: 'now that a railway crosses the whole width of India'; 'the old Rajah . . . was suddenly seen to become erect'; 'Fix was no longer [on board] to place obstacles in the way'; 'throughout that Sunday . . . his colleagues were no longer expecting him'; and '[Fogg] was now well and truly ruined . . . His bet was lost'.

All these statements are untrue. A first reaction may be that some of them are in free indirect style, that is, they are reporting the characters' words or thoughts without necessarily agreeing with them. But we are very rarely privy to the thoughts of, in particular, Fogg; and some of the instances are difficult to link with any of the characters—as indeed are the erroneous dates the narrator uses after the Pacific crossing. We are forced therefore to conclude that in at least some of the cases the narrator is reporting his own immediate 'thoughts', and that these are just as subject to delusion as the thoughts of any of the characters; sometimes, indeed, changing within a line or two.

Verne's narrator thus has the outward form of the nineteenth-century's omniscient and ubiquitous narrator, but is in fact less reliable than the twentieth-century bystander-narrator: a combination that very much undercuts the veracity and authority of his own position, and throws considerable doubt on his role as a whole. Even the late twentieth century has not accustomed us to a narratorial figure actively misleading the reader. The radical conclusion is that Verne disassociates himself from his own narrator. The novel is thus surprisingly modern, for no framework of truth can exist in any part of it.

'Face isn't the only expressive organ'

(MS1)

We have observed that the serene surface of *Around the World* hides depths of sex and violence, a fair amount of contradiction, and concerns about personal identity, love, time, and space. How is the anguish cloaked?

One answer lies in the humour, which by its nature reconciles oppositions and enables the unthinkable to be thought. Fogg's mathematical precision provides much of it—Bergson was later to emphasize the comic of the mechanical. Some of the humour also centres on his reactions to strange foreign customs and deviations from his self-imposed code of behaviour. But the difference between his personality and those of Passepartout and Fix also gives rise to much of the humour, causing misunderstandings to abound and a classical tragicomic triangle to develop. The humour then affects even the narration, which borrows many of its understated, *pince-sans-rire* characteristics from Fogg himself.

The humour never becomes biting; and indeed the novel is at times rather melodramatic. Thus the violence almost never does any harm, with the two assaults on Fix and the effect of the American Indian attack coming over as oddly detached. As if to compensate, the description of the Indians themselves torn to pieces by the train's wheels introduces a gratuitously gruesome element.

Another hidden aspect is the artistic process itself: in common with most of his century, Verne does not show the creative impulse at work, but nevertheless many of his thematic concerns coincide with those of the writer, caught between 'what he wants to say' and inchoate forces seeking expression.

The comic elements, violence, and creativity can in fact be considered part of a wider network of meaning which also englobes the 'unknowability' of the hero and the narrator's duplicities. There exists a meta-theory which, although not fully formulated in the 1870s, provides a powerful benefit-of-hindsight analysis of the novel's clandestine features. Modern psychology has indicated the existence of different areas of the mind and consequently distinct modes of behaviour. The vital missing link can thus be found in Freud's demonstration that the human personality is 'split', that the dark undercurrents of the psyche, unknown to the subject, are divorced from the publicly visible persona.

Verne demonstrated great interest in mental phenomena throughout his life. In 1850 he enthusiastically wrote to his parents about a 'magnétiseur' ('mesmerizer' or 'hypnotist') called Alexis who gave public performances. He went to these twice, and wrote that Alexis was able to deduce considerable information about the Verne family from a simple physical object, in a way that the writer describes as 'miraculous'. Starting from his early twenties, Verne suffered from paralysis in one side of his face, but was treated in 1851 by means of electricity. Following these two events, electricity and magnetism play an important part in his works, not only as 'powers at a distance', but especially as inseparably physical and psychic phenomena. Electromagnetism generates, for instance, the plot in *Antarctic Mystery* (1897); and hypnotism is used in *The Mysterious Island* (1874) to restore speech to a madman by taking him back to the traumatic events that provoked his illness. Another hypnotism scene, in *Mathias Sandorf* (1885), lists doctors specializing in mental illness, including the co-founder of modern neurology, Jean-Martin Charcot (1825–93), whom Verne himself may have consulted in the 1850s. Charcot was also renowned for his disciple Pierre Janet's development of the idea of the unconscious—and for being the first to interest one of his students, called Sigmund Freud, in the mental origins of neurosis (see note to Ch. 27 for further details). There exists, in other words, at least one link between Verne and the founder of twentieth-century psychology. And this link passes through the vital notion of the unconscious, which William James called 'the most important discovery of the nineteenth century'.

Another relevant thread may be Verne's own family. From about 1873 onwards, the physical and mental health of his only son Michel gave him great cause for concern, and resulted in his being hospitalized in 1874 in the clinic of Dr Antoine Blanche (1828–93), a renowned mental specialist who treated writers including Nerval and Maupassant. In 1886, Verne was fired on and permanently disabled by his mentally ill nephew Gaston. The author often wrote that he himself was 'misunderstood' and that he had a dark 'secret'. Whether this was sexual, psychological, or otherwise, it points in any case to murky depths in the soul, ones clearly shared with Michel and Gaston.

From the earliest works, Verne similarly suggests that his characters have hidden motivations. They are constantly prey to strong emotions which lead them into situations that their rational mind would not have chosen. This concept is not in itself surprising; but starting from the 1860s, Verne begins to use words like 'without thinking' when describing his characters' behaviour.

In the seventh edition (1867) of *Journey to the Centre of the Earth*, he adds new chapters based on the most up-to-date theories of prehistory and the origins of the human race, including a reference to a certain William Carpenter (1813–85). This polymath was not only a writer on the sea depths and the law of the circulation of the oceans, but the author of *Zoology . . . and Fossil Remains* (1857 and 1866), *The Unconscious Action of the Brain* (1866–71), 'Is Man an Automaton?' (1875), and *Mesmerism, Spiritualism, &c. . . .* (1877). Most of his findings were published in the Proceedings of the Royal Institution or the Geographical Society; and in 1873 he became a corresponding member of the Institute of France. Carpenter's sevenfold interest in France, learned societies, the fossil past, the ocean's abysses, the origins of man, automatic behaviour, and the hidden areas of the mind seems almost too perfect. His influence must be counted as a source of Verne's innovative psychology of the depths from 1867 onwards.

It should now be evident why the characters in *Around the World* have such different public and private faces, why the narrator contradicts himself so often, why the protagonists appear so often in catatonic poses, why humour plays such a prominent role, why creativity is masked in the novel, and why, above all, mental phenomena are so important. The answers lie in the unconscious.

All of the characters stand constantly divided. The collectivities are subject to 'undercurrents': changes which are not obvious on the surface, but in any case irrational. Even the boring clubmen feel simultaneously secure and insecure. Again, Fix is not only blind to motives in others, but prey to conflicting forces within himself, making him constantly do things without noticing or things he does not 'really' want to do. The scene on Kearney Station, where he solipsistically argues with himself and cannot move despite longing to do so, provides a brilliant illustration. A similar division is externalized as the Fogg–Passepartout couple: the two men successfully operate as a team, with Fogg the rational and Passepartout the instinctive part, each having his own *modus operandi*, but neither permanently in charge. In all these cases, then, the vital distinction is between the conscious and the unconscious minds.

Fogg represents indeed the archetypally repressed individual that Freud associates with the achievements of the Victorian age. This automaton remains blind to his environment and hence unprepared for the unexpected—especially from within. Repressing urges, warns Verne, just makes them bigger. Precisely because he is so dominated by his rules and regulations, Fogg remains permanently at risk.

Aouda's conversion to Fogg's cause has a corresponding language of 'almost without her knowing', 'unexplained premonition', and 'more than she realized'. Her final 'Do you want me?', with its excessive frankness, appears remarkably similar to the secret desires expressed in a canonical Freudian slip.

Generally, all four main characters are described as having battles going on within them, as oscillating between states, as being beside themselves. The following are amongst the remarkable adjectives and adverbs used: mesmerized, hypnotized, instinctively, mechanically, automatically, secretly, involuntarily, and unconsciously. The vocabulary is systematic throughout the novel. In other words, all four are credited with having motives which determine their actions but remain hidden from themselves. And Verne's use may represent an important innovation, since his term 'inconsciemment' ('unconsciously') is unrecorded in any of the dictionaries before 1876.

Previously, the unexplored past was represented by the fundamental image of the historic and prehistoric remains in the ocean and the geological layers in the Earth's crust. In *Around the World* the image is replaced by tunnels—themselves carefully hidden—but especially by the repeated analogy of 'encrustation'. This term is applied not only to the Great Salt Lake, which has got deeper as it has grown smaller, but to ideas fixing themselves in the depths of the characters' minds.

Even that great Freudian standby, uncontrollable sexuality, constantly rampages through *Around the World*—confirming that the book is not designed for callow adolescents. The sexual symbolism is so blatant that it is surprising it was allowed; and two scenes elevate it to a paroxysm. Soon after a vision of barely clothed Indian dancing-girls, twice accompanied in the French text by the word 'viole' (a 'viol' but also 'rapes' or 'violates'), four men witness a religious scene with a half-naked reclining woman as centre-piece; and sexuality immediately proceeds to have a field-day. The episode of the Long Noses again represents nothing but one extended *double entendre*. In both scenes, there also appears a worry that everything might come crashing down: a fear of impotence, connected with the female sexuality visible in the chapter on that other erotico-religious group, the Mormons. It seems appropriate, therefore, that brazen homosexual overtures occur frequently between all three male characters.

Sex thus constitutes a perfect way for Verne to illustrate that the religious impulse is not always what it seems, that the superego is not permanently in control, that the 'other' may intervene, that the mind's composition is not in the face, that Fogg's stiffness may have an ulterior explanation. 'In man, just like the animals, the members are veritable organs expressing the passions'—or as the first manuscript puts it, 'Face isn't the only expressive organ'.

The remarkable images of the novel, then, range from encrustation to systematic innuendo to scrutiny of Fogg's organ. They all combine with an explicit and repeated indication that the characters' rational minds are not in control. Verne thus produces an inventive account of human nature, involving split personality, repressed memories, neurotic behaviour, illicit impulses, sexual obsessions, and many of the concepts that would later be formalized by the psychologists. Even if many pre-Freudian ideas of repression and hidden motivation were current in the 1870s, *Around the World* is highly original in its literary formulation of them. Freud himself pointed out that most of the scientists' ideas were previously visible in literature—and the case of the unconscious would seem to confirm this.

Or as Verne wrote in 1882, 'There are two beings inside us: me and the other.'

Around the World in Eighty Days is in many ways a key work in Verne's production. All sorts of cracks run deep through the novel. The shrinking of the globe, caused notably by the closing down of the age of exploration and the building of the railways, will shatter his universe once and for all, and *Around the World* represents the breaking-point.

Science-fiction novels have made great play of adapting space and time and studying the consequences—but Verne does this within the additional constraints of his century. Without wishing to make Verne an anticipator of the theory of relativity, he does here pose the question, in subtle and above all literary fashion, of relative time-frames and hence whether an absolute time-scale can ever exist. His novel also gives a central role to anxiety about machine-based, standardized, and soon-to-be-mass travel. It introduces two important techniques involving narrative point of view and depiction of character. It thus undermines conceptions of objectivity and coherence in a manner that will become much more prevalent later. In terms of the labels currently fashionable, *Around the World* may consequently be judged startlingly modern, perhaps even verging on the post-modern.

For the reader at the turn of the millennium, all these special effects add up to a work of unparalleled readability. Verne has mastered the art of making the difficult look so easy as to appear uncrafted. His is a model of directness and accessibility. The result of all his inner turmoil is to produce a work of unique serenity. Fogg's rigidity has given unalloyed pleasure to tens of millions of readers.

Around the World in Eighty Days must rank as one of its century's most surprising achievements.

I would like to thank Greg Scott and Angela Brown for their help with the preparation of the manuscript, together with Anne Miller, Elizabeth Stewart, Gregory James, David Longworth, Cécile Compère, the Centre de Documentation Jules Verne d'Amiens, Geoff Woollen, Tim Unwin, Piero Gondolo della Riva, Betty Harless, the University of Hong Kong, and Christian Porcq. I would also like to give belated acknowledgements to Alan Brook and Barry Clifton for their help with *Journey to the Centre of the Earth*, and thank Paz for everything.

NOTE ON THE TEXT AND TRANSLATION

AT least two manuscripts of *Le Tour du monde en quatre-vingts jours* survive (the MS1 and MS2 cited here are held by the Town of Nantes and the Bibliothèque nationale, to whom grateful acknowledgements are recorded). Although often illegible, MS1 is more revealing. It bears the date '29 March 1872' on the cover (probably the date when it was begun); and it converts to note form in the middle of 'chapter 27'. MS2 is much more legible. On the front cover it bears the definitive title, plus 'Page 28'; and it reads '16,998' (the number of lines) at the beginning of the text. It is complete apart from two sheets missing in Ch. 7 and four in Ch. 18.

The uniform appearance of the two manuscripts implies that they were recopied from earlier drafts (usually in pencil underneath the ink version); but the text of both is typical of the period in being careless in spelling, use of capitals, hyphens, punctuation, and so on. Nevertheless, a few of the mistakes in the published text, for instance 'Londonner' (Ch. 1), are correct in these manuscripts.

The thirty-second sheet of the first manuscript contains a vital early sketch of Ch. 1, upside down in the left margin. In addition to containing doodles of what may be a Red Indian, of a Jewish-looking face, and of a dog, it reads:

Around the World in 80 Days

340 520

—

1.

The reform club, Pall mall, 1858 [or 183x] xxxxxxxx Burgh [in English]
60 clubs in London [these first two lines loosely crossed out]
reform club xxxx xxxxxxxxxxxxxxxxxxxxxxx ~~the fortune longxxxxx supposed/supported by [m]illion markxx xxxounds~~

1 October 1872, a 40-year-old man,

—Face isn't the only expressive organ, rem. ['obs'] gentleman/sir.
—Fog's foot never rxxxx—accordingly, given Article 29

      qux

£x banks [in English]   fog 'qine' [for 'quine'?]

Fog xxx xxxx

‒‒‒‒

16 Fog at home.

These few lines, preserved by accident, are extremely important for our understanding of the book. They show, first, that
the Reform Club, 'Fog', and money are central from the
beginning. But it is the year indicated, apparently '1858',
which is a revelation, for this fourteen-year backdating implies a radically different conception of *Around the World*.
Britain was not initially imagined in terms of the engineering,
financial, and colonial successes of the 1870s. The question
then arises whether Verne's idea was to describe a circumnavigation before the railways existed. But the date above all
points to the 1859 trip to the land of Verne's ancestors, a vital
influence on the whole of the following production.

Wey reads 'London has more than 60 clubs' and 'the heart
of the City is called "the Borough"'—proving once again his
influence.

The clearly legible '—Face isn't the only expressive organ' is
also vital. Its explicit sexual innuendo declares that the mind's
composition is not in the face, that Fogg's imperturbability
conceals the strongest impulses, and that his fate will ultimately be determined by his libido. Its laconic form betrays
Verne's haste to get his ideas down—but also prefigures the
ellipticality Fogg himself displays throughout the book.

The mention of Fogg's foot may be connected with Byron's
club-foot, or else with Fogg's habit of always going forward.
The basis for Fogg's formalism would seem to be legal: the
fascinating allusion to 'Article 29' is complemented by legal
references throughout the book—not surprising since Verne
was the son of a lawyer and a trained lawyer himself.

The reading of 'quine' for 'qine' is more hypothetical:
'quine' meant 'a winning combination of five numbers in the
state lotteries'—perhaps an allusion to Fogg's winning gamble.

This fragment, in sum, is highly revealing.

The first page of MS1 reads as follows (phrases which are not in the published version appear in italics):

Around the World in 80 Days

—

I.

In the year 1872, No. 7 Savile Row—where Sheridan died in   — had *only* been occupied *for a few months* by *a certain* Phileas Fogg, Esq., *one of the members recently admitted into the honourable association of the Reform Club.*

One of the greatest *statesmen* to have honoured—*and been honoured by*—Britain had therefore been succeeded in this residence by this Phileas Fogg, a mysterious and enigmatic figure: *his past was unknown, and no one knew where he came from, where he went to, what he did, or who he spent his time with.* Although clearly British, he was not a Londoner. He had never been spotted in the Stock Exchange, the Bank, or the City. Neither the basins of London, nor those of *St Catherine*, nor those of xxxxx xxxxx, nor the docks! *of the Company of the East [sic] Indies, nor those of the East India Company* had berthed a ship for an owner called Phileas Fogg . . . nor even the Society for the Combined Arts and Sciences which enjoys the direct patronage of Her Gracious Majesty *and whose vice-xxxxx was formerly the Duke of Wellington.* He was not a member of the associations that breed: *none, from the committee xxxxxx Hanover* [*equine xsolved?*] *to* the Entomological Society, founded chiefly with the aim of a thousand xxx xxx xxxxx, the institution for harmful insects. ~~He was~~ Phileas Fogg was a member of the Reform Club— that's all that can be said.

It was surprising to see a gentleman *so lacking in curiosity* [included?] amongst the members of this honourable association. *Accordingly, his admission was debated for a relatively long time, but in the end* he got in on the recommendation of *his xxxxxx xx, grasping, of Rotschild* [sic] *and Son* with whom he had an ~~acco~~ unlimited overdraft facility. Hence a certain 'profile' for this Fogg, whose cheques were regularly paid on sight, and his account was invariably in the black.

These three opening paragraphs contribute considerably to our understanding of the text. First, Wey had referred to 'the docks—meaning basins—of London, of St Catherine or of the East India Company'. Verne's repetition of the East Indies is greatly clarified by Wey, who also refers to the docks of 'the *West* Indies'! In other words, Verne confuses east and west, as he does throughout the novel. For every Frenchman, the Duke of Wellington was synonymous with the defeat at Waterloo; but political allusions had little chance of surviving Hetzel's censorship. The illegible—and similarly cut—reference to the House of 'Hanover' is frustrating. Again, Sheridan's downgrading from 'states[man]' to 'public speaker', and the accompanying deletion of 'honoured by' Britain, affects our perception of writers who wish to influence the commonwealth. We also see signs in this passage of the anti-Semitism visible elsewhere in the *Journeys*. In addition, one of the central themes of the book, Fogg's relationship with the Reform Club, is different here, being markedly more conflictual.

Finally, MS1 and MS2 contain a number of significant variants in points of detail. Thus in MS1 '2 October' (Ch. 1) is '1 October', and in MS2 'twenty minutes to six' (Ch. 3) is '. . . eight' (perhaps due to the different dining times in France and Britain) and all the time indications in Ch. 34 are about two hours behind. The anti-Romantic dig of the first page is reinforced in the description of 'a Byron *without passion, grown cold*, impassive . . . without ever growing *physically* old' (MS2). The portrait of Fogg is generally less complimentary in MS1, omitting the words 'fine and noble face', and occasionally possessing biblical overtones ('precision *made man*'); in MS2, in addition, the sexual allusion appears stronger, as in 'as flawless in his moving parts'. We also learn that Fogg's clock indicates 'the phases of the sun and the moon' (MS1); that he is 'forty to forty two years old' and the 'owner' rather than the 'occupant' of 7 Savile Row (MS2); and that he—most unusually—undergoes 'an anxious moment' (MS1) before the arrival of his new servant, 'who had been recommended to him at the Club' (MS2). Virtually the whole of the first paragraph about Passepartout is in fact missing from MS1, together with the exchange about his watch being slow; in MS2, he 'wish[es] to *participate again in* family life' (rather than 'try'), and is described as being 'a dyed-in-the-wool stay-at-home'. In sum, we may regret many of the published changes, which simplify the story but delete interesting facets of, especially, Passepartout's background.

The text used for the present edition is based on the illustrated 1873 one reprinted in all the modern French editions. Unlike most of the previous volumes, *Around the World in Eighty Days* was not serialized in Hetzel's *Magasin d'Éducation et de Récréation*, but in the adult review *Le Temps* (6 November–22 December 1872). It was then published in the unillustrated 18mo edition in January 1873. As usual, the illustrations (by Neuville and Benett) were only included in the more expensive first large-octavo edition (December 1873).

The present translation is an entirely new one, benefiting from the most recent scholarship on Verne and aiming to be faithful to the text. However, the use of phrases like 'he said' and 'she replied', of ellipses and exclamation marks, and of very long sentences has been slightly reduced. Also omitted are the equivalents in francs that Verne gives of the sums Fogg spends (at the variable rate of 20 or 25 francs to the pound). It is not always clear whether Verne is using French or British feet and miles, so distances here are sometimes slightly approximate.

SELECT BIBLIOGRAPHY

HACHETTE, Michel de l'Ormeraie, and Rencontre (reprinted by Edito-Service) have published the only complete editions of the *Voyages extraordinaires* since the original Hetzel one, although 44 of the books have appeared in Livre de Poche. All these editions, however, are partly out of print. In English, the overwhelming majority of translations are of an unacceptable standard, with such brilliant howlers as 'prunes' for 'plums', 'Galilee' for 'Galileo', 'St Helen's' for 'St Helena', 'mass' in a Presbyterian kirk, and 'Scotsmen, and the English in general'!

The major scholarly books on Verne in English are Andrew Martin, *The Mask of the Prophet: The Extraordinary Fictions of Jules Verne* (Oxford: Oxford University Press, 1990) and William Butcher, *Verne's Journey to the Centre of the Self: Space and Time in the 'Voyages extraordinaires'* (Basingstoke: Macmillan, 1990). Arthur B. Evans's *Jules Verne Rediscovered: Didacticism and the Scientific Novel* (Westport, Conn.: Greenwood Press, 1988) is also worth consulting.[1]

Amongst the French critics, François Raymond and Daniel Compère's *Le Développement des études sur Jules Verne* (Minard (Archives des lettres modernes), 1976) still remains the most readable introduction. There exist many stimulating collections of articles, notably: *L'Herne: Jules Verne*, ed. P.-A. Touttain (L'Herne, 1974), *Colloque de Cerisy: Jules Verne et les sciences humaines*, ed. François Raymond and Simone Vierne (Union générale d'éditions, 1979), *Modernités de Jules Verne*, ed. Jean Bessière (Presses universitaires de France, 1988), and the seven volumes of the Minard (Lettres modernes) series on Verne, especially *Machines et imaginaire* (1980) and *Texte, image, spectacle* (1983).

The following may also be useful: Jean Chesneaux, *Une lecture politique de Jules Verne* (Maspero, 1971, 1982), translated as *The Political and Social Ideas of Jules Verne* (Thames and Hudson, 1972), Simone Vierne, *Jules Verne* (Balland (Phares), 1986), Alain Froidefond, *Voyages au centre de l'horloge: Essai sur un texte-genèse, 'Maître Zacharius'* (Minard, 1988), and Olivier Dumas, *Jules Verne* (Lyons: La Manufacture, 1988).

[1] All places of publication are London or Paris unless otherwise indicated. All dates of Verne's works are those of the beginning of their first publication, usually in serial form.

The best biography is Jean Jules-Verne, *Jules Verne* (Hachette, 1973), translated and adapted by Roger Greaves as *Jules Verne: A Biography* (MacDonald and Jane's, 1976). But there are also Charles-Noël Martin, *La Vie et l'œuvre de Jules Verne* (Michel de l'Ormeraie, 1978) and Marc Soriano, *Jules Verne (le cas Verne)* (Julliard, 1978).

The only systematic secondary bibliographies are the exhaustive listing in Jean-Michel Margot, *Bibliographie documentaire sur Jules Verne* (Amiens: Centre de documentation Jules Verne, 1989) and the critical bibliography, William Butcher, 'Jules and Michel Verne', in David Baguley (ed.), *Critical Bibliography of French Literature: The Nineteenth Century* (New York: University of London (Ontario) with Syracuse University Press, 1994).

The main studies on *Around the World in Eighty Days* are:

Albors, Enrique Garcia, 'Le Coup de théâtre final du *Tour du monde en quatre-vingts jours*', *Bulletin de la Société Jules Verne*, 6: 2 (1968), 10–12.

Auden, W. H., *The Dyer's Hand and Other Essays* (New York: Random House, 1962), 139–43 (the Fogg–Passepartout relationship, which both envisage as a formal master–servant one, is transformed by the rescuing of Aouda, with each thereafter risking his life for the other; and is thus a parable of Agape).

Avrane, Patrick, *Un divan pour Phileas Fogg* (Aubier, 1989) (psychoanalytical study of Fogg).

Bradbury, Ray, 'Introduction', in *Around the World in Eighty Days* (Los Angeles: Plantin Press, 1962), vii–xii (enthusiastic piece showing that Fogg and Passepartout represent respectively thinking and doing, the eccentric genius of taste and imagination and his uncreative shadow).

Brisson, Adolphe, *Portraits intimes* (Colin, 1899), iv. 111–20 (recounts a visit in which Verne mentions a Thomas Cook 'advertisement' as the source of *Around the World*).

Cocteau, Jean, *Mon premier voyage (Tour du monde en 80 jours)* (Gallimard, 1936) (Cocteau's trip round the world following Fogg's footsteps, plus the influence of Verne on his own writing: the idea of encircling the world is a modern myth, that of reconnoitring man's domain).

Cordeau, Valérie, 'Jules Verne: Le Tour du monde en quatre-vingts jours', Maîtrise de lettres modernes, Université de Picardie, 1991.

Daudet, Alphonse, 'Le Tour du monde en 80 Jours par Jules Verne et d'Ennery', in *Pages inédites de critique dramatique* (Flammarion, 1875), 179–82.

Edgren, A. H., 'Preface, Biographical Sketch and Notes', in *Le Tour du monde en quatre-vingts jours* (Boston: D. C. Heath & Co., 1898 (student edition)), 3–5.

Evans, I. O., 'Introduction', in *Around the World in Eighty Days* (Arco, 1967), 7–9 (points to *Magasin pittoresque* article as source).

Farmer, Philip José, *The Other Log of Phileas Fogg* (New York: Daw, 1973) (science fiction based on the mythological dimension of Verne's characters, considered as heroes of our time).

Green, Alexander, 'Introduction', in *Le Tour du monde en quatre-vingts jours* (Boston: D. C. Heath, 1926), xi–xviii (claims Verne as 'literary apostle of popular science').

Martin, Andrew, *The Knowledge of Ignorance: From Genesis to Jules Verne* (Cambridge: Cambridge University Press, 1985), 142–4 and *passim* (an erudite and ironic account of the structural foundations of Verne's imagination).

Marx, Adrien, 'Introduction: Jules Verne', in *Around the World in Eighty Days* (Sampson Low, Marston & Company, 1873), 5–10 (mainly about Verne's work habits).

Mouthon, F. I., 'Le Tour du monde et Jules Verne' (1901), reprinted in *Jules Verne: Textes oubliés*, Union générale d'éditions, 1979, 379–82.

Porcq, Christian, 'NGORA, ou les images de la folie dans les *Voyages extraordinaires* de Jules Verne', unpublished thesis, University of Paris V, 1991, 134–5, 164–71 (imaginatively exposes the personal and psychoanalytic aspects of Verne's work, especially dreams, the unconscious, and hypnosis).

Raymond, François, 'L'Homme et l'horloge chez Jules Verne', in *L'Herne: Jules Verne*, ed. P.-A. Touttain (L'Herne, 1974), 141–51 (*Around the World* is a tragi-comedy; Fogg the walking chronometer becomes humanized, but Verne remains ambivalent towards mechanization, with more fluid forms of transport often seeming preferable to trains; Verne is a past master of time, but a time of poetry rather than science).

—— (ed.), *Jules Verne 1: Le Tour du monde* (Minard (Lettres modernes), 1976) (a volume uneasily balanced between the scholarly and the admirative): Jean Chesneaux, 'Le Tour du monde en quatre-vingts jours', 11–20 (readable but naïve account of 'the poetry of railways', the humanization of Fogg, and imperialist ideology in India and elsewhere); André Lebois, 'Poétique secrète du *Tour du monde en quatre-vingts jours*', 21–9 (the themes of gold, Providence, time, mathematical precision, and the influence on Jarry); Daniel Compère, 'Le Jour fantôme', 31–52 (knowledgeably traces possible sources for the initial idea of the novel); Jean-

Pierre Poncey, 'Misère de Jules Verne, ou l'échec d'un projet', 53–64 (unrelenting attack on Verne); Raymond, 'Tours du monde et tours du texte: procédés verniens, procédés rousselliens', 67–88 (entertainingly explores Verne's *tours*: both the closed circuits on the globe and the narrator's traps, bluffs, and deliberate omissions); Marie-Hélène Huet, 'Exploration du jeu', 95–108 (on bets, games, and death); Pierre Terrasse, 'Le *Tour du monde* au théâtre', 109–24 (information about the play); Jules Verne, 'Les Méridiens et le calendrier', 125–30 (lecture given at the Société de Géographie, 4 Apr. 1873, and first published in the *Bulletin de la Société de Géographie*, 6 (July 1873), 423–8); Daniel Compère, 'Bibliographie' of works on *Around the World*, 189–203.

Ricardou, Jean, *Pour une théorie du nouveau roman* (Seuil, 1971), 120–4 (studies structural constraints in *Around the World*, and observes the Poe-like use of black on white symbolism).

Sigaux, Gilbert, 'Préface', in *Le Tour du monde en quatre-vingts jours* (Lausanne: Rencontre, 1966), 5–14.

Terrasse, Pierre, 'Naissance du *Tour du monde*', *Bulletin de la Société Jules Verne*, 19: 73 (Jan.–Mar. 1985), 31–4.

Tournier, Michel, 'A Propos de Marcel Brion, *L'Allemagne romantique, III: Les Voyages initiatiques*', *La Nouvelle Critique* (June 1977), 106–7 (distinguishes between novels of confrontation and of initiation, and places *Around the World* in the former, together with *Scarlet and Black* and *Don Quixote*).

—— *Les Météores* (Gallimard, 1975), *passim* (points out the contrasting spatio-temporal ideas of Fogg and Passepartout, and brilliantly analyses the structure of the novel; also reveals that his own conceptions of symmetry and difference in human relations are drawn from the male Vernian couple).

Unwin, Timothy, *Jules Verne: 'Le Tour du monde en quatre-vingts jours'* (Glasgow: University of Glasgow, 1992) (an introduction for students that covers a wide range of topics in a lucid and fair-minded way).

Verne, Jules, *Around the World in Eighty Days* (Sampson Low, Marston & Co., 1873), also published as *The Tour of the World in Eighty Days* (Boston: J. R. Osgood, 1873), trans. Geo. M. Towle and N. d'Anvers (the first translation, of high quality; followed over the years by at least six other signed translations into English, plus a large number of unsigned ones).

—— and Adolphe d'Ennery, *Le tour du monde en 80 jours* (play), music by Jean-Jacques Debillemont, opened at the Théâtre de la Porte-Saint-Martin on 7 Nov. 1874, published by F. Debons, 1875, and Hetzel, 1881, reprinted in *Grand album Jules Verne*, ed.

Jacques Leclerc (Hachette, 1982); trans. C. Clark as *Around the World in Eighty Days* (French, 1875).

Vierne, Simone, 'Introduction' and other material in *Le Tour du monde en quatre-vingts jours* (Garnier-Flammarion, 1978) (a mine of interesting information).

A CHRONOLOGY OF
JULES VERNE

1828   8 February: birth of Jules Verne, on the Île Feydeau in
        Nantes, to Pierre Verne, a lawyer and son and grandson of
        lawyers, and Sophie, née Allotte de la Fuÿe, from a military
        line.

1829   Birth of brother, Paul, later a naval officer, but who retired
        in 1859 and became a stockbroker; followed by those of
        sisters Anna (1836), Mathilde (1839), and Marie (1842).

1834–8 Goes to school: the teacher, Mme Sambain, is the widow of
        a sea-captain, whose return she is still waiting for.

1838–41 Collège Saint-Stanislas. Performs well in geography, trans-
        lation from Greek and Latin, and singing.

1841–6 Goes to the Petit Séminaire, then to the Lycée Royal de
        Nantes. Above average; probably won a prize in geogra-
        phy. Passes *baccalauréat* without difficulty. Writes short
        pieces in prose.

1847   Studies law in Paris; his cousin, Caroline Tronson, with
        whom he has been unhappily in love for several years, gets
        engaged. Writes a play called *Alexandre VI*.

1848   June: revolution in Paris. Verne is present at the July
        disturbances. He continues his law studies, sharing a room
        at 24 Rue de l'Ancienne-Comédie. His uncle Châteaubourg
        introduces him into literary *salons*. Meets novelists
        Alexandre Dumas *père* and *fils*. Writes plays, probably
        including *La Conspiration des poudres*.

1849   Passes law degree. Father allows him to stay on in Paris.
        Writes more plays.

1850   12 June: his one-act comedy *Les Pailles rompues* runs
        for twelve nights at Dumas's Théâtre Historique, and is
        published.

1851   Publishes short stories 'Les Premiers Navires de la Marine
        mexicaine' and 'Un voyage en ballon'.

1852–5 Becomes secretary at Théâtre Lyrique. Publishes 'Martin
        Paz', 'Maître Zacharius', 'Un hivernage dans les glaces',
        and the play *Les Châteaux en Californie* in collaboration

with Pitre-Chevalier. His operette *Le Colin-Maillard*, written with Michel Carré, is performed to music by Hignard.

1856   20 May: goes to a wedding in Amiens, and meets a young widow with two children, Honorine de Viane.

1857   10 January: marries Honorine; then becomes a stockbroker in Paris, and moves house several times.

1859–60 Visits Scotland with Hignard, and is greatly marked by the experience. Writes *Voyage en Angleterre et en Ecosse*.

1861   Goes to Norway and Denmark with Hignard. 3 August: birth of only child, Michel.

1863   31 January: *Cinq semaines en ballon* appears, three months after submission to publisher Jules Hetzel, and is an immediate success. Writes *Paris au XXe siècle*, rejected by the publisher.

1864   Publication of 'Edgar Poe et ses œuvres', *Aventures du capitaine Hatteras*, and *Voyage au centre de la Terre*. Gives up his unsuccessful stockbroker practice, and moves to Auteuil.

1865   *De la Terre à la Lune* and *Les Enfants du capitaine Grant*. Death of Mme Estelle Duchêne of Asnières, close friend of Verne's.

1867   16 March: goes with brother Paul to Liverpool, thence on *Great Eastern* to United States. First English translation of any of the novels, *From the Earth to the Moon*.

1868   Buys a boat, the *Saint-Michel*. Visits London.

1869   Rents a house in Amiens. *Vingt mille lieues sous les mers* and *Autour de la Lune*.

1870   Outbreak of Franco-Prussian War: Verne is coastguard at Le Crotoy (Somme).

1871   3 November: father dies.

1872   Moves to 44 Boulevard Longueville, Amiens; becomes member of Académie d'Amiens. *Le Tour du monde en quatre-vingts jours*.

1873–4 *Le Docteur Ox*, *L'Île mystérieuse*, and *Le Chancellor*. Begins collaboration with Adolphe d'Ennery on stage adaptation of novels (*Le Tour du monde en 80 jours*, performed 1874, *Les Enfants du capitaine Grant*, 1878, *Michel Strogoff*, 1880: all highly successful).

1876–7 *Michel Strogoff, Hector Servadac,* and *Les Indes noires.*
        Buys second, then third boat, the *Saint-Michel II* and *III.*
        Gives huge fancy-dress ball. Wife very seriously ill, but
        recovers.

1878   June–August: sails to Lisbon and Algiers.

1879–80 *Les Cinq Cents Millions de la Bégum, Les Tribulations
        d'un Chinois en Chine,* and *La Maison à vapeur.* Michel,
        who had caused problems throughout his childhood, mar-
        ries an actress, despite the opposition of his father. Verne
        sails to Norway, Ireland, and Scotland, including Edin-
        burgh and probably the Hebrides.

1881   *La Jangada.* Sails to Rotterdam and Copenhagen.

1882   October: moves to a larger house at 2 Rue Charles-Dubois,
        Amiens. *Le Rayon vert.*

1883–4 *Kéraban-le-têtu.* Michel abducts a minor, Jeanne. Has two
        children by her within eleven months. Divorces, and mar-
        ries her. Verne leaves with wife for grand tour of Medi-
        terranean, but cuts it short. On the way back, is received in
        private audience by Pope Leo XIII.

1885   *Mathias Sandorf.*

1886   *Robur-le-conquérant.* 15 February: sells *Saint-Michel III.*
        9 March: his nephew Gaston, mentally ill, asks for money
        to travel to England. Verne refuses, and the nephew fires at
        him twice, making him lame for life. 17 March: Hetzel
        dies.

1887   15 February: mother dies.

1888   Is elected local councillor, on a Republican list. For next
        fifteen years attends council meetings, administers theatre
        and fairs, opens Municipal Circus (1889), and gives public
        lectures.

1889   *Sans dessus dessous* and 'In the Year 2889' (published in
        New York: signed Jules Verne but written by Michel, and
        then probably translated into English).

1890   Stomach problems.

1892   *Le Château des Carpathes.* Pays debts for Michel.

1895   *L'Île à hélice,* apparently the first novel ever written in a
        European language in the present tense and third person.

1896–7 *Face au drapeau* and *Le Sphinx des glaces.* Sued by chemist
        Turpin, inventor of melinite, who recognizes himself in
        Face au drapeau. Successfully defended by Raymond

Poincaré, later President of France. Health deteriorates. 27 August: brother dies.

1899   Dreyfus Affair: Verne is initially anti-Dreyfus, but approves of the case being reviewed.

1900   Moves back into 44 Boulevard Longueville. Sight weakens (cataracts).

1901   *Le Village aérien.*

1904   *Maître du monde.*

1905   17 March, falls seriously ill with diabetes. 24 March: dies, and is buried in Amiens.

1905–14 On Verne's death, *L'Invasion de la mer* and *Le Phare du bout du monde* are in the process of publication. Michel takes responsibility for the remaining manuscripts, and publishes *Le Volcan d'or* (1906), *L'Agence Thompson and Co.* (1907), *La Chasse au météore* (1908), *Le Pilote du Danube* (1908), *Les Naufragés du 'Jonathan'* (1909), *Le Secret de Wilhelm Storitz* (1910), *Hier et demain* (short stories, including 'L'Éternel Adam') (1910), and *L'Étonnante aventure de la mission Barsac* (1914). In 1978, it is proved that Michel in fact wrote considerable sections of these works, and between 1985 and 1993 the original (i.e. Jules's) versions are published.

Around the World in Eighty Days

CONTENTS

4   *Contents*

1

In Which Phileas Fogg and Passepartout Accept Each Other, the One as Master and the Other as Servant

IN the year 1872, No. 7 Savile Row, Burlington Gardens*—the house where Sheridan* died in 1814—was occupied by Phileas Fogg,* Esq. This gentleman was one of the most remarkable, and indeed most remarked upon, members of the Reform Club,* although he seemed to go out of his way to do nothing that might attract any attention.

One of the greatest public speakers to honour his country had thus been replaced by the aforesaid Phileas Fogg. The latter was an enigmatic figure about whom nothing was known, except that he was a thorough gentleman and one of the most handsome figures in the whole of high society.

He was said to look like Byron:* his head at least, for his feet were beyond reproach—but a mustachioed and bewhiskered Byron, an impassive Byron, one who might have lived for a thousand years without ever growing old.

Although clearly British, Mr Fogg might not have been a Londoner. He had never been spotted in the Stock Exchange, the Bank, or the City. The basins and docks of London had never berthed a ship for an owner called Phileas Fogg. This gentleman was not on any board of directors. His name had never rung out in a barristers' chambers, whether at the Temple, Lincoln's Inn, or Gray's Inn. He had never pleaded in the Courts of Chancery, Queen's Bench, or Exchequer, nor in an Ecclesiastical Court.* He was not engaged in industry, business, commerce, or agriculture. He did not belong to the Royal Institution of Great Britain, the London Institution, the Artizan Society, the Russell Institution, the Western Literary Institution, the Law Society, nor even that Society for the Combined Arts and Sciences* which enjoys the direct patronage of Her Gracious Majesty. In sum, he was not a member of any of the associations that breed so prolifically in the capital of the United Kingdom, from the Harmonic Union* to the

Entomological Society, founded chiefly with the aim of exterminating harmful insects.*

Phileas Fogg belonged to the Reform Club—and that was all.

Should anyone express surprise that such a mysterious gentleman be numbered amongst the members of that distinguished society,* it can be pointed out here that he was accepted on the recommendation of Messrs Baring Brothers,* with whom he had an unlimited overdraft facility. Hence a certain 'profile', for his cheques were always paid on sight and his account remained invariably in the black.

Was this Phileas Fogg well off? Without any doubt. But how he had made his fortune, even the best informed could not say. And Mr Fogg was the last person one would have approached to find out. In any case, while in no way extravagant, he was not tight-fisted either. Whenever support was needed for some noble, useful, or generous cause, he would provide it, noiselessly and even anonymously.

In short, the least communicative of men. He spoke as little as possible, and so seemed all the more difficult to fathom.* His life was transparent, but what he did was always so mathematically the same, that one's imagination, disturbed, tried to look beyond.

Had he travelled? Probably, because no one possessed the map of the world as he did. Nowhere was so remote that he didn't seem to have some inside knowledge of it. Sometimes he would rectify, briefly and clearly, the thousand ideas about temporarily or permanently lost travellers that spread through the clubs. He would demonstrate the most likely outcome; and he had seemed gifted with second sight, so often had the facts in the end borne out what he had said. He was a man who must have been everywhere—in his imagination at the very least.

What seemed certain, all the same, was that Mr Fogg had not been away from London for some years. Those who had the honour of knowing him a little better than most attested that, apart from the shortest route he took each day from his house to the Club, nobody could claim ever to have seen him anywhere else. His only pastimes were reading the newspapers and playing whist. It fitted his nature entirely that he often won at this silent game. His winnings, however, never stayed in his wallet, but formed instead a major part of his contributions to charity. In any case it should be pointed out that Mr Fogg clearly played for playing's sake, not so as to win. Whist was for him a challenge, a struggle against a difficulty, but one that required no action, no travel, and no fatigue—and so perfectly suited his character.

As far as anyone knew, Phileas Fogg had neither wife nor children—which can happen to the most respectable—nor friends nor relatives—admittedly much rarer. Phileas Fogg lived alone in his house on Savile Row, and no one visited. Nobody ever knew what went on inside. A single servant attended to all his needs. He took lunch and dinner at the Club at chronometrically set times, always at the same place in the same room, never inviting his colleagues, never sharing his table with anyone else.*

He never used those comfortable rooms that the Reform Club likes to place at the disposal of its members, but always went home and retired straight to bed on the stroke of midnight. He spent ten out of every twenty-four hours at home, whether sleeping or dressing and preparing to going out. If he went for a walk, it was invariably at a regular pace around the entrance-hall with its carefully laid-out parquet, or else along the circular gallery which is lit by its round cupola with blue glass and supported by twenty Ionic columns of red porphyry.* If he lunched or dined, the succulent dishes on his table were supplied by the kitchens, pantry, larder, fish store, or dairy of the Club. It was the servants of the self-same Club, serious figures in dress-coats and shoes soled with thick felt, who served him using special china on an admirable Saxony table-cloth. It was the Club crystal, from long-lost moulds, that accommodated his sherry, port, or claret, spiced with maidenhair, cinnamon sticks, and ground cassia bark. And it was Club ice, brought over at huge expense from the Great Lakes, that maintained his wine at a satisfactorily cool temperature.*

If to live in such conditions is to be an eccentric, then it has to be admitted that eccentricity has its good points!

Although not palatial, the house on Savile Row was remarkable for its level of comfort. Because of the regular habits of its occupant, the service was far from onerous. Nevertheless, Phileas Fogg demanded an extraordinary punctuality and reliability from his one servant. That very day, 2 October, he had given notice to James Forster: the fellow had made the mistake of bringing in his shaving-water at a temperature of 84°F, rather than the statutory 86. Mr Fogg was even now expecting his successor, due to report between eleven and half past.

Phileas Fogg sat squarely in his armchair, both feet together like a soldier on parade, hands firmly on knees, body erect, and head held high. He was watching the hand moving on the clock: a complicated apparatus that showed the hours, minutes, seconds, days, dates, and years. In keeping with his daily habit, Mr Fogg was due to go to the Reform Club on the stroke of 11.30.

A knock came on the door of the morning-room where Phileas Fogg was waiting. James Forster, the sacked servant, appeared.

'The new valet,' he announced.

A man of about thirty came in and bowed.

'You are French and called John?'

'Jean, if sir pleases—Jean Passepartout,* a nickname that has stuck with me and was first applied due to my natural ability to get out of scrapes. I consider myself an honest fellow, sir, but if truth be told I have had several occupations. I used to be a wandering singer and a circus rider; I was a trapeze artist like Léotard* and a tightrope walker like Blondin;* then I became a gymnastics instructor in order to make greater use of my skills; and lastly I was a sergeant in the Paris Fire Brigade. I have some remarkable fires in my c.v. But I left France five years ago: wishing to try family life, I became a personal manservant in England. Then, finding myself without a job, I heard that Mr Phileas Fogg was the most particular and stay-at-home man in the whole of the United Kingdom. I presented myself at sir's house in the hope of being able to live in peace and quiet and forget the very name of Passepartout . . .'

'Passepartout suits me very well. You have been recommended to me—I have excellent references on your account. Are you aware of my terms?'

'Yes, sir.'

'Very well, then. What time do you make it?'

'Eleven twenty-two,' replied Passepartout, pulling an enormous silver watch from the depths of his waistcoat pocket.

'Your watch is slow.'

'Pardon me, sir, but that's impossible.'

'You're four minutes slow. It is of no consequence. What matters is to note the difference. So, starting from this moment, 11.29 a.m. on Wednesday, 2 October 1872, you are in my employ.'

Whereupon Phileas Fogg got up, took his hat in his left hand, placed it on his head with the action of an automaton, and vanished without uttering another word.

Passepartout heard the front door shut once: that was his new master going out; then a second time: his predecessor James Forster leaving in turn.

He stood alone in the house on Savile Row.

2

*Where Passepartout Is Convinced That He Has
Finally Found His Ideal*

'I DO believe', he said, a little dazed at first, 'that I have bumped into blokes at Madame Tussaud's* with as much life in them as my new boss!'

It is germane to say here that the 'blokes' at Madame Tussaud's are waxworks in London, which, lacking only the power of speech, attract large numbers of sightseers.

During the short time of his interview, Passepartout had been quickly but carefully examining his future master. He was about forty years old, with a fine and noble face, tall, and none the worse for a slight tendency to stoutness. He had fair hair and sideboards, a smooth forehead with no sign of wrinkles at the temples, a complexion that was pale rather than florid, and splendid teeth. This man seemed to possess to an exceptional degree what the physiognomists call 'repose in action', a quality of all those who produce more light than heat. Calm, phlegmatic, with clear eyes and a steady gaze, he was a consummate example of those self-possessed people encountered quite frequently in Britain—Angelica Kauffmann* has painted them to perfection, captured in somewhat academic positions. In the different phases of his existence, this gentleman gave the impression of being perfectly balanced in all his parts, weighted and poised, as flawless as a chronometer by Leroy or Earnshaw.* The truth was that Phileas Fogg was precision personified. This could easily be seen in the 'expression of his feet and hands', for in man, just like the animals, the members are veritable organs that express the passions.*

Phileas Fogg was one of those mathematically precise people, never in a hurry* but always prepared, economical with his steps and movements. He never took a pace too far, and invariably found the shortest path. He never wasted glances on the ceiling. He allowed himself no unnecessary gestures. Nobody had ever seen him aroused or troubled. He was the least rushed man in the world, but always came on time. In fairness, it should be pointed out that Mr Fogg lived alone and therefore free from all social contact. He knew that in life you can't avoid rubbing against people—and since rubbing slows you down, he rubbed himself up against no one.*

As for Jean, known as Passepartout, he was a real Parisian from Paris.* But he had been working as a gentleman's gentleman in London for five years, while looking, in vain, for a master he could become attached to.

Passepartout was not one of those Frontins or Mascarilles* with shoulders shrugged and noses in the air, self-assured and steely eyed, who are nothing but impudent rascals. No, Passepartout was an honest fellow, with a pleasant physiognomy and slightly sticking-out lips always ready to taste or kiss. A gentle being, ever prepared to help, he was endowed with one of those good round heads that you like to see on a friend's shoulders. He had blue eyes, a ruddy complexion, and a face that was fat enough to see its own cheeks. He possessed a broad chest, a large frame, vigorous muscles, and a Herculean strength that the activities of his youth had admirably developed. His brown hair was a little unruly. If the Classical sculptors knew eighteen ways of arranging Minerva's tresses,* Passepartout knew only one for his: three broad-toothed comb-strokes and he was ready.

Elementary caution does not permit to say whether this fellow's expansive character would fit in with Phileas Fogg's. Would Passepartout be the thoroughly punctual servant his master required? The only way to know was to try him out.* Having spent, as has been said, a wandering youth, Passepartout was now looking for a peaceful existence. Having heard much good spoken about British methodism* and the proverbial reserve of the gentlemen, he had come to seek his fortune in England. But up till now, fate had not been kind to him. He had never been able to put roots down anywhere. He had worked his way through ten houses. In each he had found an unruly or a changeable character—running after girls or foreign parts—and such a life no longer appealed to him. His last master, young Lord Longsferry, MP, habitually spent the night in the Oyster Rooms of Haymarket,* coming back home only too often draped over policemen's shoulders. Wishing above all to be able to look up to his master, Passepartout had risked a few respectful observations, but these, unfortunately, had not been received at all well; so he left. At this point, he had learned that Phileas Fogg, Esq., was looking for a manservant. He made enquiries about this personage. A character whose life was so regular, who never spent a night out, who didn't travel, who never went away even for a day, could only suit him. He presented himself and was accepted in the manner that the reader already knows.

Eleven-thirty having struck, Passepartout found himself alone in the house on Savile Row. He immediately began an inspection, systematically working his way up from the cellar to the attic. The house was clean, well ordered, austere, puritanical, in sum designed for service; and it pleased him. The impression it made was of a fine snail's shell, but a shell lit and heated by gas, since carburetted hydrogen proved quite sufficient for all its needs. Passepartout found his bedroom on the second floor without difficulty. It met with his satisfaction. An electric bell and speaking-tubes communicated with the mezzanine and first-floor apartments. On the mantelpiece an electric clock kept perfect time with the clock in Phileas Fogg's bedroom, the two devices striking the second simultaneously.*

'This is a piece of alright, suits me down to the ground, down to the ground!' he said to himself.

He spotted a card displayed above the clock in his room. It was the schedule of his daily duties. From eight in the morning, the regulation time when Phileas Fogg got up, till half-past eleven, when he left for his lunch at the Reform Club, it specified all the details of the service he was to provide: the tea and toast at 8.23, the water for shaving at 9.37, the hairdressing at twenty to ten, etc. Then from 11.30 a.m. until twelve midnight, when the methodical gentleman went to bed, everything was noted, planned, regulated. Passepartout took great pleasure in contemplating this schedule and committing its various entries to memory.

As for *Monsieur*'s wardrobe, it was well organized and perfectly comprehensive. Each pair of trousers, waistcoat, or jacket bore an order number. This number was marked on a register of incoming and outgoing items, showing the date on which each garment was to be worn, depending on the time of the year. Likewise for the shoes.

In sum, the house on Savile Row—surely a temple to disorder in the days of the illustrious but dissipated Sheridan—constituted a well-appointed abode showing that its inhabitant was very comfortably off. There was no library and no books—of no use to Mr Fogg as the Reform Club put two libraries at his disposal, one devoted to literature, and the other to law and politics.* In the bedroom stood a safe of average size, built to withstand both fire and theft. No arms were to be found in the house, neither hunting gear nor weapons of war. Everything pointed to the most pacific of habits.

Having examined the residence in detail, Passepartout rubbed his hands together. His broad face beamed, and he exclaimed cheerfully:

'To the ground. Just what I need. We'll get on famously, Mr Fogg and me. A home-loving and regular man. A genuine piece of machinery. Well, I shan't mind serving a machine!'

3

Where a Conversation Starts That May Cost Phileas Fogg Dear

PHILEAS FOGG had left his house on Savile Row at half-past eleven and placed his right foot 575 times in front of his left and his left foot 576 times in front of his right. He had thus reached the Reform Club, a vast edifice in Pall Mall that cost no less than £120,000 to build.*

Mr Fogg immediately made his way to the dining-room, whose nine windows opened out on to a fine garden with trees already turned to gold by the autumn. There he sat at his usual table with the service laid out ready for him. Lunch consisted of an *hors d'œuvre* of steamed fish in a Reading Sauce of the highest quality, scarlet roast beef with mushrooms, rhubarb-and-gooseberry tart, and some Cheshire cheese*—all washed down with a few cups of that excellent tea specially grown for the Reform Club.

At 12.47, the gentleman got up and moved into the vast drawing-room, a sumptuous area adorned with paintings in elaborate frames. There a servant gave him an uncut copy of *The Times*,* which Phileas Fogg managed to unfold and cut with a proficiency indicating great experience of that exacting operation. Reading this newspaper occupied Phileas Fogg until 3.45, and the *Standard**—which came next—until dinner. This meal took place in the same way as luncheon, but with the addition of Royal British Sauce.

At twenty minutes to six the gentleman returned to the huge drawing-room and absorbed himself in the *Morning Chronicle*.

Half an hour later, various members of the Reform Club made their entrance and headed for the hearth, where a good coal fire was burning. These were the usual partners of Mr Phileas Fogg, like him fanatical whist players: the engineer

Andrew Stuart, the bankers John Sullivan and Samuel Fallentin, the brewer Thomas Flanagan, and Gauthier Ralph,* one of the governors of the Bank of England—figures of considerable wealth and respectability, even in this club composed of the leading lights of industry and finance.

'Well, Ralph,' asked Thomas Flanagan, 'what's the latest news on this theft business?'

'Well,' answered Andrew Stuart, 'the Bank won't see its money again.'

'I am confident, on the contrary,' intervened Gauthier Ralph, 'that we will soon be able to lay our hands on the thief. Very smart police inspectors have been sent to America, the Continent, and all the main ports of entry and exit, so that this gentleman will have quite a job escaping them.'

'But do we have the thief's description?' asked Andrew Stuart.

'First of all, he's not a thief,' Ralph replied quite seriously.

'What, not a thief, this individual who's made off with £55,000 worth of banknotes?'*

'No,' answered Gauthier Ralph.

'So he's a manufacturer, is he?' enquired John Sullivan.

'The *Morning Chronicle* assures us that he is a gentleman.'

The person making this remark was none other than Phileas Fogg, whose head now emerged from the sea of paper piled up around him. At the same time Mr Fogg greeted his colleagues, who returned the compliment.

The case in question—which the various newspapers were heatedly discussing—had taken place three days previously, on 29 September. A wad of notes amounting to the enormous sum of £55,000 had been taken from the desk of the Chief Cashier of the Bank of England.

To those surprised that such a theft could be carried out so easily, Assistant Governor Gauthier Ralph merely replied that the Cashier was at that time occupied recording a receipt of 3s. 6d., and that one cannot keep one's eyes on everything.

It is important to note—and this makes the matter slightly easier to fathom—that that remarkable establishment, the Bank of England, seems to possess the utmost regard for the public's dignity. No guards, no retired soldiers, no grills. The gold, the silver, and the notes are left lying about, at the mercy, as it were, of the first passer-by. It would be unthinkable to cast doubt on the honesty of a member of the public. One of the acutest observers of British society even recounts the following incident: he was in a room in the Bank one day, and felt the wish to examine more closely a gold bar weighing about seven or eight pounds, lying on the cashier's desk. He took the ingot, examined it, then passed it on to his neighbour, who handed it on to someone else, with the result that it went from hand to hand to the end of a dark corridor, then half an hour later returned to its normal place—without the cashier even looking up.*

But on 29 September, things didn't happen quite like that. The wad of banknotes never came back, and when the magnificent clock dominating the 'drawing-office' announced that it was five o'clock and that the offices were closing, the Bank of England had no choice but to pass £55,000 through its account of profits and losses.

Once the theft had been properly recorded, 'detectives'* chosen from among the best policemen were sent to the main ports of Liverpool, Glasgow, Le Havre, Suez, Brindisi, New York, etc. They had been promised a reward of £2,000 plus 5 per cent of the sum recovered. While waiting for the information that the promptly initiated enquiries would clearly produce, the job of the inspectors was to carefully observe everyone entering and leaving the country.

Now, as the *Morning Chronicle* had pointed out, there was in fact very good reason to believe that the thief did not belong to any of the known criminal gangs of England. During that same day of 29 September, a well-dressed gentleman with good manners and a distinguished bearing had been noticed walking to and fro in the cash room where the theft took place. The enquiries had allowed a relatively accurate description of the gentleman to be produced, and it had been immediately sent to every detective in the United Kingdom and Europe. Some optimistic souls, Gauthier Ralph amongst them, believed consequently that the thief would find it difficult to escape.

As one can imagine, this case was in the news in London and everywhere else. People discussed it and took impassioned positions for or against the Metropolitan Police being successful. The reader will not therefore be surprised to learn that the members of the Reform Club also debated the question, all the more so since one of the Bank's Assistant Governors was amongst their number.

The esteemed Gauthier Ralph did not doubt the success of the enquiries, believing that the reward on offer would ensure that the police showed due zeal and intelligence. But his colleague Andrew Stuart was far from sharing his confidence. Accordingly the discussion continued at the whist table, with Stuart partnering Flanagan and Fallentin, Phileas Fogg. During the game the players did not speak, but between the rubbers the conversation carried on all the more heatedly.

'I maintain', said Stuart, 'that the odds are in favour of the thief, who is clearly an experienced operator.'

'Come on!' answered Ralph. 'There's not a single country left he can hide in.'

'Really?'

'And where do you think he might go, then?'

'I can't say,' replied Stuart. 'But after all, the world is big enough.'

'It used to be,' Fogg said quietly.* 'Will you cut,' he added, presenting the cards to Flanagan.

The discussion was interrupted by the play. But soon Andrew Stuart said:

'What d'you mean, "used to be"? Has the Earth suddenly got smaller by some chance?'

'Unquestionably it has,' responded Ralph. 'I share Mr Fogg's view. The Earth has shrunk because it can be covered ten times as quickly now as a hundred years ago. And in the case we are discussing, this will make the search faster.'

'And the thief's escape easier!'

'Your turn to play, Mr Stuart,' observed Fogg.

But the doubting Stuart was not convinced, and once the game was over:

'You must admit, Ralph, that you have a funny way of saying the Earth has shrunk! Because you can now go round it in three months . . .'

'Eighty days,' interjected Fogg.

'Yes indeed, good sirs,' confirmed Sullivan. 'Eighty days, now they've opened the section of the Great Indian Peninsular Railway from Rothal to Allahabad. This is the calculation done by the *Morning Chronicle*:*

London to Suez via the Mont Cenis Tunnel* and Brindisi, by railway and steamship	7 days
Suez to Bombay, by steamship	13 "
Bombay to Calcutta, by railway	3 "
Calcutta to Hong Kong (China), by steamship	13 "
Hong Kong to Yokohama, by steamship	6 "
Yokohama to San Francisco, by steamship	22 "
San Francisco to New York, by railroad	7 "
New York to London, by steamship and railway	9 "
Total	80 days

'Possibly 80 days!'* exclaimed Stuart, trumping a winner in his excitement. 'But not allowing for unfavourable weather, headwinds, shipwrecks, derailments, etc.'

'All included,' said Fogg, continuing to play—for the discussion was no longer respecting the whist.

'Even if the Indians and Red Indians tear up the rails?' cried Stuart. 'Even if they stop the trains, plunder the carriages, and scalp the passengers?'

'All included,' repeated Phileas Fogg, laying down his hand. 'Two winning trumps.'

Andrew Stuart picked up the hands and started shuffling.

'In theory you may be right, but in practice . . .'

'In practice too, Mr Stuart.'

'Well I should like to see you do it.'

'Your choice. Let's go together.'

'Heaven forbid!' exclaimed Stuart. 'But I would gladly wager £4,000 that such a journey, carried out under the conditions specified, is simply not possible.'

'On the contrary, perfectly possible,' replied Fogg.

'Well do it, then!'

'Go round the world in 80 days?'

'Yes!'

'All right then.'

'Starting when?'

'Starting now.'

'It's pure madness!' cried Andrew Stuart, beginning to get annoyed by his partner's obstinacy. 'Let's get on with the game!'

'Please reshuffle, then,' said Phileas Fogg, 'because there's been a misdeal.'

Andrew Stuart picked up the cards with a shaking hand; then, suddenly laying them back down again:

'Very well, Mr Fogg. I'll bet you £4,000.'

'My dear Stuart,' said Fallentin, 'steady on. You can't be serious.'

'When I say I'll bet,' answered Stuart, 'it is always serious.'

'Very well!' said Mr Fogg, and turned to his colleagues:

'I have £20,000 in my account at Baring Brothers. I'll be glad to venture this sum.'

'Twenty thousand!' cried Sullivan. 'Twenty thousand pounds that you could lose through an unforeseen mishap!'

'The unforeseen does not exist.'

'But, Mr Fogg, this period of 80 days is merely the minimum it can be done in!'

'A properly used minimum is enough for anything.'

'But in order to do it, you'll have to mathematically jump from trains into steamships and from steamships on to trains!'

'I'll jump mathematically.'

'You must be joking!'

'An Englishman never jokes about anything as important as a bet. I hereby wager £20,000 with anyone who wishes that I will carry out the tour of the world in 80 days or less, i.e. in 1,920 hours or 115,200 minutes. Will you accept?'

'We accept,' replied Messrs Stuart, Fallentin, Sullivan, Flanagan, and Ralph after a brief discussion.

'Good. The boat-train leaves at 8.45. I'll be on it.'

'This very evening?' enquired Stuart.

'This very evening,' answered Phileas Fogg. Then, consulting a pocket diary, 'Since today is Wednesday, 2 October, I must be back in London, in this drawing-room of the Reform Club, at 8.45 p.m. on Saturday, 21 December, failing which the £20,000 presently deposited in my account at Baring

Brothers will belong to you *de facto* and *de jure*. Here is a cheque for that amount, gentlemen.'

The wager was witnessed and signed there and then by all six interested parties. Phileas Fogg had remained cool. He had certainly not bet in order to win, and he had pledged only £20,000—half his fortune—because he planned to spend the other half on this difficult, not to say impossible, undertaking. As for his adversaries, they seemed a little upset, not because of the amount at stake, but because they felt unhappy at fighting with such one-sided odds.

Seven o'clock struck. Mr Fogg was asked if he wanted to stop playing so as to make preparations for his departure.

'I'm always ready,' replied the impassive gentleman as he dealt.

'Diamonds are trumps,' he said. 'Your lead, I believe, Mr Stuart.'

4

In Which Phileas Fogg Flabbergasts His Servant Passepartout

AT 7.25 Phileas Fogg, having won a good twenty guineas, said goodbye to his honourable colleagues and left the Reform Club. At 7.50 he opened his front door and went in.

Passepartout, who had meticulously studied the schedule, was a little surprised to see Mr Fogg displaying irregularity, by appearing at this most unusual time. According to the card, the tenant of Savile Row was not due back until the stroke of midnight.

Phileas Fogg first went up to his room, and then called:

'Passepartout.'

The manservant didn't reply. The call couldn't possibly be addressed to him. It wasn't the right time.

'Passepartout,' repeated Mr Fogg, not raising his voice.

The manservant appeared.

'I had to call you twice.'

'But it's not midnight yet,' answered Passepartout, watch in hand.

'I know,' said Phileas Fogg, 'and I'm not finding fault. We're leaving for Calais in ten minutes.'*

An experimental sort of grimace appeared on the Frenchman's round face. He couldn't have heard properly.

'Is sir travelling?'

'He is,' replied Phileas Fogg. 'We're going around the world.'

Passepartout, his eyes wide-staring, his eyebrows completely raised, his arms hanging loose, his whole body sagging, showed all the signs of an astonishment verging on stupefaction.

'Around the world?' he murmured.

'In 80 days,' was Mr Fogg's rejoinder. 'There is not a moment to lose.'

'But what about the trunks?' said Passepartout, unconsciously rocking his head from side to side.*

'No trunks. Just an overnight bag. Two woollen shirts and three pairs of stockings. The same for you. We'll buy things on the way. You will bring down my mackintosh and travelling rug. Wear stout shoes. Although we'll be doing little or no walking. Off you go now.'*

Passepartout tried to reply. He couldn't. He left Mr Fogg's room, went up to his own, collapsed on to a chair, and uttered a slightly colloquial phrase from his native land:

'Well,' he said, 'I'll be blowed. And me who was looking for the quiet life!'

And, mechanically, he got ready to leave. Around the world in 80 days! Was he dealing with a madman? Unlikely . . . Was it possibly a joke? They were going to Dover, okay. Calais: won't say no. After all, that had to be nice, as he hadn't set foot on his native soil for five years. Perhaps they would even go to Paris: he would certainly be glad to see the great capital again. But a gentleman so careful with his movements would clearly stop there. . . . Yes, that had to be it. But he was going to travel all the same, this gentleman, so stay-at-home until now!

By eight o'clock, Passepartout had prepared a modest bag containing his own and his master's wardrobes. Then, his mind still troubled, he left the room, carefully closed the door, and went to find Mr Fogg.

Mr Fogg was ready. He was carrying under his arm Bradshaw's *Continental Railway, Steam Transit and General Guide*, which would provide him with all the information he needed for his travels. He took the bag from Passepartout, opened it, and dropped in a thick wad of those fine banknotes that are tender in all countries.

'You haven't forgotten anything?'

'No, sir.'

'My mackintosh and rug?'

'They're here.'

'Good, take this.'

Mr Fogg handed over the bag.

'And take care; there's £20,000 inside.'

The bag almost fell from Passepartout's hands, as if the £20,000 had been in solid gold.

Master and servant went downstairs and double-locked the front door.

There was a cab-stand at the end of Savile Row. Phileas Fogg and his servant got into a cab which headed quickly for Charing Cross Station, one of the termini of the South-Eastern Railway.*

At 8.20 the cab drew up at the station entrance. Passepartout got out. His master followed and paid the driver.

At this moment, a poor beggar-woman holding a child by the hand, barefoot in the mud, a shawl in rags over her torn clothing, and wearing a ragged hat from which drooped a single bedraggled plume, came up to Mr Fogg and asked for charity.

Mr Fogg got out the twenty guineas* he had just won at the whist table and gave them to the beggar.

'Take this, my good woman,' he said. 'I'm glad I met you.'

And then he continued on his way.

Passepartout felt a damp sensation in his eyes. His master had taken a step forward in his heart.

The two men entered the concourse. Phileas Fogg instructed Passepartout to buy two first-class tickets for Paris. Then, turning round, he noticed his five colleagues from the Reform Club.

'Gentlemen,' he said, 'I am leaving. The various visas stamped on the passport I am taking for this express purpose will allow you to verify my journey when I come back.'

'Oh, Mr Fogg!' replied Gauthier Ralph politely. 'There is no need. We shall count on your word as a gentleman.'

'Better all the same.'

'You haven't forgotten when you need to be back?' enquired Andrew Stuart.

'In 80 days,' answered Mr Fogg. 'On Saturday, 21 December 1872, at 8.45 p.m. Till we meet again, gentlemen.'

At 8.40 Phileas Fogg and his servant sat down in the same compartment. At 8.45 a whistle sounded and the train pulled off.

It was a dark night, with a drizzle falling. Phileas Fogg, sitting back in his corner, did not speak. Passepartout, still in a state of shock, was mechanically hugging the bag containing the banknotes.

But the train had not got past Sydenham,* before Passepartout produced a real cry of despair!

'What's the matter?' asked Mr Fogg.

'The matter . . . in my hurry . . . thinking about other things . . . I forgot . . .'

'What?'

'. . . to turn off the gas in my bedroom!'

'Well, my boy,' said Mr Fogg coldly, 'it's burning at your expense!'

5

In Which a New Stock Appears on the London Exchange

When he left London, Phileas Fogg probably had no idea of the sensation his departure was going to produce. But the news of the wager spread through the Reform Club and generated considerable excitement amongst the members of that august circle. Then, from the Club this agitation passed to the newspaper reporters, and from the papers to readers in London and the whole of the United Kingdom.*

This question of the Journey Round the World was commented on, discussed, and analysed with as much passion and ardour as a new *Alabama* Claim.* Some people supported Phileas Fogg; others—who soon formed a significant majority—came out against. A trip around the world, to be carried out by a deadline using the existing means of transport and not in theory nor on paper was not only impossible, it was crazy!

The Times, the *Standard*, the *Evening Star*, the *Morning Chronicle*, and twenty other large-circulation newspapers declared themselves against Mr Fogg. Only the *Daily Telegraph* supported him to a certain extent. Phileas Fogg was generally dismissed as a maniac or a lunatic, and his colleagues in the Reform Club suffered criticism for accepting this bet which showed that the person involved had undergone a decline in his mental faculties.

Articles appeared on the question that were extremely passionate but totally logical. Everyone knows the interest the British take in anything to do with geography. Accordingly there was not a single reader, of whatever social class, who did not devour the column-inches devoted to the Phileas Fogg case.

In the early days, a smattering of bold spirits backed him—mainly women—especially when the *Illustrated London News** published a likeness based on his photograph in the Reform Club files. Some gentlemen even went so far as to say, 'Well, well! But after all, why not? We've seen stranger things than that!' These were generally readers of the *Daily Telegraph*. But it soon became clear that even this newspaper's support was beginning to crumble.

The reason was that a long article had appeared in the 7 October issue of the *Proceedings of the Royal Geographic Society*.* It considered the question from every point of view, and proved that the enterprise was clear madness. According to this article, everything was against the traveller, both man-made and natural. To complete the expedition, there had to be a miraculous concordance of departure and arrival times, a concordance which did not exist and which could never exist. In most cases involving trains in Europe, one can count on arrivals at fixed times, for the distances involved were relatively short; but when one needs three days to cross India or seven for the United States, could one found the axioms of a theory on any punctuality? And what about breakdowns, derailments, collisions, bad weather, and snowdrifts—wasn't everything against Phileas Fogg? On the steamships would he not be at the mercy of the winter squalls and fogs? Was it so rare for even the fastest intercontinental liners to be two or three days late? But it only needed one delay, just one, for the chain of communication to be irreparably broken. If Phileas Fogg missed the departure of a single steamship even by a few hours, he would have to wait for the next ship, and his journey would be ruined once and for all.

This article caused a sensation. It was reprinted in almost all of the newspapers, and Phileas Fogg stocks went into free fall.

During the first few days after the gentleman's departure, considerable sums had been wagered on the chances of his enterprise. Everyone knows that those who bet in England are cleverer and subtler than those who merely gamble. Betting is in the blood. Accordingly, not only did the various members of the Reform Club place considerable sums for and against Phileas Fogg, but the general public also took part in the proceedings. Phileas Fogg was registered like a racehorse, in a sort of 'studbook'. He was listed on the Stock Exchange, and a price was immediately quoted on the London market. 'Phileas Fogg' was asked for and offered as both a share and an option, with tremendous business being carried out. But five days after his departure, and following the article in the Geographical Society's *Proceedings*, the amount on offer began to increase significantly. Phileas Fogg shot down. He was sold hand over fist. People accepted 5 to 1, then 10 to 1, and in the end he was taken only at 20 to 1, 50 to 1, and finally 100 to 1.

Only one supporter remained. This was old Lord Albermale, who was paralysed.* The noble lord, confined to his chair, would have given his fortune to be able to do the trip around the world even taking ten years! He bet £5,000 on

Phileas Fogg. Whenever people proved to him how useless the idea was, how idiotic even, he would merely reply, 'If the thing can be done at all, it is fitting that an Englishman should be the first to do it!'

Things had reached this point, with Phileas Fogg's supporters getting rarer and rarer and everybody turning against him—not without reason. He could not be bought at less than 150 to 1, then 200 to 1—when, exactly a week after his departure, a completely unexpected incident meant he wasn't taken at all.

At 9 p.m. on that day, the Commissioner of the Metropolitan Police received the following telegram:

To: *Rowan, Commissioner, Scotland Yard, London.*
Tailing bank-robber Phileas Fogg. Send arrest warrant soonest Bombay (British India).

Fix, Detective Inspector, Suez.

The effect of the telegram was considerable. The honourable gentleman vanished and his place was taken by the thief of the banknotes. His photograph, available at the Reform Club with those of all his colleagues, was duly studied. Every single feature in it appeared identical to those of the description produced by the enquiries. People remembered how mysterious Phileas Fogg's existence had been, his seclusion and his sudden departure; and it became evident that this character, inventing a journey around the world and maintaining the pretence with a senseless wager, had had no other aim than to throw the British police off the scent.

6

In Which Detective Fix Shows a Highly Justifiable Impatience

THE telegram concerning Mr Phileas Fogg had been sent under the following circumstances.

On that Wednesday, 9 October, the liner *Mongolia* was due to arrive at Suez at eleven in the morning. She belonged to the Peninsular and Oriental Steamship Company and was a screw-driven iron steamer with a spar-deck, of 2,800 tons burden and 500 hp. The *Mongolia* plied regularly between Brindisi and Bombay via the Suez Canal.* She was one of P. & O.'s quickest ships, and had always exceeded the regulation speed, ten knots between Brindisi and Suez and 9.53 knots between Suez and Bombay.

While waiting for the *Mongolia*'s arrival, two men were strolling along the quayside. They formed part of the crowd of natives and foreigners who are at present streaming into this town, formerly little more than a village, but now guaranteed a great future, thanks to the magnificent work of M. de Lesseps.*

Of the two men, one was the Consul of the United Kingdom in Suez. Despite the unfortunate predictions of the British Government and the sinister forecasts of the engineer Stephenson,* every day this official saw British ships going through the Canal, cutting the distance from Britain to the Indies via the Cape of Good Hope by half.

The other was a thin little man with a fairly intelligent face, quick nervous movements, and constantly knit eyebrows. Through his long lashes shone very bright eyes, which, however, he was able to mask at will. At this particular moment he was showing signs of impatience, pacing up and down, unable to stay in one place for long.

This man was called Fix,* and he was one of the 'detectives', or roving British policemen, who had been sent to the various ports after the theft at the Bank of England. Fix was to keep the sharpest look-out on all travellers on the Suez route, and, if one of them aroused his suspicion, to shadow him until he received a warrant for his arrest.

Exactly two days previously, Fix had received the description of the suspected thief from the Commissioner of Scotland Yard. This was the distinguished, well-dressed character who had been observed in the cash room of the Bank. The detective, very excited by the substantial reward promised in the case of success, was therefore waiting for the arrival of the *Mongolia* with understandable impatience.

'And you say', he asked the Consul for the tenth time, 'that the boat will soon be here?'

'Yes, Mr Fix. She was reported yesterday off Port Said, and it will not take long for such a fast ship to cover the 100 miles of the Canal. I repeat that the *Mongolia* has always earned the bonus of £25 awarded by the Government for any ship that passes through the Canal 24 hours ahead of schedule.'

'So this ship has come straight from Brindisi then?'

'From Brindisi, where she picked up the mail for the Indies. She left at 5 p.m. on Saturday. So please be patient, she can't be long now. But with the description you've got, I really can't see how you'll be able to spot your man, even if he is on board the *Mongolia*.'

'People of that sort, you scent rather than recognize. Flair is everything. It's like a sixth sense: a combination of hearing, sight, and smell. I've arrested more than one of these gentlemen in my time, and provided that my thief is indeed on board, I can guarantee you that he will not slip through my fingers.'

'I hope so, for it was a big theft.'

'A magnificent theft!' the policeman replied with gusto. 'Fifty-five thousand pounds! Such windfalls don't turn up very often! Thieves are getting parsimonious! The breed of Sheppard* is dying out! People go and get themselves hanged these days for a few shillings!'

'Mr Fix, you are speaking with such ardour that I sincerely wish you every success. But I repeat, I fear that your task may be difficult in the present circumstances. Do you realize that according to the description you've got, this thief looks exactly like an honest man?'

'With all due respect,' dogmatically answered the police inspector, 'great thieves always resemble honest men. It's obvious that those with wicked faces have no choice, they have to go straight, or else they would soon get themselves arrested. Honest faces are the ones you've got to take a special look at. A tough job, I must admit, and no longer a matter of experience, but a veritable art.'

One can see that the aforesaid Fix did not underestimate his own abilities.

Meanwhile the wharf was gradually becoming busier. Sailors of different nationalities, shopkeepers, brokers, porters, and fellahs were arriving in large numbers. The steamship was clearly due in soon.

The weather was quite fine, but the air felt cold, with an easterly wind. A few minarets stood silhouetted above the town by the light of a pale sun. To the south, a jetty more than a mile long stretched out like an arm into the Suez shipping lanes. On the surface of the Red Sea several fishing and coastal vessels, some retaining the elegant form of the ancient galleys, were undulating in the wind.

While wandering amongst the motley crowd, Fix stared briefly at each of the passers-by, out of professional habit.

It was half-past ten.

'But when is this ship going to arrive!' he cried on hearing the port clock strike.

'She can't be far off now,' replied the Consul.

'How long will she put in at Suez?' asked Fix.

'Four hours, the time to coal. The distance from Suez to Aden, at the other end of the Red Sea, is 1,310 nautical miles, and the boat needs to take on fuel supplies.'

'And from Suez, she goes directly to Bombay?'

'Directly, without unloading.'

'Well then,' said Fix, 'if the thief has taken this route and this boat, he must be planning to get off at Suez, so as to take a different route to the Dutch or French colonies in Asia. He must know full well that he will not be safe in India, which is British.'

'Unless he's a very cunning customer indeed,' answered the Consul. 'As you know, a British criminal is always better hidden in London than abroad.'

This observation gave the policeman food for thought, and the Consul went back to his offices close by. The inspector remained alone, full of nervous impatience. He had a funny feeling that his thief simply had to be on board the *Mongolia*. If the rascal had left Britain hoping to get to the New World, the route via the Indies, less carefully watched than the Atlantic, or at least less easily watched, surely had to be his first choice.

Fix did not spend long in his thoughts. Loud whistle blasts announced the arrival of the steamer. A whole horde of porters and fellahs headed for the quayside in a mad rush that was a little worrying for the passengers' limbs and clothing. A dozen boats put out from shore and headed off to meet the ship.

Soon the gigantic hull of the *Mongolia* came into sight, gliding along between the banks of the Canal. Eleven o'clock was striking when the steamer dropped anchor in the road while steam burst noisily out of her escape pipes.

There were quite a few passengers on board. Some remained on the spar-deck admiring the picturesque view of the town; but most got into the boats which had come alongside to meet the *Mongolia*.

Fix examined everyone landing with the utmost care.

At this moment, one of the passengers came up to him, having vigorously pushed away the fellahs assailing him with offers of service. He asked very politely if Fix could possibly tell him where to find the British Consulate. At the same time he held out a passport where he undoubtedly wished to have a British visa stamped.

Fix instinctively took the passport, and quickly read the description.

He barely managed to control an involuntary movement. The document trembled in his hands. The description in the passport was identical to the one received from the Commissioner of Scotland Yard.

'This isn't your own passport?'

'It's my master's.'

'And his whereabouts?'

'He's still on board.'

'He will need to go to the Consulate in person to establish his identity.'

'What, is that really necessary?'

'Indispensable.'

'And where are these offices?'

'On the corner of the square,' replied the inspector, pointing to a building about two hundred yards away.

'All right then, I'll go and get my master. But he won't be very pleased at being disturbed.'

Whereupon, raising his hat to Fix, he went back on board the steamer.

7

Which Shows Once More the Uselessness of
Passports as a Means of Control

THE inspector went back down to the quayside and headed quickly for the British Consulate. He was so insistent that he was immediately ushered into the Consul's office.

'Sir,' he said coming straight to the point, 'I have strong reasons for believing that our man is on board the *Mongolia*.'

And Fix recounted what had happened between him and the servant concerning the passport.

'Well, Mr Fix,' answered the Consul, 'I would be interested to see the thief's face. But I doubt whether he'll come to my office if he's the person you think he is. Thieves aren't generally very keen to leave trace of their movements behind them, and in any case passports are no longer required.'

'Sir, if he is as cunning a man as we think, he'll come!'

'To have his passport stamped?'

'Yes. Passports never serve any other purpose than to annoy honest citizens and help criminals escape. I assure you that his will be in order, but I hope very much that you will not agree to stamp it . . .'

'And why ever not? If his passport is in order,' replied the Consul, 'I have no right to refuse to stamp it.'

'Nevertheless, sir, I need to retain this man here until I get an arrest warrant from London.'

'Ah that, Mr Fix, is your problem! As far as I'm concerned, I cannot . . .'

The Consul didn't finish his sentence. At that moment, a knock came on the door, and the clerk brought in two strangers, one of them the very servant the detective had spoken to.

With him was his master, who presented his passport, laconically asking the Consul to kindly put his visa in it.

The Consul took the passport and examined it conscientiously, while from a corner of the office Fix observed, or rather devoured, the stranger.

When the Consul had finished, he asked:

'Are you Mr Phileas Fogg?'

'I am.'

'And this man is your servant?'

'He is. A Frenchman called Passepartout.'

'Have you just arrived from London?'

'Yes.'

'Heading for . . .?'

'Bombay.'

'Very good, sir. You know that stamping serves no purpose and that we no longer require the presentation of passports?'

'I do,' answered Phileas Fogg; 'but I wish to use your stamp to prove I have passed through Suez.'

'Very well, sir.'

And the Consul signed, dated, and stamped the passport. Mr Fogg paid, coolly raised his hat, and left the office followed by his servant.

'We-ell?' asked the inspector.

'Well, he seems perfectly honest!'

'Maybe,' replied Fix, 'but that is hardly the point. Did you not find, sir, that this phlegmatic gentleman is the spitting image of the thief whose description I have?'

'Quite possibly, but as you know, all descriptions . . .'

'I want to be sure. The servant seems less enigmatic than the master. He's French as well, so he won't be able to keep his mouth shut. Till we meet again, sir.'

And the detective went out in search of Passepartout.

Meanwhile Mr Fogg had left the Consulate buildings and headed back to the quayside. There he gave his servant some orders, got into a boat, returned to the *Mongolia*, and retired to his cabin. He picked up his notebook, containing the following notes:

Left London, Wednesday, 2 October, 8.45 p.m.
Arrived in Paris, Thursday, 3 October, 7.20 a.m.
Left Paris, Thursday, 8.40 a.m.
Arrived in Turin, via Mont Cenis, Friday, 4 October, 6.35 a.m.
Left Turin, Friday, 7.20 a.m.
Arrived in Brindisi, Saturday, 5 October, 4 p.m.
Took the *Mongolia*, Saturday, 5 p.m.

Arrived at Suez, Wednesday, 9 October, 11 a.m.
Total time spent: 158½ hrs, or 6½ days.

Mr Fogg wrote these dates down in a schedule divided into columns that ran from 2 October to 21 December. It indicated the month, date, and day for the expected and actual arrival times at each principal point:* Paris, Brindisi, Suez, Bombay, Calcutta, Singapore, Hong Kong, Yokohama, San Francisco, New York, Liverpool, and London. This allowed him to calculate how much he had saved or lost at each stage of his journey.

His highly methodical travel-plan thus included everything, and Mr Fogg always knew if he was ahead or behind.

Accordingly, he noted his arrival in Suez as Wednesday, 9 October. Coinciding with the scheduled arrival time, this constituted neither gain nor loss.

Then he took lunch in his cabin. As for seeing the town, he did not even think of it, being of that breed of Britons who have their servants do their sightseeing for them.

8

*In Which Passepartout Speaks Perhaps a Little
More Freely Than He Should*

Fix had quickly caught up with Passepartout on the quayside, who was strolling and looking about him, since he personally did not feel obliged to see nothing.

'Well, my friend,' said Fix. 'Is your passport now stamped?'

'Oh! It's you, sir,' answered the Frenchman. 'Much obliged. Our papers are perfectly in order.'

'And are you seeing the sights?'

'Yes, but we're doing everything so quickly that I seem to be travelling in a dream. We're in Suez, it would appear?'

'In Suez.'

'Which is in Egypt?'

'In Egypt, yes.'

'And in Africa?'

'And in Africa.'

'In Africa!' repeated Passepartout. 'I simply can't believe it. Just think, sir: I couldn't see myself going any further than Paris. I visited that wonderful city from 7.20 to 8.40 a.m., between the Gare du Nord and the Gare de Lyon. It was through the windows of a hackney cab and in the pouring rain! Such a shame. I would dearly have loved to see the Père-Lachaise Cemetery and the Champs-Elysées Circus* again!'

'So you're in a bit of hurry, are you?'

'I'm not, but my master is. Come to mention it, I must buy some socks and shirts. We left with no luggage, only an overnight bag.'

'I'll take you to a bazaar where you'll get everything you need.'

'Sir, you really are too kind!'

And the two of them set off. Passepartout was still talking.

'One thing, I must make sure I don't miss the boat.'

'You've got plenty of time, it's not twelve o'clock yet.'

Passepartout fished out his enormous watch.

'Twelve? Come on, it's only 9.52!'

'Your watch must be slow.'

'It can't be. My watch is a family heirloom, it belonged to my great-grandfather. It never loses more than five minutes a year. It's a genuine chronometer!'

'I know what's happened. You've stayed on London time, which is about two hours behind Suez. You need to remember to adjust your watch in each new country.'

'Me touch my watch? Not a chance!'

'Well it just won't agree with the sun then.'

'So much the worse for the sun, sir! The sun will be wrong!'

And the honest fellow put his watch back in its fob with a proud gesture.

A few moments later, Fix continued:

'So you left London in a real hurry?'

'I should say so! Last Wednesday, Mr Fogg came back from the club at eight in the evening, a thing he never does—and we left three-quarters of an hour later.'

'But where's he going then?'

'Straight in front of him! He's going round the world.'

'Around the world!'

'Yes, in 80 days! A bet, says he. But just between the two of us, I don't believe a word of it. It wouldn't make sense. There must be something else in it.'

'Ah, so he's an eccentric, is he, this Mr Fogg?'

'So it would seem.'

'And wealthy?'

'Obviously. He's taken a nice little packet with him, in crisp new notes. And he doesn't mind spending it, either. Why, he's promised the chief engineer of the *Mongolia* a handsome reward if we get to Bombay ahead of time!'

'And have you known your master for long?'

'For long? I entered his service on the day we left.'

One can easily imagine the effect these replies produced on the already overexcited mind of the police inspector.

Everything inevitably confirmed Fix's preconceptions: the hurried departure from London soon after the theft, the large sum being carried, the hurry to travel to faraway countries, the excuse of an eccentric bet. Fix kept the Frenchman talking, and soon he became certain that the fellow hardly knew his master at all. Fogg lived in London on his own, was said to be rich although no one knew where his money came from, was meant to be an unfathomable man, etc. Fix slowly became convinced that Phileas Fogg would not leave the ship at Suez, and that he really was heading for Bombay.

'Is Bombay very far?' asked Passepartout.

'Quite far. About ten days away by sea.'

'And where do you find Bombay?'

'In India.'

'Which is in Asia?'

'Of course.'

'Good Lord! Listen, I'm going to tell you something. There's one thing that's been bothering me . . . it's my burner!'

'What burner?'

'My gas burner. I forgot to turn it off, and so have to pay the bill myself. I've worked out that it's costing me 2*s.* every

24 hours, or 6*d.* more than I earn. So it's easy to calculate that if the journey goes on for any length of time . . .'

Did Fix understand this difficulty with the gas? Probably not. In any case, he was no longer listening, but coming to a decision. The Frenchman and he had got to the bazaar. Fix left his companion to his shopping, warned him not to miss the *Mongolia*'s departure, and rushed back to the Consulate.

Now that his mind was made up, he had totally recovered his composure.

'Sir,' he said to the Consul, 'I no longer have any doubts whatsoever. I've got my man. He's pretending to be an eccentric trying to do a trip around the world in 80 days.'

'How cunning! He's planning to return to London after throwing the police forces of two continents off his trail!'

'We'll see about that.'

'But is there no chance you've made a mistake?' asked the Consul once again.

'I'm not making a mistake.'

'Then why is this thief so keen to get a stamp to prove he's been to Suez?'

'I've got no idea, sir,' replied the detective. 'But just listen to this.'

And in a few words, he reported the gist of his conversation with the servant of the aforesaid Fogg.

'All the evidence', said the Consul, 'does seem to point against this man. But what are you going to do?'

'I'm going to send a wire to London telling them to immediately send a warrant for his arrest to Bombay. Then I'll go on board the *Mongolia*, and tail my thief as far as India. And there, on British soil, I'll politely accost him, with a warrant in one hand and the other on his shoulder.'

Having coldly pronounced these words, the policeman took leave of the Consul and headed for the Telegraph Office. There he sent the previously mentioned telegram to the Commissioner of the Metropolitan Police.

A quarter of an hour later, Fix went on board the *Mongolia*, his small bag in his hand, and plenty of money on him. Soon the steamer was running at full speed over the waters of the Red Sea.

9

Where the Red Sea and Indian Ocean Favour
Phileas Fogg's Designs

THE distance from Suez to Aden is exactly 1,310 nautical miles, and the Company's regulations assign its steamships 138 hours to cover the distance. The *Mongolia*, whose boilers were stoked up, was moving fast so as to be ahead of the regulation time.

Nearly all of the passengers taken on board at Brindisi were bound for India. Some were just going to Bombay, others to Calcutta via Bombay: now that a railway crosses the whole width of India, there is no need to sail round the tip of Ceylon.

Amongst the passengers of the *Mongolia* were various civil servants and officers of all ranks. Some belonged to the British Army in the strict sense, the others officered native Sepoy regiments—but all received very generous salaries, notwithstanding that the Government has now taken over the rights and duties of the East India Company. Second lieutenants get £280 per annum, brigadiers, £2,400, and generals, £4,000.[1]

There was consequently a luxurious lifestyle on board the *Mongolia*. This society of civil servants had a few other young Britons mixed in, who were travelling to set up businesses in faraway places with £50,000 in their pockets. The Purser, in whom the Company placed its trust—the equal of the captain on board—conducted things in style. At breakfast, at the lunch at two o'clock, at the dinner at 5.30, at the supper at eight, the tables groaned with the dishes of fresh meat and puddings provided by the liner's own butcher and kitchens. The lady passengers—there were some—changed clothes twice a day. There was music—and even dancing, when the sea allowed.

---

[1] The salary of civil servants is still higher. Mere clerical assistants on the first level of the hierarchy receive £480; judges, £2,400; high court judges, £10,000; governors, £12,000; and the Governor-General, more than £24,000. (Author's Note)

But the Red Sea is highly capricious, and too often unpleasant, like all long, narrow gulfs. When the wind blew from the Asian or the African coasts, the *Mongolia*, a long rocket with a propeller on the end, was caught abeam, and rolled terribly. At these times the ladies would disappear, the pianos fall silent, and the songs and dances stop. And yet, in spite of the squalls, despite the storms, the steamer, propelled by its powerful engine, forged ahead towards the Strait of Bab el Mandeb without pausing.

What was Phileas Fogg doing all this time? One might think he was constantly anxious and nervous, continually worrying about changes in the wind that might impede the ship's progress, about tumultuous movements of the swell damaging the engine; in short, all sorts of possible mishaps which, by making the *Mongolia* put into some port, would have threatened the success of his journey.

Not at all—or at least, if Mr Fogg did think about such possibilities, he showed nothing. He was still the impassive, the imperturbable member of the Reform Club, whom no incident or accident could surprise. He appeared no more moved than the chronometers on board. Rarely was he seen on deck. He made little effort to observe this Red Sea, so redolent in memories and the theatre of the opening scenes of human history. He did not come and observe the fascinating towns crowded along its banks, whose picturesque silhouettes sometimes appeared on the horizon. He did not even dream about the dangers of this Gulf of Arabia which the Classical historians—Strabo, Arrian, Artemidorus, and Idrisi*—always spoke of with horror. In the olden days sailors never ventured out on it without first consecrating their journey with propitiatory sacrifices.

So what did this original do, incarcerated in the *Mongolia*? First of all, he ate his four square meals a day: the pitching and rolling could never upset such a marvellously regulated machine. And secondly, he played whist.

Yes, he had found partners as fanatical as himself: a tax-collector heading for his post at Goa, a minister called the Revd Decimus Smith who was returning to Bombay, and a Brigadier-General in the British Army rejoining his regiment at Benares. These three passengers had the same passion for whist as Mr Fogg, and they played for hours on end, remaining just as silently absorbed as him.

As for Passepartout, seasickness had no effect on him. He had a cabin near the stern and took his meals seriously, just like his master. It must be said that the journey, carried out in these conditions, no longer displeased him. He was making the most of it. Well-fed and -housed, he was travelling places, and in any case, as he said to himself, this whole fantasy would certainly come to a halt at Bombay.

The day after leaving Suez, 10 October, he was on deck. It was with some pleasure that he bumped into that most obliging person whom he had addressed on landing in Egypt.

'If I'm not very much mistaken,' he said, going up with his most amiable smile, 'it really is you, sir, who were so helpful to me as a guide in Suez?'

'Yes, indeed,' answered the detective; 'I recognized you as well. Aren't you the servant of that peculiar Englishman . . .'

'Precisely. Mr . . .?'

'Fix.'

'Well, Mr Fix, delighted to find you on board. Where are you headed for?'

'Bombay, just like you.'

'All the better! Have you done this trip before?'

'Several times. I work for P. & O.'

'So you must know India?'

'Well . . . yes . . .' replied Fix, not wishing to commit himself too much.

'And this India, is it interesting?'

'Fascinating! Mosques, minarets, temples, fakirs, pagodas, tigers, snakes, Indian dancing-girls!* But with any luck you'll have some time to see the country?'

'I hope so too, Mr Fix. I'm sure you understand that a man with a healthy mind cannot spend his whole life jumping from steamships into railway carriages, and from carriages back on to steamships, on the pretext he's going round the world in 80 days! No: all these antics will have to stop at Bombay, take my word for it.'

'And is Mr Fogg keeping well?' enquired Fix in his most casual tone.

'Perfectly. Just like me. I'm eating like an ogre who's been on a diet. It must be the sea air.'

'But I never see your master on deck.'

'No. He has no curiosity.'

'Do you know, Mr Passepartout, that this so-called journey in 80 days might easily be the cover for some secret assignment . . . a diplomatic mission, for example?'

'Indeed, Mr Fix. I confess I really don't know. But to tell you the truth, I wouldn't give tuppence to find out.'

After this meeting, Passepartout and Fix often chatted. The inspector thought it important to get to know Mr Fogg's servant. It might be useful at some time. Accordingly he frequently invited him to the bar-room of the *Mongolia* for a few glasses of whisky or pale ale. The good-natured fellow accepted willingly, and even felt obliged to return the compliment—finding, indeed, that this Fix was an extremely good sort.

Meanwhile the steamer moved swiftly on. On the 13th Mocha* was sighted, with its girdle of ruined walls, and a few verdant date trees standing out above them. Amongst the distant mountains stretched vast fields of coffee trees. Passepartout was delighted to see this famous town, and even decided that it looked just like an enormous half-cup, with its round walls and its ruined fort sticking out like a handle.*

The following night, the *Mongolia* entered the Strait of Bab el Mandeb, whose name is Arabic for Gate of Tears; and, the following day, the 14th, it stopped over at Steamer Point, on the north-west side of the Port of Aden. Here it was due to stock up with fuel again.

This nourishment of steamship boilers is a serious matter at such distances from the centres of production. The Peninsular Company alone pays out about £800,000 a year on it. It has found it necessary, in fact, to establish depots in several ports on faraway oceans, with the coal costing as much as £4 a ton.

The *Mongolia* still had 1,650 miles to go before reaching Bombay, and was due to spend four hours at Steamer Point to fill its hold.

But this delay could do no harm at all to Phileas Fogg's programme, since it was allowed for. In any case the *Mongolia* had arrived in Aden in the evening of 14 October instead of the following morning: a gain of fifteen hours.

Mr Fogg and his servant went ashore. The gentleman wished to have his passport stamped. Fix followed them without being noticed. When he had completed this formality, Phileas Fogg went back on board to continue his interrupted game.

As for Passepartout, he strolled around, as was his habit, in the middle of this population of Somalis, Banians,* Parsees, Jews, Arabs, and Europeans who comprise the 25,000 inhabitants of Aden. He admired the fortifications* which make this town the Gibraltar of the Indian Ocean, as well as the magnificent cisterns on which the British engineers are still working, two thousand years after the engineers of King Solomon.

'Fascinating, it's all fascinating!' Passepartout repeated to himself as he came back on board. 'It's really useful to travel, if you want to see new things.'

At 6 p.m. the blades of the *Mongolia*'s propellers were biting into the waters of Aden harbour, then soon afterwards the Indian Ocean. A total of 168 hours were allocated for the crossing from Aden to Bombay. As it happened, the Indian Ocean provided favourable conditions, for the wind stayed north-westerly. The sails were brought into use and helped the steam.

With this additional support, the ship rolled less. The female passengers reappeared on deck in light new clothing. The songs and dances started up again.

In other words, the journey was being continued in the best possible conditions. Passepartout was delighted with the pleasant companion that chance had provided him in the person of Fix.

On Sunday, 20 October, at about midday, the Indian coast was sighted. Two hours later, a pilot climbed on board the

Mongolia. On the horizon, a background of hills appeared harmoniously against the backdrop of the sky. Soon the rows of palm trees covering the town stood out clearly. The steamship penetrated the harbour, formed by Salsette, Kolaba, Elephanta, and Butcher Islands, and at 4.30 it drew up alongside Bombay quay.

Phileas Fogg was at that moment finishing his thirty-third rubber of the day. With his partner, he had pulled off an audacious coup, making all thirteen tricks. So he was ending this fine crossing with a superb slam.

The *Mongolia* was set to reach Bombay on 22 October. It was arriving on the 20th. A gain of two days since departure from London, which Phileas Fogg duly inscribed in the profits column of his schedule.

10

Where Passepartout Is Only Too Happy To Get Off With Losing Just His Shoe

IT is well known that India—that great upside-down triangle pointing to the south—has an area of 1,400,000 square miles, with an unequally distributed population of 180 million. The British Government exercises effective power over part of this huge country. It maintains a Governor-General in Calcutta, Governors in Madras, Bombay, and Bengal, and a Lieutenant-Governor in Agra.

But British India in the strict sense only covers an area of 700,000 square miles and a population of 100–110 million. In other words, a considerable part of the territory still escapes the Queen's authority; and, indeed, amongst certain fierce and dreaded rajahs of the interior, Indian independence continues absolute.

From 1756—the date when the first British establishment was founded, on the spot now occupied by Madras—to the year when the great Sepoy Rebellion* broke out, the famous East India Company* was all-powerful. It gradually annexed the various states, bought from the rajahs for annual annuities, of which very little or nothing was ever in fact paid; and it appointed the Governor-General and all the civil and military employees. But it is no longer in existence, and the British possessions in India now come directly under the Crown.

Accordingly, the general appearance, the customs, and the linguistic and cultural patterns of the Subcontinent are changing very quickly. Formerly every traditional means of transport was used: foot, horse, cart, wheelbarrow, palanquin, men's backs, coach, etc. But now steamboats navigate on the Indus and the Ganges at a rate of knots, and a railway crosses the whole width of India, with branch lines all along its route, meaning that Bombay is only three days from Calcutta.*

This railway does not follow a straight line across the country. The distance is only 1,000 or 1,100 miles as the crow flies, and the trains wouldn't need three days to cover it even at a moderate speed; but the distance is increased at least a third by the detour the railway makes to Allahabad in the north.

The following, to sum up, are the main points on the Great Indian Peninsular Railway. After leaving the island of Bombay, it crosses Salsette, jumps on to the mainland opposite Thana, crosses the mountain range of the Western Ghats, heads north-east towards Burhanpur, runs through the more or less independent territory of Bundelkhand,* works its way up to Allahabad, cuts a chord towards the east, meets the Ganges at Benares, moves slightly away from it, and finally, running back south-east via Burdwan and the French town of Chandernagore, arrives at its terminus of Calcutta.

The passengers of the *Mongolia* landed in Bombay at 4.30, and the Calcutta train was leaving at eight sharp.

Mr Fogg took leave of his partners, left the steamer, told his servant exactly what shopping to do, and gave strict instructions to be at the station by eight o'clock. Then, with his regular pace marking the seconds like the pendulum of an astronomic clock, he headed for the Passport Office.

He did not think of visiting any of Bombay's wonders: not the Town Hall, the magnificent library, the forts, docks, cotton markets, bazaars, mosques, synagogues, Armenian churches, or the splendid pagoda of Malabar Hill* with its twin polygon-shaped towers. He had no wish to see the masterpieces of the Island of Elephanta with its mysterious *hypogea*,* hidden to the south-east of the harbour, nor the Kanheri Grottoes on Salsette,* those wonderful ruins of Buddhist architecture.

No! nothing. After the Passport Office, Phileas Fogg headed calmly for the station, and there he ordered dinner. Amongst other dishes, the head waiter ventured to recommend a certain 'local rabbit'* casserole, which he said was excellent.

Phileas Fogg ordered the casserole and carefully tasted it; but found it detestable, despite the highly spiced sauce.

He called the head waiter over.

'*Garçon*,' he said, fixing his gaze on him, 'do you call that rabbit?'

'Yes my lord,' answered the impudent wit. 'Jungle rabbit.'

'But are you sure the rabbit didn't miaow when it was killed?'

'Miaow? Your Excellency, a rabbit? I swear . . .'

'My good man,' coldly said Mr Fogg, 'do not swear, and simply remember this: Indian cats used to be considered sacred animals. That was in the good old days.'

'For cats, my lord?'

'For travellers too!'

And Mr Fogg calmly continued to eat his dinner.

Fix had left the *Mongolia* a few moments after Mr Fogg, rushing off to see the Commissioner of Police in Bombay. He presented his credentials as a detective, the mission he was carrying out, and the position concerning the supposed culprit. Had an arrest warrant arrived from London? Nothing had been received. And indeed a warrant which had left after Fogg could not have got there yet.

Fix was put out. He tried to persuade the Commissioner to give him a warrant for Mr Fogg's arrest. The Commissioner refused. The case was a matter for the Metropolitan Police, who alone could by law issue a warrant. This regard for principles, this rigorous observation of the law, is quite in accordance with British practice, which permits no bending of the rules where individual freedom is concerned.

Fix did not insist, understanding that he had to resign himself to waiting for his warrant. But he resolved to keep a watchful eye on the inscrutable ruffian throughout his whole stay in Bombay. He was in no doubt whatsoever that Phileas Fogg *would* stay—after all this was Passepartout's conviction as well. And that would allow time for the warrant to arrive.

But when Passepartout received the instructions from his master on leaving the *Mongolia*, he had realized that what had happened in Suez and Paris would happen again in Bombay. The journey wasn't going to finish here, but would continue at least as far as Calcutta, and possibly even further. And he began to wonder whether Mr Fogg's bet mightn't be serious, whether fate wasn't dragging him off, despite his longing to live so peacefully, hauling him off to girdle the Earth in 80 days?

After buying several shirts and pairs of socks, he passed the time wandering around the Bombay streets. Everywhere were great crowds of people: every nationality of European, Persians with pointed headgear, Bunhyas with round turbans, Sindhis with square caps, Armenians in long robes, and Parsees in black mitres. Today was a holiday celebrated by the Parsees, or Guebres, direct descendants of the Zoroastrians,* the most hard-working, civilized, intelligent, and austere of the Indians, the race of the rich businessmen of Bombay. They were celebrating a sort of religious carnival, with all sorts of processions and entertainments. There were Indian dancing-girls, dressed in pink gauze embroidered with gold and silver, who, to the sound of viols and the beating of gongs, performed a ravishing dance, while still remaining perfectly modest.

It goes without saying that Passepartout watched these bewitching ceremonies with eyes and ears wide open to see and hear and the expression of the most innocent 'booby' imaginable.

But unfortunately for him and his master, his curiosity took him further than it ought to have, and risked the whole journey.

Having caught a taste of the Parsee carnival, Passepartout was heading for the station, when, as he passed in front of the magnificent pagoda of Malabar Hill, the unfortunate idea came to him to look inside.

He was ignorant of two things: that to enter certain Indian pagodas is strictly forbidden to Christians; and that even the faithful must take off their shoes at the door before going in. It should be said here that, in accordance with a sensible policy, the British Government not only protects the religion of the country, but enforces respect of the most trivial observances, and severely punishes anyone who violates them.

Passepartout had gone in without wishing anyone any harm, as a simple tourist, and was admiring the dazzling tinsel of the Brahmin ornamentation in Malabar Hill, when he was suddenly thrown down on to the holy flagstones. Three priests, absolutely furious, had hurled themselves on to him, and now tore off his shoes and socks, before raining blows down on him, producing wild cries all the while.

The Frenchman used his power and agility, and got up again quickly. With a punch and a kick, he knocked down two of his adversaries, obstructed by their long robes. Racing out of the pagoda as fast as his legs would carry him, he soon left far behind the third Brahmin, who had given chase and was shouting to the crowd.

At 7.55, only a few minutes before the train left, Passepartout arrived at the railway station. His head and feet were bare, and during the fight he had lost the parcel containing the shopping.

Fix was on the platform. He had followed Fogg to the station, and had realized that the scoundrel was going to leave Bombay after all. He decided to follow him to Calcutta—and further if necessary. Passepartout did not see Fix, standing in the shadows; but Fix eavesdropped on Passepartout's brief recounting of his adventures.

'I trust this will not happen again,' said Phileas Fogg as he sat down in a compartment.

The poor fellow, in bare feet and total embarrassment, followed without a word.

Fix was about to get on the train, when a thought suddenly struck him, making him change his mind.

'No,' he said, 'I'm staying. An offence committed on Indian soil. I've got my man!'

The locomotive produced a loud whistle, and the train disappeared into the night.

11

Where Phileas Fogg Buys a Mount at a Fabulous Price

THE train had left on time. In it were a few officers, and tourists, civil servants, and opium and indigo merchants, travelling to the eastern part of the Subcontinent on business.

Passepartout was in the same compartment as his master. Another person was in the opposite corner.

It was the Brigadier-General, Sir Francis Cromarty by name, who had been one of Mr Fogg's partners from Suez to Bombay, and was now rejoining his troops outside Benares.

Tall, blond, aged about fifty, Sir Francis Cromarty had played a highly distinguished role during the last Indian Mutiny. He really deserved the term 'native' since he had lived in India from his earliest years, only putting in an occasional appearance in his country of birth. He was an educated man, who would willingly have provided information about the customs, history, and political system of India if Phileas Fogg had been the sort of man to ask for it. But this gentleman requested nothing. He wasn't travelling, he was describing a circumference. He constituted a heavy body moving in orbit around the terrestrial globe, following the rational laws of mechanics. At this very moment he was recalculating the hours expended since his departure from London: and he would have rubbed his hands, if it had been in his nature to make any useless movement.

Sir Francis Cromarty had been struck by the oddness of his travelling companion, although he had only examined him cards in hand or between two rubbers. Well might he ask himself, then, whether a human heart beat under this cold exterior, whether Phileas Fogg had a soul that was sensitive to the beauties of nature or to moral aspirations. He found it difficult to say. Amongst all the originals that the Brigadier-

General had ever encountered, none could be compared to this product of the exact sciences.

Phileas Fogg had not concealed from Sir Francis Cromarty that his project was to travel around the world, nor why and how he was doing it. The Brigadier-General merely considered this bet an eccentric whim serving no useful purpose—without the necessary *transire benefaciendo** that must guide every reasonable man. At the rate this bizarre gentleman operated, he would obviously pass through life without achieving anything, either for himself or for anyone else.

An hour after Bombay, the train passed over viaducts, crossed Salsette Island, and reached the mainland. At Kalyan Station, a branch line headed off to the right towards Khandala and Poona and the South-east of India. After Pawule Station, the train headed off into the highly ramified mountains of the Western Ghats, ranges made of trap* and basalt, and whose highest summits are covered with thick forests.

From time to time Sir Francis Cromarty and Phileas Fogg exchanged a few words. At one point the Brigadier-General, pursuing a conversation that constantly flagged, remarked:

'Some years ago, Mr Fogg, you would have undergone a delay at this point that would have probably ruined your travel plans.'

'Why so, Sir Francis?'

'Because the railway stopped at the foot of these mountains, which had to be crossed by palanquin or pony to Kandallah Station, on the far side.'*

'This delay would not have interrupted the organization of my programme in the slightest. I have planned that certain obstacles may occur.'

'However, Mr Fogg,' the Brigadier-General tried again, 'you ran the risk of having some trouble on your hands with that boy's escapade.'

Passepartout, his feet twisted under the travelling rug, was deep asleep and did not dream he was being talked about.

'The British Government is extremely severe with this sort of offence, and rightly so. It insists that the Indians' religious customs be scrupulously respected, and if your servant had been caught . . .'

'Well if he had been caught, Sir Francis, he would have been convicted, served his sentence, and then calmly come back to Europe. I fail to see how this affair could have slowed down his master's progress.'

Whereupon the conversation expired once more. During the night the train crossed the Ghats, went through Nasik, and then, the following day, 21 October, dashed across the relatively flat countryside of the State of Khandesh. The landscape was well cultivated and dotted with little towns, with the minarets of the pagodas replacing the church spires in European settlements. This fertile country was irrigated by large numbers of streams, most of them tributaries or subtributaries of the Godavari.

Passepartout had woken up and watched, unable to believe that he was crossing India on the Great Peninsular Railway. It all seemed made-up to him. And yet nothing could be more genuine!* The locomotive, with a British engine-driver and burning British coal, threw its smoke out over the plantations of red pepper, cotton, coffee, nutmeg, and cloves. The steam twisted in spirals around the thickets of palms, which sheltered picturesque bungalows, a few *viharis* (abandoned monasteries), and fantastic temples covered with the inexhaustible embellishments of Indian architecture. Next, huge expanses of countryside stretched as far as the eye could see, jungles lacking neither snakes nor tigers terrified by the whinnying of the train—and finally tropical forests, cut in two by the railway line, but still haunted by elephants, watching the tousled convoy go by with their thoughtful eyes.

That morning, the travellers passed Malegaon Station, then crossed the gloomy region so often drenched in blood by the disciples of the goddess Kali.* Not far away arose Ellora and its fantastic pagodas; not far away the famous Aurungabad, capital of the untamed Aurangzeb,* now merely a county town in one of the states separated from the Nizam's kingdom. It was this land that was under the sway of Feringhea, the chief of the Thugs, the king of the Stranglers.* His assassins, brought together into a highly elusive society in honour of the goddess of death, strangled their victims of all ages, but without ever shedding a drop of blood. There was a time when no area of this country could be turned up without discovering a body. The British Government has been able to prevent many such murders, but the terrible society still exists and still operates.

The train stopped at Burhanpur Station at 12.30, and Passepartout was able to obtain a pair of local slippers adorned with fake pearls, at an outrageous price. He put them on with unconcealed vanity.

The passengers took a quick lunch, then continued on towards Assergur Station, having briefly travelled parallel to the banks of the Tapti, a small river which comes out in the Gulf of Cambay near Surat.*

It is appropriate here to comment on the thoughts passing through Passepartout's mind. Until Bombay he had believed and hoped that things wouldn't go any further. But now, steaming across India, a reversal had happened in his mind. His natural instincts had come rushing back. The wild imaginings of his youth returned. He took his master's projects seriously, and now believed in the bet, in the trip around the world, in the deadline that had to be met. The poor boy even began to worry about delays, about accidents that might happen on the way. He felt himself caught up in this rash gamble, and trembled at the thought of the possible consequences of his inexcusable gawping the day before. As a result, being much less phlegmatic than Mr Fogg, he was also much more anxious. He counted and recounted the days which had gone by, cursed each halt, accused the train of dallying, and secretly blamed Mr Fogg for not promising the driver a reward. The good fellow did not know that what is possible on a steamer may not be on a railway, whose speed is fixed by regulations.

Towards evening, they headed into the passes of the Mountains of Sutpoor, which separate the State of Khandesh from that of Bundelkhand.

The following day, 22 October, Passepartout consulted his watch in response to a question from Sir Francis Cromarty, and replied that it was three in the morning. And indeed this wonderful watch was, quite logically, four hours slow, being still set to the Greenwich meridian, nearly 77 degrees further west.

Sir Francis therefore corrected the time given by Passepartout, and made the same observation as Fix had. He tried to make him realize that he had to adjust to each new meridian. Since he was constantly travelling eastwards, towards the sun, each time a degree was covered, the day lost four minutes. It was no use. Whether or not the stubborn fellow understood the Brigadier-General's remarks, he obstinately refused to put his watch forward, invariably maintaining it on Greenwich time. An innocent obsession in any case, and one that could do nobody any harm.

At 8 a.m., fifteen miles before Rothal Station, the train stopped in the middle of a vast clearing bordered by a few bungalows and workers' huts. The guard walked along the track shouting:

'All change! All change!'

Phileas Fogg looked at Sir Francis Cromarty, who seemed to understand nothing about this halt in the middle of a forest of tamarinds and khajurs.*

Passepartout, equally surprised, dashed out on to the track but came back almost straightaway, exclaiming:

'Sir, no railway!'

'What do you mean?' asked Sir Francis Cromarty.

'I mean that the train can't go any further!'

The Brigadier-General immediately left the carriage. Phileas Fogg followed him, but without hurrying. The two men turned to the driver.

'Where are we?' asked Sir Francis.

'At the hamlet of Kholby.'

'Are we stopping here?'

'We have to. The railway isn't finished yet.'

'What? Not finished!'

'No, there's still 50 miles to be completed between here and Allahabad, where the track starts up again.'

'But the newspapers said the railway was open right through.'

'What can I say, sir? The newspapers were wrong.'

'But you sold us tickets from Bombay to Calcutta!'

Sir Francis Cromarty was beginning to boil.

'Yes, but passengers are well aware that they have to get themselves from Kholby to Allahabad.'

Sir Francis Cromarty was furious. Passepartout would gladly have knocked down the guard, even though he was unable to do anything about the situation. He didn't dare look at his master.

'Sir Francis,' Mr Fogg said, 'we shall have to consider, with your help, how to get to Allahabad.'

'Mr Fogg, this delay has completely ruined your expedition.'

'No, Sir Francis. It was planned.'

'What, you knew that the track . . .'

'Not at all; but I knew that some sort of obstacle would appear on my route sooner or later. In any case there is no harm done. I have two days in reserve that can still be used. There's a steamer that leaves Calcutta for Hong Kong at midday on the 25th. Today is only the 22nd, so we'll arrive in Calcutta in time.'

There was nothing that could be said in response to such a confident statement.

It was only too true that the railway's operation stopped at this point. Newspapers resemble certain watches in having a mania for being fast, and they had prematurely announced the completion of the line. Most travellers knew about the break in the track. They had left the train and commandeered all the various vehicles of the small town: palki-gharries* with four wheels, carts drawn by zebus, a sort of ox with a hump, carriages resembling mobile pagodas, palanquins, ponies, etc. Accordingly, although they searched the town, Mr Fogg and Francis Cromarty returned empty-handed.

'I'll carry on on foot,' said Phileas Fogg.

At this moment Passepartout came back, frowning meaningfully at his gorgeous but flimsy slippers. Very fortunately he had been exploring as well, and announced, with some diffidence:

'Sir,' he said, 'I think I've found a means of transport.'

'What is it?'*

'An elephant. One that belongs to an Indian who lives a hundred yards from here.'

'Let's have a look at the elephant,' said Mr Fogg.

Five minutes later Phileas Fogg, Sir Francis Cromarty, and Passepartout arrived at a hut adjoining an enclosure surrounded by a tall fence. In the hut was an Indian, and in the enclosure, an elephant. At their request the Indian took Mr Fogg and his two companions into the enclosure.

There they found themselves in the presence of a half-domesticated animal being raised by its owner: not to make it a beast of burden but a fighting animal.

To achieve this he had begun to modify the elephant's naturally gentle character in such a way as to gradually lead it into the frenzied paroxysm called *musth** in the Indian language—by feeding it with sugar and butter for three months. This treatment may seem unlikely to produce the desired result, but it is none the less employed with success by the breeders. Fortunately for Mr Fogg, the elephant in question had only just been put on this diet, and so was not yet actually in *musth*.

Kiouni—for this was his name—was, like the rest of his species, able to move quickly for long periods. Since he lacked any other mount, Phileas Fogg decided to use this one.

However, elephants are expensive in India, where they are beginning to become scarce. The males, the only ones suitable for circus fighting, are highly sought after. They reproduce only rarely when kept in domesticity, so the only way of acquiring them is by hunting. They are considered very precious, and when Mr Fogg asked the Indian if he wanted to hire his elephant, he refused point blank.

Mr Fogg tried again, offering the excessive price of £10 an hour. Same refusal. Twenty pounds—yet another rebuff. Forty pounds—still a rejection. Passepartout jumped at each bid, but the Indian wasn't allowing himself to be tempted.

Nevertheless, it was a substantial amount. Assuming the elephant took fifteen hours to get to Allahabad, that would mean £600 for its owner.

Phileas Fogg, without getting worked up in any way, proposed that the Indian sell his animal, offering him £1,000.

The Indian rejected the deal. Perhaps the knave could scent a wonderful bargain.

Sir Francis Cromarty took Mr Fogg aside and urged him to consider before going any further. Phileas Fogg replied that it was not his habit to act without considering, and that ultimately a bet of £20,000 was involved. So he needed this elephant. Even if he had to pay twenty times the value, he would get him somehow.

Mr Fogg came back to the Indian, whose small eyes were alight with greed, showing full well that it was only a question of price. Phileas Fogg offered £1,200, then £1,500, then £1,800. Finally he offered £2,000. Passepartout, normally ruddy, was pale with emotion.

At £2,000 the Indian gave in.

'By my slippers,' exclaimed Passepartout, 'it's quite a price to pay for elephant-steak!'

Now that the deal had been reached, it only remained to find a guide. This proved easier. A bright-looking young Parsee offered his services. Mr Fogg accepted, and promised him a high rate of pay, which could only increase his intelligence!

The elephant was fetched and fitted out without delay. The Parsee was experienced in the profession of 'mahout' or elephant-keeper. He covered the elephant's back with a sort of saddle-cloth and arranged on each side of its body a rather uncomfortable litter.

Phileas Fogg paid the Indian in banknotes extracted from the famous bag. It really seemed as though they were being drawn from Passepartout's entrails! Then Mr Fogg offered Sir Francis Cromarty a ride to Allahabad Station. He accepted. An extra traveller couldn't possibly tire the huge beast.

Food and drink were bought in the village. Sir Francis Cromarty sat down in one of the litters and Phileas Fogg in the other. Passepartout sat astride the saddle-cloth between his master and the Brigadier-General, and the Parsee perched himself on the elephant's neck. At nine o'clock the animal left the town, and thrust its way into the thick forest of fan palms, taking the shortest route.

12

Where Phileas Fogg and His Companions Venture Through the Indian Jungle, and What Ensues

In order to shorten the distance to cover, the guide headed off to the left, away from the track where the works were still being carried out. The railway line, obstructed by the capricious ramifications of the Vindhya Range, was not the shortest path that Phileas Fogg had to take. The Parsee, perfectly familiar with the roads and tracks of the area, claimed to be able to gain about twenty miles by cutting through the forest, and his idea was accepted.

Phileas Fogg and Sir Francis Cromarty, buried up to their necks in the howdahs, were shaken around by the stiff trot of the elephant, which was moving at a considerable speed under his mahout. They endured the situation with the most British imperturbability, talking little and hardly able to see each other.

As for Passepartout on the animal's back, he received the full force of every jolt. He followed his master's recommendation, and kept his tongue well away from his teeth, for it would have been severed. The good fellow was thrown back and forth between the neck and the rump of the elephant, performing acrobatics like a clown on a trampoline. But he joked and laughed in the middle of the routine, and from time to time pulled a sugar-lump out of his bag, that the intelligent Kiouni took with the end of his trunk, without interrupting his regular trot for a moment.

After two hours' march, the guide stopped the elephant and gave him an hour's rest. The animal drank at a neighbouring pool and devoured branches and shrubs. Sir Francis Cromarty was not sorry for this halt as he was a broken man. Mr Fogg seemed as fresh as if straight out of bed.

'He's made of iron!' said the Brigadier-General, looking at him with admiration.

'Wrought iron,' answered Passepartout, as he prepared a simple lunch.

At 12.00, the guide gave the signal for departure. The countryside soon became very rugged. The great forests were replaced by thickets of tamarinds, dwarf palms, and then vast arid plains, bristling with thin shrubs and dotted with large blocks of syenite. This whole region of the Upper Bundelkhand, where travellers rarely go, is inhabited by a fanatical population inured in the most repugnant practices of Hinduism. British domination has not been able to take proper hold over a territory still under the rajahs' influence, difficult to reach in their inaccessible fastnesses of the Vindhya Range.

Several times bands of fierce-looking Indians were spotted, making angry gestures at seeing the speedy quadruped pass. The Parsee avoided them as much as possible, considering them bad company. Few animals were seen during this day: just a few monkeys, who fled with much contortion and grimacing, greatly amusing Passepartout.

One thought was especially bothering him. What would Mr Fogg do with the elephant when he got to Allahabad Station? Would he take the animal with him? Impossible! The cost of transport added to the purchase price would make it ruinous. Would he sell him; or set him free? This fine animal fully deserved proper consideration. If by chance Mr Fogg made a present of the beast, to him, Passepartout, he would be very embarrassed. He couldn't stop worrying about this.

At 8 p.m., the main range of the Vindhyas had been crossed, and the travellers halted in front of a ruined bungalow at the foot of the northern flank.

The distance covered that day was about 25 miles, the same as the distance to be covered to Allahabad Station.

The night was cold. Inside the bungalow the Parsee lit a fire of dried branches, resulting in a warmth that was greatly appreciated. Dinner consisted of the food bought at Kholby. The travellers ate in a worn-out and black-and-blue state. The conversation began with a few disjointed sentences, but soon finished up with loud snores. The guide stood watch near Kiouni, who slept standing up, leaning against the trunk of a big tree.

Nothing happened during that night. A few roars from cheetahs and panthers occasionally broke the silence, mixed with the sharp tittering of monkeys. But the carnivorous animals merely made noises, and showed no hostile behaviour towards the people in the bungalow. Sir Francis Cromarty slept heavily like a good soldier exhausted by exercises. Passepartout's sleep was agitated, continually dreaming of the somersaults of the day before. As for Mr Fogg,* he slept as peacefully as if he'd been in his quiet house on Savile Row.

At 6 a.m., the march was resumed. The guide hoped to arrive at Allahabad Station that very evening. Then Mr Fogg would have used only part of the 48 hours saved since the beginning of the journey.

The travellers were crossing the last slopes of the Vindhyas. Kiouni had resumed his rapid pace. At about midday, the guide headed towards the small town of Kallinger, situated on the Kaniah, one of the sub-tributaries of the Ganges. He avoided all inhabited areas, feeling more secure in the deserted countryside, which forms the first part of the catchment area of the great river. Allahabad Station was only twelve miles north-east. A halt was made beneath a clump of banana trees and they much appreciated their fruit which, according to travellers, has the nourishment of bread and 'the succulence of cream'.

At two o'clock the guide moved under the cover of a dense forest, through which they were going to travel for several miles. He preferred to journey in the shelter of the trees. In any case nothing untoward had happened so far; and the journey seemed about to finish without incident—when the elephant suddenly stopped dead, showing signs of uneasiness.

It was four o'clock.

'What's the matter?' asked Sir Francis Cromarty, raising his head over the howdah.

'I don't know, esteemed sir,' replied the Parsee, tuning his ears to a confused murmur coming out of the dense foliage.

Moments later, the murmur became more distinct. It might have been a concert of human voices and brass instruments, although still a long way off.

Passepartout was all eyes and ears. Mr Fogg waited patiently, without a word.

The Parsee jumped down, tied the elephant to a tree, and worked his way under the thickest undergrowth. Minutes later he was back.

'A procession of Brahmins heading our way. We should try to keep out of sight.'

The guide untied the elephant and led it into a copse, requesting the travellers not to get down. He himself stood ready to mount the animal quickly if flight seemed necessary; but he thought the troop of believers would probably pass by without noticing, since he was completely hidden by the thick foliage.

The discordant noise of voices and instruments was coming closer. Monotonous chanting mingled with the sounds of drums and cymbals. Soon the head of the procession appeared under the trees, about 50 yards from Fogg and his companions. They could distinguish the curious participants in this religious ceremony despite the branches.

In the first advancing line were priests dressed in long embroidered robes and wearing mitres. They were surrounded by men, women, and children chanting a sort of dirge, interrupted at regular intervals by the sounds of tam-tams* and cymbals. Behind them, on a car with vast wheels whose spokes and felloes were shaped like interlaced snakes, appeared a hideous statue drawn by two pairs of richly caparisoned zebus. The statue had four arms. The body was deep red, the eyes wild, the hair tousled, the tongue lolling, the lips coloured with henna and betel. Around its neck was draped a garland of death's heads, and on its waist, a girdle of severed hands. The statue was standing on a floored giant, whose head was missing.

Sir Francis Cromarty recognized the statue.

'Kali,' he murmured, 'the goddess of love and death.'

'Death I will allow, but love, never!' said Passepartout. 'The old hag!'

The Parsee motioned to him to keep quiet.

A group of old fakirs were around the statue, jumping up and down, gesticulating, and convulsing. They were painted with bands of ochre and covered in cross-shaped incisions, through which their blood was oozing drop by drop. Foolish fanatics who in the great Hindu ceremonies still throw themselves under the wheels of the Juggernaut Car.*

Behind them a few Brahmins in all the sumptuousness of their oriental costumes were dragging a woman hardly able to stand.

This woman was young, and as white as a European. Her head, neck, shoulders, ears, arms, fingers, and toes, were laden with jewels, necklaces, bracelets, earrings, and rings. A tunic of gold lamé, covered with thin muslin, revealed the curves of her waist.*

Behind the spectacle of this young woman—in violent contrast—guards armed with unsheathed sabres passed through their belts and long inlaid pistols were carrying a corpse on a palanquin.

This was the body of an old man, dressed in the rich raiments of a rajah. As in life, he wore a turban embroidered with pearls, robes of silk and gold, a belt of diamond-studded cashmere, and the magnificent weapons of an Indian prince.

Some musicians and a rearguard of fanatics, their cries sometimes drowning the deafening crash of the instruments, closed the cortège.

Sir Francis Cromarty watched this ceremony with a singularly saddened expression, then turned to the guide.

'A suttee!'*

The Parsee nodded and put a finger to his lips. The long procession slowly wound its way through the trees, and finally its last members disappeared into the depths of the forest.

The chants were also dying down. There were still a few faraway shouts, and at long last, after all this uproar, a profound silence followed.

As soon as the procession had disappeared, Phileas Fogg asked the Brigadier-General:

'A "suttee"?'

'A suttee is a human sacrifice, but a voluntary one. The woman you have just seen will be burned at daybreak.'

'Oh, the bastards!' cried Passepartout, unable to hold back his indignation.

'And the body?' enquired Mr Fogg.

'The prince, her husband's,' answered the guide, 'one of the independent rajahs of Bundelkhand.'

'Can it be?' said Phileas Fogg, his voice not betraying the least emotion. 'These barbaric customs survive in India, and the British still haven't been able to put an end to them?'

'Sacrifices don't happen any more in most of India, but we have no influence over these wild kingdoms, especially in the State of Bundelkhand. The whole northern flank of the Vindhya Range is the scene of incessant murder and pillaging.'

'The poor woman,' murmured Passepartout: 'burned alive!'

'Yes,' said the Brigadier-General, 'but if she wasn't, you wouldn't believe what miserable treatment her relatives would subject her to. They would shave off her hair, barely feed her with a few handfuls of rice, in sum repudiate her completely: she would be considered an unclean creature and would die in some corner like a mangy dog. So the prospect of such an awful existence often forces these unhappy women to self-immolation, much more than love or religious fanaticism. Sometimes, however, the sacrifice is really voluntary, and the forceful intervention of the Government is necessary to prevent it. A few years ago, when I was living in Bombay, a young widow came and asked the Governor for the authorization to be burned with her husband's body. As you can imagine, the Governor refused. The widow then left the town, took refuge with an independent rajah, and there accomplished the self-sacrifice.'

The guide had been shaking his head while the Brigadier-General talked, and at the end:

'The sacrifice to take place at dawn tomorrow is not a voluntary one.'

'How do you know?'

'It's a story everybody in Bundelkhand knows.'

'But the poor woman didn't seem to be offering any resistance!' said Sir Francis Cromarty.

'That is because she was drugged with opium and hashish fumes.'

'But where are they taking her?'

'Pillagi Pagoda, two miles from here. She'll spend the night there until the sacrifice.'

'Which will happen . . .'

'Tomorrow, at first light.'

The guide led the elephant out of the dense undergrowth and hoisted himself up on to his neck. But just as he was about to urge him forward using a special whistle, Mr Fogg stopped him, and turned to Sir Francis Cromarty.

'What about saving this woman?'

'Saving this woman, Mr Fogg?' exclaimed the Brigadier-General.

'I'm still twelve hours ahead. I can use them that way.'

'I say, you do have a heart!'

'Sometimes,' he replied. 'When I have the time.'

13

In Which Passepartout Proves Once Again That Fortune Favours the Bold

THE plan was a bold one, bristling with difficulties, perhaps impossible to execute. Mr Fogg was going to risk his life, or at the very least his liberty and hence the success of his project; but he did not hesitate. He found, moreover, staunch support in Sir Francis Cromarty.

Passepartout was also ready for anything—he could be counted on. His master's idea excited him. He detected a heart and a soul under that icy exterior. He began to like Phileas Fogg very much.

That left the guide. Whose side would he be on? Might he not support the Indians? Even if his help was not forthcoming, they had to make sure of his neutrality.

Cromarty put the question in frank terms.

'Sir,' he answered, 'I am a Parsee, and this woman is a Parsee. I'm at your orders.'

'Good man,' said Mr Fogg.

'Nevertheless, take careful note, not only are we risking our lives, but terrible torture if we are captured. So consider it carefully please.'

'We've considered,' Mr Fogg replied. 'I suppose we'd better wait for nightfall before doing anything?'

'It would be better.'

This worthy native then gave them a few particulars about the victim. She was an Indian of celebrated beauty, of the Parsee race, the daughter of rich Bombay merchants. She had received a thoroughly British education in that town, and from her manners and education, one would have thought her a European. Her name was Aouda.*

Left an orphan, she had been married against her will to the old Bundelkhandi Rajah. Three months later she had become a widow. Knowing the fate that awaited her, she escaped, but was immediately recaptured, and the Rajah's relatives, who had an interest in her death, condemned her to this sacrifice from which it seemed there was no escape.

This tale could only strengthen Mr Fogg and his companions in their generous resolve. It was decided that the guide should take the elephant towards Pillagi Pagoda, and get as near as possible.

Half an hour later, a halt was made in a copse about five hundred yards from the pagoda, and out of sight from it, although the fanatics' shouting could clearly be heard.

The men discussed the best way of reaching the victim. The guide knew this Pillagi Pagoda in which he said the young woman was imprisoned. Could they get in through one of the doors, when the whole crowd was plunged in the deep sleep of drunkenness, or would they have to make a hole in one of the walls? They could only decide that once they got there. But it was beyond doubt that the rescue had to take place that very night, because the victim would be being taken out to her final torture the following day. By then no human intervention could possibly save her.

Mr Fogg and his companions waited for the night. As soon as the shadows fell, at about six o'clock, they decided to reconnoitre the area round the pagoda. The last cries of the fakirs were dying down. As was their custom, these Indians were lost in a haze of *hang*—liquid opium mixed with an infusion of hashish—and it was perhaps possible to slip through them and reach the temple.

The Parsee, guiding Fogg, Sir Francis, and Passepartout, moved noiselessly through the jungle. After ten minutes of crawling under the branches, they arrived at a stream; and there, by the light of iron torches covered with burning resin, they saw a huge pile of wood. This was the funeral pyre, precious sandalwood already impregnated with perfumed oil. On top lay the embalmed body of the Rajah, to be consumed at the same time as his widow. A hundred yards away stood the pagoda, whose silhouetted minarets cut through the tops of the trees.

'Come,' said the guide in a low voice.

With the utmost caution, he slid silently through the tall grass, followed by his three companions.

The silence was now broken only by the murmuring of the wind in the branches.

The guide stopped at the edge of a clearing. A few resin torches provided light. The ground was strewn with groups of sleepers, overcome by drunkenness. It was like a battlefield strewn with corpses. Men and women were mixed with children, a few of the drunkards still groaning here and there.

In the background Pillagi Temple did not stand out clearly amongst the clumps of trees. To the guide's great disappointment, the Rajah's guards were keeping watch on the door, lit by sooty torches, and were wandering around with naked sabres. Priests were probably keeping watch inside as well.

The Parsee went no further. He realized that it was impossible to force entry to the temple, and so brought his companions back.

Phileas Fogg and Sir Francis had also understood that nothing could be tried in this direction.

They stopped and discussed in whispers.

'Let's wait,' said the Brigadier-General. 'It's only eight o'clock, and these guards may also give in to sleep.'

'They may,' said the Parsee.

Phileas Fogg and his companions stretched out at the foot of a tree and waited.

The time seemed to go by very slowly. Now and then the guide left them and went to watch from the edge of the clearing. The Rajah's guards were still keeping watch in the light of the torches, and a faint light trickled through the pagoda's windows.

They waited until midnight. The situation did not change, for the same watch continued outside. It was clear that they could not count on the guards falling asleep. They had probably been spared the drunken stupor of the *hang*. Something else had to be tried, like making a hole in the walls of the pagoda. It still remained to be seen whether the priests inside were continuing to watch over their victim as carefully as the soldiers at the temple door.

After a final discussion, the guide said he was ready to start. Mr Fogg, Sir Francis, and Passepartout followed him, making a long detour to reach the pagoda via its apse.*

At about 12.30 they had reached the foot of the walls without attracting any attention. No watch had been set on this side, where, it must be said, there were no windows or doors.

The night was dark. The moon, in its last quarter, had hardly risen above the horizon, which was shrouded with clouds; and the tall trees made it even darker.

But to get to the foot of the wall wasn't enough: they still had to make a hole in it. For this operation, Phileas Fogg and his companions had no tools apart from their pocket knives. Luckily the temple walls were made of a mixture of bricks and wood, probably not difficult to penetrate. Once the first brick had been removed, the others would come away easily.

Work started, as quietly as possible. The Parsee on one side and Passepartout on the other worked at loosening the bricks, so as to make a hole two feet wide.

Their work was already under way, when a cry rang out inside the temple, with almost immediately shouts replying from outside.

Passepartout and the guide stopped. Had they been spotted? Had the alarm been given? The most elementary prudence meant beating a retreat, which all four did. Once again they crouched under the cover of the wood, waiting for the alarm, if it was one, to die down, ready then to start their operation again.

But—by a catastrophic piece of bad luck—the guards appeared at the apse of the pagoda, and took up a position preventing anyone approaching.

It would be difficult to describe the disappointment of the four men, interrupted in the middle of their work. Now that they couldn't get to the victim, how could they save her? Sir Francis Cromarty was biting his nails and Passepartout was beside himself, making it difficult for the guide to hold him back. Fogg waited impassively, concealing his feelings.

'Is there nothing we can do but leave?' whispered the Brigadier-General.

'There is nothing we can do but leave,' answered the guide.

'Wait!' said Fogg. 'I only need to be in Allahabad by midday.'

'But what can you hope for?' replied Sir Francis Cromarty. 'In a few hours it'll be daybreak . . .'

'The luck against us now may come back at the decisive moment.'

The Brigadier-General would have liked to be able to read Phileas Fogg's eyes.

What was this cold Briton thinking about? Did he plan to rush towards the young woman at the vital moment and flagrantly tear her from her executioners' grasp?

That would be pure madness, and it was hard to believe that the man was as mad as that. All the same Sir Francis Cromarty agreed to wait until the terrible drama reached its climax. The guide, however, would not let his companions stay where they were, and led them back towards another part of the clearing. From there, they could watch the slumbering groups of men, while sheltered by a group of trees.

But Passepartout, perched on the lowest branches of a tree, was mulling over an idea that had flashed through his mind like lightning, and then obstinately lodged in his brain.

Having started by saying to himself, 'What madness!', he was now muttering, 'Why not, after all? It's a chance, perhaps the only one, and with such brutes . . .'

Passepartout did not express his thoughts in any other form, but soon, as supple as a snake, he slithered along to the lowest branches of the tree, which bowed down almost to the ground.

The hours went by, and soon a few lighter streaks announced the approach of daybreak, although it still remained completely dark.

This was the moment. It was as though a resurrection had taken place in the sleeping crowd. The groups came to life; the sounds of the tam-tam rang out, and chants and cries burst forth again. The time had come for the unfortunate woman to die.

The doors of the pagoda opened and a bright light flooded out. Mr Fogg and Sir Francis Cromarty were able to see the brilliantly illuminated victim: she was being dragged out by two priests. It even seemed that, shaking off the stupor of intoxication through supreme self-preservation, the unfortunate woman was trying to escape from her executioners. Sir Francis Cromarty's heart leapt, and he gripped Phileas Fogg's hand with a convulsive movement, then realized the hand was holding an open knife.

The crowd started to get going. The young woman had collapsed back into the stupor produced by the hashish fumes. She passed through the ranks of the fakirs, who escorted her while maintaining their religious intoning.

Phileas Fogg and his companions joined up with the last ranks of the crowd, and followed her.

Two minutes later they arrived at the edge of the stream, and stopped less than 50 yards from the funeral pyre where the Rajah's body was lying. In the half-light they saw the victim, absolutely motionless, stretched out beside the body of her husband.

Next a torch was brought up. The wood, soaked with oil, caught fire straightaway.

Sir Francis Cromarty and the guide had to hold Phileas Fogg back, for in a moment of selfless madness, he was thrusting himself towards the pyre.

Fogg had already pushed them aside—when the scene abruptly changed. A cry of terror arose. The entire crowd threw themselves to the ground, petrified.

Was the old Rajah not dead then?—for he was suddenly seen to stand erect like a ghost. Then he took the young woman in his arms, and, spectre-like, climbed down from the pyre through the swirling smoke.

The fakirs, the guards, and the priests, in the grip of a sudden terror, lay face down, not daring to contemplate such a miracle!

The inanimate victim was carried in the strong arms of the person bearing her, and appeared almost weightless. Mr Fogg and Sir Francis had remained standing, while the Parsee bowed his head and Passepartout was doubtless just as flabbergasted . . .

This apparition risen from the dead reached the spot where Mr Fogg and Sir Francis Cromarty were standing; and there, succinctly said:

'Let's move!'

It was Passepartout himself who had crept to the pyre in the midst of the thick smoke! It was Passepartout who, under the cover of darkness, had snatched the young woman from the jaws of death. It was Passepartout who had played his role with bold fortune, and passed through the universal terror!

A moment later the four had disappeared into the wood, with the elephant carrying them away at a rapid trot. But shouts, cries, and then a bullet, making a hole in Phileas Fogg's hat, told them that their ruse had been discovered.

The old Rajah's body could now be seen on the blazing pyre. The priests had recovered from their terror, and had realized that an abduction had taken place.

They immediately rushed into the jungle with the guards hot on their heels. A volley had been fired, but the kidnappers were moving too fast, and a few moments later were out of range of the arrows and bullets.

14

In Which Phileas Fogg Travels the Whole Length of the Wonderful Ganges Valley Without Even Considering Seeing It

THE bold abduction had been successful and an hour later Passepartout was still chuckling at his triumph. Sir Francis Cromarty had shaken the hand of the brave fellow, and his master had said to him, 'Well done'—which from Mr Fogg was tantamount to praise indeed. Passepartout answered that all the credit in this affair was his master's. He himself had only had a funny idea. He laughed at the thought that for a few moments he, Passepartout, former gymnast, ex-sergeant in the Fire Brigade, had been an embalmed old rajah and the husband of a beautiful woman!

As for the young Indian woman, she was not conscious of what had happened. Wrapped up in the travelling rugs, she was resting in one of the howdahs.

Meanwhile the elephant, guided with great skill by the Parsee, was moving very quickly through the still-dark forest. An hour after leaving Pillagi Pagoda it was crossing an immense plain, and by seven o'clock a halt was called. The young woman was still in a state of utter exhaustion. The guide made her swallow a few mouthfuls of water and brandy, but the effects of the stupor weighing down on her had not yet passed.

Sir Francis Cromarty knew about the effects of the intoxication produced by inhaling hashish fumes, and he had no worries about her.

Although the Brigadier-General had no doubt about the young woman's recovery, he was more worried about her future. He did not hesitate to tell Phileas Fogg that if Mrs Aouda remained in India, she would inevitably fall into the hands of her executioners. These fanatics were to be found everywhere in the Subcontinent, and would certainly be able to recapture the victim, whether at Madras, Bombay, or Calcutta—and regardless of any action the British police might take. In support of his argument, Sir Francis quoted a similar case that had occurred recently. In his opinion the young woman would not be safe until she left India.

Phileas Fogg replied that he would look into it.

At about ten the guide said they were getting near Allahabad Station. The railway line started up again there, with trains going from Allahabad to Calcutta in less than 24 hours.

Fogg would therefore arrive in time for the boat for Hong Kong, due to leave at noon the following day, 25 October.

The young woman was placed in a room in the station, and Passepartout was given the task of going to buy various items of clothing for her: a dress, a shawl, furs, etc., whatever he could find. His master gave him unlimited credit.

Passepartout left immediately and worked his way through the streets of the town. Allahabad is the City of God, one of the holiest cities in India; it is built on the confluence of two venerated rivers, the Ganges and the Jumna, whose waters attract pilgrims from the whole Subcontinent. According to the legends in *The Ramayana*, the source of the Ganges is in heaven, from where, through the grace of Brahma,* the river flows down to Earth.

While doing his shopping, Passepartout had soon seen the town, formerly defended by a magnificent fort that is now a state prison. There is no commerce or industry left in the town, previously an industrial and trading centre. Passepartout looked for a fancy-goods shop, as if he had been in Regent Street just down from Farmer & Co. But he was out of luck, and could only find a small shop run by a tough old Jew. What he bought was a dress made of Scottish material, a huge cloak, and a magnificent pelisse of otter fur, for which he did not hesitate to pay £75. Then he returned to the station in triumph.

Mrs Aouda was beginning to regain consciousness. The influence of the drugs administered by the priests of Pillagi was slowly disappearing, and her beautiful eyes were regaining all their Indian softness.

When the poet-king, Yusuf'Adil,* extols the charms of the Queen of Ahmadnagar, he expresses himself as follows:

'Her shining head of hair, symmetrically divided, forms a frame to the harmonious contours of her delicate pale cheeks, glowing with polish and freshness. Her ebony brows have the form and power of the bow of Kama, the god of love,* and beneath her long silky lashes, in the black pupils of her big limpid eyes, swim, as in the sacred lakes of the Himalaya, the purest reflections of celestial light. Her teeth, small, even, and white, gleam between her smiling lips, like dewdrops within the half-closed heart of a pomegranate flower. Her delicate ears with their symmetrical whorls, her rosy hands, and her tiny feet, curved and tender like lotus buds, shine with the brilliance of the finest Sinhalese pearls or the most exquisite Golconda diamonds. Her slim and supple waist, which a hand can encircle, sets off the elegant arch of her rounded loins and the richness of her breast, where blossoming youth displays its most perfect treasures; and under the silky folds of her tunic, she seems to have been sculpted in pure argent by the divine hand of Vicvakarman, the eternal sculptor.'*

Even without all this elaboration, it is enough to say that Mrs Aouda, the widow of the Bundelkhandi Rajah, was an attractive woman in the full European meaning of the word. She spoke excellent English, and the guide had not exaggerated when he said that this young Parsee had been transformed by her upbringing.

The train was about to leave Allahabad Station and the Parsee was waiting. Mr Fogg paid him his wage at the agreed rate, but not a farthing more. This surprised Passepartout, as he knew how much his master owed to the guide's devotion. The Parsee had voluntarily risked his life in the Pillagi adventure, and if the Hindus ever learned of this, he would find it extremely difficult to escape their vengeance.

There was also the question of Kiouni. What could be done with this elephant bought at such a price?

But Phileas Fogg had already decided what to do.

'Parsee,' he said to the guide. 'You have been most devoted and helpful. I have paid for your service but not for your commitment. Would you like this elephant? If so, he is yours.'

The guide's eyes shone.

'Your Honour is giving me a fortune!'

'Take it, guide; and I will still be in your debt.'

'Go on!' exclaimed Passepartout. 'Take him my friend! Kiouni is a good and plucky animal.'

And going up to the animal, he gave him a few sugar-lumps.

'Here, Kiouni, here!'

The elephant gave a few grunts of satisfaction and then, taking Passepartout by the waist and coiling him up in his trunk, lifted him up to his head. Passepartout, not at all frightened, gave the animal a good stroke, and was then deposited gently back down on the ground. To the trunk-shake offered by the noble Kiouni, the honest fellow returned his own hearty handshake.

A few moments later Fogg, Sir Francis, and Passepartout settled into a comfortable compartment, where Mrs Aouda occupied the best seat, and left at full steam for Benares.

This town is at most 80 miles from Allahabad, a journey of two hours.

The young woman recovered completely during the ride, and the soporific clouds of the *hang* disappeared completely.

She was astonished to find herself on a train, in this compartment, dressed in European clothes, and surrounded by travellers completely unknown to her.

Her companions lavished their attention on her, bringing her back to life with a few drops of brandy. Then the Brigadier-General told her what had happened. He emphasized the devotion shown by Phileas Fogg, who had not for one moment hesitated to risk his life to save her, as well as the finale of the adventure due to the daring imagination of Passepartout.

Mr Fogg let him speak without uttering a word. Passepartout, highly embarrassed, kept repeating, 'Not worth mentioning!'

Mrs Aouda thanked her saviours effusively with her tears, rather than her words. Her beautiful eyes expressed this gratitude, much more than her lips. Then her thoughts carried her back to the scenes of the suttee, her eyes refocused on this land of India where so many dangers still lay in wait for her; and she was overcome with shudders of terror.

Phileas Fogg realized what was passing through Mrs Aouda's mind. To reassure her, he offered, very coldly, to take her to Hong Kong, where she could stay until the affair blew over.

Mrs Aouda accepted the offer with gratitude, as one of her relatives in fact lived in Hong Kong: a Parsee like her, and one of the most important businessmen of that town, which is wholly British, although situated on the Chinese coast.

At half-past twelve the train halted at Benares Station. The Brahmin legends maintain that this town is built on the spot where Kasi* was situated, suspended in space between the zenith and the nadir, like Mohammed's Tomb. However, in this more down-to-earth age, Benares, which the Orientalists call the Athens of India, was quite prosaically reposing on terra firma. Passepartout caught a brief glimpse of its brick houses and wattle huts, which gave it a very desolate appearance, without any local colour.

This was where Sir Francis Cromarty was due to get off, for the troops he was joining were encamped a few miles to the north of the town. Accordingly the Brigadier-General said goodbye to Phileas Fogg, wishing him every possible success and expressing the wish that he could carry out his journey again in less original but more useful fashion. Mr Fogg shook hands with his companion briefly. Mrs Aouda's leave-taking was more affectionate. Never would she forget what she owed Sir Francis. As for Passepartout, he was honoured by a real handshake from the Brigadier-General. Deeply moved, he wondered where and when he could offer him his services. Then the travellers went their separate ways.

Starting from Benares, the railway roughly followed the Ganges Valley. Through the panes of the compartment appeared the varied countryside of Bihar. The weather was quite bright. The mountains were covered with greenery, fields of barley, sweet corn, and wheat, plus streams and ponds inhabited by greenish alligators, smartly kept villages, and forests that were still verdant. A few elephants and zebus with big humps came and bathed in the waters of this sacred river, as well as groups of Hindus of both sexes, who performed their holy ablutions piously in spite of the lateness of the season and the cool temperature. These devotees, relentless enemies of Buddhism, are fervent followers of the Brahmin religion, which is incarnate in three personages: Vishnu, the solar divinity, Shiva,* the personification of the natural forces, and Brahma, the supreme master of the priests and legislators. But what must Brahma, Shiva, and Vishnu have thought of this India, now 'Britannicized', when some steamboat passed on the Ganges: neighing, churning up the sacred waters, and frightening the seagulls skimming over the surface, the tortoises swarming over its banks, and the devout stretched out along its shores.

This whole panorama flew past like a flash, although often a cloud of white steam masked the details.* The travellers hardly saw the fort of Chunar, twenty miles south-east of Benares; nor the ancient fortress of the rajahs of Bihar; Ghazipur with its important rosewater factories; Lord Cornwallis's Tomb,* which stands on the left bank of the Ganges; the fortified town of Buxar; and the large industrial and business city of Patna, where the principal opium market in India is held. They could hardly glimpse Monghyr, a town which is more than European, being as British as Manchester or Birmingham, renowned for its iron foundries and its factories for edge tools and knives, and whose tall chimneys choked the sky of Brahma with their black smoke—a veritable punch delivered to the land of dreams!

Then night came, and the passengers sped on in the midst of the roars of the tigers, bears, and wolves fleeing before the locomotive. Nothing else could be seen of the wonders of Bengal: not Golconda,* the ruins of Gour, Murshidabad, formerly the capital, nor Burdwan, Hooghly, nor even Chandernagore: that French outpost on Indian territory, where Passepartout would have been proud to see his country's flag fluttering.

They finally reached Calcutta at seven in the morning. The steamship for Hong Kong was not due to weigh anchor until twelve, so Phileas Fogg had five hours ahead of him.

According to the gentlemen's programme, he was scheduled to arrive in the capital of India on 25 October, 23 days after leaving London; and he had got there on the planned day. So he was neither ahead nor behind. As the reader already knows, the two days he had gained between London and Bombay had unfortunately been lost during this crossing of the Indian peninsula.

But we may reasonably assume that Phileas Fogg did not regret them.

15

Where the Bag of Banknotes Is Again Lightened by a Few Thousand Pounds

THE train stopped at the station. Passepartout left the compartment first, followed by Mr Fogg, who helped his young companion out on to the platform. Fogg planned to head directly for the Hong Kong steamship and settle Mrs Aouda in comfortably, as he did not wish to leave her alone in a country so dangerous for her.

But just as he was leaving the station, a policeman came up.

'Mr Phileas Fogg?'

'Yes?'

'Is this man your servant?'

'Yes.'

'Would you both be good enough to follow me?'

Mr Fogg showed no sign of surprise. This man was a representative of the law, and the law is sacred for every Briton. Passepartout tried to argue, in the French manner—but the policeman touched him with his truncheon, and Phileas Fogg motioned to him to obey.

'Can this young lady accompany us?' asked Mr Fogg.

'Yes.'

And the policeman led Fogg, Aouda, and Passepartout towards a palki-gharrie, a sort of four-wheeled carriage with four seats, drawn by a pair of horses. It set off and no one said anything during the twenty-minute journey.

The carriage first crossed the 'black town' with its narrow streets lined with hovels swarming with a cosmopolitan population, squalid and in rags. It then crossed the European quarter, made of brick houses sheltered under coconut trees and bristling with masts, where elegant riders and magnificent horse and carriages were already out exercising, despite the early hour.

The palki-gharrie stopped in front of a building of simple appearance, but clearly not a private residence. The policeman asked the prisoners—they could really not be called by any other name—to get down and conducted them into a chamber with barred windows.

'You will appear before Judge Obadiah* at 8.30.'

He went out, closing the door.

'So,' cried Passepartout, 'they've caught us'; and dropped on to a chair.

Mrs Aouda spoke to Mr Fogg immediately, in a voice where she sought in vain to disguise her emotion.

'Sir, you must abandon me! You're being prosecuted on my account! It's because you saved me!'

Phileas Fogg merely replied that it was simply not possible. Prosecuted for that affair of suttee? Inconceivable! How could the plaintiffs dare come forward? There was surely a misunderstanding. Mr Fogg added that under no circumstance would he abandon the young woman, and that he intended to take her to Hong Kong.

'But the boat leaves at twelve!' observed Passepartout.

'We'll be on board by twelve,' replied the impassive gentleman.

This was asserted so firmly that Passepartout couldn't help saying to himself, 'By Jove, the thing's certain! We'll be on board by twelve!' However, he was far from reassured.

At half-past eight the door of the chamber opened. The policeman led the prisoners into the adjoining room. It was a courtroom;* and a large number of people, Europeans and natives, already filled the public benches.

Fogg, Aouda, and Passepartout sat down on a bench opposite the seats reserved for the judge and the clerk.

Judge Obadiah came in almost straightaway, followed by his clerk. He was a stout, round man. He unhooked a wig hanging on a nail and slid it on to his head.

'The first case.'

Then, raising hand to head:

'But this is not my wig!'

'Indeed, Mr Obadiah, it's mine,' answered the clerk.

'My dear Mr Oysterpuf,* how do you expect a judge to be able to pass a good sentence when he's wearing a clerk's wig?'

The wigs were swapped round. During these preliminaries Passepartout was boiling with impatience, for the hand on the large clock in the courtroom seemed to be moving terribly fast.

'The first case!' repeated Judge Obadiah.

'Phileas Fogg?' said clerk Oysterpuf.

'Yes.'

'Passepartout?'

'Present.'

'Good,' said Judge Obadiah. 'Prisoners at the bar, we've been watching out for you on all the trains from Bombay for two days.'

'But what are we accused of?' exclaimed Passepartout impatiently.

'You'll learn in due course,' replied the judge.

'Sir,' said Mr Fogg at this point. 'I am a British subject and I am entitled . . .'

'Have you been ill-used in any way?' asked Mr Obadiah.

'Not in the least.'

'Well then, show in the plaintiffs.'

On the judge's order, a door opened and an usher brought in three Hindu priests.

'Just as I thought,' murmured Passepartout. 'Those scoundrels who wanted to burn our young lady.'

The priests stood in front of the judge as the clerk read out the charge against Phileas Fogg, Esq., and his servant, accused of violating a place consecrated by the Brahmin religion.

'Do you understand this charge of desecration?' the judge asked Phileas Fogg.

'Yes, sir,' answered Mr Fogg, consulting his watch, 'and I confess.'

'Ah, so you confess?'

'I confess, and I would like these three priests to confess in their turn what they intended doing at Pillagi Pagoda.'

The priests looked at each other. They didn't seem to be able to make head or tail of what the defendant was saying.

'Yes!' shouted Passepartout impetuously. 'At that Pagoda in Pillagi, where they were going to burn their victim.'

Renewed stupefaction from the priests, and total astonishment of Judge Obadiah.

'What victim?' he burst out. 'Burn whom? In the very heart of Bombay?'

'Bombay?' Passepartout shouted back.

'Yes; we're not talking about Pillagi Pagoda, but Malabar Hill Pagoda in Bombay.'

'And as Exhibit Number One, here is the desecrator's footwear,' added the clerk, placing a pair of shoes on the desk in front of him.

'My shoes!' exclaimed Passepartout, in total surprise and unable to keep back this involuntary exclamation.

It is easy to understand the confusion in the minds of the master and servant. They had completely forgotten about the incident in the pagoda in Bombay, but it was this same incident that had brought them before the Calcutta magistrate.

Fix the detective had realized the advantage he could draw from this unfortunate affair. He had put his departure off by twelve hours, and appointed himself adviser to the Brahmins of Malabar Hill. He had promised them substantial damages, knowing full well that the British Government acted very firmly against this sort of offence. Later, he had sent them off to pursue the profaner's trail by taking the next train. But because of the time spent rescuing the young widow, Fix and his Hindus had arrived in Calcutta before Phileas Fogg and his servant. The magistrates were instructed by telegram to arrest them as soon as they got off the train. One can imagine Fix's disappointment when he learned that Phileas Fogg had not arrived in the capital. He must have thought that his thief had stopped at an intermediate station on the Peninsular Railway, and taken refuge in one of the northern states. For 24 hours, Fix had kept watch on the station, in a state of terrible anxiety. He had been delighted when, that very morning, he had seen him getting out of a carriage, in the company, it is true, of a young woman whose presence he could not explain. He immediately set a policeman on him; and that was how Mr Fogg, Passepartout, and the widow of the Bundelkhandi Rajah were brought before Judge Obadiah.

If Passepartout had been less engrossed by this affair, he would have spotted the detective in a corner of the public benches. Fix was following the debate with an interest easy to understand—for in Calcutta, just as in Bombay and Suez, he still didn't have his arrest warrant!

Judge Obadiah had, however, noted the confession that had blurted from Passepartout's lips, who would have given everything he owned to take back the rash words.

'Are the facts admitted?' enquired the Judge.

'They are,' replied Mr Fogg coldly.

'Inasmuch', said the judge, 'inasmuch as British law has the duty of protecting all the religions of the peoples of India equally and rigorously, and inasmuch as the offence has been admitted by Mr Passepartout, Esq., who stands convicted of having violated the floor of Malabar Hill Pagoda in Bombay with a sacrilegious foot on 20 October, we sentence the aforesaid Passepartout to two weeks' detention at Her Majesty's Pleasure and a fine of £300.'

'Three hundred pounds?' shouted Passepartout, only concerned about the fine.

'Silence in court!' yelped the clerk.

'And', added Judge Obadiah, 'inasmuch as collusion between the servant and the master is not satisfactorily proven, but inasmuch as the master must in any case be held responsible for the acts and deeds of a servant in his employ, I hereby detain the aforesaid Phileas Fogg and sentence him to seven days' imprisonment and a fine of £150. Call the next case!'

Fix in his corner experienced inexpressible satisfaction. Phileas Fogg detained for a week in Calcutta would leave more than enough time for the warrant to arrive.

Passepartout was dumbfounded. This sentence had ruined his master. A bet of £20,000 lost, and all because he had gone into that cursed pagoda as a gawking tourist!

Phileas Fogg appeared as much in command of himself as if the sentence had concerned someone else, not even frowning. But just as the clerk was calling the following case, he got up.

'I wish to offer bail.'

'You are entitled to do so,' answered the judge.

Fix felt a cold shiver run down his back, but his confidence soon came back when he heard the judge pronounce that, 'inasmuch as Phileas Fogg and his domestic are foreigners', he was fixing the bail at the enormous sum of £1,000 each.

This meant that Mr Fogg would have to pay £2,000 if he didn't want to serve his sentence.

'I'll pay,' said the gentleman.

From the bag Passepartout carried he drew a wad of banknotes and deposited it on the clerk's desk.

'This sum will be returned to you when you leave prison,' said the judge. 'You are now released under bail.'

'Come,' said Phileas Fogg to his servant.

'At least give me my shoes back!' howled Passepartout, with an angry gesture.

His shoes were duly returned.

'Expensive footwear,' he murmured. 'More than £1,000 apiece, and they don't even fit properly!'

Passepartout was utterly crestfallen as he followed Mr Fogg, who had offered the young woman his arm. Fix was still hoping that his thief wouldn't be able to let the sum of £2,000 go, and that he would do his week in prison. He therefore rushed out, following in Fogg's tracks.

Mr Fogg hailed a carriage, and Mrs Aouda, Passepartout, and he got in. Fix ran behind the carriage, which soon stopped on one of the quaysides of the town.

The *Rangoon* lay at anchor, half a mile out in the roadstead, her departure flag hoisted to the top of the mast. Eleven o'clock was striking: Mr Fogg was an hour early. Fix saw him get out of the carriage and into a boat, together with Mrs Aouda and his servant. The detective stamped the ground.

'The scoundrel!' he cried. 'He's leaving. Two thousand pounds thrown away. He's spending money like a thief! Oh, I'll tail him to the ends of the Earth if need be—but at the rate he's going, all the stolen money will have disappeared!'

The police inspector's thoughts were well founded. Since Phileas Fogg had left London, he had already scattered more than £5,000 *en route*, on travelling expenses or rewards, the elephant, or bail and fines. The percentage of the sum recovered, the one given to the detectives, was decreasing all the time.

16

Where Fix Gives the Impression of Not Knowing
About Events Reported to Him

THE *Rangoon*, one of the steamships P. & O. employ on the China Seas and the Sea of Japan, was a screw-driven iron steamer, of 1,770 tons burden and a nominal 400 hp. She was the equal of the *Mongolia* for speed, but not for comfort. Mrs Aouda was therefore far from as well looked after as Phileas Fogg would have liked—but in any case the crossing was only 3,500 miles, taking about eleven or twelve days, and the young woman was not a demanding passenger.

During the first few days of the crossing, Mrs Aouda started to get to know Phileas Fogg better. She showed him deep gratitude at all times. The phlegmatic gentleman listened to her, apparently with great coldness, without a single intonation or gesture betraying the least emotion. He made sure that the young woman lacked for nothing. At fixed times each day, he would come, if not to talk at least to listen to her. He was unfailingly polite, but with the grace and spontaneity of an automaton, whose movements could have been contrived for such a purpose. Mrs Aouda hardly knew what to think; but Passepartout had tried to enlighten her on his master's eccentric character. He told her about the gamble, which was why the gentleman was travelling round the world. Mrs Aouda had smiled—but she owed him her life after all, and gratitude necessarily made her think better of her saviour.

Mrs Aouda confirmed the touching story related by the Indian guide. She did indeed belong to that race which occupies the highest level amongst the native races. Several Parsee businessmen had made great fortunes in the Indies from the cotton trade. One of them, Sir James Jeejeebhoy,* a wealthy individual who lived in Bombay, had in fact been given his title by the British Government. Mrs Aouda was a relative of his; it was even a cousin of Sir James Jeejeebhoy's, the Hon. Jejeeh, that she hoped to meet in Hong Kong. Would he give her protection and assistance? She could not say for certain. Mr Fogg replied that she had no need to worry, and that everything would sort itself out mathematically! That was the word he used.

Did the young woman understand this horrible adverb? It is difficult to say. However, her large eyes gazed at Mr Fogg's, her large eyes as 'limpid as the sacred lakes of the Himalaya'. But the uncompromising Mr Fogg, as buttoned up as ever, did not appear to be the sort of man to throw himself into these lakes.

The first part of the *Rangoon*'s crossing took place in excellent conditions, as the weather was good. This section of the immense bay sailors call 'the Fathoms of Bengal' presented perfect conditions for the steamship to move ahead. The *Rangoon* came into view of Great Andaman, the main section of the archipelago, whose picturesque mountain of Saddle Peak, 2,400 feet high, is a landmark for navigators for a long distance around.

The ship hugged the coast quite closely. The Papuan savages of the island did not show themselves. These are beings placed on the lowest rung of the human scale, although it is not correct to say that they are cannibals.*

The panorama of the islands was superb. Huge forests of fan palms, areca palms, bamboo, nutmeg, teaks, gigantic mimosas, and arborescent ferns filled the foreground of this countryside, with the elegant silhouettes of the mountains appearing behind. On the coast swarm millions of those precious salanganes, whose edible nests* form a much sought-after delicacy throughout the Celestial Empire. But the varied spectacle of the Andaman Islands was soon out of sight, and the *Rangoon* headed swiftly towards the Strait of Malacca, the way through to the South China Sea.

During the crossing, what was Inspector Fix doing, so unfortunately caught up in this voyage of circumnavigation? Before leaving Calcutta, he had given instructions for the warrant, if it finally arrived, to be sent on to him in Hong Kong. He had then managed to embark on the *Rangoon* without being spotted by Passepartout, and he hoped to remain concealed until the steamer arrived. It would indeed have been difficult for him to explain why he was on board, without making Passepartout suspicious, for he must have thought he was still in Bombay. However, he was compelled to meet up again with the worthy fellow by the force of circumstance. How? This will be seen shortly.

All the inspector's hopes and desires were now concentrated on a single point of the globe, Hong Kong, since the steamship didn't stop in Singapore long enough for him to be able to operate there. So the arrest of the thief had to take place in Hong Kong, or he would be lost irretrievably.

Hong Kong was indeed yet another British territory, but the last one encountered on the route. Beyond, China, Japan, and America offered Fogg a virtually secure refuge. But in Hong Kong Fix would arrest him and place him in the hands of the local police—provided the arrest warrant arrived, and it *was* clearly following him. No problem. But after Hong Kong, a mere warrant wouldn't be enough. An extradition order would be necessary. Hence delays, slowness, obstacles of all sorts, which the scoundrel would use to escape once and for all. If the operation failed in Hong Kong, it would be extremely difficult, if not impossible, to start again with any chance of success.

'So', he repeated to himself during the long hours he spent in his cabin. 'So either the warrant is in Hong Kong and I can arrest my man, or it isn't, and then this time I really must put off his departure at all costs. I failed in Bombay, I failed in Calcutta! If I miss the chance in Hong Kong, my reputation will be ruined. Whatever the price, I must succeed. What can I do to delay this accursed Fogg's departure, if I have to?'

As a last resort Fix had made up his mind to admit everything to Passepartout, and tell him what sort of master he was serving: he couldn't possibly be an accomplice. Once this information was revealed, Passepartout would surely be afraid of getting involved, and had to come over to Fix's side. But it really was a risky expedient, only to be employed as a last resort. A word from Passepartout in his master's ear would be enough to spoil everything.

The police inspector was therefore extremely undecided, when Mrs Aouda's presence in Phileas Fogg's company on board the *Rangoon* gave him new food for thought.

Who was this woman? What circumstances had made
her Fogg's companion? The encounter had obviously happened between Bombay and Calcutta—but at what point on
the Subcontinent? Was it chance that had brought Phileas
Fogg and the young woman together? Had the journey across
India not been undertaken by the gentleman with the express
aim of meeting this captivating being? For captivating she
was, as Fix had seen from his public seat in the Calcutta
courtroom.

It was easy to understand how intrigued the detective
was. He wondered if there mightn't be some element of
criminal abduction in this affair. Yes, that had to be it! The
idea encrusted itself in Fix's brain, as he realized all the
mileage that could be extracted from the situation. Whether
or not the young woman was married, there was abduction—
and in Hong Kong he might easily be able to create problems for the kidnapper that couldn't be solved by financial
means.

However, waiting for the *Rangoon* to reach Hong Kong
wasn't feasible. This Fogg man had the abominable habit of
jumping from one boat on to another: before the operation
was set up, he might be far away.

It was therefore essential to notify the British authorities of
the approach of the *Rangoon* before it actually got to Hong
Kong. This was easy to do, since the steamship was due to
make a stopover at Singapore, which is connected to the
Chinese coast by a telegraph cable.

However, before taking any action, Fix decided to question
Passepartout, so as to be able to operate with greater safety.
He knew that it was easy to make him talk, and so he decided
to drop the disguise he had maintained until then. There was
no time to be lost, as it was now 30 October, and the *Rangoon*
was due to put into Singapore the next day.

Accordingly, Fix came out of his cabin and went up
on deck, with the intention of greeting Passepartout first,
with signs of the greatest surprise. Passepartout was strolling
near the front when the inspector suddenly rushed up,
exclaiming:

'You? Here on the *Rangoon*!'

'Mr Fix on board?' replied Passepartout, amazed to recognize his companion from the crossing on the *Mongolia*. 'What, I left you at Bombay, and I find you again on the way to Hong Kong! But are you travelling round the world as well?'

'No, no, no,' answered Fix. 'I'm planning to stop at Hong Kong—at least for a few days.'

'Ah!' said Passepartout, who seemed nonplussed for a moment. 'But how is it I haven't seen you on board since we left Calcutta?'

'On my word, I didn't feel too well . . . a bit seasick . . . I was lying down in my cabin. The Bay of Bengal doesn't suit me half as well as the Indian Ocean. But what about your master, Mr Phileas Fogg?'

'In perfect health, and as punctual as his schedule! Not a day behind. Ah! Mr Fix, you don't know, but we also have a young lady with us.'

'A young lady?' answered the detective, who really seemed not to understand what his interlocutor meant.

Passepartout had soon recounted the tale. He described the incident at the pagoda in Bombay, the purchase of the elephant for £2,000, the affair of the suttee, the abduction of Aouda, the court sentence in Calcutta, and the release on bail. Fix, who knew the last part of the story, nevertheless gave the impression of not knowing any of it, and Passepartout gave in to the pleasure of narrating his adventures to a listener who showed so much interest in him.

'But doesn't your master intend to take this young woman to Europe eventually?'

'Not at all, Mr Fix, not at all! We are quite simply going to entrust her to one of her relatives, a rich merchant in Hong Kong.'

'Nothing doing!' muttered the detective to himself, hiding his disappointment. 'How about a glass of gin, Mr Passepartout?'

'With pleasure, Mr Fix. That's the least we can do: drink to our meeting on board the *Rangoon*.'

17

*Where a Number of Things Happen During the
Journey From Singapore to Hong Kong*

FROM that day onwards, Passepartout and the detective met
frequently, although the detective maintained an extreme reserve towards his companion, and made no further attempt to
make him talk. Once or twice he caught a glimpse of Mr Fogg,
who usually stayed in the main saloon of the *Rangoon*, keeping Mrs Aouda company or indulging in his unvarying habit
of playing whist.

As for Passepartout, he had started to reflect very seriously
about the remarkable coincidence that once again Fix was
following his master's route. It was indeed more than astonishing. This gentleman, very friendly and certainly very generous, who one meets first at Suez, who boards the *Mongolia*,
then gets off again at Bombay where he says he's going to stay,
who one meets again on the *Rangoon* heading for Hong
Kong: in sum, following Mr Fogg's programme step by step—
that gave food for thought. It was at the very least a strange
coincidence. What was Fix's game? Passepartout was ready to
wager his slippers—he had carefully kept them—that Fix
would leave Hong Kong at the same time as them, and probably on the same boat.

Passepartout could have thought for a hundred years without ever guessing the detective's mission. He could never have
imagined that Phileas Fogg was being tailed around the Earth
as a thief. But since it is human nature to produce an explanation for everything, the following is how Passepartout, after
a sudden brainwave, interpreted Fix's continual presence; and
really his interpretation was very plausible. He decided that
Fix was none other, could be nothing else, than an agent. He
had been put on Mr Fogg's trail by his colleagues at the
Reform Club, to make sure that the journey around the world
was properly completed, along the agreed route.

'It's obvious, it's so obvious!' the worthy fellow repeated,
proud of his own perspicacity. 'He's a spy that these
gentlemen have put on our trail. But it's not right. And

Mr Fogg so honest, so upstanding! Putting a detective to spy on him. Ah, gentlemen of the Reform Club, you will pay for this!'

Passepartout, delighted by his discovery, resolved nevertheless to say nothing about it to his master, for fear that he might be offended by his opponents' suspicion. However, he vowed to make fun of Fix on occasion, by allusion and without jeopardizing his own position.

During the afternoon of Wednesday, 30 October, the *Rangoon* entered the Strait of Malacca, which separates the Malayan peninsula from the large island of Sumatra. The island itself was hidden from the view of the passengers by small, very steep, mountainous islands that were extremely picturesque.

At four the following morning the *Rangoon* dropped anchor at Singapore so as to stock up with coal, having gained half a day on its timetabled crossing.

Phileas Fogg inscribed the saving in the credit column. This time he went ashore, keeping Mrs Aouda company, as she had said she wanted to go for a drive for a few hours.

Any action by Fogg seemed suspect to Fix, so he followed him without being seen. As for Passepartout, he laughed to himself at Fix's manœuvres, and went out for his usual shopping.

Singapore Island is neither large nor imposing. It has no mountain profiles. Nevertheless, it is charming in its brevity, resembling a park criss-crossed with fine roads. A fine carriage drawn by elegant horses imported from New Holland* conveyed Mrs Aouda and Phileas Fogg. They passed through groves of palm trees with blooming foliage and clove trees whose cloves are formed of the half-opened flowers of the bud itself. Groves of pepper-plants replaced the thorny hedges of the European landscape. Sago trees and large ferns with their superb boughs lent variety to the appearance of the tropical countryside. Nutmeg trees with veneered leaves saturated the air with their penetrating scent. There was no shortage of alert and grimacing bands of monkeys in the trees, nor perhaps tigers in the jungles. If anyone were to express surprise on learning that these terrible carnivores had not been hunted down to the last one in this small island, one can reply that they came from Malaya by swimming across the strait.

Having visited the countryside for two hours, Mrs Aouda and her companion—who looked without seeing very much—went back into the town, a vast conglomeration of heavy low houses surrounded by charming gardens, full of mangosteens, pineapples, and all the best fruit in the world.

At ten o'clock they arrived back at the steamship, having been unobtrusively followed by the inspector, who had had to pay for the hire of a carriage of his own.

Passepartout was waiting for them on the deck of the *Rangoon*. The good fellow had bought a few dozen mangosteens: nearly as large as apples, with dark brown outsides, bright red insides, and whose white flesh, melting between the lips, gives real gourmets incomparable pleasure. Passepartout was only too happy to offer them to Mrs Aouda, who thanked him with considerable grace.

At eleven o'clock, the *Rangoon* had taken on all its coal, and cast off. A few hours later, the passengers had lost sight of the high mountains of Malaya, whose jungles shelter the finest tigers on Earth.

Singapore is about 1,300 miles from the island of Hong Kong, a small British territory detached from the Chinese coast. It was important for Phileas Fogg to cover the distance in six days at most, so as to catch the boat due to leave Hong Kong on 6 November for Yokohama, one of the chief ports of Japan.

The *Rangoon* was heavily laden. Numerous passengers had come on board at Singapore: Indians, Ceylonese, Chinese, Malays, and Portuguese, for the most part occupying the second-class accommodation.

The weather had been quite fine, but now changed with the last quarter of the moon, and a high sea blew up. The wind was sometimes quite strong, but very fortunately from the south-east quarter, helping the steamer's headway. When practicable, the captain unfurled the sails. The *Rangoon*, rigged as a brig, often sailed using its two topsails and foresail, and its speed increased under the joint action of the steam and the wind. In this way it hugged the coasts of Annam and Cochin China,* on a short wave that was sometimes very tiring.

This was the *Rangoon*'s fault rather than the sea's, and the passengers, most of whom were seasick, should have blamed the boat for their fatigue.

The reason was that P. & O. ships on the China Seas route have a serious construction fault. The ratio of their draught when laden to their depth was badly calculated, and as a consequence they only offer a small resistance to the sea. The volume that is closed and watertight is insufficient. They are 'drowned', to employ the maritime expression, and as a consequence of their structure just a few large waves overboard are enough to affect their operation. These ships are in fact highly inferior, if not in engines and steam apparatus, at least in construction, to the designs used by the French Postal Service, such as the *Impératrice* and the *Cambodge*. According to the engineers' calculations, these two ships can take on board a mass of water equal to their own weight before sinking, but the P. & O. boats, the *Golconda*, *Korea*, and *Rangoon*, can absorb less than a sixth of their own weight before dropping to the bottom.

So when the weather was bad, the *Rangoon* needed to be very careful. It sometimes had to run before the wind under a small amount of steam. Hence a delay, which did not seem to affect Phileas Fogg at all, but which infuriated Passepartout. At such moments he denounced the captain, the chief engineer, and the Company, and cursed all those who get mixed up in transporting passengers. The thought of the gas-lamp continuing to burn at his expense in the house on Savile Row may also have contributed somewhat to his impatience.

'But you really are in a hurry to reach Hong Kong,' the detective said one day.

'Most definitely!'

'D'you think that Mr Fogg is in a rush to catch the steamer for Yokohama?'

'An enormous rush.'

'So you now believe in this bizarre journey round the world?'

'Totally. Don't you, Mr Fix?'

'Me? Not a word of it!'

'Joker!' replied Passepartout, winking at him.

This made the policeman think. The word worried him, but without his really being able to say why. Had the Frenchman seen through his disguise? He really didn't know what to think. But how had Passepartout been able to recognize his profession as detective, since he had kept it entirely secret? And yet, in speaking like that, he must have been thinking of something definite.

Then one day Passepartout happened to go further, constitutionally unable as he was to hold his tongue.

'You don't mean to say, Mr Fix!' he said in a mischievous tone. 'Do you mean that once we get to Hong Kong we will no longer have the pleasure of your company?'

'Well', answered Fix, a little embarrassed, 'I don't know.... It may happen that...'

'Ah, if you were to come with us, I'd be delighted. Come on, a P. & O. agent shouldn't stop halfway: you were only going to Bombay, and here you are about to reach China! America isn't very far—and from America to Europe is hardly any distance at all.'

Fix scrutinized his interlocutor's face, with its amiable expression; and decided to join in his laughter. But Passepartout was in a good mood, and asked if it paid a great deal, that job of his?

'Yes and no,' replied Fix, not batting an eyelid. 'Some things work out better than others. But as I'm sure you're aware, it's all on expenses!'

'Oh, I'm quite sure it is!' exclaimed Passepartout, laughing more than ever.

Fix returned to his cabin and started thinking seriously. He had obviously been found out. Somehow or other, the Frenchman had realized that he was a detective; but had he told his master? And whose side was he on in all this? Was he an accomplice or not—was the secret out and therefore all hope lost? The policeman spent a few difficult hours on this, first believing that everything was lost, then hoping that Fogg remained unaware of the situation—and finally not knowing what to think.

His brain calmed down again, however, and he decided to be frank with the servant. If conditions weren't right to arrest Fogg in Hong Kong, and if Fogg was planning to leave British soil, for good this time, then he, Fix, would tell Passepartout everything. Either the servant was in league with his master—who therefore knew everything, and the case was ruined—or else he had nothing to do with the theft, in which case it would be in his interests to abandon the thief.

Such was the position of the two men; but above them Phileas Fogg moved in majestic indifference. He was following his own rational orbit around the world, without bothering at all about the asteroids gravitating around him.

And yet there was in the neighbourhood a disturbing body—to use the astronomers' expression—which ought to have produced certain disturbances on the gentleman's heart. But no! Mrs Aouda's beauty had no effect, to Passepartout's great surprise. And the disturbing forces, if they existed, would have been harder to calculate than those of Uranus, which led to the discovery of Neptune.*

Passepartout was astonished to read so much gratitude every day towards his master in the young woman's eyes! Decidedly Phileas Fogg only had a heart when it was needed for behaving heroically, not tenderly. As for worries that he might have about the journey's success, he showed no trace of any. Passepartout himself was on perpetual tenterhooks. One day he was leaning on the guard-rail of the engine-room, watching the powerful machine: from time to time, when the ship pitched violently, the propeller would spin wildly above the water, making the engine run away. Steam would then burst out of the valves, making the worthy fellow hopping mad.

'The valves aren't weighted down enough!' he kept bellowing. 'We're not moving at all! Just like the British. If this was an American vessel, we might easily blow up, but at least we'd be going faster!'*

18

*In Which Phileas Fogg, Passepartout, and Fix Each
Go About Their Business*

DURING the last few days of the voyage, the weather
worsened. The wind strengthened considerably and settled in
the north-west, slowing the steamship down. The *Rangoon*,
rather unstable, rolled a great deal, and the passengers had
every right to feel a grudge against the long, devitalizing waves
that the wind produced on the open sea.

During 3 and 4 November, a storm blew up. A violent
squall whipped up the sea. The *Rangoon* had to heave to for
half a day, maintaining only ten revolutions of its screw to
keep its position, and thus travel obliquely across the waves.
All sails had been furled, but it was still too much for the
rigging, which whistled in the gusts.

The steamship's overall speed was considerably reduced,
and it could be calculated that it would arrive in Hong Kong
twenty hours behind schedule—or even more if the storm
didn't abate.

An impassive Phileas Fogg contemplated this spectacle of a
furious sea, apparently conspiring against him. His face
showed no discouragement, although a loss of twenty hours
could put his whole journey in danger by making him miss the
Yokohama steamship. This nerveless man felt neither impatience nor annoyance. It really seemed as though the storm
formed part of his schedule: that it was foreseen. Mrs Aouda
discussed the setback with her companion and found him as
calm as ever.

Fix didn't view the situation in the same way. On the
contrary. The storm in fact pleased him. His satisfaction
would have known no bounds if the *Rangoon* had been
forced to run before the storm. Any delays suited him,
for they meant that Mr Fogg would have to remain in Hong
Kong for some days. The heavens were at last giving him a
good hand, with their squalls and strong gusts. He felt ill, but
that didn't matter. The number of times he was sick was
beyond counting; but each time his body was doubled up

with seasickness, his mind was rejoicing with an immense satisfaction.

As for Passepartout, one can imagine with what ill-concealed anger he spent this testing time. Everything had gone so well until now. Land and sea had seemed to bow down before his master. Steamers and trains had obeyed his every wish. Wind and steam had joined forces to help him on his journey. Had the time for disillusionment finally come? Passepartout could no longer breathe, as if the £20,000 bet was drawn from his own bag. This storm exasperated him; the squalls put him beside himself; and he would have gladly whipped this disobedient sea.* The poor fellow! Fix was careful to hide his personal satisfaction: and was wise to do so, for if Passepartout had guessed Fix's secret contentment, he would have been in deep trouble.

Passepartout remained on the deck of the *Rangoon* for the whole duration of the storm. He wouldn't have been able to stay below. He climbed up the rigging; he astonished the crew as he helped with everything with the skill of a monkey. A hundred times he questioned the captain, the officers, and the sailors, who couldn't help laughing at the man's annoyance. Passepartout insisted on knowing how long the storm would last. He was told to go and have a look at the barometer, which obstinately refused to rise. Passepartout kept shaking it; but nothing made any difference; neither shaking the barometer, nor the curses which he heaped on the irresponsible instrument.*

The gale finally abated. During the daytime of 4 November the state of the sea changed. The wind shifted two points round to the south and became favourable once more.

Passepartout's serenity returned with the weather. The topsails and lower sails were unfurled again and the *Rangoon* continued on its route at a fine speed.

However, not all the lost time could be regained. The inevitable had to be faced up to, and 'Land ahoy!' was heard only at 5 a.m. on the 6th. Phileas Fogg's programme indicated the arrival of the steamship as the 5th. A delay of 24 hours had occurred, and the departure for Yokohama was going to be missed.

At six o'clock the pilot climbed on board the *Rangoon* and took his place on the navigation bridge in order to steer the ship through the channels to Hong Kong harbour.

Passepartout was dying to question the man, to ask if the Yokohama steamship had left, but he didn't dare, preferring to keep some hope until the last moment. He shared his worries with Fix, who—foxily—tried to console him, telling him that Mr Fogg could get off and take the next steamship. This put Passepartout into a towering rage.

But although Passepartout didn't dare question the pilot, Mr Fogg consulted his *Bradshaw*, and then blandly asked the pilot if he knew when a boat was leaving for Yokohama.

'Tomorrow, on the morning tide.'

'Hm,' said Mr Fogg, not showing the least surprise.

Passepartout, who was present, would have liked to give the pilot a hug, whilst Fix wanted to wring his neck.

'And what is the name of this steamer?' asked Mr Fogg.

'The *Carnatic*.'

'Was she not due to sail yesterday?'

'Yes sir, but they had to repair one of the boilers, and so the departure was put off until tomorrow.'

'Thank you very much,' answered Mr Fogg, and went back down to the *Rangoon*'s saloon with his automatic movements.

As for Passepartout, he seized hold of the pilot's hand and shook it vigorously.

'Thank you, pilot, you're a good man!'

The pilot probably never understood why his reply had produced such a show of friendship. On a whistle-blow, he went back up to the navigation bridge and steered the steamship through the flotilla of junks, Tanka boats,* fishing-boats, and ships of all natures crowding the narrows of Hong Kong.

At one o'clock the *Rangoon* was at the quayside, and the passengers were going ashore.

On this particular occasion, luck had wonderfully served Phileas Fogg, it had to be admitted. Without the need to repair its boilers, the *Carnatic* would have left on 5 November, and the travellers would have had to wait a whole week for the next steamship to Japan. Mr Fogg was now 24 hours late, it

was true, but this delay wouldn't have undesirable consequences for the rest of the journey.

The reason was that the Pacific steamer from Yokohama to
San Francisco connected directly with the steamship from
Hong Kong, and thus could not leave before it arrived. Obviously they would be 24 hours behind at Yokohama, but it
would be easy to make them up during the 22 days of crossing
the Pacific. Accordingly, 35 days out from London, Phileas
Fogg had satisfied the stipulations of his travel-plan, give or
take 24 hours.

Since the *Carnatic* was not due to leave until 5.00 the
following morning, Mr Fogg had sixteen hours ahead of him
to deal with his business, or rather Mrs Aouda's. Getting off
the ship, he offered the young woman his arm and led her to
a palanquin. He asked the porters to recommend a hotel, and
they indicated the hotel of the Club.* The palanquin set off,
followed by Passepartout, and twenty minutes later reached
the hotel.

A suite was reserved for the young woman, and Phileas
Fogg saw to it that she had everything she might need. Then
he told Mrs Aouda that he was going to set off straightaway
in search of the relative to whose care he was planning to
entrust her in Hong Kong. He also directed Passepartout to
remain in the hotel until he got back, so that the young
woman wasn't left alone.

The gentleman drove to the Stock Exchange. There they
would certainly know a personality like the Hon. Jejeeh, who
was one of the richest businessmen in town.

The broker Mr Fogg introduced himself to did indeed know
the Parsee merchant, but he had not been living in China for
the last two years. Having made his fortune, he had settled in
Europe—Holland, it was thought: he had had many contacts
with that country during his business career.

Phileas Fogg returned to the hotel of the Club. He sent a
message to Mrs Aouda, asking permission to enter her suite,
and, coming straight to the point, told her that the Hon. Jejeeh
was no longer living in Hong Kong, and was now probably
resident in Holland.

At first Mrs Aouda made no reply. She put her hand to her forehead, and thought for a few moments. Then in her gentle voice:

'What am I to do, Mr Fogg?'

'It's quite simple. Come back with us to Europe.'

'But I cannot abuse your . . .'

'You're not abusing, and your presence doesn't slow my programme down one bit. . . . Passepartout?'

'Sir?'

'Go to the *Carnatic* and book three cabins.'

Enchanted at the idea of continuing the journey with the young woman who was so kind to him, Passepartout left the hotel of the Club.

19

Where Passepartout Takes Too Lively an Interest in His Master, and What Happens as a Consequence

HONG KONG is but a small island, which the Treaty of Nanking transferred to Great Britain after the war of 1842.* In a few years the British genius for colonization had founded an important town there, and created a port, Victoria Harbour. The island is situated at the mouth of the Canton River,* only 60 miles from the Portuguese city of Macao on the opposite shore. Hong Kong was bound to overtake Macao in the commercial arena, and now the majority of Chinese imports and exports pass through the British town. Docks, hospitals, wharves, godowns, a Gothic cathedral, a Government House, and surfaced roads—everything made you think that one of the many market towns in Kent or Surrey had passed right through the terrestrial sphere and popped out at this point in China, almost at the antipodes.

Passepartout, hands in pockets, headed for Victoria Harbour, examining the palanquins, the wind-driven wheelbarrows still in use in the Celestial Empire,* and the large crowds of Chinese, Japanese, and Europeans filling the streets. With a few exceptions, it was Bombay, Calcutta, or Singapore all over

again, that the worthy fellow was finding on his route. There
is a trail of British towns right round the world.

Passepartout arrived at the Harbour. There, at the mouth of
the Canton River, teemed ships of all nations: British, French,
American, Dutch, warships and cargo ships, Japanese and
Chinese, junks, sampans, Tanka boats, and even flower
boats,* covering the waters like so many floating flowerbeds.
As he strolled around, Passepartout noticed a number of
residents dressed in yellow, all very elderly. Going into a
barbers' shop to be shaved in the Chinese fashion, he
learnt from the local barber, who spoke quite good English,
that these men were all at least 80 years old, and that at this
age they had the privilege of wearing yellow, the imperial
colour. Passepartout found this very amusing, without quite
knowing why.*

Freshly shaven, he headed for the quay the *Carnatic* was
due to sail from. He spotted Fix there, walking up and down,
but was not at all surprised. However, the police inspector's
face showed signs of terrible disappointment.

'Good! Everything is working out badly for the gentleman
of the Reform Club!'

He greeted Fix with his joyous smile, ignoring his companion's annoyance.

The policeman certainly had good reason to curse the infer-
nal luck dogging his footsteps. He still had no warrant! It was
obvious that the warrant was hot on his tracks, but could only
catch up with him if he stayed in town for a few days. And
since Hong Kong was the last British territory on the route,
Mr Fogg would escape his clutches for ever if he didn't manage to keep him there.

'Well, Mr Fix, have you decided to come with us to
America?'

'Yes,' replied Fix through gritted teeth.

'Come, come!' shouted Passepartout, with peals of laughter. 'I knew perfectly well that you wouldn't be able to bear
splitting up from us. Let's go and book your seat. Come on!'

And the two of them went into the shipping office and
booked cabins for four people. The clerk informed them that
since the repairs to the *Carnatic* were now finished, the steam-

ship was leaving at eight o'clock that very evening, and not the following morning as had previously been announced.

'Perfect!' said Passepartout. 'My master will be delighted. I'll go and tell him.'

At this moment Fix decided on an extreme course of action. He resolved to tell Passepartout everything. It was perhaps the only way he had of keeping Phileas Fogg in Hong Kong for a few more days.

On leaving the office, Fix offered his companion a drink. As Passepartout had plenty of time, he accepted the invitation.

There was a tavern with a welcoming appearance opening on to the quayside, so the two of them headed in. They found a huge, finely decorated room, at the end of which was stretched out a camp-bed equipped with cushions. Several people were sleeping on it.

In the large room about thirty customers were sitting at small tables made out of rattan. Some were downing pints of British beer—ale or porter—others flagons of spirits—gin or brandy. Most were also smoking long pipes of red clay, filled with small pellets of opium mixed with attar of roses. From time to time some smoker overcome by the fumes would slide under the table. The waiters of the establishment, taking him by his head and feet, would then carry him to the camp-bed, and lay him down beside a fellow smoker. About twenty of these inebriates were already laid out side by side, totally incapacitated.

Fix and Passepartout understood that they were in a den frequented by these wretches: besotted, emaciated, and reduced to idiocy, to whom each year a grasping Britain sells £11,000,000 worth of that lethal drug called opium. These are sad millions, derived from one of the most deadly vices of human nature.

The Chinese Government tried its utmost to put a halt to such abuse by introducing severe laws, but in vain. From the rich classes, for whom opium was at first strictly reserved, the usage moved down to the lower classes, and the havoc could no longer be stopped. Opium is smoked everywhere and at all times in the Middle Kingdom. Men and women alike are addicted to this deplorable passion, and once they have got accustomed to smoking, they can no longer give it up without suffering from appalling stomach contractions. A heavy smoker can consume up to eight pipes a day, but dies within five years.

So it was into one of these smoking dens, visible everywhere even in Hong Kong, that Fix and Passepartout had gone looking for a drink. Passepartout had no money on him, but gladly accepted the kind offer of his companion, planning to reciprocate on an appropriate occasion.

Two bottles of port were ordered, to which the Frenchman did full justice, while Fix, more restrained, observed his companion with keen attention. They chatted about this and that, but especially about the excellent idea that Fix had had of taking the *Carnatic*. Reminded about this steamer, whose departure had been brought forward by a few hours, Passepartout got up to go and tell his master, since the bottles were empty.

Fix held him back.

'A moment please.'

'What is it, Mr Fix?'

'I wish to discuss a serious matter with you.'

'A serious matter?' cried Passepartout, emptying the last drops at the bottom of his glass. 'We'll talk about it tomorrow. I don't have time today.'

'Wait! It's to do with your master.'

At these words, Passepartout carefully examined Fix's face. His expression seemed curious. He sat down again.

'So what have you got to say to me?'

Fix put a hand on his companion's arm and lowered his voice.

'Maybe you've guessed who I am?'

'But of course I have!' said Passepartout, smiling.

'Then I'll confess completely . . .'

'Now that I know everything, my good chap? Thank you very much! Oh, go on, I suppose you might as well. But let me tell you that those gentlemen have wasted their money!'

'Wasted? You're speaking out of the top of your hat. You obviously don't know how much is involved!'

'Yes, I do: 20,000!'

'*Fifty-five!*' said Fix, taking the Frenchman by the hand.

'What? Did Mr Fogg dare? £55,000? Well, all the more reason not to lose a single moment!' he said, getting up again.

'Fifty-five thousand,' repeated Fix, forcing Passepartout to sit down once more while at the same time ordering a flagon of brandy. 'And if I succeed I shall get a reward of 2,000. Do you want 500 for helping me?'

'Helping you?' exclaimed Passepartout, his eyes wide open.

'Yes, for helping me keep Fogg in Hong Kong for a few more days.'

'But', said Passepartout—'but what are you saying? Not content with having my master followed and doubting his honesty, those gentlemen even want to place obstacles in his way? Shame on them!'

'Whatever do you mean?'

'I mean it's the same as foul play. They might as well have stripped Mr Fogg and taken the money from his pocket!'

'But that's exactly what we're hoping to do!'

'But it's a plot!' exclaimed Passepartout, getting excited under the influence of the brandy Fix was pouring, and which he was drinking without noticing. 'A real set-up. Claiming to be gentlemen! And colleagues!'

Fix was beginning to feel out of his depth.

'Colleagues and members of the Reform Club! Let me tell you, Mr Fix, that my master is an honourable man, and that once he has made a bet, he tries to win it honestly.'

'But who on Earth do you think I am?' asked Fix, fixing his eyes on Passepartout.

'*Parbleu!* A detective sent by the members of the Reform Club to check on my master's route, which is an absolute disgrace! I have been careful not to tell Mr Fogg, although I guessed some time ago who you were.'

'So he knows nothing?' Fix enquired keenly.

'Nothing,' answered Passepartout, emptying his glass once more.

The inspector rubbed his forehead. He took his time before speaking again. What should he do? Passepartout's mistake seemed genuine, but it made his plan more difficult. The fellow was clearly speaking in entire good faith, and was not his master's accomplice as he might have feared.

'Well', he said to himself, 'since he's not his accomplice, he'll help me instead.'

The detective had once more decided on a course of action. In any case there was no time to lose. Fogg had to be arrested in Hong Kong at any cost.

'Listen,' said Fix firmly, 'and listen carefully. I am not who you think I am, a detective that the Reform Club members . . .'

'Bah!' said Passepartout looking at him mockingly.

'I am a police inspector, sent on a mission by the Metropolitan Police.'

'You . . . a police inspector?'

'Yes, and I can prove it. Here is my warrant.'

And producing a document from his pocket-book, the detective showed his companion some papers signed by the Commissioner of Police. A dumbfounded Passepartout stared at Fix, unable to say a word.

'Mr Fogg's bet was only a trick to fool you and his colleagues at the Reform Club, because it was in his interest to have your unconscious collaboration.'

'But why?'

'Listen. On 28 September, £55,000 was stolen from the Bank of England by an individual whose description was noted. Here it is: Fogg's down to the last detail!'

'Nonsense!' exclaimed Passepartout, striking the table with his hefty fist. 'My master is the most upright person in the world!'

'But how do you know? You don't even know him! You started work the day he left; and he went hurriedly, on a mad pretext, without any luggage, carrying a huge sum in banknotes! And you still dare tell me he's an honest man?'

'Yes, yes!' repeated the poor fellow mechanically.

'So you want to be arrested as an accomplice, do you?'

Passepartout had buried his head in his hands. He was unrecognizable. He didn't dare look at the inspector. Phileas Fogg a thief? The man who had saved Aouda, a brave and generous soul? But what a lot of evidence there was against him! Passepartout tried to fight the suspicion creeping into his mind. He didn't want to believe his master was guilty.

'But what do you want of me?' he asked the policeman, holding himself back with a supreme effort.

'The following. I've tailed Mr Fogg as far as here, but I still haven't got the arrest warrant I need from London. So you must help me keep him here in Hong Kong.'

'Me? You want me to . . .'

'And I'll split the reward of £2,000 from the Bank of England!'

'Never!' replied Passepartout trying to get up, but feeling his reason and strength abandoning him.

'Mr Fix,' he stammered. 'Even if everything you've told me was true . . . even if my master really was the thief you're looking for . . . which I deny . . . I have been . . . I *am* in his service. . . . He has been good, generous. . . . Betray him? . . . Never. . . . Not for all the tea in China. . . . Where I come from, we don't do such things.'

'So you refuse?'

'I refuse.'

'Then please forget what I said, and let's drink.'

'Yes, let's have another drink!'

Passepartout felt himself more and more overcome by the alcohol. Fix realized that he had to separate him from his master at all costs, and wanted to finish him off. On the table were a few pipes of opium. Fix pushed one into Passepartout's hand, who took it, lifted it to his lips, lit it, took a few puffs, and then slumped down, his head weighed down by the narcotic.

'So,' said Fix when he saw Passepartout collapse. 'Mr Fogg will not be told about the *Carnatic*'s departure in time, and even if he does manage to leave, at least it will be without this confounded Frenchman!'

Then he paid the bill and left.

20

In Which Fix Enters Into a Direct Relationship With Phileas Fogg

DURING this scene so critical for his future, Mr Fogg was accompanying Mrs Aouda on a tour of the streets of the

British quarter. Since Mrs Aouda had accepted his offer to take her to Europe, he had had to think a great deal about all the little matters involved in such a long journey. It might be perfectly possible for a Briton like him to go on a trip around the world with just a light bag, but a lady could not be expected to carry out the undertaking in such conditions. Hence the need to buy the clothing and other items needed for the journey. Mr Fogg performed the task with his usual composure, replying to all excuses or objections from the young widow, flustered by such assistance, with:

'It's conducive to the success of my journey, it's part of my schedule.'

Once the shopping was over, Mr Fogg and the young woman went back to the hotel and had dinner, sumptuously served at the manager's table. Then Mrs Aouda, a little tired, shook her imperturbable saviour's hand 'in the English manner', and retired to her suite.

As for the honourable gentleman, he engrossed himself all evening in *The Times* and *Illustrated London News*.

If he had been the sort of man to wonder about anything, he might have been surprised not to have seen his servant appear at bedtime. But knowing that the Yokohama steamer wasn't due to leave Hong Kong until the next morning, he didn't give it a second thought. In the morning, however, Passepartout failed to arrive when Mr Fogg rang.

What the honourable gentleman thought on learning that his servant hadn't come back to the hotel, nobody could have said. Mr Fogg merely picked up his bag, sent word to Mrs Aouda, and ordered a palanquin.

It was eight o'clock. High tide, which the *Carnatic* needed to thread its way through the channels, was due at 9.30.

When the palanquin arrived, Mr Fogg and Mrs Aouda got into this comfortable vehicle, with the luggage following behind on a wheelbarrow.

Half an hour later, the travellers were at the quayside—and learned that the *Carnatic* had left the night before.

Mr Fogg, expecting both steamship and servant, was going to have to make do without either. But no sign of disappoint-

ment appeared on his face, and with Mrs Aouda looking at
him anxiously, he simply answered:

'A trifling incident, madam, nothing more.'

At that moment a person who had been watching him
closely came up. It was Inspector Fix, who now greeted Mr
Fogg.

'Are you not in the same situation as myself, sir? Weren't
you a passenger on the *Rangoon* which arrived yesterday?'

'Yes,' replied Mr Fogg coldly, 'but I do not believe that I
have had the honour . . .'

'Pardon me, sir, but I thought I would be able to find your
servant here.'

'Do you know where he is?' asked the young lady eagerly.

'What!' answered Fix, feigning surprise. 'Is he not with
you?'

'No, we haven't seen him since yesterday. Might he possibly
have gone on board the *Carnatic* without us?'

'Without you, madam? Please pardon the question, but
were you planning to catch this steamship?'

'We were.'

'So was I, madam, and I feel very disappointed. The
Carnatic finished its repairs and left Hong Kong twelve hours
early without telling anybody, and now we have to wait a
whole week for the next ship!'

As he spoke, Fix felt his heart leaping with joy. A whole
week! Fogg held back in Hong Kong for seven whole days!
The warrant would have time to arrive. Luck was finally on
the side of the representative of the law.

One can therefore imagine the stunning blow when he
heard Phileas Fogg speaking in his usual calm voice.

'But it seems to me there are other ships in Hong Kong
harbour.'

And Mr Fogg, offering his arm to Mrs Aouda, headed for
the docks in search of a ship about to set sail.

A flabbergasted Fix followed. It was as if he was attached to
this man by a cord.

Nevertheless, luck seemed to have deserted the person it
had served so well up until now. For three hours Fogg worked
his way around the port, prepared if necessary to charter a

boat to transport him to Yokohama. But all the boats he saw were being loaded or unloaded and were therefore unable to sail. Hope began to return to Fix.

Mr Fogg did not panic, however, and was just about to carry on with his systematic search, even if it meant going as far as Macao, when a sailor accosted him on the Outer Harbour.

'Is Your Honour looking for a boat?' he said, taking off his cap.

'Do you have one ready to sail?'

'Yes, Your Honour. Pilot-boat No. 43, the best in the fleet.'

'Is she fast?'

'Eight to nine knots, near enough. Would you like to see her?'

'Yes.'

'Your Honour will be pleased. A sea-trip?'

'No, a voyage.'

'A voyage?'

'Will you agree to take me to Yokohama?'

The sailor just stood there, his arms hanging limp and his eyes wide open.

'Your Honour must be joking?'

'No. I missed the *Carnatic*, and must be in Yokohama by the 14th at the latest, in time for the San Francisco steamship . . .'

'I'm sorry,' replied the pilot, 'but it can't be done.'

'I'll pay £100 per day, and a reward of 200 if I arrive on time.'

'Are you in earnest?'

'Deadly.'

The pilot stood aside for a few moments. He gazed seawards, plainly torn between the desire to earn such an enormous sum of money and the fear of venturing so far. Fix was on tenterhooks.

Fogg turned to Mrs Aouda.

'You won't be afraid, madam?'

'With you there, no.'

The pilot had come back, turning his cap in his hands.

'Well, pilot?'

'Well, Your Honour. I cannot risk my men, myself, or yourself on such a long crossing at this time of the year on a boat of scarcely twenty tons. In any case, we wouldn't arrive on time, for it's 1,650 miles from Yokohama to Hong Kong.'

'Sixteen hundred.'

'It comes to the same thing.'

Fix breathed again.

'But', added the pilot, 'we might arrange it some other way.'

Fix stopped breathing.

'How?' enquired Fogg.

'By doing the 1,100 miles to Nagasaki, at the southern end of Japan, or only going to Shanghai, 800 miles from Hong Kong. In the latter case, we would stay close to the Chinese coast, which is quite an advantage, especially as the currents head north.'

'Pilot,' answered Phileas Fogg, 'Yokohama is where I have to catch the boat for America, not Shanghai or Nagasaki.'

'Why? The steamship for San Francisco doesn't start from Yokohama. It calls at Yokohama and Nagasaki, but it starts from Shanghai.'

'Are you certain?'

'Yes.'

'And when does it leave Shanghai?'

'At 7 p.m. on the 11th. We've got four days. Four days makes 96 hours, and doing an average of eight knots, we can cover the 800 miles to Shanghai—if we are lucky, if the wind stays south-easterly, and if the sea remains calm.'

'And when could you leave?'

'In an hour. We need to buy food and get under sail.'

'Very well. Are you the skipper?'

'Yes. John Bunsby of the *Tankadère*.'*

'Would you like an advance?'

'If it's not inconvenient to Your Honour.'

'Here is £200 on account. Mr Fix,' he added, 'if you care to avail yourself . . .'

'Sir,' he resolutely replied, 'I was just going to ask you this favour.'

'Good. On board in half an hour.'

'But what about your poor servant . . .' said Mrs Aouda, extremely worried about Passepartout's disappearance.

'I shall do everything I can for him,' answered Fogg.

And while Fix, jittery, feverish, angry, headed for the pilot-boat, the two of them made their way to Hong Kong Police Station. Phileas Fogg provided a description of Passepartout and left money for him to be repatriated. The same was done at the French Consulate, and then the palanquin passed by the hotel, picked up the luggage, and took the travellers back to the Outer Harbour.

Three o'clock was striking. Pilot-boat No. 43, with its crew on board and food and water loaded, was ready to set sail.

The *Tankadère* was a charming little schooner: twenty tons with fine bows, a very easy appearance, and graceful lines. You would have said a racing yacht. Her shining brass railings, her galvanized iron fittings, and her deck as white as ivory, showed that skipper John Bunsby knew how to keep her in good condition. Her two masts leaned back a little. She was carrying spanker, mizzen, forestay, jib, and topsails, and could rig indefinitely with a following wind. Her speed was clearly outstanding, and she had in fact won several prizes in pilot-boat races.

The crew of the *Tankadère* consisted of John Bunsby plus four men. They were sturdy seamen who knew these seas admirably well and who ventured out in all weathers to bring ships in. John Bunsby was a man of about forty-five, vigorous, almost black with sunburn, a lively expression, an energetic face, sturdily balanced, comfortable in his movements: he would have inspired confidence in the most fearful.

Phileas Fogg and Mrs Aouda went on board. Fix was already there. The stern hatchway of the schooner led down to a square cabin, whose sides bulged out to form bunks above a circular divan. In the middle, a table lit by a hurricane lamp. It was small but clean.

'I'm sorry not to have anything better to offer you,' Mr Fogg said to Fix, who bowed without replying.

The police inspector felt a sort of humiliation in benefiting from Fogg's kindness.

'I must say he's a very polite scoundrel,' he thought, 'even if he is a scoundrel all the same!'

At ten past three the sails were hoisted. The Union Jack flapped on the schooner's gaff. The passengers sat on deck. Mr Fogg and Mrs Aouda scanned the quayside one last time to see whether Passepartout might appear.

Fix was a little worried, for chance might have brought to that very spot the unfortunate fellow he had treated so badly, and then an argument would have broken out, in which the detective would have suffered some disadvantage. But the Frenchman did not show up: he was undoubtedly still under the influence of the narcotic.*

Skipper John Bunsby finally headed out for the open sea. The *Tankadère* caught the wind under its spanker, mizzen, and jib sails, and shot forward as it bounded over the waves.

21

Where the Skipper of the Tankadère *Runs a Considerable Risk of Losing a Bonus of £200*

SUCH a voyage of 800 miles, on a ship of twenty tons, was a dangerous expedition, above all at this time of the year. These China seas are generally squally, exposed as they are to terrible gusts of wind, especially during the equinox periods—and it was still early November.

It would unquestionably have been in the skipper's interest to take his passengers on to Yokohama, since he was paid by the day. But he would have been very reckless to attempt the journey in such conditions, since to make for Shanghai was already an audacious, almost foolhardy act. However, John Bunsby had confidence in the *Tankadère*, which rose to the waves like a seagull, and perhaps he had good reason to do so.

As the day came to a close, the *Tankadère* navigated through the capricious channels leading out of Hong Kong. She behaved admirably at all speeds, whether tacking into the wind or running with the wind behind.

'I have no need,' said Fogg to the helmsman as the schooner reached the open sea, 'to advise you of the need for the greatest possible speed.'

'Your Honour can leave everything to me. We are carrying all the canvas the wind will allow. Our topsails would not help at all for they would only "knock down" the ship and slow her down.'

'You're the expert, skipper, not me, and I put my trust in you.'

Phileas Fogg, standing upright, his legs apart and balanced like a sailor, watched the rough sea without flinching. The young woman, sitting at the stern, felt moved as she contemplated this ocean already darkened by dusk, that she was braving on a frail ship. Above her head spread the white sails, carrying her into space like huge wings. The schooner, lifted up by the gust, seemed to be flying through the air.

Night fell. The moon was moving into its first quarter, and its thin light would soon disappear into the mists of the horizon. Clouds were gathering in the east and had already covered part of the sky.

The skipper had lit the navigation lights—an essential safeguard in these seas crowded with land-bound shipping. Collisions between ships are quite common, and, at the speed the schooner was doing, she would have broken up at the least contact.

Fix was dreaming at the prow of the ship. He was keeping himself to himself, knowing that Fogg was not naturally talkative. In any case, he felt reluctant to speak to this man whose help he had accepted. He was also thinking about the future. It now seemed certain that Fogg wouldn't stop at Yokohama, that he would immediately catch the steamship for San Francisco, since America's vast spaces would guarantee him sanctuary and impunity. Phileas Fogg's plan struck him as perfectly simple.

Instead of heading straight for the United States like a common or garden criminal, this Fogg had done a Grand Tour three-quarters of the way round the globe. He would thus reach North America more safely, having thrown the police off the trail, and would live quietly there on the Bank's

80,000. But once in the United States, what should Fix do? Should he give up on his man? No, a hundred times no! Until he got an extradition order, he would stay hot on his heels. It was his duty, and he would do it to the end. In any case, some progress had been made: Passepartout was no longer with his master. Especially after the secrets he had been told, it was essential that master and servant never saw each other again.

As for Fogg, he too was thinking about his servant who had vanished so mysteriously. On reflection it seemed possible that, as the result of some misunderstanding, the poor fellow had embarked on the *Carnatic* at the last moment. This was Mrs Aouda's opinion as well, who very much missed the good servant she owed so much to. They might possibly meet up with him again in Yokohama—it would be easy to find out if he had arrived there on the *Carnatic*.

At about ten, the wind got stronger. It would perhaps have been prudent to reef, but the master studied the state of the sky, and left the sails rigged. The *Tankadère* had a considerable draught, and so was able to bear the sails admirably; in any case, everything was ready to be brought down rapidly if a squall did blow up.

At midnight Phileas Fogg and Mrs Aouda went down to their cabin. Fix was already there, stretched out on one of the wooden bunks. As for the skipper and his men, they stayed on deck all night.

At sunrise the following day, 8 November, the schooner had covered more than 100 miles. The log-line, often dropped, showed that the average speed was between eight and nine knots. The sails of the *Tankadère* had the wind behind and were all carrying, and with this setting, she was moving at her maximum speed. If the wind and general conditions held, she had an excellent chance of making it.

The *Tankadère* stayed in touch with the coast all day, following the currents round. She kept five miles out at most, and the irregular profile of the shoreline was sometimes visible over her port side during clearer conditions. Since the wind came from the land, the sea was less turbulent closer in—fortunately for the schooner, as boats of small tonnage often suffer from a swell which cuts their speed, 'kills' them, to use the marine expression.

At about midday, the wind softened slightly and veered south-east. The skipper set the topsails, but two hours later they had to be taken down again, for the wind had freshened once more.

Mr Fogg and the young woman were fortunate not to suffer from seasickness, and so ate with a hearty appetite the preserved food and biscuits customary on board. Fix was invited to share their meal and was forced to accept, knowing that stomachs need ballasting as much as boats; but it galled him all the same! Travelling at the expense of this man and living off his food, he found rather treacherous. He ate—or rather nibbled—but eat he did.

When the meal was over, he thought it his duty to take Fogg aside.

'Sir . . .'

This 'Sir' scorched his lips, and he had to stop himself from taking hold of 'sir's' collar!

'Sir, you have been most kind in offering me passage on board this ship, and although my means do not allow me to act as generously as yourself, I intend to pay my full share.'

'Let's not discuss that.'

'But yes, I must insist.'

'No,' repeated Fogg, in a tone which brooked no reply. 'It's all included in running expenses!'

In a state of suffocation, Fix bowed, went to stretch out at the bows of the schooner—and said not another word for the rest of the day.

The ship was flying ahead. John Bunsby had high hopes. Several times he told Mr Fogg they would reach Shanghai in time. Mr Fogg merely replied that he hoped so. In any case the whole crew of the little schooner were working as hard as they could. The bonus spurred on these experienced men. There was not a sheet that was not properly taut, not a sail that was not vigorously set. The man at the helm could not have been blamed for a single yaw. They couldn't have manoeuvred more accurately at a Royal Yacht Club regatta.

In the evening the skipper used the log-line to confirm that they had done 220 miles since Hong Kong. Mr Fogg could now hope that on arrival in Yokohama, he would not have any delay to write in his programme. The first serious setback encountered since leaving London looked as though it would cause him no serious harm.

Late that night, the *Tankadère* entered the Fokien Strait, between the large island of Formosa and the Chinese coast, and crossed the Tropic of Cancer. The sea was very difficult in this strait, full of the eddies caused by opposing currents. The schooner laboured a great deal. The choppy waves broke its momentum. It became almost impossible to remain standing on deck.

At dawn, the wind freshened further. The sky gave evidence of a gale building up. The barometer also announced that the atmosphere was going to change: its behaviour became irregular after daybreak, with the mercury oscillating capriciously. In the south-east the sea could be seen heaving itself into long surges which 'smelt of a storm'. The night before, the sun had gone down in a red mist, disappearing into the ocean in phosphorescent flickers.

The captain examined the threatening appearance of the sky for a long time, muttering barely intelligible things between his teeth. On one occasion, he found himself beside his passenger.

'May I tell Your Honour frankly what is on my mind?' he said in a low voice.

'Yes.'

'Well we're going to have a storm.'

'Will it come from the north or the south?'

'From the south. Look, you can see the typhoon building up!'

'Let's go with the typhoon from the south, since it's in the right direction.'

'If that's the way you look at it, then there's nothing more can be said.'

John Bunsby's inkling was correct. If it had been a less advanced season, the typhoon might have spent itself in a luminous cascade of electric flames—to quote a celebrated meteorologist—but near the winter equinox it was to be feared that it would break with great violence.

The skipper took every precaution he could. He had all the sails on the schooner furled and the yards brought down to deck. The poles were struck and the boom taken in. The hatches were securely battened down, so that not a drop of water could get into the hull. A single triangular sail, a storm jib of strong canvas, was hoisted as a foretop staysail, so as to keep the schooner stern to the wind. Then they waited.

John Bunsby had urged the passengers to go down to their cabin; but in such a confined space, virtually airless and with all the jolts and jerks from the waves, this imprisonment would have been rather unpleasant. Neither Mr Fogg nor Mrs Aouda, nor even Fix, consented to leave the deck.

At about eight, a raging storm of rain and wind swooped down on the ship. Although it had only a tiny amount of sail, the *Tankadère* was lifted up like a feather. The wind beggars description when it blows up into a storm. To say that its speed is four times a locomotive's at full steam only conveys part of the truth.

The vessel ran northwards all day, borne on by the monstrous waves, but fortunately maintaining the same speed as them. Twenty times it was on the point of being overtaken by the mountains of water that rose up at the stern; but a deft twist on the helm by the captain, and catastrophe was prevented each time. The passengers were sometimes completely covered in spray, but took it stoically. Fix undoubtedly cursed; but the intrepid Aouda kept her eyes fixed on her companion, whose composure she couldn't help admiring, and showed herself worthy of him as she braved the storm at his side. As for Fogg himself, the typhoon seemed to be part of his programme.

Until then the *Tankadère* had been heading continuously north; but as feared, the wind veered three-quarters in the evening, and became north-westerly. The schooner, its flank exposed to the waves, was buffeted terribly. The sea hit it with a violence that would have been frightening had one not known how solidly the parts of a ship are joined together.

As night fell the tempest grew worse. Seeing the darkness come down while the storm increased, John Bunsby felt seriously worried. He wondered whether it might be time to put into port, and consulted his crew.

Then Bunsby approached Mr Fogg.

'Your Honour, we would do well to make for one of the coastal ports.'

'I think so too.'

'Ah, but which one?'

'I only know one,' Mr Fogg tranquilly answered.

'Namely . . .'

'Shanghai.'

For a minute the captain could not understand what this reply meant—how much obstinacy and tenacity it involved. Then he exclaimed:

'Yes, Your Honour is quite right. To Shanghai!'

And the *Tankadère* was steadfastly maintained on a northerly course.

It was a terrible night. Only by a miracle did the little schooner avoid capsizing. Twice she was on the point of leaning right over, and everything would have been carried off if the lashings had failed. Although Mrs Aouda was completely worn out, she made no complaint. More than once Mr Fogg had to rush to protect her from the violence of the waves.

Day broke again. The storm was still unleashing its force with a dreadful fury. However, the wind fell back to the south-east. This was more favourable, and the *Tankadère* started to move fast over the raging sea whose waves were now colliding with those previously produced by the wind. Hence a conflict of swells and counter-swells that would have crushed a less solidly constructed ship.

From time to time the coast could be glimpsed through the torn mists, but not a ship in sight. The *Tankadère* was alone on the high seas.

At midday, a few signs of calm appeared, which became more pronounced as the sun went down.

The shortness of the storm had been due to its very violence. The passengers, absolutely exhausted, were able to eat a little and take some rest.

The following night was relatively peaceful. The skipper unfurled the sails again to low reef. The ship remained moving fast. At daybreak on the following day, the 11th, the coast was sighted, and John Bunsby confirmed that they were less than 100 miles from Shanghai.

A hundred miles, but only today to cover them in! Mr Fogg had to reach Shanghai that very evening if he wanted to catch the steamship for Yokohama. Without the storm which had lost him several hours, he would have been less than 30 miles from port.

The wind dropped appreciably, but fortunately the sea fell at the same time. All sails were unfurled. Topsails, staysails, foretop staysail: all caught the wind, and the sea foamed under the stem of the ship.

At midday, the *Tankadère* was only 45 miles from Shanghai. The Yokohama steamship was not due to leave port for another six hours.

Great suspense could be felt on board. Everyone wanted to come into port at any price. Everyone could feel his heart pounding with impatience—everyone that is except Fogg. The tiny schooner had to maintain an average of nine knots and the wind was still abating! It was a fitful breeze, with capricious gusts coming off the coast and leaving the sea smooth again as soon as they had passed.

However, the current helped and the ship was so light, its sails so lofty, of such fine fabric, so good at picking up the mad breezes, that at six o'clock John Bunsby was able to calculate they were only ten miles from the Shanghai River—for Shanghai itself is situated more than twelve miles above the mouth.

At seven they were still three miles out. A gruesome oath escaped from the lips of the skipper: the £200 bonus was going to slip from his grasp. He looked at Mr Fogg. The gentleman was impassive, even though his entire fortune was at stake.

At this moment a long black rocket crowned with a banner of smoke appeared over the water-line. It was the American steamship, leaving at the regulation time.

'Damn and blast!' cried John Bunsby, pushing away the helm with a desperate arm.

'Signal!' shouted Fogg.

A small brass canon lay on the foredeck of the *Tankadère*, used for sending messages when it was foggy.

The canon was quickly loaded to the muzzle, but just as the skipper was about to apply a glowing coal to the touch-hole:

'Flag at half-mast,' said Mr Fogg.

The flag was brought halfway down. This was a distress signal, in the hope that the American steamer would see it and change its route slightly to come and meet the ship.

'Fire!'

And the blast of the little brass canon hit the air.

22

Where Passepartout Realizes That Even at the Antipodes, It Is Wise To Have Some Money in One's Pocket

THE *Carnatic* had left Hong Kong at 6.30 p.m. on 7 November, and was heading at full steam towards Japan. It was carrying a full load of merchandise and passengers. Only two cabins at the stern remained empty: those reserved for Mr Phileas Fogg.

The following morning the men at the bow were rather surprised to notice a passenger with eyes half-dazed, a shaky walk, and tousled hair. He emerged from the second-class companionway and went to sit down on a pile of gear, tottering all the while.

This passenger was Passepartout. The following is what had happened.

Shortly after Fix left the opium den, two attendants had lifted Passepartout up as he slept, and laid him down on the bunks reserved for the smokers. But three hours later, haunted by a fixed idea even in his nightmares, Passepartout woke up again and began to fight against the stupefying effect of the narcotic. The thought of duty undone cut through his torpor. He left the addicts' bed, and, stumbling, leaning against the walls, falling down and getting up again, always and irresistibly pushed on by a sort of instinct, he left the den, shouting all the while as if in a dream, 'The *Carnatic*! *Carnatic*!'

The steamship was ready with her steam up. Passepartout had only a few steps left to take. He threw himself on the gangway, managed to work his way up it, and fell down insensible on the foredeck just as the ship cast off.

The sailors were used to this sort of scene and carried the poor fellow down into a second-class cabin. Which is where he woke up the following morning, on board the *Carnatic*, 150 miles off the Chinese coast.

Thus Passepartout discovered himself on deck that morning, breathing in mouthfuls of the fresh sea breeze. The pure air sobered him up, and he began to put his thoughts together, not without a certain difficulty. At last he remembered the scenes of the day before: Fix's secrets, the smoking den, etc.

'I must have been abominably drunk. Whatever will Mr Fogg say? But at least I didn't miss the boat, and that's the main thing.'

Then he thought about Fix.

'Let's hope we've said good riddance to that fellow, and let's hope he hasn't dared follow us on to the *Carnatic*, after that proposition he made me. A police inspector, a detective, shadowing my master and claiming that he is suspected of stealing from the Bank of England. What a load of rubbish! If Mr Fogg's a thief then I'm a murderer!'

But should he tell his master the tale? Should he describe the part that Fix had played in the affair? Wouldn't he be better waiting until London, and then telling him that a policeman from Scotland Yard had tailed him right round the world, and laugh about it with him then? That might perhaps be best. In any case, he would think it over. What needed doing first was to go and find Mr Fogg and offer apologies for his inexcusable behaviour.

Passepartout got up. The sea was rough, and the steamer rolling a great deal. The worthy fellow, whose legs still didn't feel very steady, somehow made his way to the stern of the ship.

He saw nobody on deck looking like his master or Mrs Aouda.

'Oh well, at this time of the day Mrs Aouda will still be in bed. As for Mr Fogg, he's bound to have found someone to play whist with, as he always does, and . . .'

With these words, he went down to the saloon. Mr Fogg wasn't there. Passepartout now had only one choice left: to ask the Purser what cabin Mr Fogg was in. The Purser told him he didn't know of any passenger of that name.

'Please let me explain,' said Passepartout, repeating his question. 'He's a gentleman, tall, cold, not very communicative. He's travelling with a young lady . . .'

'There are no young ladies on board. Here's the list of passengers. You can check for yourself.'

Passepartout scanned the list. His master's name wasn't on it.

For a moment his head whirled. Then an idea shot through his brain.

'Good Lord! I am on the *Carnatic*, am I?'

'You are.'

'Bound for Yokohama?'

'Yes indeed.'

He had been afraid he had got on the wrong boat! But if he really was on the *Carnatic*, it seemed clear that his master wasn't.

Passepartout collapsed into a deck chair. It was a crushing blow. But suddenly, it all came rushing back to him. The departure time of the *Carnatic* had been brought forward, he was meant to have told his master, but he hadn't. It was all his fault if Mr Fogg and Aouda had missed the boat.

His fault, yes, but even more the double-crosser's who had got him drunk, so as to separate him from his master and make sure Mr Fogg stayed in Hong Kong! He finally understood the inspector's trick. And now Mr Fogg had lost his bet, he was ruined, arrested, even perhaps in prison. . . . At these thoughts Passepartout tore at his hair. Ah, if ever Fix came within striking distance, what a settling of scores there would be!

But in the end, after the first moment of despair, Passepartout recovered his composure, and examined the situation. It was not good. The Frenchman found himself on the way to Japan. He would certainly get there, but how would he come back? His pockets were empty: not a shilling, not even a penny. Admittedly, his passage and food on board had been paid for in advance. So he had five or six days before him to make a decision. Accordingly, during the whole journey he ate and drank to an indescribable degree. He ate for his master, Mrs Aouda, and himself. He ate as if Japan was a desert island, entirely devoid of edible substances.

On the 13th, the *Carnatic* entered Yokohama Harbour on the morning tide.

This town is an important port of call for the Pacific. All the steamers put in here to pick up and set down post and travellers from North America, China, Japan, and the Malaysian Archipelago. Yokohama is on the Bay of Edo,* with the immense town of Edo itself, the second capital of the Empire of Japan, close by. It was formerly the residence of the Taikun*—the Civil Emperor, since abolished—and was a rival to Miyako,* the immense city where the Mikado resided—the Ecclesiastical Emperor, descended from the gods.

The *Carnatic* came alongside Yokohama quay, near the jetties of the port and the customs sheds, amidst large numbers of ships from all nations.

Passepartout set foot without enthusiasm in this curious land of the Children of the Rising Sun. He had nothing better to do than to take chance as his guide, and wander through the streets.

At first he found himself in an absolutely European city: houses with low fronts adorned with verandas on top of elegant colonnades. Its streets, squares, docks, and warehouses covered the whole area between the Treaty Promontory and the river. As in Hong Kong and Calcutta, a jumble of all races swarmed, Americans, Britons, Chinese, Dutch—merchants ready to buy or sell anything. The Frenchman felt himself as high and dry as if he had been cast suddenly into the land of the Hottentots.

Passepartout had one remaining option: to go to the French or British Consulates in Yokohama. But he was reluctant to recount his story, so intimately mixed up with his master's; and before resorting to that, he wanted to exhaust all other possibilities.

So, after crossing the European quarter without chance having come to his help, he went into the Japanese part, resolved if necessary to walk as far as Edo.

This native portion of Yokohama is called Benten, from the name of a sea goddess* worshipped on the neighbouring islands. Here there appeared magnificent avenues of firs, sacred gateways to an exotic architecture, bridges hidden in the midst of bamboo and reeds, temples sheltering under the spacious, melancholic cover of ancient cedars, monasteries in whose depths stagnated Buddhist priests and followers of Confucianism, and interminable streets where you could have gathered a harvest of children all with pink complexions and red cheeks: little fellows who looked cut out of some native screen, and who played amongst short-legged poodles and yellowish tail-less cats, very lazy and very affectionate.

In the streets, nothing but a swarming, incessant movement: processions of monks beating on their monotonous drums and tambourines, *yakunin*—customs or police officers—in pointed hats encrusted with lacquer and carrying two sabres in their waistbands, infantrymen dressed in blue cotton with white stripes and armed with percussion guns,* men from the Mikado's Household Guard in their sack-like silk doublets and their chain-mail tunics and shiny coats of mail; together with soldiers of all ranks—for in Japan, the military profession is as honoured as it is looked down upon in China. Then mendicant friars, pilgrims in long robes, and ordinary people, all with hair as shiny black as ebony, big heads, long trunks, thin legs, short statures, complexions anywhere between the darker shades of copper and matt white, but never yellow like the Chinese, from whom the Japanese essentially differ. Finally, amongst the carriages, the palanquins, the horses, the porters, the wind-powered wheelbarrows, the *norimono* with their lacquered sides, the soft *kago*, veritable litters made of bamboo; and, moving around with little steps of their little feet, in canvas shoes, straw sandals, or clogs made out of carved wood, a few not very pretty women, with slant eyes, flattened breasts, and fashionably blackened teeth,* but gracefully wearing the national dress, the kimono: a sort of dressing-gown crossed with a silk sash, whose wide belt opens out behind into an extravagant bow—as seems to have been borrowed by the most up-to-date *Parisienne*.

Passepartout wandered for a few hours amongst this motley crowd, looking at the quaint, luxurious shops, the bazaars with their piles of gaudy Japanese jewellery, the eating-houses decorated with streamers and banners which he was not in any position to enter, the tea-houses where repeated cups of odorous hot water are drunk together with *sake* (alcohol from fermenting rice), and those snug smoking dens where a fine tobacco is consumed, not opium, virtually unknown in Japan.

Then Passepartout found himself in the fields, amongst huge rice paddies. Here bloomed flowers shedding their last colours and their last scents, dazzling camellias on trees rather than bushes, and bamboo enclosures containing cherry trees, plums, and the apples that the Japanese cultivate more for their blossom than their fruit, defended by grimacing scare-crows and noisy whirligigs against the beaks of sparrows, pigeons, crows, and other predators. Every majestic cedar sheltered its broad eagle; every weeping willow some heron, melancholically balancing on one leg; and everywhere stood rooks, ducks, hawks, wild geese, and a multitude of those cranes called 'Lordships' by the Japanese, representing long life and happiness.

The wandering Passepartout spotted a few violets in the grass.

'Good,' he said. 'There's my supper.'

But having smelled them, he found that they had no fragrance.

'No luck!'

Certainly the worthy fellow had anticipated by eating as copiously as he could before leaving the *Carnatic*; but after a day's walk, his stomach felt very hollow. He had noticed that mutton, goat, and pork were totally missing from the displays of the native butchers. And as he knew that it was a sacrilege to kill cattle, strictly reserved for agricultural tasks,* he had concluded that meat was rare in Japan. He was right; but if he couldn't have butcher's meat, his stomach would have very much welcomed a joint or two of wild boar or deer, a few partridges or quails, or some poultry or fish, which, with rice, are almost the only things that the Japanese eat. But he had to make the best of a bad job and put off to the morrow the task of finding food.

Night came. Passepartout returned to the native quarter, and roamed the streets amongst the multicoloured lanterns, watching the groups of wandering acrobats perform their amazing tricks and the open-air astrologers drawing large crowds around their telescopes. He caught sight of the harbour again, dotted with fishermen's lanterns, drawing fish in with the glow of their flaring resin lamps.

The streets got emptier. The crowds gave way to *yakunin* doing their rounds. In magnificent costumes and surrounded by their retinues, these officers looked like ambassadors; and each time he met some dazzling patrol, Passepartout quipped:

'Hello! Another Japanese embassy leaving for Europe!'

23

In Which Passepartout's Nose Becomes Inordinately Long

THE following day, a famished and exhausted Passepartout told himself that he needed to eat at all costs, and the sooner the better. He did have one last resource, to sell his watch, but he would rather have died of hunger. It was now or never for the worthy fellow to use the strong, if not melodious, voice given him by nature.

He knew a few French and English songs, and resolved to try them out. The Japanese were surely music-lovers, since everything is done to the sound of cymbals, tam-tams, and drums, and they could but appreciate the talents of a European virtuoso.

But perhaps it was a bit early to organize a concert, and the audience, unexpectedly woken up, might perhaps not pay the singer by showering down money with the Mikado's effigy on it.

Passepartout decided to wait for a couple of hours. Then, as he made his way along, he decided he was too well dressed for a wandering artist, and resolved to exchange his clothes for cast-offs more in keeping with his present position. This exchange would also produce some money, which he could immediately use on filling himself up.

Having taken such a decision, he still had to implement it. Only after long searches did Passepartout discover a native second-hand shop, where he made his request. The European clothing pleased the shopkeeper; and soon Passepartout emerged decked out in an old Japanese robe and a sort of ribbed turban, faded with age. But a few silver coins were jingling in his pocket.

'Oh well,' he thought. 'I'll just have to pretend there's a carnival going on.'

Passepartout's first action, thus 'Japanesed', was to go into a tea-house of modest appearance. There, chicken scraps and some rice provided him with a lunch fit for a man for whom dinner was still a problem to be solved.

'And now', he said, when he had eaten his fill, 'one mustn't lose one's head. I can no longer sell these cast-offs for ones still more Japanese. As soon as possible, therefore, I must find a way out of this Land of the Rising Sun which will leave me with such terrible memories.'

Passepartout thought then about visiting the steamships leaving for America. He planned to offer his services as a cook or a servant, the only pay being the food and passage. Once in San Francisco, he would consider how to get out of the spot he was in. The most important thing was to cross the 4,700 miles of Pacific between Japan and the New World.

Since Passepartout was not a man who liked an idea to languish, he headed for the port of Yokohama. But as he approached the docks, his project, which had seemed so simple when he had first thought of it, appeared more and more difficult to actually execute. Why would a servant or cook be needed on board an American steamship, and what confidence could he inspire dressed in this way? What letters of recommendation could he produce? What referees could he quote?

While thinking, his eyes fell on a huge poster that a sort of clown was parading through the streets of Yokohama. The poster was in English, and it read as follows:

TROUPE OF JAPANESE ACROBATS
UNDER
THE HON. WILLIAM BATULCAR

———

LAST FEW PERFORMANCES
Before the Departure for the United States of America
of the
LONG NOSES—LONG NOSES
Under the Special Protection of the God Tengu
GREAT ATTRACTION!

'The United States of America!' read Passepartout. 'Just the job.'

And he followed the sandwich-man back towards the Japanese quarter. Fifteen minutes later he stopped in front of a huge shed crowned with several bunches of streamers: its outside walls portrayed a whole band of jugglers, without any sense of perspective but in violent colours.

This was the establishment of the Hon. William Batulcar, a sort of American Barnum,* manager of a troupe of showmen. It had jugglers, clowns, acrobats, gymnasts, and tightrope walkers, giving, as the poster said, their last few performances before leaving the Land of the Rising Sun for the United States.

Passepartout walked through the colonnade fronting the shed, and asked for Mr Batulcar. This gentleman appeared in person.

'What do you want?' he said, taking Passepartout for a native.

'Do you need a servant?'

'A servant?' exclaimed this Barnum, stroking the thick grey goatee proliferating under his chin. 'I already have two that are obedient and devoted, have never left me, and serve me for free, provided that I feed them well. . . . And here they are,' he added, showing two strong arms, lined with veins as thick as the strings on a double-bass.

'So there's nothing I can do for you?'

'Nothing.'

'That's a terrible shame. I would have been only too pleased to leave with you.'

'Hold on!' said the Hon. Batulcar. 'You're Japanese if I'm a monkey! Why are you dressed up like that?'

'One dresses as best one can!'

'True, that. Frenchman, aren't you?'

'Yes, a Parisian from Paris.'

'Then you must know how to poke faces?'

'Yes,' replied Passepartout, annoyed to see his nationality produce this question. 'We French do know how to make faces, but no better than the Americans!'

'Nicely put. Well, if I don't take you on as a servant, you could do as a clown. Please understand me, my good man. In France they exhibit foreign jesters; and abroad, French buffoons!'

'I see!'

'Are you strong by any chance?'

'Especially with a good meal inside me.'

'And can you sing?'

'Like a bird,' answered Passepartout, who had done his time in street concerts.

'But do you know how to sing while standing on your head, with a top spinning on the sole of your left foot and a sabre balanced on the right one?'

'Why of course!' replied Passepartout, remembering his exercises as a youth.

'That, you see, is what is essential,' answered the Hon. Batulcar.

The deal was struck there and then.

Passepartout had finally found employment. He was now a jack of all trades in the celebrated Japanese troupe. It was not very flattering, but within a week he would be on his way to San Francisco.

The performance, noisily announced by the Hon. Batulcar, was due to start at three o'clock; and soon the formidable instruments of a Japanese orchestra, complete with drums and tam-tams, were reverberating at the door. It will be understood that Passepartout had not been able to rehearse his part:

his solid shoulders were to provide support for the grand scene of the 'Human Pyramid' performed by the Long Noses of the god Tengu.* This 'Great Attraction' was to bring the performance to an end.

By three o'clock spectators had filled the huge shed. Europeans and Asians; Chinese and Japanese; men, women, and children; all rushed on to the narrow benches and into the boxes near the stage. The musicians had taken up their places, and the full orchestra, with gongs, tam-tams, bone castanets, flutes, tambourines, and bass drums, was playing furiously.

The performance was like all exhibitions of acrobats. But it must be said that the Japanese are the best equilibrists in the world. One of them, armed with a fan and small pieces of paper, performed the gracious scene of the butterflies and the flowers. Another used the scented smoke from his pipe to rapidly write in the air a series of bluish words, forming a compliment to the audience. Another juggled with lighted candles, which went out as they passed before his lips and which he relit from one another without interrupting his marvellous juggling for a single moment. Yet another produced the most implausible combinations by means of spinning tops: under the guidance of his hand, each of these rumbling machines seemed to take on a life of its own, so interminably spinning were they. They ran through pipes, along sabre edges, on to hair-thin iron wires stretched across the stage; they worked their way round the rims of great crystal vases, they climbed bamboo ladders, they spread out into all the corners, whilst producing bizarre harmonic effects by combining their various tones. The jugglers juggled with them as they span in the air. They used wooden rackets to throw them like shuttlecocks, and still they span; they thrust them into their pockets, and when they took them out again, they were still turning—until the uncoiling of a spring made them burst out into set-piece sprays.*

There would be little point in describing here the acrobats' and gymnasts' extraordinary manœuvres. The tricks they did with the ladder, perch, balls, casks, etc., were performed with a remarkable precision. But the main attraction was the display by the 'Long Noses': amazing equilibrists that have never been seen in Europe.

These Long Noses formed a distinct corporation placed under the special protection of the god Tengu. Dressed like heralds from the Middle Ages, their shoulders bore a splendid pair of wings. But their special trademark was the long noses adorning their faces, and above all the use they made of them. The noses were really pieces of bamboo five, six, or even ten feet long, some of them straight, others bent, some smooth, others covered with warts. And they performed their balancing feats while perched on these appendages, solidly fixed. A dozen of the followers of the god Tengu would lie flat on their backs and their comrades would come and frolic on their noses, erect like lightning-conductors—jumping, vaulting from one to the other, carrying out the most incredible performances.*

For the finale, the audience had heard a special announcement of a human pyramid, with about fifty Long Noses representing the 'Juggernaut Car'.* But instead of forming this pyramid by climbing on one another's shoulders, the artistes of the Hon. Batulcar were to be fitted together using nothing but their noses. Now, a member of the bottom row of the Car had left the troupe, and since all that was needed was strength and skill, Passepartout had been chosen to replace him.

Certainly, the worthy fellow felt dejected when—a sad remembrance of his youth—he put on this attire from the Middle Ages, adorned with multicoloured wings, and a six-foot nose had been applied to his face. But this nose was his livelihood, so he had to make the best of it.

Passepartout went on stage and lined up with his colleagues to form the bottom row of the Juggernaut Car. They all lay down on the ground with their noses straight up in the air. A second row of acrobats came and rested on these long appendages, then a third formed a layer above, then a fourth; and using these noses which were only touching at their ends, a human monument soon rose right up to the eaves of the theatre.

The applause was just increasing and the orchestra's instruments bursting like claps of thunder, when the pyramid sud-

denly jerked to and fro, the equilibrium was lost, one of the
noses in the bottom row faltered, and the whole structure
came crashing down like a house of cards.

It was all Passepartout's fault. Abandoning his post, leaping
over the floodlights without even using his wings, clambering
up to the right-hand balcony, he fell at the feet of one of the
spectators, shouting:

'Oh! My master, my master!'

'Can it be you?'

'It is!'

'Well. In that case, to the steamship, my good fellow!'

Fogg, Aouda, and Passepartout rushed through the corri-
dors and into the open air. There they discovered the Hon.
Batulcar raging and demanding damages for the 'breakage'.
Phileas Fogg calmed him down by throwing a handful of notes
at him. And at 6.30, just as it was about to leave, Fogg and
Aouda set foot on the American steamship, followed by a
Passepartout with wings on his back and a six-foot nose he
had still not managed to remove from his face.

24

In Which the Pacific Is Crossed

WHAT had happened off Shanghai is easy to understand. The
Tankadère's signals had been spotted by the Yokohama steamship. Seeing a flag flying at half-mast, the captain had steered
towards the little schooner. A few moments later, Phileas Fogg
paid his passage at the price agreed by putting £550 into
skipper John Bunsby's pocket. Then the honourable gentleman, Mrs Aouda, and Fix had climbed on board the steamer,
which had immediately set sail for Nagasaki and Yokohama.

Arriving that very morning, 14 November, on schedule,
Phileas Fogg left Fix to deal with his affairs, and went on
board the *Carnatic*. There, to Mrs Aouda's great joy—and
perhaps also his, although he showed nothing—he learned
that the Frenchman Passepartout had indeed arrived at
Yokohama the day before.

Fogg was due to leave again for San Francisco that same evening, so set off in search of his servant. He enquired at the French and British Consulates, but to no avail. Having explored the streets of Yokohama, he was just about to give up hope of finding Passepartout again, when chance, or perhaps a sort of premonition, made him go into the Hon. Batulcar's shed. He would never have recognized his servant under the eccentric heraldic get-up; but even from his horizontal position, Passepartout had recognized his master on the balcony. He was unable to prevent a movement of his nose. Hence the disruption of the equilibrium and what ensued.

Passepartout learned this from Mrs Aouda, who also told him they had taken the schooner the *Tankadère* from Hong Kong to Yokohama in the company of a certain Fix.

At this name, Passepartout didn't bat an eyelid. He was thinking that this was not the best moment to tell his master about what had happened between the police inspector and himself. Accordingly, in the story Passepartout told of his adventures, he blamed himself and offered his apologies merely for opium intoxication in a smoking den in Yokohama.*

Mr Fogg listened coldly to this tale without replying; then he opened sufficient credit for his servant to buy some more suitable clothing on board. And an hour had not gone by before the worthy fellow, having cut off his nose and trimmed his wings, no longer showed any sign of having been a follower of the god Tengu.

The steamship from Yokohama to San Francisco belonged to the Pacific Mail Steamship Company, and was called the *General Grant*. It was a huge paddle-steamer with a capacity of 2,500 tons, fully equipped and capable of considerable speed. An enormous rocking lever alternately rose and fell above the deck: at one of its extremities was articulated a piston rod, and at the other a push-rod which connected directly to the wheel shaft, transforming straight-line motion into circular. The *General Grant* was rigged as a three-masted schooner with a large expanse of canvas, which helped the steam tremendously. At a speed of twelve knots the steamer would take at most 21 days to cross the Pacific.* Phileas Fogg therefore had good reason to hope that he could reach San Francisco by 2 December, then New York for the 11th, and London by the 20th—thus beating that fateful deadline of 21 December by a few hours.

There were quite a few passengers on board, Britons, plenty of Americans, a veritable emigration of Chinese labourers, and a certain number of Indian Army officers using their leave to travel round the world.

The voyage was quite uneventful from the nautical point of view. The steamship was braced by its large wheels and steadied by its expanse of sail, and so rolled very little. The Pacific Ocean justified its name. Mr Fogg was as calm and uncommunicative as ever. His young companion felt herself more and more attached to this man by ties other than gratitude. This silent nature, so generous in reality, impressed her more than she realized, and it was almost without knowing that she gave in to feelings which did not, however, seem to influence the enigmatic Fogg at all.

Mrs Aouda took tremendous interest in the gentleman's plans. She worried about the obstacles affecting the success of his journey. Often she chatted with Passepartout, who was able to read between the lines of her heart. This good fellow now had a faith in his master that would move mountains; he never stopped praising the honesty, the generosity, the devotion of Mr Fogg; and he reassured Mrs Aouda about the outcome of the journey, repeating that the most difficult part had been done, that they had got out of those fantastic countries of China and Japan, that they were on their way back to civilization, and that a train from San Francisco to New York and a liner from New York to London would undoubtedly be enough to complete that impossible trip around the world in time.

Nine days after leaving Yokohama, Phileas Fogg had gone round exactly half the terrestrial globe.

On 23 November the *General Grant* crossed the 180th meridian, the one which, in the southern hemisphere, stands at the antipodes of London. Out of the 80 days allotted to him, Mr Fogg, it is true, had used up 52, and now only had 28 left. But if the gentleman was halfway round according to the meridians, he had in reality covered more than two-thirds of the distance. How many forced detours between London and Aden, Aden and Bombay, Calcutta and Singapore, Singapore and Yokohama! If Fogg had followed the 50th parallel round from London, the circular route would only have been about 12,000 miles; whereas he was being forced by the caprices of the various means of transport to cover 26,000, of which he had done about 17,500. But now, on this 23 November, the route lay straight ahead, and Fix was no longer there to place obstacles in the way.

That 23 November, Passepartout experienced a great joy. It will be remembered that the stubborn individual had insisted on keeping his revered family heirloom on London time, considering the times of all the countries visited to be wrong. And today, although he had put it neither forwards nor back, his watch agreed with the chronometers on board.

That Passepartout was over the moon, can easily be understood. He very much wanted to know what Fix would have to say had he been present.

'That rascal who told me lots of nonsense about meridians, the sun, and the moon. Amazing! If we heeded that kind of person, we'd have wonderful clocks! I was sure that one fine day the sun would decide to synchronize with my watch. . . .'

What Passepartout didn't know was that if the face of his watch had been divided into 24 hours like Italian clocks, he would have had no reason to exult. When it was 9 a.m. on board, the hands of his watch would have shown 9 p.m., or 21 hours after midnight—the difference between the two being precisely the same as between London and the 180th meridian.

But if Fix had been able to explain this purely physical effect, Passepartout would undoubtedly have been unable to accept it, even if he had understood. In any case if by some infinitely remote chance the inspector had suddenly shown himself on board at this very moment, it was probable that Passepartout, with good reason irate, would have raised a slightly different subject and treated it in a somewhat different manner.

Now, where was Fix at this precise moment?

Fix was in fact on board the *General Grant*.

On arriving at Yokohama, the policeman had deserted Mr Fogg, whom he planned to meet up with later in the day, and immediately headed for the British Consulate. There he had finally found the warrant which had been following him since Bombay, and which was now 40 days old: the warrant sent to him from Hong Kong on the same *Carnatic* he was meant to have been on. One can imagine the detective's disappointment: the warrant was now useless! Mr Fogg, Esq., had left British soil. An extradition order was now needed to arrest him.

'So be it!' Fix had said to himself after the first moment of anger. 'My warrant is no longer any use here, but it will come back into its own in Britain. This scoundrel looks very much as if he's returning home imagining he's thrown the police off the trail. Well I'll follow him all the way. As for the money, God grant that some is left! What with voyages, bonuses, court cases, fines, an elephant, and expenses of all sorts, my man has already strewn more than £5,000 on the way. But the Bank can afford it.'

Having made up his mind, he had gone straight on board the *General Grant*. He was already there when Mr Fogg and Mrs Aouda arrived. He had been amazed when he recognized Passepartout in his heraldic costume. He immediately hid himself in a cabin to avoid a scene that would have ruined everything. Thanks to the number of passengers, he had been hoping not to be noticed by his enemy—when that very day he came face to face with him on the foredeck.

Passepartout jumped at Fix's throat without further explanation, and, to the considerable pleasure of some Americans who had immediately started laying bets on him, gave the unfortunate inspector a superb thrashing (which demonstrates, incidentally, the great superiority of French over British boxing).

When Passepartout had finished, he found himself calmer and almost relieved of his worries. Fix got up again, in rather poorer condition, looked at his adversary, and asked him coldly:

'Have you finished?'

'For the time being.'

'Then come and have a word . . .'

'You want me to . . .'

'. . . in the interests of your master.'

Vanquished by such composure, Passepartout followed the police inspector, and sat down near the bows of the steamer.

'You've given me a good hiding,' said Fix. 'Well now listen to me. Until recently I was Mr Fogg's adversary, but now I'm on his side.'

'Ah, finally! So you think he's an honest citizen?'

'No,' replied Fix coldly. 'I believe he's a criminal. . . . Hush! Keep still and let me continue. As long as Mr Fogg was on British soil, it was in my interests to hold him back while waiting for the warrant to arrest him. I spared no effort towards that end. I set the Bombay priests on to him, I got you drunk in Hong Kong, I separated you from your master, and I made him miss the Yokohama steamship.'

Passepartout was listening, his fists clenched.

'Now it looks as though Mr Fogg may head back for England. Fine. I'll follow him, but from now on I'm doing my best to remove obstacles from his route as much as I was trying to place them there before. My game has changed, you see, and it has changed because my interests require it. I will add that your interests are the same as mine, for only in Britain will you find out whether you're in the service of a criminal or an honest man!'

Passepartout had listened carefully to Fix, and felt convinced that he was speaking in entire good faith.

'Are we friends?'

'Friends, no,' answered Passepartout. 'Only allies. And only for the present accounting period, since I'll twist your neck at the least evidence of treachery.'

'Agreed,' said the police inspector calmly.

Eleven days later, on 3 December, the *General Grant* entered Golden Gate Bay and drew up in San Francisco.

Mr Fogg had neither gained nor lost a single day.

25

Where Some Slight Impression Is Given of
San Francisco on an Election Day

IT was seven in the morning when Fogg, Aouda, and Passepartout set foot on the North American Continent*—or
rather on a floating quayside. These quays move up and down
with the tide, and so help with the loading and unloading.
Clippers of all sizes tie up alongside, steamers of every nationality, plus multi-storey steamboats serving the Sacramento
and its tributaries. Products are piled up from a trade covering
Mexico, Peru, Chile, Brazil, Europe, Asia, and all the islands
of the Pacific.

To express his joy on finally reaching America,
Passepartout thought it a good idea to disembark by means of
a perfect somersault. But when he landed on the quay, he
almost fell through the worm-eaten planks. Put out by the
way he had set foot on the new continent, the worthy fellow
produced a formidable yell. He frightened away an uncount-
able flock of cormorants and pelicans, the usual occupants of
the mobile quays.

As soon as he had got off, Mr Fogg enquired when the first
train left for New York. It departed at 6 p.m. He therefore had
an entire day to spend in the capital of California.* He hailed
a carriage for Mrs Aouda and himself. Passepartout climbed
on top, and at $3 a ride, the vehicle headed for the Inter-
national Hotel.*

From his elevated position, Passepartout watched the large
American town with curiosity: wide streets, low houses in
neat rows, Protestant and Catholic churches in Anglo-Saxon
Gothic style, immense docks, warehouses like wood or brick
palaces; lots of carriages, omnibuses, and tramway cars in the
streets; and on the crowded pavements Americans and
Europeans, but also Chinese and Indians—in total a population of more than 200,000.

Passepartout was surprised at what he saw. He had still not
got away from the idea of the legendary city of the 'forty-
niners',* the town of bandits, arsonists, and murderers, all

attracted by the discovery of gold nuggets: an immense pigsty where every down-and-out came and gold-dust was won and lost, with a revolver in one hand and a knife in the other. But these so-called good old days had passed. San Francisco now had the appearance of a large commercial town.

The tall tower of the Town Hall, where look-out men kept watch, dominated this collection of streets and avenues cutting each other at right angles, with green squares spreading out and a Chinatown looking as if imported from the Celestial Empire in a box of toys. No sombreros left, no red shirts in the fashion of the gold-diggers, no feathered Indians; but instead silk hats and black suits, worn by large numbers of gentlemen engaged in all-consuming activity. Certain streets had splendid shops, displaying goods from the whole world. Prominent amongst them was Montgomery Street, the local Regent Street, Boulevard des Italiens, or Broadway.

Passepartout felt as if he had never left England, when he reached the International Hotel.

The ground floor of the hotel was occupied by an immense 'bar', a sort of buffet freely open to passers-by. Cured meats, oyster soup, biscuits, and Cheshire cheese were provided there without customers having to open their wallets at all. If they wished by any chance to take liquid refreshment, they paid only for their drink—ale, port, or sherry. All this seemed most American to Passepartout.

Mr Fogg and Mrs Aouda sat down in the comfortable restaurant. They were copiously served on Lilliputian plates* by Blacks of the finest ebony colour.

Afterwards, they headed out of the hotel to have Fogg's passport stamped at the British Consulate. Passepartout was on the pavement outside, and asked Fogg if, before taking the Pacific Railroad, it mightn't be safer to buy a few dozen Enfield rifles and Colt revolvers. Passepartout had heard of the Sioux and Pawnee Indians who stopped trains like Spanish highway robbers.* Mr Fogg said that there was no point in such precautions, but he left him free to act as he wished. Then he headed for the Consulate.

Phileas Fogg had not gone a hundred yards before, by an astonishing coincidence, he bumped into Fix. The inspector was flabbergasted. Amazing: Mr Fogg and he had crossed the Pacific together and they had not met on board! But Fix could only be honoured to meet once more the gentleman to whom he owed so much; and since his work was taking him back to Europe, he would be delighted if he might continue his journey in such delightful company.

Mr Fogg replied that the honour was his, whereupon Fix— who very much wanted to keep him in his sights—asked his permission to join him in visiting this interesting town of San Francisco. Permission was granted.

So Aouda, Fogg, and Fix went strolling through the streets. They soon found themselves in the midst of huge crowds on Montgomery Street. People milled about on the pavements, in the middle of the roadway, on the tram-tracks despite the continual passage of coaches and omnibuses, in the doorways of the shops, at the windows of all the houses, and even on the rooftops. Sandwich-men walked around amongst the crowds. Banners and streamers waved in the wind. Shouts rang out from all directions.

'Hooray for Kamerfield!'

'Hooray for Mandiboy!'

It was a political meeting. This at least was Fix's idea, and he mentioned it to Mr Fogg.

'It might be as well, sir, if we didn't get mixed up in the mob. We would only get attacked.'

'Indeed and fisticuffs, even when political ones, are still fisticuffs!'

Fix thought it politic to smile at the remark. In order to see without getting caught up in the free-for-all, Aouda, Fogg, and he made for the top landing of a staircase leading to a terrace on an upper level of Montgomery Street. In front of them, on the other side of the road, spread a large open-air committee centre. It was between the wharf of a coal mer-chant and a petroleum store, and the various currents of the crowd seemed to be converging on it.

But what was the point of this meeting? For what occasion was it being held? Phileas Fogg had no idea. Was it to appoint a high-ranking military or civil official, a State Governor, a Member of Congress? Such conjectures were justified, given the extraordinary excitement in the town.

At this moment a considerable movement occurred in the crowd. Everybody's hands shot up into the air. Some, firmly clenched, seemed to rise and fall quickly as the shouts rang out—an energetic way, presumably, of expressing a vote. Swirls agitated the mass, flowing back and forth;* banners waved, disappeared for a moment, then reappeared in shreds. The swell swept rhythmically on to the staircase while the white horses of people's heads billowed on the surface, like a sea abruptly moved by a gust of wind. The number of hats was diminishing visibly, and most of them seemed to have lost their normal height.

'It's obviously a political meeting,' said Fix, 'and the subject must be a very important one. I wouldn't be surprised if they weren't still discussing the *Alabama* Claim, although it's been settled.'

'Possibly,' was all that Mr Fogg said.

'In any case, there are two champions in the ring, the Hon. Kamerfield and the Hon. Mandiboy.'

Mrs Aouda, on Phileas Fogg's arm, watched this tumultuous scene with wonder, and Fix was just about to ask a neighbour why this popular effervescence was happening, when a more pronounced movement became apparent. The hoorays got louder, with curses added now. The poles of the banners became offensive weapons. No palms left, but fists everywhere. From the tops of the halted carriages and blocked omnibuses, punches were liberally exchanged, all sorts of objects thrown, boots and shoes sent in very low trajectories through the air, and it even seemed as if a few revolvers were adding their national shots to the crowd's bellowing.

The mob reached the staircase and flowed on to the lowest steps. One of the factions was clearly being repulsed, but without mere spectators being able to tell if it was Mandiboy or Kamerfield who was winning.

'It might be rather a good idea to withdraw,' said Fix, afraid his man might be attacked or suffer some untoward incident. 'If all this has anything to do with Britain and we are recognized, we might be at risk in a free-for-all!'

'A British subject . . .'

But Fogg couldn't finish. Behind him, from the terrace at the top of the staircase, came frightening roars of 'Hip, hip, hooray! Mandiboy!' It was a company of electors riding to the rescue, outflanking Kamerfield's supporters.

Fogg, Aouda, and Fix were caught between the two lines of fire. It was too late to run. Armed with studded sticks and clubs, this torrent of men proved irresistible. Fogg and Fix protected the young woman, and were horribly shoved and pushed. Mr Fogg, no less phlegmatic than usual, tried to defend himself with those natural weapons that nature has put at the end of the arms of every Briton, but in vain. A great strapping man with broad shoulders, a red goatee, and a ruddy complexion—apparently the leader of the mob—raised his formidable fist against Mr Fogg. He would have done considerable damage if Fix had not devoted himself and taken the blow in his place. A huge bump immediately developed under the detective's silk hat, now converted into a flat cap.

'Yankee!' said Mr Fogg, giving his adversary a look of deep contempt.

'Limey!'

'We should meet to settle this question!'

'Whenever you want. Your name?'

'Phileas Fogg. And yours?'

'Colonel Stamp W. Proctor.'*

After this exchange, the tide passed. Fix was knocked down, but got up again without serious injury. His travelling coat had split into two unequal parts, and his trousers resembled those pantaloons that certain Indians—devotees of fashion—put on only after removing the seat. But Mrs Aouda had been spared, and only Fix had suffered from the punch he had received.

'Thank you,' said Mr Fogg, as soon as they were out of the crowd.

'Don't mention it. Just follow me.'

'Where?'

'To a tailor's.'

The visit did indeed seem opportune. Fogg and Fix's clothes were in rags, as if these two gentlemen themselves had been fighting for Messrs Kamerfield and Mandiboy.

An hour later, they were properly dressed and kempt once more. They returned to the International Hotel.

Passepartout was waiting for his master. He was armed with half a dozen six-shot central-percussion revolvers with built-in daggers. When he noticed Fix with Mr Fogg, his brow darkened; but Mrs Aouda recounted in a few words what had happened, and Passepartout calmed down. Fix was clearly no longer an enemy, but an ally. He was keeping his word.

Once dinner was finished, a coach was ordered to take the travellers and luggage to the station. As he was getting into the carriage, Mr Fogg asked Fix:

'You haven't seen Colonel Proctor again, have you?'

'No.'

'I'll have to come back to America to find him again,' said Phileas Fogg coldly. 'It would not be seemly for a British gentleman to permit himself to be treated in such a manner.'

The inspector smiled and did not reply. But as can be seen, Mr Fogg was of that race of Britons who fight duels abroad when their honour is at stake, although banning them at home.

At 5.45 the wayfarers reached the station and found the train ready to leave.

Just before getting on, Mr Fogg went up to a porter.

'My friend, was there not a little trouble today in San Francisco?'

'A meeting, sir.'

'Nevertheless, I thought I noticed a certain animation in the streets.'

'Just an election meeting.'

'For a field marshal?'

'No sir, a JP.'

Phileas Fogg got in, and the train left at full steam.

26

In Which We Catch a Pacific Railroad Express

'OCEAN to ocean,' say the Americans—and this should logically be the name of the grand trunk line that crosses America at its widest point. But in reality, the Pacific Railroad is divided into two distinct parts: the Central Pacific from San Francisco to Ogden, and the Union Pacific from Ogden to Omaha. At Omaha five different lines fan out, connecting with New York by frequent trains.

New York and San Francisco are thus now joined by an uninterrupted metal line measuring no less than 3,786 miles. Between Omaha and the Pacific, the railway crosses a land still frequented by Indians and wild animals: a vast stretch of territory that the Mormons began to colonize in about 1845, after being expelled from Illinois.

Formerly, it took at the very least six months to get from New York to San Francisco. It now takes seven days.

It was in 1862 that the railroad route was planned to run between the 41st and 42nd parallels, despite the opposition from the representatives of the South, who wanted a less northerly line. President Lincoln, of regretted memory, himself established the railhead of the new network as the town of Omaha, Nebraska. Work was immediately started, and continued with that American hustle which is against both paperwork and red tape. The speed of response did not mean that the railway was poorly constructed. On the prairie, the progress was a mile and a half a day. A locomotive, running on the rails of the day before, brought the rails for the following day, and moved forward on them as they were laid down.*

The Pacific Railroad sends branch lines off into the States of Iowa, Kansas, Colorado, and Oregon. On leaving Omaha, it runs beside the left bank of the Platte as far as the mouth of the North Platte, then follows the South Platte, crosses the Laramie Mountains and the Wasatch Range, works its way round the Great Salt Lake, arrives at the Mormons' capital of Salt Lake City, heads off into the valley of the Tooele, skirts the Great Salt Lake Desert, Mounts Cedar and Humboldt, the Humboldt River, the Sierra Nevada, and then descends again by way of Sacramento to the Pacific—without ever encountering a gradient of more than 1 in 50, even while crossing the Rocky Mountains.

Such was this long artery that trains take seven days to cover, and which was going to allow the esteemed Phileas

Fogg—or so he hoped—to catch the Liverpool steamship from New York on the 11th.

The carriage occupied by Phileas Fogg was a sort of long omnibus resting on two undercarriages, each with four wheels, whose movements allow sharp curves to be negotiated. There are no compartments inside: just a row of seats on each side, perpendicular to the passageway, which leads to the toilets and other rooms within each carriage. Throughout the whole length of this train, gangways connected the carriages, and the passengers could thus move from one end to the other, gaining access on the way to saloon carriages, observation carriages, restaurant carriages, and bar carriages.* The only thing missing was theatre carriages. But one day they will have them.

People constantly moved up and down the gangways, selling books, newspapers, and other goods, hawking alcoholic drinks, things to eat, and cigars, and there was no lack of customers.

The travellers had left Oakland Station at 6 p.m. It was already dark: a cold night, murky with a lowering sky and clouds threatening snow. The train was not going very fast. Including stops, it was not doing more than twenty miles an hour—this would, however, allow it to cross the United States on schedule.

There was little conversation in the carriage. In any case, it would soon be time for the travellers to sleep. Passepartout had been found a place beside the police inspector, but didn't speak to him. Since the recent events, their relationship had got significantly colder. All sympathy and intimacy had disappeared. Fix had not changed his manner, but Passepartout now maintained an extreme reserve, ready to strangle his former friend on the least suspicion.

An hour after the train had left, some snow began to fall: a fine snow, which would fortunately not check the train's progress. Soon all that could be seen through the windows was a measureless white covering, with the steam of the locomotive appearing ashen as its spirals unwound.

At eight, a steward came in and announced the time to retire. This carriage was a sleeping-car, and was transformed into a dormitory in a matter of minutes. The backs of the seats were lowered, carefully wrapped couchettes were let down using an ingenious system, compartments were improvised in a few moments, and each traveller soon had a comfortable bed at his or her disposal, with thick curtains to prevent indiscreet glances. The sheets were white, the pillows soft. The only thing left to do was to go to bed and sleep—which everyone did, as if they had been in the comfortable cabin of a liner. The train meanwhile headed at full steam across the State of California.

In the portion of territory between San Francisco and Sacramento, the ground is more or less level. This part of the line, called the Central Pacific Road, started at first from Sacramento, then was extended eastwards to meet the line coming from Omaha. From San Francisco to Sacramento, the railway headed directly north-east, running alongside the American River which comes out in San Pablo Bay. The 120 miles between these two major cities were covered in six hours, and the travellers passed through Sacramento at about midnight, while still in their first sleep. They saw nothing of this important town, the seat of government of the State of California: not its fine quays, its wide streets, its splendid hotels, its squares, nor its Protestant churches.

Next, the train passed through the stations of Junction,* Rochin, Auburn, and Colfax, and headed up into the Sierra Nevada. At seven in the morning Cisco Station was reached. An hour later the dormitory had returned to being an ordinary carriage, and the travellers could watch the delightful scenery of this mountainous country. The track followed the caprices of the Sierra, now hanging on to the flanks of the mountain, now suspended above precipices, but avoiding sharp angles by means of audacious curves, suddenly throwing itself into narrow gorges that looked as though they had to be cul-de-sacs. The locomotive was as sparkling clean as a reliquary, with its large headlight giving out yellow rays, its polished silver bell, its cowcatcher projecting like a spur or ram; and it mingled its whistling and roaring with those of the torrents and waterfalls as it sent its smoke spiralling round the inky branches of the firs.

Almost no tunnels, and no bridges on the line. The railroad worked its way round the sides of the mountains, not seeking to cut straight across the shortest distance from one point to another, not violating nature.

At about nine o'clock, the train entered the State of Nevada through Carson Sink, still heading north-east. At twelve it left Reno, where the companions had taken twenty minutes for lunch.

At this point, the railway line, running alongside the Humboldt River, heads north for a few miles. Then it curves east, still following the watercourse up as far as the Humboldt Ranges, where the stream has its source, almost at the eastern confines of Nevada.

After lunch, Mr Fogg, Mrs Aouda, Fix, and Passepartout settled back down in their carriage. Comfortably seated, the four travellers watched the varied scenery passing before their eyes—vast prairies, mountains standing up on the horizon, creeks with foaming waters. Sometimes a large herd of bison would mass in the distance, resembling a moving dike. In fact these countless armies of ruminants often present an insurmountable barrier to the passage of trains. Thousands of these animals have been seen streaming over the railway track for hours at a time, serried rank upon serried rank—with the locomotive forced to stop and wait for the line to be clear again.

This was what happened on this occasion. At about three in the afternoon, a herd of 10,000–12,000 head blocked the railroad. The locomotive slowed down, then tried to push its ram into the side of the immense procession, but had to stop again in the face of the impenetrable mass.

These ruminants—'buffaloes', as the Americans incorrectly call them—could be seen plodding calmly by, producing a formidable bellowing from time to time. They were bigger than European bulls, with short legs and tails, withers forming a bulging muscular hump, the bases of their horns set wide apart, and heads, necks, and shoulders covered with a mane of long hair. The idea of stopping this migration could not even be contemplated. Once bison have chosen a particular direction, nothing can stop or slow down their movement. They form a torrent of living flesh no dam could ever hold back.

The travellers, spread out along the platforms, watched this curious sight. But the one who should have been in the greatest hurry of them all, Mr Phileas Fogg, remained in his seat and philosophically waited for the buffalo to deign to let him past. Passepartout was furious at the delay the mass of animals was causing. He wanted to discharge his whole arsenal of revolvers into it.

'What a country!' he cried. 'Common or garden cows that stop trains and amble along in an enormous parade no more hurriedly than if they weren't blocking the traffic! *Pardieu!* I would very much like to know if Mr Fogg foresaw *this* setback to his schedule! And what about the engine-driver who hasn't enough pluck to send his machine right into these obstructive cattle?'

The driver had in fact been wise not to try to overcome the obstacle. He would undoubtedly have crushed the first buffalo with the ram of the locomotive, but however powerful it was, the machine would soon have come to a stop. A derailment would have happened, and the train come to grief.

It was best therefore to wait patiently, even if this meant trying to catch up lost time by speeding the train up later. The procession of bison lasted three long hours, and the track only became free again as night was falling. As the last stragglers crossed the rails, the leaders were disappearing below the southern horizon.

At eight o'clock the train crossed over the pass of the Humboldt Ranges, and at 9.30 penetrated the Territory of Utah. This was the region of the Great Salt Lake and the peculiar realm of the Mormons.

27

In Which Passepartout Attends a Lesson on Mormon History at Twenty Miles an Hour

DURING the night of 5 to 6 December, the train headed southeast for about fifty miles, and then north-east towards the Great Salt Lake for the same distance.

At about nine, Passepartout came out to take some morning air on the outside passageway. The weather was cold, and the sky grey, but the snow was no longer falling. The disc of the sun, enlarged by the mist, seemed like an enormous gold coin. Passepartout was in the middle of calculating its value in pounds sterling, when he was distracted from this useful occupation by the appearance of rather a strange personage.

This person had caught the train at Elko Station. He was tall and very dark: a black moustache, black stockings, a black silk hat, a black waistcoat, black trousers, a white tie, and dog-skin gloves. He looked like a minister. He was going from one end of the train to the other, using sealing wafers to stick a handwritten notice on the door of each carriage.

Passepartout went up to the notice and read that, taking advantage of his presence on Train No. 48, the distinguished elder William Hitch, a Mormon missionary, was giving a lecture on Mormonism from 11.00 to 12.00 in Car No. 117— inviting all gentlemen desirous of being instructed in the holy mysteries of the religion of the Latter-day Saints to come and listen.

'I'm definitely going,' Passepartout said. He knew virtually nothing about Mormonism apart from its polygamous practices, the foundation of its society.

The news spread rapidly through the train. Of the approximately hundred passengers, at eleven about thirty filled the seats of Car No. 117, drawn by the lure of the lecture. Passepartout was in the front row of the faithful. His master and Fix had not thought it worth bothering.

At the appointed hour, the elder William Hitch got up and exclaimed in a rather irritated voice, as if he had been contradicted in advance:

'I tell you personally that Joe Smith is a martyr, that his brother Hyrum is a martyr, and that the persecution of our prophets by the Federal Government will also make a martyr out of Brigham Young!* Who dares oppose this notion?'

Nobody ventured to contradict the missionary, whose exaltation contrasted with his naturally calm face. But his anger could undoubtedly be explained by the rude tribulations that Mormonism was experiencing at that time. The Government of the United States had just overcome these independence fanatics, not without considerable difficulty. It had taken control of Utah, submitted it to the laws of the Union, and imprisoned Brigham Young, accused of rebellion and polygamy. Since then his disciples had redoubled their efforts and, while not yet proceeding to actions, they were resisting Congress's demands in words.

It was clear that the elder William Hitch was trying to make converts, even on a railway.

He then recounted the story of Mormonism, starting from biblical times, making his tale more exciting by raising his voice and exaggerating his gestures: 'how, in Israel, a Mormon prophet of the Tribe of Joseph published the Annals of the new Religion, and bequeathed them to his son Moroni; how, many centuries later, a translation of this priceless book written in Egyptian hieroglyphs was made by Joseph Smith, Jr., a farmer by trade in the State of Vermont, and who revealed himself in 1825 as a mystical prophet; how a Heavenly Messenger appeared before him in a shining forest and gave unto him the Annals of the Lord.'

A few listeners, not really interested in the missionary's retrospective narration, left the carriage at this point. But William Hitch carried on, recounting 'how Joseph Smith, Jr., gathering together his father, two brothers, and a few disciples, founded the religion of the Latter-day Saints—a religion which is practised not only in America, but also in Great Britain, Scandinavia, and Germany, and which includes amongst its devotees craftsmen as well as large numbers of people from the liberal professions; how a colony was founded in Ohio; how a church was built at the cost of $200,000, and a town constructed at Kirtland; how Smith became a daring banker and how a mere mummy showman gave him a papyrus containing a Chronicle written in the hand of Abraham and other renowned Egyptians.'*

As this tale was proving a little long, the audience had been thinning out, and was now down to about twenty.

But the elder didn't seem worried by these desertions, and recounted in detail 'how Joe Smith suffered bankruptcy in 1837, how his ruined shareholders covered him with tar and feathers, how he was found again a few years later in Independence, Missouri, more honourable and more honoured than ever, the leader of a flourishing community of no less than 3,000 disciples, and how then, pursued by the hatred of the Gentiles, he had to flee into the Far West.'

Ten listeners remained, amongst them the worthy Passepartout, listening with all his ears. He thus learned 'how, after long persecutions, Smith re-emerged in Illinois, and founded Nauvoo-la-Belle in 1839, on the banks of the Mississippi, with a population of as many as 25,000 souls; how Smith became its Mayor, Chief Justice, and Commander-in-Chief; how in 1843, he stood for the Presidency of the United States; and how finally, lured into an ambush in Carthage, he was thrown into prison and murdered by a band of masked men.'

Passepartout was now absolutely alone in the carriage. The elder, looking him straight in the eyes, hypnotizing him with his words,* reminded him that two years after the murder of Smith, his successor, the inspired prophet Brigham Young, left Nauvoo, and came to settle on the shores of the Salt Lake; and that there, in this wonderful land of Utah, in the midst of this fertile country, on the route of emigrants crossing to California, the new colony expanded tremendously, thanks to the polygamous principles of the Mormons.

'And that is why', added William Hitch, 'that is why Congress was so jealous of us; why the soldiers of the Union marched into the Territory of Utah; and why our leader, the prophet Brigham Young, was cast into prison, totally illegally! Will we cede to force? Never! Driven out of Vermont, of Illinois, of Ohio, of Missouri, of Utah, we will discover yet another independent territory where we can pitch our tents. ... And you, my faithful one,' added the elder, fixing angry looks on his sole listener, 'will you pitch yours in the shade of our banner?'

'No,' bravely answered Passepartout as he fled in turn, leaving the zealot preaching in the wilderness.

During this lecture the train had been speeding along, and at about 12.30 it reached the Salt Lake at its north-western point. From there, one could see a vast perimeter of this interior sea, also called the Dead Sea, which has an American River Jordan flowing into it. It forms a beautiful lake, surrounded by magnificent wild rocks with large bases encrusted with white salt. This superb stretch of water formerly covered a much larger space, but its banks have slowly risen, and have now reduced its area at the same time as increasing its depth.

The Great Salt Lake, about 70 miles long and 35 wide, is 3,800 feet above sea level. It is very different from the Asphaltic Lake,* in a depression of 1,200 feet below sea level. It is highly saline for its waters contain in solution a quarter of their weight in solid matter. It has a specific gravity of 1.170, compared to 1.000 for distilled water. Accordingly fish cannot live in it. Those brought in by the Jordan, the Weber, and the other creeks soon die; but it is not true that the density of the waters reaches such a level that a man cannot dive or swim in it.

Around the lake, the countryside is beautifully cultivated, for the Mormons are good at agriculture: ranchos and corrals for domesticated animals, fields of wheat, sweet corn, sorghum, lush meadows, everywhere hedgerows of wild roses, and clumps of acacias and euphorbia—such would have been the appearance of the countryside six months later. But at that time the ground was invisible under a thin layer of snow, deposited as a light powder.

At two o'clock, the passengers got off at Ogden Station. The train was not due to leave again until six, and so Fogg, Aouda, and their two companions headed for Salt Lake City, via the little branch line from Ogden Station. Two hours were enough to visit this thoroughly American town, built on the pattern of every city in the Union: huge chessboards with long cold lines, infused with 'the lugubrious sadness of the right angle', as Victor Hugo says. The founder of the City of the Saints has been unable to break away from the need for symmetry that characterizes the Anglo-Saxons. In this peculiar country, where the people are not nearly so distinguished as their institutions, everything is done straight down the line: the towns, the houses, and the mistakes.

At three o'clock the travellers were strolling through the city streets, built between the banks of the Jordan and the first waves of the Wasatch Range. They saw almost no churches, but instead monuments like the House of the Prophet, the Court-House, and the Arsenal. They discovered houses in bluish brick with verandas and balconies, surrounded by gardens bordered with acacias and palm and carob trees. A wall built of clay and pebbles, dating from 1853, encircled the town. In Main Street, where the market is held, there stood a few mansions adorned with flags, and amongst them, Salt Lake House.

Mr Fogg and his companions did not find the city very busy. The streets were almost deserted, except for the part near the Temple, which could only be reached after passing through several areas surrounded by high fences. Large numbers of women were visible, due to the remarkable composition of Mormon families. It should not be thought, however, that all Mormons are polygamous. People are free to do as they wish: it is in fact the female citizens of Utah who are particularly keen to get married since, in the Mormon religion, Heaven does not allow unmarried women to accede to its joys. These wretched creatures did not seem well off or happy. A few of them, undoubtedly the richest, wore black silk jackets open at the waist under a highly modest hood or shawl. The others were dressed only in cotton print dresses.

As for Passepartout—a confirmed bachelor—it was not without a certain panic that he contemplated these lady Mormons whose duty it was to band together to make a single man happy. To his good sense it was the husband who was to be especially pitied. It seemed shocking to have to guide so many ladies at once through the vicissitudes of life, to herd them, as it were, towards the Mormon paradise—with the prospect of finding them there for all eternity in the company of the glorious Smith, surely present as the crowning ornament of that place of every delight.* Decidedly, he could not feel any vocation for such a life; and he found—perhaps mistakenly—that the ladies of Salt Lake City were examining his person in a slightly worrying manner.

Fortunately his sojourn in the City of the Saints was not to last long. At a few minutes to four, the travellers were back at the station, and soon sitting down again in their seats.

A whistle blew. But as the driving wheels of the locomotive, skidding on the rails, were beginning to give the train some speed, cries rang out: 'Stop! Please do stop!'

Moving trains do not stop. The gentleman shouting in this way was obviously a late Mormon. He ran as fast as his lungs would go. Fortunately for him, the station had neither gates nor barriers. He rushed on to the track, reached the bottom step of the last carriage, and eventually fell back in a seat, completely out of breath.

Passepartout had followed these acrobatics with some emotion, and went over to examine this latecomer. He took an immense interest when he learned that the citizen of Utah had taken flight because of a domestic dispute.

When the Mormon had caught his breath again, Passepartout ventured to enquire politely how many wives he had, all on his own—judging from the way he had just left that he had to have at least twenty.

'One, sir!' replied the Mormon, raising his arms to the sky. 'One, and it is quite enough!'

28

In Which Passepartout Is Unable To Make Anyone Listen to Reason

ON leaving the Great Salt Lake and Ogden Station, the train headed north for about an hour, as far as the River Weber, about 900 miles from San Francisco. From that point, it headed east across the rugged mass of the Wasatch Range. It is on this part of the route, between these mountains and the Rockies in the strict sense, that the American engineers encountered the greatest difficulties. The subsidy from the Federal Government was accordingly $48,000 per mile for this stretch, compared with only $16,000 on the plains. But as has been said, the engineers did not violate nature, they used cunning to win her over, working their way round obstacles. To reach the main drainage basin, a tunnel 14,000 feet long was bored, but it is the only one on the whole route.*

The highest altitude reached so far was at the Salt Lake itself. From this point on, the line would describe a very gentle curve, heading down towards Bitter Creek Valley, before climbing up again to the point where the waters of the Atlantic and Pacific divided. There were numerous streams in this mountainous region, and culverts were necessary to cross the Muddy, the Green, and many others. Passepartout had become more impatient as he got nearer the journey's end. For his part, Fix would also have liked to be out of this formidable country already. He was worried about delays, frightened of accidents—in more of a hurry to set foot on British soil than Phileas Fogg himself!

At 10 p.m. the train stopped very briefly at Fort Bridger Station, and then, twenty miles further on, reached the State of Wyoming, the former Dakota. It followed the whole of Bitter Creek Valley, which provides some of the water for the hydrographic system of Colorado.

The following day, 7 December, there was a quarter of an hour's stop at Green River Station. During the night the snow had fallen quite heavily, but since it was mostly sleety, it could not disrupt the train's progress. Nevertheless, this bad weather continued to worry Passepartout, for an accumulation of snow might make the carriage wheels get stuck, which would certainly have compromised the journey.

'What an idea of my master's, to travel in winter! Couldn't he have waited for the good weather to improve his chances?'

But while the worthy fellow was so absorbed in the state of the sky and the drop in temperature, Mrs Aouda was suffering more serious fears from a different source. Some of the travellers had got out while the train was halted, and were strolling along the platform of Green River Station. Through the window the young woman recognized Colonel Stamp W. Proctor, that American who had behaved so rudely to Mr Fogg at the meeting in San Francisco. Not wishing to be seen, Mrs Aouda jumped back.

This recognition made quite an impression on the young woman. She had grown attached to the man who gave her evidence every day of the most absolute devotion—however coldly. She probably did not understand the full depths of feeling her saviour awoke in her, and gratitude was still the only name she gave it. But without her knowing, there was more to it than that. So her heart stopped when she recognized that coarse brute from whom Mr Fogg wished to seek, sooner or later, satisfaction. Obviously it was pure coincidence that Colonel Proctor had taken the train, but there he was, for whatever reason, and it was absolutely vital to prevent Phileas Fogg from seeing his adversary.

Once the train had started off again, Mrs Aouda took advantage of a moment when Mr Fogg was dozing to bring Fix and Passepartout up to date.

'That man Proctor on our train?' exclaimed Fix. 'Well rest assured, madam, that before dealing with, er, Mr Fogg he will have to deal with me! I rather think that in that affair I received the worst insults!'

'And', said Passepartout, 'I'll also take care of him, colonel or not.'

'Mr Fix,' said Mrs Aouda, 'Mr Fogg will let nobody take on the task of avenging his honour. He has said he is quite prepared to come back to America to find the source of the offence. So if he notices Colonel Proctor, we shan't be able to prevent an encounter, which might have dreadful consequences. He simply mustn't be allowed to see him.'

'You're right, madam,' answered Fix; 'an encounter might ruin everything. Win or lose, Mr Fogg would waste time, and . . .'

'And', said Passepartout, 'that would please the gentlemen of the Reform Club only too well. We'll be in New York in four days! Well, if my master doesn't leave the carriage for the next four days, we can only hope that he won't bump by chance into this cursed American, the devil take him! Now there is one way of stopping him . . .'

The conversation was interrupted as Mr Fogg had just woken up. He started watching the countryside through the snow-streaked window. But later, without being overheard by his master or Mrs Aouda, Passepartout asked the police inspector:

'Would you really fight for him?'

'I'll do anything to bring him back to Europe alive!' replied Fix, in a tone indicating implacable determination.

Passepartout felt a sort of shiver running through his body, although his belief in his master did not waver.

But was there a way of keeping Mr Fogg in the carriage, and so preventing an encounter with the colonel? This shouldn't be difficult, since the gentleman was not naturally energetic or curious. The police inspector thought he had found a way, for a few moments later he said to Phileas Fogg:

'These are long and tortuous hours, sir, that we're spending in the train.'

'Indeed, but they do pass.'

'I believe you used to play some whist on the steamships?'

'Yes indeed, but here it would be difficult. I have neither cards nor partners.'

'Oh, we'd easily be able to get some cards. They sell everything on American trains. And as for partners, if by any chance madam . . .'

'Certainly, sir,' Mrs Aouda eagerly answered, 'I can play whist. It's part of a British education.'

'And I too', said Fix, 'think I can claim to play this game fairly well. Now with three of us and a dummy . . .'

'Perfect,' replied Fogg, delighted to play his favourite game again, even on a train.

Passepartout was sent in search of the steward, and soon came back with two packs, score cards, counters, and a folding baize-covered table: everything needed. The game started. Mrs Aouda was very proficient at whist, and she even received compliments from the stern Phileas Fogg. As for the inspector, he was quite simply first-rate and a worthy match for Mr Fogg.

'Now we've got him,' murmured Passepartout to himself. 'He won't budge!'

At eleven, the train reached the dividing line of the waters of the two oceans. It was at Bridger Pass, at a height of 7,524 feet above sea level, one of the highest points reached by the line in the Rocky Mountains. After another 200 miles, the travellers would find themselves on those long plains stretching all the way down to the Atlantic, which nature has made so suitable for the laying of railway lines.

The first small streams were already beginning to flow down the slopes of the Atlantic watershed, all of them tributaries or sub-tributaries of the North Platte. The whole horizon to the north and east was filled by the huge semi-circular curtain of the northern Rocky Mountains, dominated by Laramie Peak. Between this curve and the railway line stretched vast plains, generously watered. On the right of the railroad rose the first layered slopes of the mountain range which curved round to the south as far as the source of the Arkansas River, one of the largest tributaries of the Missouri.

At half-past twelve, the passengers caught a brief glimpse of Fort Halleck, which commands this region. In a few hours' time, the crossing of the Rocky Mountains would be over. It was possible to hope that this difficult terrain would produce no problems. The snow had stopped falling. The weather was becoming cold and dry. Large birds, frightened by the locomotive, flew off into the distance. No wild animals, no bears or wolves, could be seen on the plain. Nothing but a totally exposed wilderness.

After a comfortable lunch served at the seats themselves, Mr Fogg and his partners had just resumed their interminable card-game, when loud whistle blasts were heard. The train stopped.

Passepartout put his head out of the window, but couldn't see anything that might have caused the halt. There was no station in sight.

For a moment Mrs Aouda and Fix were afraid that Mr Fogg might think of getting out. But the gentleman merely told his domestic:

'Please go and see what it is.'

Passepartout rushed out of the carriage. About forty people had already left their seats, including Colonel Stamp W. Proctor.

The train had pulled up at a stop signal. The engine-driver and guard, who had already got off, were having a lively discussion with a track watchman, sent to meet the train by the stationmaster at Medicine Bow, the next stop. The passengers were taking part, amongst them the aforementioned Colonel Proctor with his loud voice and overbearing gestures.

Passepartout joined the group, and heard the watchman say:

'There's no way you can get across! Medicine Bow Bridge is already shaky and can't take the weight of the train.'

The bridge being discussed was a suspension bridge built over rapids, a mile ahead of where the train had stopped. According to the watchman, several of the cables were broken, the bridge was threatening to collapse, and so it was impossible to reach the other side. The watchman wasn't exaggerating one bit. In any case, with the devil-may-care attitude of the Americans, one can say that when they play safe, one would be crazy not to play safe as well.

Passepartout did not dare go and tell his master. He listened, his teeth clenched and his body as motionless as a statue.

'Good Lord,' exclaimed Colonel Proctor, 'we're not going to stay here, I hope, until we take roots in the snow!'

'Colonel,' answered the guard, 'we telegraphed Omaha Station to get a replacement train, but it probably won't arrive in Medicine Bow for another six hours.'

'Six hours!' exclaimed Passepartout.

'And anyhow,' said the guard, 'it'll take us all that time to reach the station on foot.'

'On foot?' cried the passengers in unison.

'But how far is this station, then?' one of them asked.

'Twelve miles, on the other side of the river.'

'Twelve miles in the snow?' exclaimed Stamp W. Proctor.

The colonel produced a whole string of oaths, swearing indiscriminately at the railway company and the guard; and Passepartout, in his fury, almost joined in. This time the obstacle was a material one, one that all his master's banknotes could not remove.

But all the passengers were in fact annoyed for, not even counting the time wasted, they now had about fifteen miles to walk across a snow-covered plain. So there was a brouhaha, an outcry, a general shouting, which would have certainly caught Fogg's attention had he not been absorbed in his game.

Even so, Passepartout still needed to tell him and he was just heading for the carriage, his head lowered, when the engine-driver—a true Yankee named Forster—roared at the top of his voice:

'Gentlemen, there may be a way to get across after all.'

'Over the bridge?'

'Over the bridge.'

'With our train?'

'With our train.'

Passepartout had stopped and was drinking in the engine-driver's words.

'But the bridge is falling down!' said the guard.

'Never mind about that. My idea is that by sending the train hurling along at full speed we might have some chance of crossing.'

'Heavens!' said Passepartout.

Some of the passengers, however, had immediately been won over by the suggestion.* It particularly pleased Colonel Proctor. This hothead found the idea perfectly feasible. He even pointed out that certain engineers had had the notion of crossing rivers without a bridge at all by using rigid trains hurled at full speed, etc. And in the end, all those discussing the question ended up on the driver's side.

'We have a 50 per cent chance of getting across,' said one man.

'Sixty,' said another.

'Eighty . . . 90 per cent!'

Passepartout was horrified. Although he was ready to try anything to get across Medicine Creek, the idea still seemed to him a little too 'American'.

'In any case, there is a much simpler way that these people haven't even thought of!'

'Sir,' he said to one of the passengers, 'the method proposed seems a little risky to me, but . . .'

'Eighty per cent chance!' replied the passenger, turning his back on him.

'I know,' replied Passepartout, addressing another gentleman, 'but a moment's thought . . .'

'No thinking, there's no point!' retorted the American, shrugging his shoulders. 'The driver says we can get across.'

'Probably,' Passepartout tried again; 'but mightn't it be safer . . .'

'What do you mean, "safer"?' shouted Colonel Proctor, outraged at the word, overheard by chance. 'At full speed, I tell you. Don't you understand? FULL SPEED!'

'I do understand,' said Passepartout, still unable to finish his sentence, 'but it would still be safer or, since the word shocks you, at least more natural . . .'

'Who?—What?—How?—What's the matter with him, with his "natural"?' The exclamations came from all directions.

The poor fellow no longer knew who to turn to.

'You're afraid, aren't you?' said Colonel Proctor.

'Me, afraid?' exclaimed Passepartout. 'Well, all right. I'll show these people that a Frenchman can be just as American as they are!'

'All aboard! All aboard!' shouted the guard.

'Yes, yes, all aboard,' repeated Passepartout. 'And quick about it! But no one can stop me thinking that it would have been more natural for us passengers to have crossed the bridge on foot first, and then the train afterwards!'

But nobody heard this wise thought, and in any case nobody would have thought it made any sense.

Everybody was back on the train. Passepartout sat down without saying anything about what had happened. The players were still absorbed in their whist.

The locomotive whistled vigorously. The driver, putting the train into reverse, brought it back for about a mile, retreating like an athlete who wishes to gain speed.

Then, on a second whistle blast, it moved forward again; it accelerated; and soon the speed became terrifying. All that could be heard was a continuous whinnying from the locomotive; the pistons were pumping twenty times a second; the axles of the undercarriages smoked in their grease-boxes. It could be felt that the whole train, moving at 100 miles an hour, no longer weighed on the rails, so to speak. Gravity was absorbed by the speed!

And they made it across! It happened just like greased lightning. Nothing could be seen of the bridge. The train leaped—the only term—from one bank to another, and the driver only managed to stop his runaway engine five miles past the station.

But hardly had the train crossed the river than the bridge, now completely demolished, crashed noisily down into Medicine Bow Rapids.

29

Where a Tale Is Told of Diverse Incidents That Could Happen Only on the Railroads of the Union

THAT same evening, the train continued on its way without meeting any further obstacles, went past Fort Sanders, crossed Cheyenne Pass, and arrived at Evans Pass. At this spot the railroad reached the highest point on its route: 8,091 feet above sea level.* It was now downhill all the way to the Atlantic, over those endless plains levelled by nature.

Leading off the grand trunk was a branch line to Denver, the chief town of Colorado. This territory is rich in gold and silver mines, and more than 50,000 people have already moved there.

Thirteen hundred and eighty-two miles had been covered since San Francisco, taking 72 hours. Four more nights and days would in all probability be enough to reach New York. Phileas Fogg was still within the statutory time.

During the night Camp Walbah passed by on the left. Lodgepole Creek flowed parallel to the track, following the straight-line frontier between the States of Wyoming and Colorado. At eleven o'clock, the train entered Nebraska, passed near Sedgwick, and arrived at Julesberg, on the South Platte river.*

It was at this point that on 23 October 1867 the Union Pacific Railroad was inaugurated, the chief engineer being General J. M. Dodge.* Two powerful locomotives had stopped there, after hauling the nine carriage-loads of guests, amongst them the railroad vice-president Mr Thomas C. Durant.* There, cheers rang out; there, Sioux and Pawnees provided the spectacle of a little Indian War; there, fireworks were set off; and there, the first number of the *Railway Pioneer** was published on a portable printing press. The inauguration of the great railway was thus celebrated, and an instrument of progress and civilization thrown across the desert, designed to link towns and cities that had not yet come into existence. The whistle of the locomotive, more powerful than Amphion's Lyre,* would soon make them sprout from the American soil.

At 8 a.m. Fort McPherson was left behind. Omaha was 357 miles away. The iron road followed the capricious sinuosities of the left bank of the South Platte. At nine the train arrived at the important town of North Platte, built between the two arms of the great watercourse, which closed again around it to form a single artery. The Platte is a major river whose waters join the Missouri a little above Omaha.

The 101st meridian had been reached.

Mr Fogg and his partners had started their game again. Not one of them complained about the length of the journey—not even the dummy. Fix had begun by winning a few guineas, which he was now losing again, but he did not show any less passion than Mr Fogg. That morning, luck singularly favoured the gentleman. Trumps and honours rained down from his hands. At one point, having thought out a bold plan, he was just about to play a spade when a voice was heard behind his seat.

'Personally, I would play a diamond.'

Mr Fogg, Mrs Aouda, and Fix looked up. Colonel Proctor was standing beside them.

Stamp W. Proctor and Phileas Fogg recognized each other instantly.

'Ah, so it's you, the Limey,' exclaimed the colonel. 'You were going to play a spade!'

'And I am playing it,' Phileas Fogg replied coldly, putting down a ten.

'Well, I'd have been happier with a diamond,' said Colonel Proctor in an irritated tone of voice.

And he moved to pick up the card, adding:

'You know nothing about this game.'

'Perhaps I'll prove more skilful at another,' said Fogg getting up.

'It's up to you if you want to try, son of John Bull!' answered the uncouth individual.

Mrs Aouda had gone quite pale: all the blood had rushed to her heart. She seized Phileas Fogg's arm, but he pushed her away gently. Passepartout stood ready to throw himself at the American, who was staring at his adversary with the most insulting expression. But Fix had also risen, gone up to Colonel Proctor, and said:

'You forget that I am the one you must deal with, sir. You have not only insulted, but struck me!'

'Mr Fix,' said Mr Fogg. 'Forgive me, but this is my affair. When he claimed that I was wrong to play a spade, the colonel insulted me again; and he will have to give me satisfaction.'

'When you like, where you like,' replied the American, 'using whatever weapon you like.'

Mrs Aouda tried in vain to hold Mr Fogg back. The inspector attempted to take over the quarrel, but again without success. Passepartout would have thrown the colonel out of the door, but stopped at a sign from his master. Phileas Fogg left the carriage, and the American followed him out on to the platform.

'Sirrah,' said Mr Fogg to his adversary, 'I am in a hurry to return to Europe, and any delay would be most prejudicial to my interests.'

'What's that got to do with me?'

'Sir,' answered Mr Fogg very politely, 'after our encounter in San Francisco, I planned to come back to America to meet you, as soon as I had finished my business in the Old World.'

'Really?'

'Will you agree to meet me in six months' time?'

'Why not six years?'

'I say six months, and I will be there without fail.'

'You're just trying to put me off!' cried Stamp W. Proctor. 'Straightaway or not at all.'

'As you wish. Are you going to New York?'

'No.'

'Chicago?'

'No.'

'Omaha?'

'Never you mind. Do you know Plum Creek?'

'No,' replied Mr Fogg.

'The next stop. The train will be there in an hour. It will stop for ten minutes. Quite a few revolver shots can be exchanged in ten minutes.'

'As you wish. I'll stop at Plum Creek.'

'And I believe you'll stay there!' said the American with unbelievable insolence.

'Who knows, sir?' answered Mr Fogg, returning to his carriage, as cold as usual.

The gentleman began by reassuring Mrs Aouda, telling her that show-offs were never to be feared. Then he asked Fix to act as his second in the encounter about to take place. Fix couldn't refuse, and Phileas Fogg continued his interrupted game, playing spades with total calm.

At eleven, the locomotive whistle announced that they were getting near Plum Creek Station. Mr Fogg got up and, with Fix following, moved out on to the platform. Passepartout went with them carrying a pair of revolvers. Mrs Aouda remained in the carriage, as pale as a corpse.

The door of the other carriage opened, and Colonel Proctor appeared on the platform, followed by his second, a Yankee of the same mould. But just as the two foes were going to step on to the track, the guard ran up and shouted:

'No getting down, sirs.'

'Why not?' asked the colonel.

'We're twenty minutes late, and the train's not waiting.'

'But I have to fight this gentleman.'

'I'm sorry, sir. We're leaving immediately. There's the bell!'

The bell was indeed ringing, and the train moved off again.

'My apologies, gentlemen,' said the guard. 'In any other circumstances, I'd have been glad to oblige you. But since you didn't have time to fight here, what's stopping you fighting on board the train?'

'Perhaps sir might not like that!' sneered Colonel Proctor.

'I like it perfectly,' replied Phileas Fogg.

'You can see that we're really in America', thought Passepartout, 'and that the guard is a perfect gentleman!'

And he followed his master.

Preceded by the guard, the two duellists and their seconds headed for the rear of the train, passing through all the carriages. The last one was occupied by only about a dozen travellers. The guard asked if they would be so kind as to vacate the room for a few minutes for two persons who had a question of honour to settle.

Yes indeed—they were only too happy to be able to oblige the two gentlemen; and retired to the platforms.

This carriage, about fifty feet long, was perfect. The two adversaries would be able to advance on each other between the rows of seats and blunderbuss each other to their hearts' content. Never was a duel easier to arrange. Mr Fogg and Colonel Proctor, each equipped with two six-shooters, entered the carriage. Their seconds, remaining outside, shut them in. On the first whistle blast from the locomotive, they were to open fire. . . . Then, after exactly two minutes, what remained of the gentlemen would be removed from the carriage.

Nothing could have been simpler. It was so simple, in fact, that Fix and Passepartout felt their hearts beating as if they would break.

They were waiting for the whistle—when suddenly savage shouts rang out. Shots could also be heard, but not from the carriage reserved for the duellists. On the contrary, they came from the front and whole length of the train. Cries of terror were heard from the middle carriages.

Colonel Proctor and Mr Fogg, revolver in hand, immediately came out of the carriage and rushed towards the front, where shots and cries were now coming even louder.

They had realized that the train was being attacked by a band of Sioux.

This was not the first time these brave Indians had tried—and more than once already they had held up trains. As was their wont, about a hundred leaped on to the footboards without waiting for the train to stop, and climbed up the outside of the carriages like clowns on galloping horses.

The Sioux were armed with rifles. Hence the shots, to which the passengers, almost all armed, were replying with revolver shots. The Indians had started by rushing the locomotive. The driver and the fireman had been half-killed by club blows. A Sioux chief, trying to stop the train but not knowing how to operate the handle of the governor, had completely opened the steam up instead; and the locomotive had bolted and was travelling on at a frightening speed.

At the same time the Sioux had invaded the carriages—they were running like enraged monkeys over the roofs of the coaches, knocking in the doors, and fighting hand-to-hand with the passengers. The luggage van had been forced and pillaged, and bags and trunks were being thrown out on to the track. The cries and shots did not stop.

But the travellers defended the train courageously. Some of the carriages, barricaded, underwent a siege like veritable moving forts, while carrying on at a speed of 100 miles an hour.

From the beginning of the attack, Mrs Aouda had behaved fearlessly. Revolver in hand, she had defended herself hero-ically, firing through the broken windows whenever some savage came into view. A score of Sioux, fatally wounded, had fallen on to the track, and the carriage wheels crushed like worms those who slid from the platforms on to the rails.

Several travellers, seriously wounded by bullets or clubs, lay stretched out on the seats.

Something had to be done. This battle had been going on for ten minutes already, and could only finish to the Sioux's advantage if the train didn't stop. Fort Kearney Station was only two miles away. This was an American military out-post—but, once past it, the Sioux would be masters of the train until the following station.

The guard was fighting at Mr Fogg's side when a bullet knocked him flat. As he fell, he shouted:

'We're lost if the train doesn't stop in the next five minutes!'

'It will stop!' said Phileas Fogg, rushing out of the carriage.

'Wait, sir,' shouted Passepartout. 'This one's for me!'

Phileas Fogg didn't have time to stop the brave fellow opening a door without being seen by the Indians and sliding underneath the carriage. And while the battle raged, while the bullets criss-crossed over his head, recovering his agility, his clown's suppleness, he worked his way along under the carriages, hanging on to the chains, using the brake-levers and undercarriage rods to help him along, crawling from one carriage to another with wonderful skill; and thus reached the head of the train. He hadn't been seen, there was no way he could have been.

And then, using one hand to hang on between the luggage van and the tender, he unhooked the safety chains with the other; but, because of the traction, he would never have been able to disconnect the coupling pin if a jolt of the locomotive hadn't jerked it free. The carriages, detached, gradually fell behind, as the locomotive fled on at increasing speed.

Carried on by the momentum, the train continued for a few minutes. But the brakes were soon applied from inside the carriages, and the train finally stopped less than a hundred yards from Kearney Station.

The soldiers from the fort had heard the shots, and ran up quickly. The Sioux hadn't waited for them: before the train had finally stopped, the whole band had cleared off.

But when the travellers did a roll-call on the station platform, they realized that several of them were missing—amongst them the brave Frenchman whose devotion had saved their lives.

30

In Which Phileas Fogg Simply Does His Duty

THREE passengers had disappeared, including Passepartout. Had they been killed in the struggle? Were they prisoners of the Sioux? It was too soon to say.

There were quite a number of wounded, but it was quickly realized that none were fatally injured. One of the most seriously hurt was Colonel Proctor, who had fought gallantly, and been knocked down by a bullet in the groin. He was moved to the station with the other travellers whose condition required immediate attention.

Mrs Aouda was safe. Phileas Fogg, who had not spared himself, was totally unharmed. Fix had been hit in the arm, but the wound was not serious. However, Passepartout was missing, causing tears to flow from the young woman's eyes.

All the passengers had left the train. The carriage wheels were stained with blood, and loose shreds of flesh hung off the hubs and spokes. As far as the eye could see, long red trails stretched over the white plain. The last of the Indians were disappearing to the south, in the direction of the Republican River.

Mr Fogg remained motionless, his arms crossed. He had a serious decision to make. Mrs Aouda was beside him, looking at him without a word. . . . He understood this gaze. If his servant was a prisoner, did he not have to risk everything to rescue him from the Indians?

'I will find him, dead or alive.'

'Oh, sir . . .!' exclaimed the young woman, taking hold of her companion's hands which she covered with her tears.

'Alive,' said Mr Fogg, 'if we don't waste any time!'

Through this decision, Phileas Fogg sacrificed himself completely. He had just pronounced his own ruin. A single day's delay would make him miss the steamship in New York. His bet was irrevocably lost. But at the thought, 'My duty!' he hadn't hesitated.

The captain commanding Fort Kearney was present. His soldiers—about a hundred in all—had taken up defensive positions in case the Sioux mounted a direct attack against the station.

'Sir,' Mr Fogg told the captain, 'three passengers have disappeared.'

'Dead?'

'Dead or prisoners. We must find out. Do you intend to pursue the Sioux?'

'That would be a serious matter, sir. Those Indians might flee beyond the Arkansas River! I can't abandon the fort under my command.'

'Sir,' said Phileas Fogg, 'the lives of three men are at stake.'

'Certainly. . . . But can I risk the lives of fifty to save three?'

'I don't know if you can, sir, but you must.'

'Sir,' answered the captain, 'no one here should tell me what my duty is.'

'As you wish,' said Phileas Fogg coldly. 'I'll go alone then!'

'You, sir?' exclaimed Fix, who had arrived. 'Pursue the Indians alone?'

'Do you want me to let the poor man die, who everyone here owes their lives to? I have to go.'

'You will not go alone!' exclaimed the captain, moved in spite of himself. 'You are a brave man. Thirty volunteers!'

The company stepped forward as one. The captain simply had to choose from amongst these intrepid men. Thirty soldiers were designated, and an old sergeant placed himself at their head.

'Thank you, captain!' said Mr Fogg.

'Will you allow me to accompany you?' Fix asked.

'You can do as you wish,' replied Fogg. 'But if you care to do me a favour, you will stay with Mrs Aouda. Should something happened to me . . .'

A sudden pallor covered the inspector's face. Split up from the man he had doggedly followed step by step, and let him wander off into the wilderness? Fix carefully examined the gentleman. He couldn't help it, but had to lower his eyes before this calm and frank expression—in spite of his reservations, in spite of the battle going on inside him.

'I'll stay.'

A few moments later Mr Fogg shook the young woman's hand. Then he handed the precious travelling bag over to her, and left with the sergeant and the little company.

But before leaving he had said to the soldiers:

'My friends, £1,000 if we save the prisoners!'

It was a few minutes past twelve.

Mrs Aouda retired to a room in the station, and there she waited alone, thinking of Phileas Fogg, his great and simple generosity, his quiet courage. Mr Fogg had sacrificed his fortune, and now he was gambling with his life: without hesitation, through a sense of duty, without empty words. In her eyes Phileas Fogg was a hero.*

Inspector Fix did not share the same view; and could not contain an inner turmoil. He agitatedly walked up and down the platform. For a moment crushed, his true character was coming out again. Now that Fogg had left, he understood his stupidity in letting him go. What, the very man he had followed around the world: he had allowed himself to be separated from him! His real nature had now regained the upper hand. He blamed himself, he criticized himself, he called himself names as if he had been the Commissioner of Metropolitan Police, ticking off a policeman guilty of a simpleton's blunder.

'What a fool I've been!' he thought. 'That man must have told him who I was! Now he's gone, and he won't come back. How will I ever be able to catch him again now? How could I let myself be mesmerized like that? Me, Fix, with the arrest warrant in my pocket! I really am a complete idiot!'

Thus debated the police inspector, while the hours went slowly by. He really didn't know what to do. At times he was tempted to tell Mrs Aouda everything. But he realized how the young woman would respond. So what should he do? He was tempted to head off in pursuit of Fogg over the great white plains. It wouldn't be impossible to find him again. The party's tracks were still printed on the snow. But soon the imprints were erased under a new sheet.*

Then Fix got discouraged. He felt an irresistible longing to give up the whole game. And precisely that chance of leaving and continuing the journey which had produced so many disappointments now presented itself.

At about 2 p.m., as the snow fell in large flakes, long whistles were heard coming from the east. An enormous shadow, preceded by a tawny light, was advancing slowly, magnified considerably by the fog, giving it a fantastic aspect.

But no train was expected from the east. The help asked for by telegraph couldn't have arrived so soon, and the train from Omaha to San Francisco was not due until the following day. But the mystery was soon solved.

This slow-moving locomotive, sending out great blasts, was the one detached from the train, which had continued with such frightening speed, carrying off the unconscious driver and fireman. It had shot along the rails for several miles; then the fuel had run out and the fire had died down. The steam had expired and an hour later the locomotive had gradually slowed down, and finally stopped twenty miles beyond Kearney Station.

Both fireman and driver were still alive, and after being unconscious for quite a while they had come to again.

By this time the machine had stopped. The engine-driver found himself in the middle of the wilderness, with the locomotive no longer drawing any carriages behind it; but he soon understood what must have happened. How the locomotive had got detached from the train he couldn't guess, but it was clear to him that the train left behind was in trouble.

The driver didn't hesitate. To return to the train, that the Indians might still be pillaging, was dangerous; and to continue towards Omaha would have been safer. Never mind! Shovelfuls of coal and wood were thrown into the firebox, the flames roared up again, the pressure rose, and at about two the machine reversed through the fog into Kearney Station, whistling all the while.

The passengers were delighted to see the locomotive taking up its position at the head of the train. They were going to be able to continue their journey so unfortunately interrupted.

When the locomotive arrived, Mrs Aouda came out of the station building and spoke to the guard.

'Are you leaving?'

'Very soon, madam.'

'But the prisoners . . . our unfortunate companions . . .'

'I can't hold up the service,' answered the guard. 'We're three hours late as it is.'

'And when does the next train arrive from San Francisco?'

'Tomorrow evening, madam.'

'Tomorrow evening? But that will be too late! You must wait . . .'

'That's impossible. If you want to come with us, please get in.'

'I can't!'

Fix had overheard the conversation. A few moments earlier, without any means of transport, he had decided to leave Kearney. But now that the train was there, ready to leave, and all he had to do was get into the carriage, an irresistible force tied him to the ground. The station platform burned his feet, but he could not tear himself away. The battle inside him began again. The anger from his lack of success was choking him. He wanted to fight to the end.

But meanwhile the passengers and the wounded—amongst them Colonel Proctor, in serious condition—had got into the train. The overheated boiler was roaring noisily, and steam was escaping through the safety valves. The driver blew the whistle as the train started off. It had soon disappeared, mingling its white steam and smoke with the whirling masses of the snowflakes.

Inspector Fix had not moved.

A few hours went by. The weather was severe, the cold biting. Fix, seated on a bench in the station, did not move. He looked as if he was sleeping. Every few minutes Mrs Aouda kept leaving the room placed at her disposal, in spite of the storm. She would go to the end of the platform, trying to see through the blizzard, wanting to pierce this fog narrowing the horizon around her, listening out to see whether some noise might be heard. But there was nothing. She would go back in chilled to the bone, then come back out again a minute or two later, but each time in vain.

Evening came down. The little detachment had still not come back. Where were they at this precise moment? Had they caught up with the Indians? Had there been a battle, or were the men lost in the fog and wandering around at random? The captain of Fort Kearney was very worried, although he tried not to show it.

Night fell, and less snow came down, but the cold increased. The most intrepid gaze could not have contemplated this immense darkness without fear. Absolute silence reigned over the plain. No birds flew past, and no wild animals prowled nearby to trouble the infinite stillness.

All night, Mrs Aouda wandered on the edge of the prairie, her mind full of sinister foreboding, her heart full of anguish. Her imagination carried her far away, showing her a thousand dangers. What she suffered during those long hours cannot easily be expressed.

Fix remained motionless on the same spot, but without sleeping either. At one point a man had come up and said something, but the detective had shaken his head and dismissed him.

The night went by. At dawn, the half-extinguished disc of the sun rose over a misty horizon. None the less, the distance visible now was perhaps as much as two miles. Phileas Fogg and the detachment had headed south. . . . But the landscape in that direction was absolutely deserted. It was seven in the morning.

The captain, extremely worried, didn't know what to do. Should he send a second detachment to rescue the first? Should he risk more men with so little chance of saving those who had sacrificed themselves in the first place? He did not hesitate for long, however, but called for one of his lieutenants, and was just giving the order to make a reconnaissance in the south—when shots rang out. Was it a signal? The soldiers rushed out of the fort, and saw a little troop returning in good order about half a mile away.

Mr Fogg was marching at the head, and with him Passepartout and the other two passengers snatched from the hands of the Sioux.

There had been a fight ten miles south of Kearney. A few moments before the detachment had arrived, Passepartout and his two companions were already struggling with their captors; the Frenchman had knocked three out with his fists, when his master and the soldiers came rushing to their help.

Both the saviours and the saved were welcomed at Kearney with great shouts of joy. Phileas Fogg distributed the reward that he had promised the soldiers, while Passepartout repeated, not without justification:

'You have to admit I'm costing my boss a pretty packet!'

Fix looked at Mr Fogg without saying a word: it would have been difficult to analyse the feelings fighting inside him at this moment. As for Mrs Aouda, she had taken the gentleman's hand, and was squeezing it between hers, unable to produce a single word!

Passepartout had looked for the train, as soon as he had arrived. He had assumed that it would still be in the station, ready to head off for Omaha at full speed, and he had hoped that the time lost could still be caught up again.

'The train, the train!' he shouted.

'Gone,' said Fix.

'And when does the following train arrive?' asked Fogg.

'Not until this evening.'

'I see,' replied the impassive gentleman.

31

In Which Inspector Fix Takes Phileas Fogg's Interests Very Seriously

PHILEAS FOGG was twenty hours behind schedule. Passepartout, the involuntary cause of the delay, was in a state of despair. He had ruined his master!

At this moment the inspector came up to Mr Fogg, and looking him straight in the eye:

'Seriously, sir, are you in a hurry?'

'Seriously, I am.'

'I repeat, do you really want to be in New York by 9 p.m. on the 11th, when the Liverpool steamship leaves?'

'I really do.'

'And if your journey had not been interrupted by the Indians' attack, you would have been in New York by the morning of the 11th?'

'Yes, twelve hours ahead of the departure.'

'Fine. Well, you are now twenty hours behind. Take twelve from twenty gives eight. You have eight hours to catch up. Would you like to try?'

'On foot?' asked Mr Fogg.

'No by sledge, or rather land-yacht. Someone has suggested this means of transport to me.'

(This was the man who had spoken to the inspector during the night, and whose offer he had refused.)

Phileas Fogg did not at first reply; but when Fix pointed out the man strolling in front of the station, the gentleman went up to him. A moment later Phileas Fogg and this American, who was called Mudge,* went into a cabin below Fort Kearney.

Mr Fogg examined a remarkable vehicle, a sort of frame built on two long beams slightly raised at the bows, like the runners of a sledge, and with room for five or six people. About a third of the way along, at the front, stood a very tall mast, on which was spread a huge spanker sail. This mast, solidly attached with metal rigging, was attached to an iron stay which served to hoist a huge jib. At the stern a kind of scull-rudder allowed the apparatus to be steered.

It was a sort of sled rigged as a sloop. During the winter, when the trains are stopped by the snows, these vehicles travel extremely quickly over the icy plains, linking one station to the next. They carry a prodigious amount of sail—even more than a racing cutter, which risks capsizing—and, with the wind behind, they glide over the surface of the prairies with a speed equal to the express trains, perhaps even greater.

In a few moments, a bargain had been struck between Mr Fogg and the skipper of this land-vessel. The wind was favourable, blowing quite strongly now from the west. The snow had hardened, and Mudge was confident he could get Mr Fogg to Omaha Station within a few hours. Trains are frequent there, with many lines leading to Chicago and New York. It was possible the delay might be caught up. There was no reason, therefore, to hesitate to try this adventure.

Mr Fogg did not want to expose Mrs Aouda to the great discomfort of a trip in the open air, especially in this cold that the speed would make even harder to bear, and so suggested that she remain under Passepartout's protection at Kearney Station. The worthy fellow's duty would be to accompany the young woman to Europe by some better route and in more suitable conditions.

Mrs Aouda refused to be separated from Mr Fogg, which made Passepartout very happy. Nothing in the world could have made him want to leave his master when Fix was accompanying him.

As to what the police inspector was thinking, it would have been difficult to say. Had his conviction been shaken by Fogg's return, or did he think him an extremely clever criminal who, when he had completed his trip round the world, would think he was perfectly safe in Britain? Perhaps Fix's opinion of Phileas Fogg had changed. But he was still as determined as ever to do his duty: he was the most impatient of them all, intending to use all his energy to speed up their return to Britain.

At 8 a.m. the sled was ready to leave. The travellers—one would be tempted to call them the passengers—got on and carefully wrapped themselves up in travelling rugs. The two huge sails were hoisted and, pushed on by the wind, the vehicle moved off over the hardened snow, reaching a speed of 40 knots.

The straight-line distance between Fort Kearney and Omaha is two hundred miles at most, as the bee flies—as the Americans say.* If the wind held, this distance could be covered in five hours. If there were no incidents, the sled would be in Omaha by one o'clock.

What a trip! The travellers huddled together, unable to speak. The cold, increased by the speed, would have taken their words away. The sled glided over the plain as lightly as a vessel on the surface of the waters—but without the swell. When the wind blew stronger and close to the ground, it seemed as if the sled was lifted from the ground by its sails, vast wings of a huge span. Mudge the tillerman kept a straight line, and would use a scull-stroke to correct the yaws that the machine tended to make. Every sail caught the wind. The jib had been perked and was no longer shielded by the spanker. A top-mast was sent up; and a topsail, stretched by the wind, added its driving force to the other sails. It was not possible to estimate with mathematical precision, but the speed of the sled was certainly not less than 40 knots.

'If it all holds together,' said Mudge, 'we'll make it!'

And it was in Mudge's interests to get there on time, since Mr Fogg, faithful to his system, had enticed him with the promise of a good bonus.

The sled cut a straight line over the prairie, as flat as the sea. It was exactly like an immense lake covered with ice. The railroad serving this region headed up from the south-west to the north-west, via Grand Island, Columbus a major town of

Nebraska, Schuyler, Fremont, and then Omaha. Its route closely followed the right bank of the Platte. The sled, however, took a shorter route, following the chord of the arc described by the railway line. Mudge was not afraid of being stopped by the Platte, at the loop it performs before Fremont, as its water was frozen. The route was therefore wholly free of obstacles, and Phileas Fogg had only two things to worry about: damage to the vessel, or a change or drop in the wind.

But the wind did not fall—on the contrary. It blew hard enough to bend the mast, held solidly in place by the iron rigging. These metal ropes vibrated like a stringed instrument, as if a bow had been run across them. The sled flew on in the midst of a plaintive harmony of remarkable intensity.

'These strings are producing the fifth and the octave,' Mr Fogg declared.

And these were the only words he pronounced during the whole crossing. Mrs Aouda, carefully wrapped up in furs and travelling rugs, was protected from the cold's reach as far as was possible.

As for Passepartout, he was sniffing the biting air, his face as red as a sun setting through mists. With his bedrock of unshakeable confidence, he had begun to hope again. Instead of getting to New York in the morning, they would arrive in the evening, but there was still a chance the steamship mightn't have left for Liverpool.

Passepartout had even felt a strong wish to shake his ally Fix's hand. He hadn't forgotten that it was the inspector who had got hold of the land-yacht, the only way for them to reach Omaha before it was too late. But because of some unexplained premonition, he carefully maintained his reserve.

In any case, one thing Passepartout would always remember was the sacrifice that Mr Fogg had unhesitatingly and spontaneously made to rescue him from the Sioux. Mr Fogg had risked his life and fortune. . . . No, his valet would never forget!

While each of the travellers was lost in these diverse thoughts, the sled flew on over the huge carpet of snow. If it went past a few creeks, tributaries or sub-tributaries of the

Little Blue River, no one noticed. The fields and watercourses had disappeared under a uniform whiteness. The plain was absolutely deserted. Lying between the Union Pacific Railroad and the branch line due to connect Kearney and St Joseph, it produced the effect of a large desert island. Not a village, not a station, not even a fort. From time to time, a frowning tree would pass in a flash, a white skeleton twisting in the wind. Sometimes flocks of wild birds would take off as one. Sometimes too, large packs of prairie wolves, lean and hungry, forced on by a fierce desire, would race the sled. On such occasions, Passepartout, his revolver in hand, stood ready to fire at the closest pursuants. If some accident had stopped the sled at this moment, the travellers, attacked by the ruthless carnivores, would have been in terrible danger. But the sled held good, it gradually pulled ahead, and each time the whole howling pack was left behind.*

At midday Mudge recognized from a few signs that he was crossing the frozen Platte. He didn't say anything, but he was now sure they would reach Omaha Station, only twenty miles away.

And indeed it was not yet one o'clock when this resourceful pilot let go of the helm, rushed to the halyards, and pulled them back to careen, while the sled, carried on by its irresistible momentum, glided another half-mile under its bare poles. But finally it stopped, and Mudge pointed towards a cluster of snow-covered roofs.

'We're there.'

There indeed, at that station which, with its frequent trains, is in daily contact with the East of the United States!

Passepartout and Fix had jumped down and were easing the pins and needles out of their legs. They helped Mr Fogg and the young woman get down. Phileas Fogg paid Mudge generously, Passepartout shook his hand like a friend, and they all rushed off towards Omaha Station.

This major city of Nebraska is where the Pacific Railroad in the strict sense stops, having connected the catchment area of the Mississippi to the Pacific. To get from Omaha to Chicago the railway takes the name Chicago–Rock Island Railroad, and heads directly east, serving fifty stations on the way.

A through train was leaving. Phileas Fogg and his companions just had time to throw themselves into a carriage. They had seen nothing of Omaha, but Passepartout told himself that there was no reason for regret, that sightseeing was not the point at all.

Moving extremely quickly, the train entered Iowa via Council Bluffs, Des Moines, and Iowa City. During the night, it crossed the Mississippi at Davenport and headed into Illinois via Rock Island. At 4 p.m. on the following day, the 10th, it arrived in Chicago, already arisen from its ruins* and standing prouder than ever on the splendid banks of Lake Michigan.

Chicago is 900 miles from New York. There was no lack of trains in Chicago. Mr Fogg immediately switched to one. The frisky locomotive of the Pittsburgh–Fort Wayne–Chicago Railroad set off at full steam, as if it realized that the honourable gentleman had no time to waste. Like a flash, it crossed Indiana, Ohio, Pennsylvania, and New Jersey, passing through towns with ancient names, some with streets and trams but no houses built in them as yet.* Finally the Hudson appeared; and at 11.15 p.m. on 11 December, the train pulled up in the station on the right bank of the river, in front of the pier for the Cunard Line steamers—otherwise known as the British and North American Royal Mail Steam Packet Company.

The *China*, bound for Liverpool, had left 45 minutes before!

32

In Which Phileas Fogg Engages in a Direct Fight Against Ill-Fortune

THE *China* seemed to have carried away Phileas Fogg's last hope with it.

None of the other steamships plying between America and Europe were of any use. Neither the French liners, nor the ships of the White Star Line,* nor the steamers of the Inman

Company, nor those of the Hamburg Line, nor any others, could serve the gentleman's ambition.

Indeed the *Pereire* of the French Transatlantic Company*— whose magnificent ships are as fast as all the other lines, without exception, and invariably more comfortable—was not due to leave for another two days, on 14 December. And in any case it did not go directly to Liverpool or London, but Le Havre, like those of the Hamburg Line; and the additional journey from Le Havre to Southampton would have been too slow for Phileas Fogg, destroying his final efforts.

As for the Inman steamships, one of them, the *City of Paris*, was sailing the following day, but it didn't even bear thinking about. These ships are mainly used for carrying emigrants, and their engines are not very powerful; they travel as much by sail as by steam, having a modest speed. They take longer to go from New York to England than Mr Fogg had left to win his bet.

The gentleman fully realized all this when he consulted his *Bradshaw*, which contained details of cross-ocean navigation for each day.

Passepartout was staggered by the news: to have missed the steamship by 45 minutes crushed him. It was his fault, entirely his, since instead of helping his master, he had done nothing but place obstacles in the way! And as his mind ranged over the various incidents of the journey, while he calculated the sums of money spent exclusively on him but to no avail, as he thought of that enormous bet combined with the expenses of the now useless journey which was completely ruining Mr Fogg, he showered reproaches upon himself.

Mr Fogg, however, did not reproach him and, as they left the transatlantic liner pier, merely said:

'We'll see about it tomorrow. Come along.'

Mr Fogg, Mrs Aouda, Fix, and Passepartout crossed the Hudson on the Jersey City ferry, and got into a hackney cab which took them to the St Nicholas Hotel on Broadway. They were given rooms. The night went by: a short one for Phileas Fogg who slept perfectly, but very long for Mrs Aouda and her companions whose agitation didn't allow them to rest.

The following day was 12 December. From 7 a.m. on the 12th to 8.45 p.m. on the 21st, there still remained 9 days, 13 hours, and 45 minutes. If, therefore, Phileas Fogg had left the day before on the *China*, one of the fastest ships of the Cunard Line, he would have arrived at Liverpool and London within the allotted time.

Mr Fogg left the hotel alone, after asking his servant to wait for him and to request that Mrs Aouda be ready at any time.

He headed for the banks of the Hudson and searched for ships that were leaving amongst those tied up on the quay or anchored in mid-river. Several ships had their departure burgees displayed and were getting ready to set sail on the morning tide, for in this immense and wonderful port of New York, not a day goes by without a hundred ships setting off for every part of the globe. But most of them were sailing ships and couldn't satisfy Phileas Fogg's needs.

The gentleman seemed about to fail in his last attempt, when he noticed moored in front of the Battery, at a cable's distance at most, a screw-driven merchantman with elegant lines. Her funnel, sending out large whorls of smoke, showed that she was preparing to get under way.

Phileas Fogg hailed a small boat, and a few strokes later was climbing up the *Henrietta*'s ladder. She was a steamer with an iron hull, but with upper works made entirely of wood.

The *Henrietta*'s captain was on board. Phileas Fogg went up on deck and asked for him. He appeared at once.

He was about fifty years old, a sort of sea-dog, grouchy and surely an awkward customer. Large eyes, a complexion of oxidized copper, red hair, with a bull neck—nothing of the demeanour of a man of the world.

'The captain?'

'Yes.'

'I am Phileas Fogg of London.'

'And I am Andrew Speedy of Cardiff.'*

'You are leaving . . .'

'In an hour's time.'

'Where are you heading?'

'Bordeaux.'

'And your cargo?'

'Stones in the belly. No freight. I'm travelling ballasted.'

'Do you have any passengers?'

'No passengers. Never any passengers. Merchandise that takes up room and argues.'

'Is your ship a fast one?'

'Eleven to twelve knots. The *Henrietta*, well known.'

'Can you transport me to Liverpool, with three other people?'

'Liverpool! Why not China?'

'I said Liverpool.'

'No.'

'No?'

'No. I am heading for Bordeaux, and Bordeaux is where I'm heading for.'

'At any price?'

'At any price.'

The captain had spoken in a tone that brooked no reply.

'But the owners of the *Henrietta* . . .'

'The owners are me,' answered the Captain. 'The ship is mine.'

'I'll charter it from you.'

'No.'

'I'll buy it.'

'No.'

Phileas Fogg didn't bat an eyelid. The situation looked serious, however. New York wasn't Hong Kong, and the captain of the *Henrietta* was not the skipper of the *Tankadère*. So far, the gentleman's money had always overcome every obstacle. But this time, money wasn't working.

Nevertheless, some way of sailing across the Atlantic had to be found—unless it was to be crossed by balloon—which would have been highly risky and, in any case, impossible.

Phileas Fogg seemed to have an idea.

'Well, could you take me to Bordeaux?'

'Not even if you paid me $200!'

'I'm offering you 2,000.

'Per person?'

'Per person.'

'And there are four of you?'

'Four.'*

Captain Speedy began to scratch his head, as if trying to remove the skin. Eight thousand dollars up for grabs, without even changing route: worth putting aside his pronounced aversion for any variety of passenger. Passengers at $2,000 apiece are no longer passengers, but precious merchandise.

'I'm leaving at nine,' was all he said. 'If you and yours happen to be there . . .'

'We'll be there!' Mr Fogg replied no less simply.

It was half-past eight. Getting off the *Henrietta*, into a cab, heading for the St Nicholas Hotel, bringing back Mrs Aouda, Passepartout, and even the inseparable Fix, to whom he offered a complimentary passage—all this was done by the gentleman with that calm that never abandoned him under any circumstances.

When the *Henrietta* got under way, all four were on board.

On learning what this last voyage was costing, Passepartout produced one of those extended *Oh*s that pass through every note on the descending chromatic scale!

As for Inspector Fix, he told himself that the Bank of England couldn't possibly come out of this affair in one piece. Even if they did arrive, even if Fogg didn't cast further handfuls of money on to the sea, more than £7,000 would be missing from the bag of banknotes!

33

Where Phileas Fogg Shows Himself Equal to the Occasion

AN hour later, the steamer *Henrietta* passed the lightship marking the mouth of the Hudson, worked its way round the headland of Sandy Hook, and put out to sea. During the day, it first hugged the coast of Long Island, seawards of the lighthouse on Fire Island, and then headed rapidly eastwards.*

At midday on the following day, 13 December, a man went up on bridge to take the bearings. It will certainly be assumed that this man was Captain Speedy—but it wasn't. It was Phileas Fogg, Esq.*

As for Captain Speedy, he had quite simply been locked up in his cabin, and was producing a howling indicating a fully understandable anger taken to its highest paroxysm.

What had happened was simple enough. Phileas Fogg wanted to go to Liverpool. The captain didn't want to take him there, so Phileas Fogg had agreed to take passage for Bordeaux. Then, in the 30 hours he had been on board, he had so cleverly manœuvred with his banknotes that the crew of sailors and engineers—a slightly shady crew, on rather bad terms with the captain—were entirely his. And that was how Phileas Fogg commanded in place of Captain Speedy, locked into his cabin, and why the *Henrietta* was at last heading for Liverpool. It was obvious, on seeing Mr Fogg manœuvre, that he had been a sailor before.

How the adventure would finish, only time would tell. Nevertheless, Mrs Aouda was constantly worried, though she said nothing. As for Fix, he had at first been flabbergasted. Passepartout had found it a splendid piece of work.

'Eleven to twelve knots,' Captain Speedy had said, and the *Henrietta* in fact remained on average within this range.

If the sea did not become too rough, if the wind did not switch to the east, if—what a lot of *if*s!—the ship did not have an accident, if the boiler held up, the *Henrietta* could possibly cover the 3,000 miles from New York to Liverpool in the nine days from 12 December to the 21st. It was true that once they arrived, the gentleman could be in a worse mess than he might like, with the *Henrietta* case coming on top of the Bank business.

For the first few days, the navigation continued in excellent conditions. The sea was not too difficult, the wind seemed settled in the north-east, the sails had been hoisted, and under its trysails, the *Henrietta* moved like a real transatlantic liner.

Passepartout was delighted. His master's latest exploit, with consequences he didn't dare consider, fired him with enthusiasm. The crew had never seen a fellow more cheerful or active. He was friendly with the sailors in many different ways and astonished them with his acrobatic turns. He showered them with kind names and attractive drinks. To his mind, the sailors manœuvred like gentlemen, the stokers stoked like heroes. His good mood, highly infectious, was caught by everybody. He had forgotten about the problems and dangers of the past. He thought only of the goal, so near to completion—and sometimes he steamed with impatience, as if he had been heated by the ship's boilers. Often, too, the worthy fellow circled round Fix, looking at him with an expression which spoke a thousand words; but he did not talk to him, for all intimacy had been lost between the two friends.*

In any case, it must be said that Fix no longer understood anything! The *Henrietta* taken by force, the purchase of its crew, Fogg's manœuvring like a born sailor: all this bewildered him, and he no longer knew what to think. But after all a gentleman who had begun by purloining £55,000 could easily end up stealing a ship. And Fix deduced quite logically that the *Henrietta*, navigated by Fogg, was not heading for Liverpool at all, but for some other part of the world. The thief, having turned pirate, would then be in perfect safety! It must be admitted that this hypothesis was extremely plausible, and the detective began seriously to regret embarking on this whole affair.

Captain Speedy had continued to howl in his cabin. Passepartout's duty was to take him his food, but he only did this after taking the greatest precautions, however strong he was. Mr Fogg himself didn't look as if he even thought there was a captain on board.

On the 13th, the tail-end of the Great Banks of Newfoundland was passed. These are dangerous waters. In the winter especially, there are very frequent fogs, and the storms are formidable. The day before the barometer had gone down abruptly, and it was now giving warning of an impending change in the atmosphere. And indeed the temperature changed during the night, the cold became sharper, and at the same time the wind veered to the south-east.

This was a setback. In order not to be pushed off route, Mr Fogg had to furl the sails and increase steam-pressure. All the same, the speed of the ship was reduced, due to the state of the sea and the long waves breaking against the stem. The vessel pitched very badly, further reducing its progress. The wind was slowly becoming a hurricane, and a situation could already be foreseen where the *Henrietta* would not be able to continue head-on to the sea. But, should they have to run before the storm, they would be facing the unknown, with all its risks of danger.

Passepartout's face clouded with the sky, and for two days the worthy fellow was on terrible tenterhooks. But Phileas Fogg was a bold mariner, able to stand up to the sea, and he continued on his way without even cutting back on the steam. When the *Henrietta* wasn't able to rise to the waves, she cut through them, and her deck was swept right across; but she passed through all the same. Sometimes also, when a mountain of water raised the stern out of the waves, the screw emerged, beating the air wildly with its blades, but the ship kept on moving forward.

The wind did not become as forceful as might have been feared. This was not one of those 90 mile-an-hour hurricanes. The wind remained quite strong, but unfortunately it was blowing obstinately from the south-east and did not allow the sails to be unfurled. And yet, as will be seen, it would have been very useful if it had been able to help the steam.

The sixteenth of December was the seventy-fifth day since leaving London. The *Henrietta* wasn't really worryingly late. Approximately half the crossing had been completed, and the most dangerous waters were behind. In the summer, success would have been guaranteed. But in winter, they were at the mercy of the weather. Passepartout did not say what he thought. But in his heart of hearts he was still optimistic, and if the wind failed, he counted on the steam to get them there.

That day, the chief engineer had gone up on deck, approached Mr Fogg, and discussed something with him quite keenly.

Without knowing exactly why—undoubtedly through some sort of foreboding—Passepartout felt vaguely worried. He would have given one of his ears to hear what was being said—with the other ear. He was nevertheless able to catch a few phrases of his master's voice.

'Are you sure of what you're saying?'

'I'm sure, sir. Don't forget that we've been burning all our furnaces ever since we left, and though we had enough coal to get from New York to Bordeaux at low steam, we haven't got enough to get to Liverpool at full steam!'

'I will think it over.'

Passepartout had understood. He was seized by a mortal anxiety: they were going to run out of coal!

'Ah, if my master gets out of that one, he really is extraordinary!'

And having bumped into Fix, he couldn't help bringing him up to date on the situation.

'So', answered the policeman through gritted teeth, 'you really think we're going to Liverpool?'

'Good Lord, yes!'

'You idiot!' And the inspector went off, shrugging his shoulders.

Passepartout thought about retorting sharply to this epithet, whose real meaning he couldn't in any case understand. But he said to himself that poor old Fix must be feeling deeply disappointed and humiliated, after so foolishly following a false trail around the world; and he therefore forgave him.

What was Phileas Fogg going to do? It was difficult to know. However, it seemed that the phlegmatic gentleman did come to a decison, for he sent for the chief engineer that very evening.

'Heap up the fires, and carry on until there's no fuel left.'

A few moments later, the funnel of the *Henrietta* was pushing forth torrents of smoke.

So the ship continued to move forward at full steam. But on the 18th, as announced two days earlier, the chief engineer said that the coal would run out at some point during the day.

'Don't let the fires die down. On the contrary: the valves must be kept filled.'

At about midday, Phileas Fogg took a bearing to calculate the ship's position, then sent for Passepartout, who was to go and fetch Captain Speedy. It was as if the good fellow had been told to unchain a tiger, but he went down into the poop.

'He'll be in a positive rage!'

Indeed a few minutes later a bomb arrived on the poop deck amidst shouts and swear-words. This bomb was Captain Speedy. It was clear that he was soon going to explode.

'Where the hell are we?' were the first words he said, in the midst of suffocations of anger; and had the worthy man been very slightly apoplectic, he might never have survived.

'WHERE ARE WE?' he repeated, his face very red.

'Seven hundred and seventy miles from Liverpool,' replied Mr Fogg with an imperturbable calm.

'Pirate!' exclaimed Andrew Speedy.

'I sent for you, sir . . .'

'Buccaneer!'

'. . . to ask you to sell me your ship . . .'

'No! By all the devils, NO!'

'. . . because I am going to be obliged to burn it.'

'Burn my ship?'

'At least its upper works, since we are running out of fuel.'

'Burn my ship!' bellowed Captain Speedy, not even able to pronounce the syllables any more. 'A ship worth $50,000!'

'Here's 60,000', and Phileas Fogg offered the captain a wad of notes.

This had a tremendous effect on Andrew Speedy. No American can look at $60,000 and remain entirely unmoved. In a moment the captain forgot his anger, the imprisonment, all his grievances against his passenger. His ship was twenty years old. It might be a gold mine . . . Already the bomb was unable to explode. Mr Fogg had ripped away the fuse.

'The iron hull remains mine of course,' he said in a remarkably softened tone of voice.

'The iron hull and the boiler. Agreed?'

'Agreed', as Andrew Speedy grabbed the wad of notes, checked it, and thrust it into his pocket.

During this scene, Passepartout had gone white. Fix had almost had a stroke. Nearly £20,000 spent, and still this Fogg was leaving the vendor the hull and boiler, by far the most expensive parts of the ship. Admittedly the sum stolen from the Bank was £55,000!

Andrew Speedy finished pocketing the money.

'Kind sir,' Mr Fogg said, 'do not be surprised. I stand to lose £20,000 if I'm not back in London by 8.45 p.m. on 21 December. I missed the steamship in New York, and as you refused to take me to Liverpool . . .'

'I did the right thing, by the fifty thousand devils of hell,' interjected Andrew Speedy, 'since I'm making a profit of at least $40,000.'

He had calmed down somewhat.

'Do you know something,' he added, 'Captain . . .'

'Fogg.'

'Well, Captain Fogg, you have Yankee blood in you.'

And having paid what he thought a compliment, he was just heading off, when Phileas Fogg spoke.

'So this ship now belongs to me?'

'Certainly, from the keel to the masthead, at least everything that's made of wood!'

'Good. Have the interior fittings demolished and stoke with the result.'

One can imagine how much dry wood needed to be consumed to keep the steam at pressure. That day the poop, the deckhouse, the cabins, the crew's quarters, and the orlop deck all disappeared.

The following day, 19 December, the spars were burnt, together with the spare masts and yards. The masts were cut down and sectioned using axes. The crew worked incredibly hard. Passepartout chopped, hewed, sawed; he did the work of ten men. He was a frenzy of demolition.

The next day, the 20th, the rails, the bulwarks, the deadworks, and most of the deck were devoured. The *Henrietta* was now razed and was no more than a pontoon.

But that day, the Irish coast and Fastnet Lighthouse had been sighted.

Nevertheless, at 10 p.m. the ship was still off Queenstown. Phileas Fogg had only 24 hours to reach London! But that was the time needed by the *Henrietta* to reach Liverpool—even at full steam. And steam was finally going to run out for the intrepid gentleman!

'Sir,' said Captain Speedy—who was now interested in the schedule—'I feel really sorry for you. Everything against you! And we're still only at Queenstown.'

'Ah,' said Mr Fogg, 'that's Queenstown, is it, those lights we can see?'

'Yes.'

'Can we get into harbour?'

'Not for three hours. Only at full tide.'

'We'll wait,' Fogg calmly answered. He did not let his face show that by a supreme inspiration he was going to try and overcome ill-fortune once more.

Queenstown, on the Irish coast, is the port where the liners coming from the United States drop their mailbags off on their way past. The letters are taken to Dublin by express trains always ready to leave. From Dublin they travel to Liverpool on high-speed steamers—thus beating the fastest ships of the ocean-going companies by twelve hours.*

These twelve hours saved by the post from America, Phileas Fogg wanted to save as well. Instead of reaching Liverpool the following evening, he would arrive at midday, and so could be in London by 8.45 p.m.

At about 1 a.m., the *Henrietta* entered Queenstown on the high tide, and Phileas Fogg, after Captain Speedy had shaken his hand vigorously, left him on the razed carcass of his ship, still worth half what he had sold it for.

The passengers got off immediately. At this moment, Fix felt a terrible desire to arrest Fogg. He didn't, however, for some reason. What battle was raging inside him? Had he changed his mind about Mr Fogg? Had he finally realized that he'd made a mistake? Whatever the answer, Fix did not give up on Mr Fogg. Accompanying the gentleman, Mrs Aouda, and Passepartout, who was no longer taking the time to breathe, he got on a train in Queenstown at 1.30 a.m., arrived in Dublin as day broke, and immediately embarked on one of those steamers—real steel rockets, nothing but machine— which, not bothering to rise for the waves, invariably cut through them.

At twenty to twelve on 21 December, Phileas Fogg landed at Liverpool Docks. He was six hours from London.

At this moment, Fix came up, put a hand on his shoulder, and showed his warrant.

'Is your name Phileas Fogg?'

'It is.'

'In the Queen's name, I arrest you.'

34

*Which Provides Passepartout With the Opportunity
To Make an Atrocious Pun, Possibly Never
Heard Before*

PHILEAS FOGG was in prison. He had been locked up in the Custom House in Liverpool, where he would have to spend the night until his transfer to London.

During the arrest, Passepartout had wanted to throw himself on the detective. Policemen held him back. Mrs Aouda was horrified by the brutality of the proceedings, as she knew nothing, and could not begin to understand the situation. Passepartout explained to her: Mr Fogg, that honest and courageous gentleman to whom she owed her life, was being arrested as a thief. The young woman protested against such an allegation, her heart was filled with indignation. Tears flowed from her eyes when she saw that there was nothing she could do, nothing she could try, to save her saviour.

As for Fix, he had arrested the gentleman because his duty commanded him to do so, guilty or not. The law courts would decide.

But then a thought came to Passepartout, a dreadful thought: he was the real cause of the whole problem! Why had he hidden his adventure from Mr Fogg? When Fix had revealed that he was not only a police inspector, but on an official mission, why had he decided not to tell his master? If he had known, he would undoubtedly have given Fix proof of his innocence—he would have convinced him of his mistake. But in any case, he wouldn't have transported this wretched policeman at his expense and in his luggage, this policeman whose first thought had been to arrest him as soon as he set foot on the soil of the United Kingdom.* Thinking about his blunders, the dangers he had caused, the poor fellow was wrung with terrible remorse. He sobbed piteously. He wanted to crack his head wide open!

In spite of the cold, he and Mrs Aouda had stayed under the portico of the Custom House. Neither of them would leave the place. They hoped to see Mr Fogg one more time.

That gentleman was now well and truly ruined, just when he was about to achieve his goal. This arrest made him lose without fail. Having arrived at Liverpool at 11.40 on 21 December, he'd had until 8.45 to show up at the Reform Club, that is nine and a quarter hours—and he only needed six to reach London.

At this moment, anyone who by chance had gone into the Custom House would have found Mr Fogg motionless, sitting on a wooden bench, not angry, imperturbable. Whether he was resigned was impossible to say, but this last blow hadn't been able to disturb him, at least not visibly.* Had there built up inside him one of those secret rages, terrible because they are kept in, and which explode with an irresistible force at the very last moment? It was impossible to say. But Phileas Fogg sat there, calm, waiting . . . waiting for what? Did he still have any hope left? Did he still believe he might win? Even though the prison gate had clanged shut behind him?

What was certain was that Mr Fogg had carefully placed his watch on a table and was contemplating the hands moving round. Not a word passed his lips, but his eyes were singularly fixed.

In any case the situation was a terrible one, and for anybody who could not read his consciousness, it could be summed up as follows:

If Phileas Fogg was an honest man, he was ruined.

If he was a criminal, he had been caught.

Did he think of escaping? Did he wonder whether he could find a way out? Did he contemplate running away? The idea seemed probable for, at one stage, he walked around the room. But the door was securely locked and the window covered with iron bars. So he came back and sat down again, taking the travel schedule from his pocket-book. He perused the line reading:

'Saturday, 21 December, Liverpool';
and added the words:

'80th day, 11.40 a.m.'

Then he waited.

The Custom House clock struck one. Mr Fogg noted that his watch was two minutes ahead.

Then two o'clock! If he had caught an express at that very moment, he could still have reached London and got to the Reform Club by 8.45 p.m. His brow wrinkled slightly.*

At 2.33 a din came from outside, a loud noise of doors being thrown open. Passepartout's voice was heard, together with Fix's.

Phileas Fogg's eyes brightened for a moment.

The door opened, and he saw Mrs Aouda, Passepartout, and Fix rushing towards him.

Fix was out of breath, his hair all over the place. He couldn't speak.

'Sir ... sir ... beg pardon ... most unfortunate resemblance. ... Thief arrested three days ... you ... free!'*

Phileas Fogg was free! He went up to the detective. He looked him straight in the eyes. Then, making the only rapid movement he had ever made or would ever make in his whole life, he drew his arms back, and with the precision of an automaton, punched the wretched inspector with both fists.

'Well hit!' exclaimed Passepartout. Indulging in an atrocious pun, as only a Frenchman can, he added, '*Pardieu!* That is what you might call a fine English punch and judy!'

Fix, knocked flat out, didn't say a word. He had only got what he deserved. Fogg, Aouda, and Passepartout quickly left the Custom House. They jumped into a cab and arrived at Liverpool Station a few minutes later.

Phileas Fogg asked whether there was an express ready to leave for London.

It was 2.40. The express had left 35 minutes ago.

Phileas Fogg then ordered a special train.

There were several high-speed engines with steam up. But given the traffic arrangements, the special train couldn't leave the station until three o'clock.

At 3 p.m., Phileas Fogg, having mentioned to the driver a certain bonus to be won, was heading for London together with the young woman and his faithful servant.

Liverpool to London had to be covered in five and a half hours: perfectly possible when the line is clear all the way. But there were unavoidable delays—and when the gentleman got to the terminus, 8.50 was striking on all the clocks of London.

Having completed his journey round the world, Phileas Fogg had arrived five minutes late.

He had lost.

35

In Which Passepartout Does Not Need To Be Told Twice by His Master

THE following day, the people living in Savile Row would have been highly surprised to learn that Mr Fogg was back home again. The doors and windows stayed firmly shut. Nothing had changed in the outward appearance of the house.*

After leaving the station, Phileas Fogg had instructed Passepartout to go out and buy some food, and he had returned home.

This gentleman had borne the blow with his usual imperturbability. Ruined! Through the fault of that bumbling police inspector! After confidently travelling that long road, overcoming a thousand obstacles, braving a myriad dangers, still finding the time to do some good on the way—to fail in port itself by an act of brute force that could not have been foreseen and could not be helped: it was appalling! Of the substantial sum he had taken away with him, there remained only a negligible amount. His total fortune consisted of the £20,000 deposited at Baring Brothers, and he owed this £20,000 to his colleagues at the Reform Club. After so many expenses, winning the wager would undoubtedly not have made him a rich man. It was indeed probable that he was not even trying to become wealthy—being one of those men who bet for honour's sake—but the lost wager ruined him completely. In any case, the gentleman had made his mind up. He knew what he had to do now.

Mrs Aouda had been given a room in the house on Savile Row. The young woman was in a state of despair. From the few words that Mr Fogg had said, she deduced that he was planning some fatal project.

It is well known what desperate ends British monomaniacs sometimes resort to under the pressure of a fixed idea. Consequently Passepartout kept a close watch on his master, although without appearing to do so.

But first the good fellow had gone up to his room, and turned off the gas, burning for 80 days. He had found a bill from the Gas Company in the letter-box, and he thought it was high time to stop this expenditure for which he was responsible.

The night went by hour after hour. Mr Fogg had gone to bed, but did he sleep? Mrs Aouda couldn't get a single moment's rest. As for Passepartout, he watched like a dog outside his master's door.

The following day Mr Fogg called for him, and told him, without more ado, to see to Mrs Aouda's breakfast. He himself would have just a cup of tea and a piece of toast. Mrs Aouda would be so kind as to excuse him for breakfast and dinner, for all his time would be devoted to putting his affairs in order. He would not be coming down. Only in the evening would he ask Mrs Aouda to be so good as to speak with him for a moment.*

Having received his instructions for the day, Passepartout had no choice but to conform to them. He gazed at his master, as impassive as ever, and he couldn't make up his mind to leave the room. His heart was heavy, his conscience racked with remorse, for he blamed himself more than ever for the irretrievable disaster. If only he had warned Mr Fogg, if only he had disclosed the detective's plans, Mr Fogg would certainly not have taken Fix with him all the way to Liverpool, and then . . .

Passepartout couldn't stand it any more.

'My master! Mr Fogg!' he cried. 'Curse me. It's all my fault . . .'

'I blame nobody,'* replied Fogg in the calmest possible tone. 'Now go.'

Passepartout left the room and went to see the young woman, whom he told about his master's plans.

'Ma'am, there is nothing I can do on my own, nothing! I have no influence over my master's mind. But you, perhaps . . .'

'What influence could I possibly have? Mr Fogg undergoes none! Has he ever realized that my gratitude was full to overflowing! Has he ever looked into my heart . . . My friend, you mustn't leave him alone, not even for a moment. You tell me that he plans to speak with me tonight?'

'Yes, ma'am. No doubt he plans to safeguard your position in Britain.'

'Let's wait and see then,' she said, remaining very pensive.

So during the whole of that Sunday, the house on Savile Row was as if empty. For the first time* since he had lived there, Phileas Fogg didn't head for his Club when half-past eleven sounded from the tower in Westminster.*

And indeed why should the gentleman have gone to the Reform Club? His colleagues were no longer expecting him there. At 8.45 the evening before, on that fateful day of Saturday, 21 December, Phileas Fogg failed to appear in the drawing room of the Reform Club. So his bet was lost. He didn't even need to go to his bank to draw out the £20,000. His opponents held in their hands a cheque bearing his signature; all that was needed now was to pass a single item through Baring Brothers' books, and the £20,000 would be transferred to their account.

Mr Fogg had no reason to go out, and so did not go out. He stayed in his room, putting his affairs in order. Passepartout didn't stop going up and down the staircase of the house on Savile Row. Time stood still for the poor fellow. He listened out at the door of his master's room, and he didn't think he was being at all indiscreet. He even looked through the key-hole—and imagined that he had the right to do so! He feared a catastrophe at any moment. Sometimes he thought about Fix, but his attitude had changed towards him. He could no longer bear a grudge against the police inspector. Fix had made the same mistake as everybody else, and when he shadowed Phileas Fogg, when he arrested him, he had only been doing his duty, whilst he himself . . . The thought overwhelmed him, and he felt the most wretched of men.

When, at last, Passepartout became too miserable at being alone, he would knock on Mrs Aouda's door, go into her room, and sit in a corner without saying a word. He would just look at the young woman, who was still wrapped in thought.

At about half-past seven, Mrs Aouda was asked if she could receive Mr Fogg, and a few minutes later, the young woman and he were alone in her room.

Phileas Fogg took a chair and sat down near the fire, opposite Mrs Aouda. His face showed no emotion. The Fogg that had come back was exactly the same as the Fogg that had left. The same calm, the same imperturbability.

He remained five minutes without saying a word. Then he looked at Mrs Aouda again.

'Madam, how can you ever forgive me for bringing you to England?'

'Forgive you, Mr Fogg?' replied Mrs Aouda, compressing the throbbing of her heart.

'Please allow me to finish. When the idea came to me of taking you away from that country that had become so dangerous for you, I was a rich man, and planned to place part of my fortune at your disposal. Your life would have been happy and free. But now I am ruined.'

'I know, Mr Fogg,' she answered; 'and I'll ask *you*: can you forgive me for accompanying you and—who knows—possibly contributing to your ruin by slowing you down?'

'Madam, you could not stay in India. Your life was safe only if you went far enough away from those fanatics for them to be unable to kidnap you again.'

'So, Mr Fogg, not content with snatching me from a horrible death, you also thought yourself duty-bound to look after my position abroad?'

'Yes, madam, but events have turned against me. Still, may I request your permission to give you the little I have left?'

'But you yourself, Mr Fogg, what is to become of you?'

'Madam,' the gentleman coldly replied, 'I need nothing.'

'But how, sir, are you going to face the future ahead of you?'

'As it is fitting to do.'*

'In any case, a man like you is beyond the reach of poverty. Your friends . . .'

'I have no friends, madam.'

'Your relatives . . .'

'I have no relatives left.'

'Then I'm truly sorry for you, Mr Fogg, for loneliness is a sad thing. Not a single heart to share your problems with! When there are two of you, they say, even lack of money is bearable!'

'So they say.'

'Mr Fogg,' said Aouda, getting up and stretching out her hand, 'would you have someone who would be both a relative and a friend? Do you want me for your wife?'

Mr Fogg, at this question, had also got up. There was an unusual light in his eyes, and his lips seemed to be almost trembling. Mrs Aouda gazed at him. The sincerity and honesty, the firmness and gentleness in the beautiful eyes of a noble woman who risks all to save the man she owes everything to, astonished him at first, then penetrated his being. He shut his eyes for a moment, as if to stop the gaze going any further in. . . . Then he opened them again.*

'I love you!' was all he said. 'Yes, in truth, by everything that is most sacred in the world, I love you, and I'm entirely yours!'

'Oh . . .' sighed Mrs Aouda, placing a hand on her heart.

Passepartout was rung for. He arrived immediately. Mr Fogg was still holding Mrs Aouda's hand in his. Passepartout understood, and his broad face beamed like the tropical sun at its height.

Mr Fogg asked him if it was not too late to go and give notice to the Revd Samuel Wilson* of the Parish of Marylebone.

Passepartout smiled his best smile.

'Never too late.'

It was only five past eight.

'It'll be for tomorrow, Monday, then?' he said.

'Tomorrow, Monday?' asked Mr Fogg, looking at Mrs Aouda.

'Yes, tomorrow, Monday!' the young woman replied.

And Passepartout left, running all the way.

36

In Which Phileas Fogg Is Again Quoted on the Options Market

THE moment has come to recount the complete change of opinion that had happened in Great Britain when the arrest of the real bank-robber became known: a certain James Strand, in Edinburgh on 17 December.*

Three days before, Phileas Fogg had been a criminal pursued by the police with all their power, and now he was the most honest of gentlemen, mathematically performing his eccentric voyage around the world.

What an impact, what a brouhaha in the newspapers! All the people betting for or against him in the affair, and who had completely forgotten about it, came magically back to life. All the transactions became valid again. All the promissory notes resuscitated; and, it must be added, the bets began again with a new vigour. The name of Phileas Fogg was at a premium on the market once more.

The gentleman's five colleagues at the Reform Club spent the next three days in a state of some anxiety. This Phileas Fogg, put out of their minds, reappeared before their eyes! Where was he at this moment? On 17 December—the day of James Strand's arrest—it was 76 days since Phileas Fogg had left, and there had been absolutely no news of him since then! Was he perhaps dead? Had he given up the struggle, or was he continuing his journey as in the agreed programme? And was he going to appear at the door of the main drawing-room of the Reform Club at 8.45 p.m. on Saturday, 21 December, like the god of punctuality?

It is impossible to describe the anxiety the whole upper strata of British society lived in for three days. Telegrams were sent to America and Asia asking for tidings of Phileas Fogg. And each morning and evening somebody was sent to observe the house on Savile Row. But to no avail. Even the police knew nothing of the doings of their detective Fix, who had so haplessly thrown himself on to a false scent. But this did not stop bets being made again, on a vastly increased scale. Like a racehorse, Phileas Fogg was coming to the last bend. He was no longer quoted at 100, but at 20, at 10, then at 5 to 1. The old paralytic Lord Albermale bet on him at evens.

On the Saturday night, accordingly, there was a huge crowd on Pall Mall and the surrounding streets. It was exactly as if a vast troop of stockbrokers had taken up permanent residence round the approaches to the Reform Club. The traffic was blocked. There were discussions, there were arguments, and the market price of 'Phileas Fogg' was shouted out just like government bonds. The police had great difficulty keeping the crowds back, and as the time approached when Phileas Fogg was due to arrive, the excitement increased tremendously.

That evening, the gentleman's five colleagues had been assembled in the main drawing-room of the Reform Club for nine hours.* The two bankers John Sullivan and Samuel Fallentin, the engineer Andrew Stuart, the member of the Board of the Bank of England Gauthier Ralph, the brewer Thomas Flanagan—all were waiting anxiously.

At the moment the clock in the main room indicated 8.25, Andrew Stuart got up.

'Gentlemen, the deadline agreed between Mr Phileas Fogg and ourselves will expire in twenty minutes.'

'What time did the last train arrive from Liverpool?' asked Thomas Flanagan.

'Seven twenty-three,' replied Gauthier Ralph. 'And the next one only arrives at ten past twelve.'

'Well, gentlemen,' continued Andrew Stuart. 'If Phileas Fogg had come in on the 7.23, he would have been here by now. We can therefore consider the wager won.'

'Let's wait, let's not commit ourselves,' interjected Samuel Fallentin. 'As you know, our colleague is an eccentric of the first order. His precision in everything is well known. He never arrives too soon or too late, and I wouldn't be at all surprised if he turned up at the very last moment.'

'I personally', said Andrew Stuart, highly excited as usual, 'wouldn't believe it even if I saw him.'

'I agree,' concurred Thomas Flanagan. 'Phileas Fogg's project was crazy. However punctual he tried to be, he wouldn't have been able to prevent delays, and a delay of only two or three days was enough to ruin his journey.'

'You will notice too, I may add,' said John Sullivan, 'that we have had no news at all of our colleague, and yet there was no shortage of telegraphic wires along his route.'

'He's lost, gentlemen,' repeated Andrew Stuart, 'he's lost a hundred times over! As you know, the *China* arrived yesterday—the only steamship from New York that he could have caught to Liverpool. Now here is a list of passengers published by the *Shipping Gazette*,* and Phileas Fogg's name is not on it. Even if he had been extremely lucky, our colleague could scarcely have arrived in America yet. I reckon that he will be at least twenty days late, and that old Lord Albermale has lost his £5,000!'

'It's obvious,' answered Gauthier Ralph; 'and all we have to do is present Mr Fogg's cheque at Baring Brothers tomorrow.'

At this moment the drawing-room clock struck 8.40.

'Five more minutes,' said Andrew Stuart.

The five colleagues looked at each other. One may surmise that their hearts were beating slightly faster since the stake was a big one even for such bold gamblers! But they didn't want it to show, and followed Samuel Fallentin's suggestion that they sit down at a card-table.

'I wouldn't sell my £4,000 share in this bet', said Andrew Stuart, sitting down, 'even for £3,999!'

The hands indicated 8.42 at this moment.

The players picked up the cards; but their eyes strayed to the clock every few seconds. One may safely say that however secure they felt, never had minutes seemed so long to them!

'Forty-three,' said Flanagan, cutting the pack that Ralph had placed in front of him.

There came a moment of silence. The huge club room was quiet. But the hubbub of the crowd could be heard outside, dominated sometimes by shrill shouts. The pendulum of the clock beat every second with mathematical regularity. Each of the players counted the sexagesimal units reaching his ear.

'Eight forty-four!' said John Sullivan, in a voice where emotion could be heard, even though he tried to hide it.

Only a minute to go, and the bet was won. Stuart and his colleagues were not playing any more. They had laid their cards down. They were counting the seconds.

At the fortieth second, nothing. At the fiftieth, still nothing.

At the fifty-fifth, a sound like thunder could be heard outside, the sound of clapping, of hoorays, even of swear-words, spreading as a continuous roll.

The players got to their feet.

On the fifty-seventh second, the door of the drawing-room opened. Before the pendulum could beat the sixtieth second, Mr Phileas Fogg appeared, followed by a delirious crowd forcing its way into the Club. A calm voice was heard.

'Here I am, gentlemen.'

37

In Which It Is Proved that Phileas Fogg Has
Gained Nothing From His Journey Around the
World Unless It Be Happiness

YES! Phileas Fogg in person.*

It will be recalled that at 7.55 p.m.—about 25 hours after the travellers had arrived in London—Passepartout had been told to inform Revd Samuel Wilson about a certain wedding to take place the very next day.

Passepartout had left, absolutely over the moon. He headed quickly for Revd Samuel Wilson's house, but the clergyman had not come home yet. Passepartout waited, of course: he waited at least twenty good minutes.

In the end, it was 8.35 before he left the Reverend's house. But in what a state! Hair all over the place, no hat, running, running, as nobody had ever run in human memory, knocking passers-by down, moving like a whirlwind through the streets!

Three minutes later, he was back in Savile Row, staggering, completely out of breath, into Mr Fogg's room.

He couldn't speak.

'But what's the matter?'

'Master's . . .' spluttered Passepartout, '. . . wedding . . . impossible.'

'Impossible?'

'Impossible . . . tomorrow.'

'But why?'

'Tomorrow . . . Sunday!'

'Monday,' said Mr Fogg.

'No. . . . Today . . . Saturday.'

'Saturday? Impossible!'

'Yes, YES, YES!' screamed Passepartout.* 'Your calculations were a day out! We arrived 24 hours early. But there are only ten minutes left!'

Passepartout had taken hold of his master's collar, and was dragging him out with an irresistible force!

Phileas Fogg, thus transported, not having the time to think, left his room, left his house, jumped into a cab, promised the driver £100, and, after running two dogs over and hitting five carriages, reached the Reform Club.

When he appeared in the large drawing-room, the clock was just striking 8.45. . . .

Phileas Fogg had completed his journey around the world in 80 days.

Mr Fogg had won his bet of £20,000.

And now, how had such a precise man, such a meticulous gentleman, not known what day it was? How had he come to think it was the evening of Saturday, 21 December, when he arrived in London, when it was in fact Friday, 20 December, only 79 days after his departure?*

Here is the reason for the mistake. It is quite simple.

Phileas Fogg, 'without beginning to suspect', had gained a day on his programme—simply because he had gone round the world *eastwards*. He would, on the contrary, have lost this day if he had gone in the opposite direction, namely *westwards*.

By heading towards the east, Phileas Fogg had gone towards the sun, and consequently his days were four minutes shorter for each degree of longitude covered in this direction. Now there are 360 degrees on the Earth's circumference, and this 360, multiplied by 4 minutes, makes exactly 24 hours—in other words the day gained unconsciously.* This means that while Phileas Fogg, heading eastwards, saw the sun cross the meridian *80 times*, his colleagues remaining in London saw it cross only *79 times*. And this was why, on that very same day, Saturday, and not Sunday as Mr Fogg believed, they were waiting for him in the drawing-room of the Reform Club.

And this was what Passepartout's famous watch—permanently kept on London time—would have read if, as well as the minutes and hours, it had shown the days!

Phileas Fogg had therefore won his £20,000. But as he had spent about £19,000 *en route*, the proceeds were insignificant. Notwithstanding, and as we have already pointed out, the eccentric gentleman simply sought a challenge through his bet, not to make his fortune. Even the remaining £1,000, he split between the good Passepartout and the hapless Fix, whom he was unable to bear a grudge against. All the same, and to keep matters straight, he charged his servant for the 1,920 hours of gas consumed through his negligence.

That same evening, as imperturbable and as phlegmatic as ever, Mr Fogg asked Mrs Aouda:

'And does this marriage still suit you, madam?'

'Mr Fogg,' she replied, 'it should be me asking you that question. You were ruined, and now you're rich . . .'*

'Pardon me, madam, the fortune is yours. If you hadn't had the idea of getting married, my servant wouldn't have gone to Revd Samuel Wilson's house, I wouldn't have been told about my mistake, and . . .'

'Dear Mr Fogg . . .'

'Dear Aouda.'*

It goes without saying that the wedding took place 48 hours later, and Passepartout, magnificent, shining, dazzling, gave the young bride away. Had he not saved her, and so earned this honour?

But the following day at the crack of dawn Passepartout began to hammer at his master's door.

The door opened, and the impassive gentleman appeared.

'What's the matter, Passepartout?'

'The matter, sir! The matter is that I've just learned a second ago . . .'

'What, then?'

'That we could have done the trip around the world in only 78 days.'

'Undoubtedly,' answered Mr Fogg, 'by not passing through India. But if I hadn't crossed India, I wouldn't have saved Mrs Aouda, she wouldn't have been my wife, and . . .'

And Mr Fogg quietly shut the door.*

So Phileas Fogg had won his bet. He had completed the journey round the world in 80 days. To do so, he had used every means of transport: steamship, train, carriage, yacht, cargo vessel, sled, and elephant. In all this the eccentric gentleman had displayed his marvellous qualities of composure and precision. But what was the point? What had he gained from all this commotion? What had he got out of his journey?

Nothing, comes the reply? Nothing, agreed, were it not for a lovely wife, who—however unlikely it may seem—made him the happiest of men!*

In truth, wouldn't anyone go round the world for less?

THE END

APPENDIX A

PRINCIPAL SOURCES

A LARGE number of sources have been suggested for *Around the World in Eighty Days*. The following are the main possibilities for the idea of the trip around the globe, the time-limit of the 80 days, and the gain of the 24 hours.

The idea of travelling round the known world goes back indefinitely. In *Journey to the Centre of the Earth*, Verne refers to Pausanias, the Greek traveller and topographer (*c.*100 AD), whose best-known work was translated as *Pausanias; ou voyage historique de la Grèce. Nouvelle édition augmentée du 'Voyage autour du monde', par Scylax* (1797). Verne's friend, Jacques Arago, had written a *Voyage autour du monde* (1853), which had been a huge popular success. But, because of developments in transport, the idea was very much in the air in 1869–72. In 1871 alone there appeared an *Around the World by Steam, via Pacific Railway*, by the Union Pacific Railroad Company, and an *Around the World in A Hundred and Twenty Days*, by Edmond Planchut; and an American called W[illiam] P[erry] *Fogg* (b. 1826) went around the globe in 1869–71, describing his tour in a series of letters to the *Cleveland Leader*, published as *Round the World: Letters from Japan, China, India and Egypt* (1872).

A great deal has been made of Thomas Cook's organizing of the first tourist trip around the globe: he published a brochure in June 1872 announcing a round-the-world trip in 102 days; the trip left on 20 September 1872 and returned seven months later. Cook described the journey in letters to the *Daily Mail*, and to *The Times* from 27 November 1872 (dated 31 October, San Francisco) to 27 May 1873. These were reissued in 1873 as *Letters from the Sea and from Foreign Lands, Descriptive of a Tour Round the World*, published by T. Cook & Son. Although neither Cook nor Verne refers to the other, and Cook travelled via Ceylon, a number of common points are visible. In the first letter alone appear references to the rebuilding of Chicago, the Sioux on the move, the highest pass across the Rockies, the repeated adjustment of watches and change of day in the Pacific, the White Star Line across the Atlantic, and the general ease and comfort of a journey round the world.

Despite these similarities, it has been argued that Thomas Cook's trip happened too late to influence Verne. Nevertheless, Verne himself, according to Brisson's 1898 account, refers to a Thomas Cook advertisement ('annonce') as the source of his book, an idea repeated by the biographers Allotte de la Fuÿe and Bernard Frank. In interviews in 1894 and 1904, on the other hand, Verne says the source was, respectively, through reading 'one day in a Paris café' and 'due merely to a tourist advertisement seen by chance in the columns of a newspaper'. *Around the World* itself says that the origin was a newspaper article—and Verne often candidly indicates his sources. All four of these accounts are in fact possibly derived from the same idea of a Thomas Cook 'advertisement', although it is far from clear whether this appeared on a hoarding, in brochure form, or in a newspaper.

But also, the periodical *Le Tour du monde* of 3 October 1869 contained a short piece entitled 'Around the World in Eighty Days' ['Le tour du monde en quatre-vingts jours'], which refers to '140 miles' of railway not yet being completed between 'Alahabad [*sic*]' and Bombay. It cites in its bibliography the *Nouvelles Annales des Voyages, de la Géographie, de l'Histoire et de l'Archéologie* (August 1869), whose Contents page is also reproduced, again including the title 'Around the World in Eighty Days'. The *Nouvelles Annales* are quoted in *Five Weeks in a Balloon*: they were written by Conrad Malte-Brun (1775–1826) and his son Victor-Adolphe (1816–89), whose *Atlas complet du précis de la Géographie universelle* (1810–28, revised regularly until the 1870s) is lyrically referred to in *Backwards to Britain*. Although the 80-day journeys suggested in 1869 start and end in Paris and run westwards, the identity of title with Verne's work, the all-important reference to the incomplete railway, and the fact that Verne is known to have consulted *Le Tour du monde* throughout his career prove the use of either it or the *Nouvelles Annales*. However, the *Nouvelles Annales* were themselves merely repeating facts previously established in *De Hollandsche Illustratie* of 30 July 1869, for this issue tabulates the successive stages of an 82-day journey westwards, starting with 'Amsterdam—Paris . . . 1 day', and also refers to '*180 miles*' of track missing between 'Alahabad' and Bombay. But finally, the 12 November 1869 issue of *Le Tour du monde* refers to the opening of the Suez Canal on 17 November, and further gives an itinerary:

Paris to Port Said, head of the Suez Canal, railway and steamer	6 days
Port Said to Bombay, steamer	14 "
Bombay to Calcutta, railway	3 "

Calcutta to Hong Kong, steamer	12	"
Hong Kong to Edo, steamer	6	"
Edo to Sandwich Islands, steamer	14	"
Sandwich Islands to San Francisco, steamer	7	"
San Francisco to New York, Pacific Railroad now completed	7	"
New York to Paris, steamship service	11	"

Total 80 days

This is similar to Verne's successive versions, which run eastwards and omit Ceylon. The main differences are that it still starts from Paris, refers to Port Said and Edo rather than Suez and Yokohama, passes through the Sandwich Islands (Hawaii), and allocates different time intervals from Verne's versions. Many further periodicals have in fact been discovered referring to trips around the world, whether or not in 80 days. *Le Magasin pittoresque* of April 1870, for instance, plagiarizes the above schedule; and *L'Année scientifique et industrielle, 1869* (1870) also features a trip in 80 days: 'Out of the whole of this immense journey, there are only 140 miles, between Allahabad and Bombay, that one is obliged to cover without using steam; but this lacuna will soon be filled in.'

Another possible source is the appropriately named George Francis Train, who made four trips around the world, the first in two years, and the second in 80 days in 1870. Like Cook, Train went westwards; but similarities with Fogg's adventures include the hire of a private train and his being imprisoned. Train was in France in 1870–1, had previously built railways in America, and ran for the American Presidency in 1872—all ideas that are echoed in *Around the World in Eighty Days*. Train later claimed Verne 'stole my thunder. I'm Phileas Fogg.'

As for the idea of losing or gaining a day, Verne's own account of the origin, as reported by Sherard in 1894, was, 'I have a great number of scientific odds and ends in my head. It was thus that, when, one day in a Paris café, I read in the *Siècle* that a man could travel round the world in eighty days, it immediately struck me that I could profit by a difference of meridian and make my traveller gain or lose a day in his journey. There was my dènouement [*sic*] ready found. The story was not written until long after. I carry ideas about in my head for years—ten or fifteen years, sometimes—before giving them form.' Again, in 1895 Belloc reported Verne's account as 'I have often carried an idea in my brain for years before I had occasion to work it out on paper: ... *Round the World in Eighty Days* was the result of reading a tourist advertisement in a newspaper. The paragraph which caught my attention mentioned the fact that nowadays it would be quite possible for a man to travel round the world in eighty days.' In 1901, Stiegler reported that 'it was an article in the *Siècle*, read by chance fifteen years before, that provided [Verne] with the *idée génératrice*'.

In his lecture in April 1873, 'The Meridians and the Calendar', Verne replies to a question about where the change of day actually happens in the Pacific (the word 'date-line' only became current in 1880 and the Greenwich prime meridian was adopted internationally in 1884). He cites an article in *Nature* in 1872 and Poe's short story 'Three Sundays in a Week' (1841), which is also predicated on the difference of a day due to going round the world, with the gain again closely linked to a marriage at the end. When Verne analyses this story in his major essay 'Edgar Poe and His Works' (1864), he analyses in detail the temporal consequences of going round the world, and confuses east and west in the same way as he does in both MS1 and MS2.

It will therefore be seen that there are many competing candidates for the sources of the novel. None in fact can be excluded, although intermediaries would have been necessary for all those in English. Many of the ideas were common currency at the time; and going round the world in the early 1870s would have been difficult without passing through Suez, Hong Kong, San Francisco, and New York. Even the minimum of 80 days seems to have been a commonplace. One curious detail is that Cook's true account and Verne's fictional account were, for about a month, being serialized simultaneously, respectively in *The Times* and *Le Temps* ('The Times').

To conclude, either the periodical *Le Tour du monde* of 3 October and 12 November 1869 or the *Nouvelles Annales des Voyages, de la Géographie, de l'Histoire et de l'Archéologie*, W. P. Fogg, probably Thomas Cook, and probably a periodical article would seem to constitute the main sources for *Around the World*—the *Extraordinary Journeys* often synthesized ideas from a number of origins. Poe certainly seems to be a basis for the idea of gaining or losing a day. On the other hand, Verne seems to contradict himself in his claim that the central idea for *Around the World* came to him many years before *and* was due to Thomas Cook. We will probably, therefore, never know the complete truth on the question of sources.

APPENDIX B

THE PLAY

THE play entitled *Around the World in 80 Days* was largely based on the novel, and undoubtedly illuminates it.

It was in fact claimed that Verne was not the sole author of the book. Before writing *Around the World*, Verne sent the playwright Édouard Cadol (1831–98) an outline so that he could produce a play from it. (Cadol is credited with Verne and Charles Wallut as co-author of *A Nephew from America*, performed in April 1873.) But Cadol was unable to place the play and, once the novel was finished, Adolphe d'Ennery was enlisted instead: d'Ennery is credited as co-author in the published version of the play, although he may in fact have had the dominant role (and in any case received seven-twelfths of the royalties). But Cadol sent a letter to *Le Figaro* in January 1874 stating that the novel was partly his work; Verne wrote to Hetzel that 'He made absolutely no contribution to the book'; however, Cadol did establish copyright on the play, and as a result received royalties on it thereafter.

The play opened in November 1874 for 415 nights, first at the Porte-Saint-Martin Theatre and then at the Châtelet; and then continued on and off until the Second World War, marking generations of French people.

The play differs from the book in significant respects. It is generally less subtle and polished, and the plot demonstrates considerable differences. It involves two shipwrecks and several new characters, including Nakahira the Queen of the Charmers, a servant called Margaret who marries Passepartout, and Aouda's sister Néméa who marries an American called Archibald Corsican, previously blackballed by the Club. (The same name is used for the captain in *A Floating City*.) The play also contains an impassioned speech by a Pawnee Chief protesting at the rape of the Indian lands by the Palefaces.

In his review of 18 October 1874, the poet Mallarmé wrote of 'this drama . . . this fairy-delight . . . One really must see the Snake Grotto, the explosion and sinking of the steamer, and the ambush of the train by the Pawnee Indians'.

Of the ten million francs that the play made, Verne later complained that he received 'much less than his fair share'—and also claimed to have sold the novel for 'a tenth of its value'.

APPENDIX C

AROUND THE WORLD AS SEEN BY THE CRITICS

1. 'We will only remind readers en passant of *Around the World in Eighty Days*, that *tour de force* of Mr Verne's—and not the first he has produced. Here, however, he has summarized and concentrated himself, so to speak . . . No praise of his collected works is strong enough . . . they are truly useful, entertaining, poignant, and moral; and Europe and America have merely produced rivals that are remarkably similar to them, but in any case inferior.' (Henry Trianon, *Le Constitutionnel*, 20 Dec. 1873)

2. '. . . upon which the young readers can embark for *The Fur Country* and *Around the World*, under the flag of Captain Jules Vernes [*sic*]. The interest and the success of the *Extraordinary Journeys* are well known. Their marvels outdo Sinbad the Sailor's; and they are as valuable as the accurate ideas contained in the naturalists' and geographers' narrations.' (Paul de Saint-Victor, *Le Moniteur*, 27 Dec. 1873)

3. 'He dramatizes science, he throws himself into fantastic imaginations, based none the less on new scientific data. In sum, they really are novels, and novels that are more adventurous and imaginary than ours [i.e. the Naturalists']. . . . I will not discuss the genre, which seems to me liable to garble our children's entire knowledge. . . . I am simply forced to note their success, which is stupefying. . . . But in any case that has no importance whatsoever for present-day literary trends. Spelling- and prayer-books also have considerable sales.' (Émile Zola, *Le Figaro littéraire*, 22 Dec. 1878)

4. 'I'm not surprised Dumas *fils* likes Verne: Verne is a sort of Dumas *père* by telephone. Such books cannot be summed up, because the storyteller has the power to keep you under his charm by means of a thousand unexpected, surprising creative details. . . . Mr Jules Verne has a rare merit in his novels and plays, that of *inventing*. . . . That's another similarity between Verne and Dumas. . . . And these travel books, these tales of adventure have their own originality, a captivating lucidity and vivacity. . . . They are very French, to say the word. . . . I know that those who are more ambitious in the analysis of human beings, refined people, say, "He's just a storyteller!".

'But a storyteller who charms and captivates a whole generation is *someone*, of that you can be sure.' (Jules Claretie, *Jules Verne: Célebrités contemporaines*, Quantin, 1883)

5. 'His first books, the shortest, *Around the World* or *From the Earth to the Moon*, are still the best in my view. But the works should be judged as a whole rather than in detail, and on their results rather than their intrinsic quality. Over the last forty years they have had an influence unequalled by any other books on the children of this and every country in Europe. And the influence has been good, in so far as can be judged today.' (Léon Blum, *L'Humanité*, 3 Apr. 1905)

6. 'Jules Verne's masterpiece, under its red-and-gold book-prize cover, and the play derived from it, behind its red-and-gold curtain in the Châtelet, stimulated our childhood and taught us more than all the atlases: the taste of adventure and the love of travel. "Thirty thousand banknotes for you, Captain, if we reach Liverpool within the hour." This cry of Philéas Fogg's remains for me the call of the sea.' (Jean Cocteau, *Mon premier voyage (Tour du monde en 80 jours)*, Gallimard, 1936)

7. 'Jules Verne leaves no sentence unturned. He creates the world anew with each line. . . . The Earth has seven continents: Europe, Africa, Asia, North and South America, Australasia—and Jules Verne. Every person born this century was brought up on white milk and red books. The golden edges of the Hetzel edition of the *Extraordinary Journeys* cut the history of human imagination into two.' (Claude Roy, *Le Commerce des classiques*, Gallimard, 1953)

8. 'Leo Tolstoy loved his works. "Jules Verne's novels are matchless," he would say. "I read them as an adult, and yet I remember they excited me. Jules Verne is an astonishing past master at the art of constructing a story that fascinates and impassions the reader. And if you'd heard how excitedly Turgenev speaks of him! I don't remember Turgenev being so enthusiastic about anyone as much as Verne."' (Cyril Andreyev, 'Preface to the Complete Works', trans. François Hirsch, *Europe*, 33: 112–13, 22–48)

9. 'Jules Verne's work is nothing but a long meditation, a reverie on the straight line—which represents the predication of nature on industry and industry on nature, and which is *recounted* as a tale of exploration. Title: the adventures of the straight line. . . . The train . . . cleaves through nature, jumps obstacles . . . and constitutes both the actual journey—whose form is a furrow—and the perfect embodiment of human industry. The machine has the additional advantage here of not being isolated in a purpose-built, artificial place, like the factory or all similar structures, but of remaining in permanent and direct contact with the variety of nature.' (Pierre

Macherey, *Pour une théorie de la production littéraire*, Maspero, 1966)

10. '[Verne] was probably my first [literary] contact with psychology ... The person who travels is a man who is searching for something he cannot find. In my view, the reason Phileas Fogg leaves is not because he has bet money, but because he has made a wager against himself. ... His novels are about heroes rather than about scientific adventure.' (J.-M.-G. Le Clézio, *Arts et loisirs*, 27, 8–10, 1966)

11. 'Fogg's project proposes more than a simple maximization of global speed, as specified by the wager: it challenges the contingency of the material world ... that chance opposes to the sequential clarity and temporal rigour of *Bradshaw* ... Fogg's preferred reading matter. ... Fogg's itinerary, exhausting all available means of transport, binding the globe with a "chain of communication", seeks to encompass and interconnect discrete locations. ... Circumnavigation is the encyclopedic manœuvre par excellence, and the diagrammatic incarnation of the Vernian quest for a totalization of knowledge. Truth for Verne ... is a circle.' (Andrew Martin, *The Knowledge of Ignorance*, Cambridge: Cambridge University Press, 1985)

12. 'The book of his childhood, the book of his life, was Verne's *Around the World in Eighty Days*, the fundament of his whole philosophy of travel.

' "Phileas Fogg never travelled at all," he would explain to me. "He was the archetype of the sedentary man, the stay-at-home, the maniacally house proud. He possesses knowledge of the whole of the Earth, but of a peculiar nature: from reading every continent's yearbooks, timetables, and almanacs, which he knows off by heart. An *a priori* knowledge. From these tomes he deduces that you can go around the globe in 80 days. Phileas Fogg isn't a human being at all, he's a walking clock. His religion is precision. At the opposite extreme, his servant Passepartout is an inveterate wanderer who has tried every occupation, including that of acrobat. His impersonations and exclamations stand in permanent contrast to Phileas Fogg's frozen phlegm. Fogg's bet is endangered by two sorts of delay: Passepartout's blunders and the changeability of the weather. But they are in fact one and the same: Passepartout equals meteorological man, thus constituting a foil to his master, who is chronological man. Fogg's schedule means that he mustn't arrive either early or late: his journey shouldn't be confused with a race around the world. This is shown by the episode where the Indian widow is saved from the pyre and the fate she was destined to share with her husband. Phileas Fogg uses her to fill up an annoying gain in his schedule. He's not trying to go round the world in 79 days!

' " 'What about saving this woman?'

' " 'Saving this woman, Mr Fogg?' exclaimed the Brigadier-General.

' " 'I'm still twelve hours ahead. I can use them that way.'

' " 'I say, you do have a heart!'

' " 'Sometimes,' he replied. 'When I have the time.'

"Phileas Fogg's journey is really time's attempt to establish mastery over the weather. The timetable must be applied despite the tide that waits for no man. Phileas Fogg only does his trip round the world to show that he's Passepartout's master."

'I listened to his theories with mitigated amusement.... He had this way of starting from an apparently puerile datum—*Around the World*—but considering it absolutely seriously, imperturbably, and hence proceeding to abstract considerations that verged on the metaphysical. It all made me think. Later I learned the reason: for Jean everything grew out of a distant reality going back into his earliest childhood: more precisely his relationship with his brother Paul. In the Phileas Fogg–Passepartout couple, it was easy to see that he identified with the very sympathetic and very French Passepartout....' (Michel Tournier, *Les Météores*, Gallimard, 1975)

Some of these quotations were first cited by Simone Vierne in her edition of *Le Tour du monde en quatre-vingts jours* (Garnier-Flammarion, 1978), to whom grateful acknowledgements are recorded here.

EXPLANATORY NOTES

Note on names

Significant proper names used by Verne are indicated in individual notes. Other names have no clear referent, like the clubman Samuel Fallentin, the showman William Batulcar, the Californian politicians Kamerfield and Mandiboy, the Revd Decimus Smith, or the domestic James Forster (MS1: 'Iain Forster') (the surname is reused for the Yankee engine-driver). Lord Longsferry may come from 'the Royal Borough of Queensferry' (*Backwards to Britain (BB)*, Ch. 27); and Sir Francis *Cromarty* seems to be another of the many people-places in Verne's works.

Real names of places, people, and ships have been amended in this edition: 'Montgomery Street' for 'Montgommery Street', 'Kirtland' for 'Kirkland', 'Tooele' for 'Tuilla', 'Fort Sanders' for 'Fort Sauders', 'Salt Lake City' for 'Lake Salt City', 'Independence' for 'Independance', 'Cardiff' for 'Cardif', 'Hyrum' [*sic*] for 'Hvram', the *Golconda* for the *Golgonda*, the *Korea* for the *Corea*, 'Inman' for 'Imman', and so on. A few of the English terms Verne uses have also been modified, although not in cases like the 'studbook' and the 'drawing-office' in the Bank.

Note on apparent errors in Verne's text

Despite its pedagogical aims, *Around the World* seems to contain many substantive errors. The biggest category, surprisingly, is geographical.

Thus the map in the illustrated edition shows longitudes calculated on the Paris meridian, whereas the text uses the London meridian; Suez is described as being 'nearly 77 degrees' east of Greenwich (in fact exactly 33 degrees); the Green River is crossed twice within three paragraphs; the travellers cross the Muddy, which in fact seems to be situated further south; in describing the border between Wyoming and Utah, Verne seems to be using the one valid in the 1860s; and the State of Colorado and the Colorado River are apparently confused.

Many of the places mentioned have not been found in the atlases, including the all-important 'Rothal', 'Kholby Hamlet', and 'Pillagi' (anglicized from Verne's 'Pillaji'); clearly this could be deliberate, but it also applies to supposedly real-life localities like 'Camp Walbah'. Yet others exist, but not in the specified place, including

'Fort Halleck', 'Fort McPherson' (Verne: 'Fort Mac-Pherson'), 'Mounts Cedar and Humboldt', and the 'Carson Sink'. The author also seems to consider Hong Kong an intergral part of China.

Many errors involve confusion of left and right or north and south, especially in Chs. 26–8. These include: 'The Platte['s] . . . waters join the Missouri a little above Omaha' (in reality a little below); 'the Platte, at the loop it performs before Fremont' (after); 'the railroad . . . headed up from the south-west to the north-west' (north-east); the transcontinental line both goes through Salt Lake City (Ch. 26) and doesn't (Ch. 27); 'Wyoming, the former Dakota' (Wyoming was created from Oregon, Dakota, Utah, and Idaho, with the Dakotas continuing to exist); and 'the Arkansas River, one of the largest tributaries of the Missouri' (the Arkansas flows into the Mississippi— although Verne may have been anticipating the modern conclusion that the Mississippi is, in all logic, a tributary of the Missouri). The scope of the tendency is shown by Verne's corrections of 'from east to west' and 'from west to east' in MS1 and MS2 to 'eastwards' and 'westwards' in the published version—in a passage of a didactic nature (Ch. 37).

Such an inclination to mirror imaging might be because the narrator traces the Pacific Railroad both from Omaha and from the Pacific; it may also be connected with the India–America symmetry and disorientation of going round the world that together govern the book. But in *Journey to the Centre of the Earth* as well, east and west are often confused. And in the decidedly seminal *Backwards to Britain*, the topos of switching is systematic, 'explained' by the fact that the protagonists are travelling 'backwards' (via Bordeaux). This left–right inversion is surprising in such a spatially fixated writer; it may indicate a mental disturbance connected with the 'dizziness' that many of his heroes experience and, more generally, with deep anxieties about the 'world out there'.

Yet other lapses relate to common sense: Fogg's water for shaving at 86°F seems rather cool; Stuart is presented as Fogg's opponent at cards, but then as his partner; the travellers' luggage seems to be sent for twice in Hong Kong; and 'the drawing-room clock [strikes] 8.40' and 8.50 strikes 'on all the clocks of London'.

Even the time sequence contains a large number of inconsistencies, mostly connected with Fogg's schedule. Does the bank robbery take place on 28 (Ch. 19) or 29 September (Ch. 3); is the *Carnatic* due to leave Hong Kong on 5 (Ch. 18), 6 (Ch. 17), or 7 November (Chs. 3 and 22); does Fogg plan to arrive in San Francisco on 3 (Ch. 24) or 5 December (Chs. 3 and 26); and is the *China* scheduled to leave New

York on 11 (Ch. 31) or 12 December (Ch. 3)? Clearly Cocteau's famous 'fantom day' is playing tricks with the chronology throughout the book.

Other mysteries include Fogg's conversation with Bunsby in Hong Kong, which seems to take about three hours; Fogg's last utterance in the opening chapter, which apparently takes three minutes; and the calculation that from 11.40 to 8.45 is 'nine and a quarter hours'. Also, if Passepartout's watch is a family heirloom, and he has never touched it, why doesn't it read Paris time? How did Fix's warrant catch up—which boat did it travel to Hong Kong on? How does Ralph intend to present Fogg's cheque on a Sunday? And finally, why does Fogg deduct 80 days' worth of gas from Passepartout's wages, and not 79?

7 *Savile Row, Burlington Gardens*: (Verne: 'Saville' throughout, repeated in most editions) Savile Row, W1, on the Burlington Estate, famous for its tailors since mid-century. From 1870 onwards No. 1 was occupied by the Royal Geographical Society, mentioned in Ch. 5 and the scene of the opening chapter of *Five Weeks in a Balloon*.

Sheridan: Richard Brinsley, born 1751, died in fact in 1816. Influential Anglo-Irish playwright, and a politician of note. Significantly, he was ruined by his gambling, and died in poverty. He lived in fact at No. 14 Savile Row.

Phileas Fogg: 'Phileas' as a first name seems unattested before the poet Phileas Lebesgue, born on 26 November 1869. Verne possibly derived it from Phineas T. Barnum (cf. note to Ch. 23); from the Greek sculptor Phidias mentioned twice by Wey—in the context of Byron; and from the Classical figure Phileas. Simone Vierne presents the latter as a Greek geographer of the fifth century BC, author of a *Périple* ('Long Journey'); but unfortunately provides no other reference. Searches have produced instead only a St Phileas (in French 'Philéas'), author of the fragmentary *Excerptum ex Epistola ad Thmuiras* ('Excerpt from an Epistle to the Thmuirans'), reprinted in France in 1856 under the title *Scripta quae supersunt* ('Surviving Writings'). St Phileas may represent, then, a fascinatingly spiritual source for Phileas Fogg. Other interpretations include the Greek *-phile* ('-lover') or French *filer* ('to tail') + *as* ('ace') (Fogg loves aces; he is an ace tailed round the world), *filer à l'anglaise* ('to take French leave, to flee like a thief in the night'), and *fil* ('thread' or 'wire', visible in many scenes in the book). In MS1 and MS2, the hero is often referred to simply as 'Phileas' (or 'Philéas' (the spelling used in the play)).

7 *Fogg*: (beginning of MS1: 'Fog') probably derived from *fog*, associated with nineteenth-century London, and from W. P. Fogg, author of *Around the World* (1872). In an interview in 1902, Verne said that 'Fogg means nothing but *brouillard*', 'but it was especially the Phileas that gave such value to the creation'. In any case Wey had already depicted the essence of our hero in 1854: the British are 'timid, a little touchy . . . indifferent to feminine beauty, and present the appearance of a pronounced coldness'; 'the Englishman, who does not wish to appear subordinate to events, never runs. . . . When he walks, he counts each step.'

Reform Club: 105 Pall Mall, SW1; founded by radicals in 1832 or 1836. Verne's description of the Reform apparently contains a number of errors. *Five Weeks in a Balloon* cites the Traveller's Club, and *Backwards to Britain* refers to four clubs on Pall Mall (Ch. 40), but does not mention the Reform. On its opening page, however, Verne acknowledges major influences from Francis Wey (1812–82), *Les Anglais chez eux: Esquisses de mœurs et de voyage* (1854) (*A Frenchman Sees the English in the Fifties*). This book was serialized in the *Musée des familles* (Nov. 1850–May 1851), which Verne contributed to during the period 1851–4.

Byron: George Gordon, 6th Baron of Rochdale (1788–1824), a prominent Romantic, and author of the long poem *Don Juan*. Born with a club-foot, he was notorious for his amorous adventures. In contrast with the earlier works, *Around the World* acknowledges very few writers or books, quoting mainly periodicals.

Courts of Chancery . . . Ecclesiastical Court: by the Judicature Act of 1873, the Court of Chancery became the Chancery Division of the High Court of Justice; *Queen's Bench*: one of the divisions of the High Court, from which appeals go to the High Court of Justice: its status was changed in the Judicature Act of 1873; *Exchequer*: since 1830, the Court of Exchequer Chamber had been a court of appeal intermediate between the three common-law courts and Parliament; ecclesiastical courts administered ecclesiastical law and maintained discipline within the Established Church.

the Royal Institution of Great Britain . . . Arts and Sciences: the Royal Institution, founded in 1799 to promote scientific knowledge; Sir Humphry Davy, mentioned repeatedly in *Journey to the Centre of the Earth*, worked there from 1801 to 1823; *the London Institution*: founded in 1806 'for the Advancement of Literature and the Diffusion of Useful Knowledge'—but Verne may have been equally interested in its large library of geographical books; *the Artizan [sic] Society*: published *The Artizan* (1843–72), about steam-driven ships and locomotives; *the Russell Institution*: the Russell Institution for the Promotion of Literary and Scientific Knowledge, with publications listed in the British Library Catalogue [BL] until 1854; *the Western Literary Institution*: also known as the Western Literary and Scientific Institution, founded 1825, publication in the BL in 1834; *the Law Society*: Chancery Lane, WC2, founded in 1825; *Society for the Combined Arts and Sciences*: possibly the Royal Society of Arts, Manufactures, and Commerce.

the Harmonic Union: publication in the BL in 1852.

8 *the Entomological Society, founded chiefly with the aim of exterminating harmful insects*: founded 1833, publications in the BL from 1847 to 1916; the aim ascribed here is clearly ironic.

In listing all these societies, Verne's emphasis seems to be on Fogg's unclubbability (a trait shared by the hero of his first novel); but it is interesting to note that most of the institutions are jointly literary and scientific—Verne's own combination of interests—with the scientific aspect subordinate to the textual.

Should anyone express surprise that such a mysterious gentleman be numbered amongst the members of that distinguished society: this phrase conceals considerable bitterness. MS1 tells us that Fogg had only recently been '*admitted*' (my italics; the word is repeated) to the Reform; that the Club is 'honourable' (repeated), and its members 'highly respected'; and that his entry was accomplished with considerable difficulty, surmounted only by using money from a 'grasping' Jewish bank. This passage may also be aimed at the Académie Française, as witness Fogg's quasi-'immortality' (the *Académiciens* are known as *Les Immortels*), his surprising membership, and his whole relationship with his 'colleagues', often described as 'adversaries' or 'opponents'. Great pleasure is in fact taken throughout in demonstrating the inane conformism of all collectivities, from the Stock Exchange and the Royal Geographical Society to 'the known criminal gangs of England' and the 'highly elusive society in honour of the goddess of death'. But the Long Noses, especially, are dressed like 'heralds from the Middle Ages' and form a self-supporting 'corporation', with the whole episode infused with unexpectedly strong feelings; and above all, a member of the bottom row has 'left' and needs replacing (the method by which the Académie appoints new members). The idea of replacement also occurs in the way Fogg 'succeeds' Sheridan in the house on Savile Row; with the word for a 'seat' at the Académie, 'fauteuil', also occurring prominently in the French text.

8 *Baring Brothers*: a family financial firm (1763) which had interests in marine insurance and the East India Company, and is still active today.

difficult to fathom: MS1 adds: 'whatever he did, [he] never discussed, having no doubt observed that discussion never convinces anyone'.

9 *with anyone else*: MS1 adds: 'reading *The Times* and *Daily Telegraph* every day from the first line of the first article to the final line of the last classified advertisement.'

comfortable rooms . . . twenty Ionic columns of red porphyry: Wey: 'The lower floor contains . . . bedrooms [for the members] . . . The entrance hall . . . is surrounded by columns supporting a wide gallery, and is covered with carefully laid-out parquet . . . a broad staircase of white marble . . . The cupola, with blue panes . . . is supported by twenty Ionic columns, whose bases of red porphyry . . . This gallery, where one goes for a walk as if in a covered cloister . . .' The phrase 'staircase of white marble' is reproduced in MS1, but omitted in the published version, although, without it, it is not absolutely clear whether Fogg's perambulations happen in his house or at the Club.

If he lunched or dined . . . a satisfactorily cool temperature: Wey: 'pantry . . . dairy . . . fish store . . . servants in dress-coats . . . their shoes soled with thick felt. . . . Saxony cloth . . . crystal and china produced for the exclusive use of the Club. Wine is drunk at the Reform Club in the Classical manner, that is with certain spices mixed in. The sherry, port, or claret . . . combined with a little maidenhair . . . cinnamon sticks, ground cassia bark . . . with ice . . . that the Reform Club brings over from a distant part of America.'

10 *Jean Passepartout*: a *passe-partout* is a 'skeleton key, or other object that can pass everywhere'. In MS2 the character is called 'Jean Fernandez', 'Jean Fricaudet' (cf. *fricoter* ('to stew, to plot, to be on the fiddle, or to sleep with')), 'Master Jean', 'John', or

most frequently 'Jean'; in MS1, 'Jean X' three times, and thereafter 'Jean Tirouflet' (possibly from *tir-au-flanc* ('skiver') + *girofle* ('clove') + *camouflet/camoufler* ('affront'/'camouflage')). Previous to MS1, he was 'Jean Français'.

Léotard: Jules (1830–70), French acrobat and gymnast. He invented the flying trapeze, exhibiting it at the Winter Circus in 1859; and also gave his name to the garment popular today.

Blondin: Charles (1824–97), French acrobat. He tightrope walked over the Niagara Falls in 1859, and repeated the feat on subsequent occasions while performing various acrobatics.

11 *Madame Tussaud's*: Madame Tussaud (1761–1850), born Marie Grosholtz in either France or Switzerland. She established her wax museum in 1835 and managed it until 1850.

12 *Angelica Kauffmann*: (MS1: 'his compatriot Angelica Kaufman'; Wey: 'paintings of Angelica Kaufmann, quite nastily academic') (1741–1807), in fact a Swiss painter. One of the most important neoclassical artists, she specialized in historical subjects, settling in Britain in 1766, then in Rome in 1781.

Leroy or Earnshaw: Julien Leroy (1686–1759) or his son Pierre Leroy (1717–85), French clockmakers; Thomas Earnshaw (1749–1829), British watchmaker, amongst whose inventions was the 'free detent escapement' (the escapement, with a sexual connotation, is at the heart of the early short story 'Master Zacharius' (1854)).

the members are veritable organs that express the passions: the *double entendre* is that societies like the Reform are composed of unreflecting and irresponsible male members.

never in a hurry: MS2: 'who never came too late or too early', with blatant sexual reference.

no one: MS2 adds: 'as for his phlegm, his coolness, his imperturbability, one cannot imagine them existing to a higher degree. To employ a popular expression, he was one of those men who chill a bottle of champagne merely by looking at it.'

Parisian from Paris: MS1 adds: 'As for Jean Tirouflet, he was a Frenchman, born and bred in the Orne, the department where one lives longest. He had been living in England for ten years.'

Frontins or Mascarilles: Frontin was an unscrupulous but ingenious valet, fond of repartee, in eighteenth-century comedy, especially Lesage's *Le Turcaret*. Mascarille was similarly an insolent but clever servant, serving his own and his master's interests, in Molière's *Les Précieuses ridicules* and other plays.

13 *Minerva's tresses*: the Roman goddess of wisdom, the arts, handicrafts, and warfare; and one of the three beautiful goddesses Paris had to choose between by presenting an apple.

try him out: MS2 adds: '~~This worthy fellow, although French through and through, was of a calm temperament.~~'

methodism: (MS1: 'conformism of the British, he had wanted to try his hand') Littré: 'doctrine of the methodist doctors, in which every illness depended on "tightening" or "relaxing"'. *Méthodiste* is also the 'name that Buffon gives to authors using various methods in natural history. A methodist insists that every single species, however anomalous, fit into his method.' *Oxford English Dictionary* (*OED*): 'methodism: adherence to fixed methods; excessive regard for methods'. Verne's use of the word provides an invaluable clue to Fogg's character, whether in reinforcing the human-animal metaphor or in anticipating modern psychoanalytical concepts of tension and release.

the Oyster Rooms of Haymarket: (Verne: 'the "oysters-rooms" of Hay-Market') although daytime Haymarket is described as 'elegant' by Verne (*BB*, ch. 41), at night he mentions 'scenes of drunkenness and debauchery, interspersed with fights and even murders', together with flagrant prostitution (ch. 43). Wey: 'the streets given up to base pleasures, and the oyster-rooms where eating continues until morning. When dawn breaks, the policemen collect from the road the drunkards of both sexes and—alas!—all levels of society.'

14 *An electric bell and speaking-tubes . . . an electric clock . . . the two devices striking the second simultaneously*: in addition to the sexual connotation, Fogg's domestic arrangements announce the magical spatio-temporal qualities of the telegram, with its use of electricity, its communication-at-a-distance, and the question it raises of extended simultaneity.

two libraries at his disposal, one devoted to literature, and the other to law and politics: Wey: 'two libraries . . . one devoted to literature, the other to law and politics'.

15 *a vast edifice in Pall Mall that cost no less than £120,000 to build*: Wey: 'The edifice . . . cost more than £120,000 to build.'

the dining-room, whose nine windows . . . some Cheshire cheese: Wey: 'the dining room . . . lit by nine windows opening out on

to a fine garden... Dinner invariably consists of main fish
and roast-meat dishes... with diverse sauces and condiments
much appreciated in Britain... rhubarb or green-gooseberry
tart... Cheshire cheese'. *Reading Sauce*: (Verne:'reading') a
sharp sauce flavoured with onions, spices, and herbs. Mrs
Beeton's recipe for it (1861) contains 'Indian soy'. The 'Royal
British Sauce' (in English in Verne's text) of the following
paragraph has not been traced, but 'English sauce' is the French
for 'custard', and Verne jokes elsewhere about the predilec-
tion of northern countries for putting sweet sauces on meat.

the vast drawing-room... an uncut copy of 'The Times': Wey:
'the vast dining room, glittering with paintings and gold... *The
Times* cannot be considered a newspaper: it has reached the
heights of an institution'.

'Standard': MS2: *'Daily Telegraph'*.

16 *Andrew Stuart... John Sullivan... Thomas Flanagan... Gauthier
Ralph*: Verne often derived his names from authors. Here the
possibilities include: Andrew Stuart (1724/5–1801), who pub-
lished extensively, including *Letters to the Directors of the East
India Company* (1773), or else Andrew Stuart (1786–1840),
who published in English and French on North American
affairs, including *Nebraska and Kansas* (1854); John Sullivan
(1749–1839), who wrote books about India, or else John
Sullivan (flourished 1844–54), who also wrote books about
India; Thomas Flanagan, author of various publications about
Church matters in the 1850s; Gauthier (MS2 sometimes
'Gautier') clearly refers to the death in 1872 of Théophile
Gautier (b. 1811), like Verne a travel-writer and a Romantic
influenced by Hoffmann. Gautier was one of the first reviewers
of Verne, in 1866.

£55,000 *worth of banknotes*: MS2: '£40,000 worth of
banknotes'.

17 *the utmost regard for the public's dignity... without the cashier
even looking up*: Wey: 'One is struck by the confidence reigning
during the transactions. At the Bank, no sentinels, no guards
... no grills. Inside, low desks, within reach of the first passer-
by... In one room containing gold bars, I was offered one
weighing about eight pounds for my curiosity.... A bystander
took the ingot after me, and passed it to his neighbour, who then
handed it on to someone else; and thus it disappeared down a
corridor giving out on to the street... When the bar returned,

the cashier took it . . . having apparently in the interim forgotten about its existence.'

17 '*detectives*': Verne's term, 'des "détectives"', was first recorded in 1871. In English, *OED* lists Dickens as first using the word, in 1850. But the underlying concept had existed at least since Poe's 'Murders in the Rue Morgue' (1841).

18 '*It used to be,' Fogg said quietly*: MS2: ~~retorted Gauthier Ralph~~'.

19 '*Yes indeed . . . "Morning Chronicle"*': this whole paragraph is attributed to Fogg in MS2. *Great Indian Peninsular Railway*: company founded in 1845, built the first Indian railway from Bombay to Thana in 1853. The line from Bombay to Calcutta was completed on 7 March 1870. The *Morning Chronicle* stopped publication on 19 March 1862.

the Mont Cenis Tunnel: the first tunnel under the Alps, running between Italy and France, 8.5 miles long (1857–71). The combination of the artificial and the natural fascinates Verne, from the coal-mines under the North Sea at Newcastle to Brunel's Rotherhithe Foot Tunnel (the first tunnel under a river) graphically described in *Backwards to Britain* (ch. 44).

'*Eighty days,' interjected Fogg . . . 'Possibly 80 days!*': MS1:

' "Eighty!"
' "Yes. Here is the timetable xxxx xxxx:

~~London~~ Suez via Brindisi, by railway and steamer   „
Suez Bombay   „
Cal. Hong.   „
Hon. Yokh.   „
Yokh. S. Fr.   „
S. Fr. New Y.   „
New Y. ~~London~~ [with Liverp. superimposed]   „
Liverp. London   „

' "Yes. Eighty days!"'

22 '*Passepartout.'* . . . '*We're leaving for Calais in ten minutes*': MS2: ' "~~John. John,~~" repeated Mr Fogg, not raising his voice. | ~~John then appeared, and said: "'Jean', if sir pleases, and not 'John'. I would be most obliged if sir would be so good as to retain my nationality by calling me by my French name." | "Yes, Jean," replied Mr Fogg, "Jean, we're leaving for Calais in ten minutes."~~'

unconsciously rocking his head from side to side: Passepartout is here reproducing the movement of the main protagonist of

'Master Zacharius' (1854), the revealing tale illustrating Verne's views on time and the psychology of the creative artist. The clockmaker *is* time, having put himself into his clocks, and then fallen in love with them: quite logically, he dies with them at the end. Some of Fogg's features derive from the grotesque Pittonachio, whose face is a clock-face, heart a pendulum, and who 'walks in jerks, without ever turning round. If one chanced to follow him, one learned that he covered a league an hour, and that his march was approximately circular.' Amongst the other connections between the two works are the mimicking of man's sexuality and the conclusion that time has no independent existence.

The term 'unconsciously' ('inconsciemment') is used again for Fogg's final 'day gained unconsciously'. These are apparently the first recorded occurrences of the term in French. (The word is also used twice in *The Mysterious Island* (1874), which includes a scene of hypnotism, and in the same paragraph of *Mathias Sandorf* (1885) as the name of the mental specialist Charcot.)

'*No trunks. Just an overnight bag . . . Off you go now.*': this, the longest speech by Fogg in the book, is a minor masterpiece. It mixes the ridiculous and the sublime; and by pointing to Passepartout's reactions, suggests the intimate relationship that will develop between the two men.

23 *Charing Cross Station, one of the termini of the South-Eastern Railway*: although Verne mentions 'Charing-Cross, where royal coronations used to take place' (*BB*, ch. 40), he himself leaves London from the 'Brighton Railway Station in Duke Street' (ch. 47).

a poor beggar-woman . . . twenty guineas: Wey: 'In Trafalgar Square, I was accosted by a beggar-woman wearing rags and a hat. I gave her a halfpenny.' MS2: 'Phileas Fogg got out ~~a guinea, and held it out~~ to the beggar-woman. | ~~"Do you have any change?"~~ | ~~"No xxx xxxx," was all that the woman murmured.~~ | ~~"Well then," Mr Fogg replied coldly, "if you do not have any change for this guinea, then you do need it xxxx xxxx xxxx"~~ | xxxx xxxx xxxx Jean felt something like a tear in his eye'.

24 *Sydenham*: Sydenham is the last stop before Suez, and Passepartout's horrified reaction humorously underlines the passage to the East. Sydenham also represents the end of *Backwards to Britain*. But in neither case is mention made of its most important building: the Crystal Palace! Built in 1851 for the Great

Exhibition at Hyde Park, this huge futuristic structure was re-erected at Sydenham in 1854, complete with dinosaurs in the grounds, and was normally visible from the railway.

The omission of the whole section from Sydenham to Suez is so ingeniously disguised that most readers do not even realize the trick. One consequence is that any description of France is absent, apart from Fogg's uninformative 'Arrived in Paris, Thursday, 3 October, 7.20 a.m. | Left Paris, Thursday, 8.40 a.m.' and Passepartout's dream of revisiting Paris and his subsequent memory of a wet cab ride. Such an omission allows reference to the traumatic events of the Paris Commune (1871) to be avoided.

The other omission is the Canal itself! Verne performs the feat of taking his hero from London to Suez without describing one of the greatest engineering accomplishments of the age—proving his reputation as an unadulterated techno-freak to be unfounded.

25 *United Kingdom*: absent in MS1 is the whole of Ch. 5, with complex consequences for the plot.

At the end of Ch. 4, we saw Fogg and Passepartout passing through Sydenham (2 October). MS1 then jumps to the morning of 9 October with Fix waiting for the boat in Suez, and continues on up to the evening of the 9th and his sending of the telegram (Chs. 6–8 in the published work). The new material introduced as Ch. 5 covers from 7 October to the evening of the 9th, and describes reactions in London to Fogg's mad bet. It closes with the receiving of the telegram from Suez.

The new material is thus a flashback which then carries on past the starting-point, transforming Chs. 6–8 in Suez into a second flashback. In sum, Verne started by placing a big spatio-temporal hole in his otherwise straightforward narration, corresponding to the entire journey from Sydenham to Suez. In the published version, he then disguises the hole by cutting from Sydenham back to London and then jumping directly to Suez for so long that readers forget they are in a flashback.

The hole is camouflaged by using a method of communication which is in two places at the 'same' time—although in Verne's relativistic world not even the narrator seems to realize this. The telegram therefore crosses time and space in three ways: within the fictional world; within the narrative structure; and in Verne's process of adding to the manuscript. Its effect precedes its cause: both within the fiction, for it is received in London before being sent in Suez; and because the fiction successfully predicts the real public's reaction to Fogg's bet!

a new 'Alabama' Claim: the *Alabama* was a Confederate vessel, built and fitted out in Liverpool during the Civil War (1861–5), and commanded by Raphael Semmes (1809–77). Captain Semmes became a hero in the South in 1862 for his disruption of Union commerce from the West Indies to Singapore, but his ship was sunk near Cherbourg in 1864. The United States considered that Britain had broken its neutrality, and a series of angry exchanges ensued. On 8 May 1871 the Treaty of Washington was signed, and on 14 September 1872 an international tribunal in Geneva concluded that Britain had acted illegally, and awarded the United States $15,500,000 damages. Ch. 25 mentions the *Alabama* Claim again (and Fix also remarks on the danger for British citizens in America), but now says 'it was settled recently'.

Surprisingly, these allusions are virtually the only ones to the war that had recently torn the United States apart.

the 'Illustrated London News': founded as a general weekly publication in 1842 and still in existence today.

the 'Proceedings of the Royal Geographic Society': published from 1857 to 1892.

26 *old Lord Albermale, who was paralysed*: in 1873 the Earl of Albermarle [*sic*] exhibited in London a painting by Angelica Kauffmann of his daughter the Countess of Albermarle; there is also an Albemarle Street parallel to Burlington Street. In *Twenty Thousand Leagues* Verne mentions the ship the *Albermale*.

28 *the Suez Canal*: completed by the French on 17 November 1869, almost halving the distance from London to Bombay. Britain acquired an interest in the canal in 1875.

now guaranteed a great future, thanks to the magnificent work of M. de Lesseps: Ferdinand-Marie, vicomte de Lesseps (1805–94), French diplomat responsible for the building of the Suez Canal. Verne's Cross of the Légion d'honneur in 1870 was proposed by de Lesseps—hence perhaps the praise here.

the engineer Stephenson: Robert (1803–59), son of George (1781–1848). The Stephensons built the *Rocket* and the Liverpool and Manchester Railway, including the first railway tunnel. Robert Stephenson's remark was made in a Commons debate in 1858.

Fix: presumably from his *idées fixes*; but also perhaps because he tries to *fix* Fogg and time.

29 *Sheppard*: Jack (alias John) Sheppard (1702–24), a robber who managed four spectacular acrobatic escapes from London prisons before being publicly executed.

34 *at each principal point*: MS2: 'these dates, Mr Fogg busied himself copying down in a schedule, which it may be appropriate to reproduce here, for it might be useful to those wishing to attempt a journey round the world in the same conditions.' There follows a table of times and dates, headed 'Around the World in 80 days, or 1920 hours, or 115200 minutes, or 6912000 seconds', with the following column-heads: 'Month', 'Date', 'Day', 'Scheduled Arrival', 'Actual Arrival', 'Days Gained', 'Days Lost', 'Days Used', and 'Remarks'. It differs from the *Morning Chronicle*'s table in the published version (Ch. 3): in having the times of departure and arrival at London as 10.35 p.m.; in containing lines for Brindisi (5 October) and Singapore (31 October); and in allowing twelve days for Calcutta to Hong Kong and ten for New York to London.

Amongst the many people who took up the challenge of imitating Fogg, Verne gave his blessing to the author of *Nellie Bly's Book: Around the World in 72 Days* (1890) (real name: Elizabeth Cochran, 1867–1922). In his novel *Claudius Bombarnac* (1892), he also refers to a 'Mrs Bisland' as having done the trip in 79 days.

35 *Père-Lachaise Cemetery . . . Circus*: a famous cemetery in the north-east of Paris where writers and statesmen are buried; *Champs-Elysées Circus*: also called the Summer Circus (1841–1900).

39 *Gulf of Arabia . . . Idrisi*: Verne is not here referring to the modern Persian/Arabian Gulf, but translating Sinus Arabicus, the Classical name for the Red Sea; *Strabo*: (64 BC–AD ?21) author of a *Geography*, travel-writer, and writer about volcanoes, especially in Southern Italy—all traits shared with Verne; *Arrian*: or Flavius Arrianus, a Greek historian of the second century AD, author of the *Anabasis*, a life of Alexander the Great, and the *Indica*, about India; *Artemidorus*: flourished 100 BC, Greek geographer of the Mediterranean and author of writings about India and a systematic geography in eleven volumes, extensively borrowed from by Strabo; *Idrisi*: Arabic geographer, scientist, and poet (?1099–?1164), author of an influential *Geography* (1154) describing the whole known world, with a major section on Sicily.

40 *'Fascinating! . . . Indian dancing-girls!'*: the Vernian list generally has the function of conveying large amounts of information;
this one, in the mouth of an uncultured policeman, reduces even
Indian exoticism to a mere jumble of harmless curiosities.

41 *Mocha*: in modern Yemen, origin of Mokka coffee.

*just like an enormous half-cup, with its round walls and its
ruined fort sticking out like a handle*: Verne humorously makes
the link between the coffee and the cup, the effect being again to
debunk exoticism.

42 *Banians*: according to *OED*, a Banian is 'a Hindu trader, especially one from the province of Gujerat; sometimes applied by
early writers to all Hindus in Western India.' It is a variant of the
form 'Bunhya' (or 'Bunnia'), that Verne uses in Ch. 10, apparently without realizing that the two forms are consonant. But
the term also forms part of the 'banian-tree', 'a remarkable East
Indian tree, the branches of which drop shoots to the ground,
that take root and support their parent branches' (*OED*), a
hyper-Vernian object that is quoted with relish in *The Steam
House* (1879).

fortifications: MS2: 'fortifications ~~restored by the British~~'.

43 *the great Sepoy Rebellion*: more often known as the Indian
Mutiny (1857–8): a revolt by Indian troops that led to the
transfer of the country's administration from the East India
Company to the British Crown.

the famous East India Company: chartered in 1600 by the
British Government to trade in the East Indies, dissolved in
1874. Verne's information about India may be influenced by his
reading of Henry Russell-Killough's *Seize mille lieues à travers
l'Asie et l'Océanie: Voyage exécuté pendant les années 1858–
61 . . .*, cited in *The Steam House*.

44 *Calcutta*: MS2 adds: '~~This is the railway the opening of the last
section of which between Bombay and Allahabad the newspapers had recently announced, an announcement which was
at the origin of the unprecedented wager drawn up between
Phileas Fogg and his colleagues of the Reform Club~~'.

Bundelkhand: historic region of central India, comprising the
hilly Vindhya region, now part of Madhya Pradesh state.

45 *Malabar Hill*: (Verne: 'Malebar Hill') a 180-foot high eminence
in Bombay, between the Harbour and the Arabian Sea.

the Island of Elephanta with its mysterious 'hypogea': now
known as Gharapuri, Elephanta contains a colossal stone ele-

phant and six Hindu temples dedicated to the phallic cult of the god Shiva; the largest temple, called the Great Cave, is a vast interior space with rows of massive pillars; *'hypogea'*: underground vaults, especially ones used for burials.

45 *the Kanheri Grottoes on Salsette*: containing gigantic Buddhist sculptures dating from the second to the ninth century.

rabbit: MS2 has ~~'lion'~~ throughout this scene.

46 *Parsees, or Guebres, direct descendants of the Zoroastrians*: Parsee, Guebre, and Zoroastrian all refer to fire-worshippers from Persia who fled to India in the seventh and eighth centuries to escape Muslim persecution.

49 *'transire benefaciendo'*: 'to do good while passing through [this world]'.

trap: *Journey to the Centre of the Earth* (ch. 12): 'the horizontal strata of superimposed [eruptive] rocks called *trapps* in the Scandinavian languages'.

the railway stopped at the foot of these mountains, which had to be crossed by palanquin or pony to Kandallah Station, on the far side: the idea of the railway not being complete here anticipates the following chapters. But the idea remains mysterious, for no trace of a 'Kandallah' can be found on the railway line. Four paragraphs previously, however, the French text uses an identical name, 'Kandallah', for an authentic station *south* of Bombay (amended in this edition to the modern name of 'Khandala').

50 *unable to believe that he was crossing India . . . yet nothing could be more genuine!*: this echoes Passepartout's earlier 'I seem to be travelling in a dream.' The characters betray the anxiety of being mere actors in a book or a play, their plausibility only guaranteed by the (fictional) narrator's insistence that they are genuine.

the goddess Kali: the Hindu goddess of time and of destruction, a form of Devi, the supreme goddess, consort of Shiva, and head of a cult characterized by savagery and cannibalism; she is often shown covered with blood, dancing on the inert body of her consort.

the untamed Aurangzeb: Mogul Emperor of India (1618–1707), responsible for the destruction of countless Hindu temples and shrines.

the chief of the Thugs, the king of the Stranglers: the Thugs or Thuggees (Sanskrit *sthaga*, 'a scoundrel', or *sthagati*, 'to conceal') were devoted to Kali, and strangled travellers. The Thuggee gangs seem to have been eliminated by 1872. Verne's account seems to derive from Eugène Sue (1804–57), *The Wandering Jew*, since both adopt the unusual spelling 'Feringhea' (= Frenchman) for the chief.

51 *having briefly travelled . . . near Surat*: the redundancy of this information may perhaps be explained by the Gulf of Cambay's resemblance to female sexual parts. The Red Sea is similarly described as 'highly capricious, and too often unpleasant, like all long, narrow gulfs' (Ch. 9); and the pendulous shape of Florida attracts much ribald attention throughout Verne's works.

52 *Phileas Fogg looked at Sir Francis Cromarty, who seemed . . . khajurs*: MS2: 'Phileas Fogg frowned briefly. Sir Francis ~~looked at him,~~ who seemed'; *khajurs*: (Verne: 'khajours') possibly from Khajuraho, a town in Bundelkhand, the site of Hindu and Jain erotic temples dating from AD 950–1050; or else 'kajus' or 'cajuputs' (in French 'cajeputs'), trees that were introduced into Southern India in the 1870s.

53 *palki-gharries*: OED: 'a carriage shaped somewhat like a palanquin on wheels' (1872).

    'What is it?': MS2: ' "What is it, ~~John?" | "Jean.' "~~ | "What is it, ~~Jean?" repeated Mr Fogg.~~'

54 *'musth'*: (Verne: 'mutsh') < *must* (Urdu) < the Persian for 'drunk'. *Collins Dictionary*: 'a state of frenzied sexual excitement in the males of certain large mammals, especially elephants, associated with a discharge from a gland between the ear and eye'. Verne smuggles the remarkable notion of the elephant's 'frenzied paroxysm' past Hetzel's eagle eye; and then compounds the felony by having Passepartout feed the animal some sugar, the 'elephant produc[ing] a few grunts of satisfaction', and then give 'the animal a good stroke' between the ear and the eye.

    In *The Steam House*, Verne sardonically comments that 'since the time when the playwrights ran completely out of tricks, and had the bright idea of exhibiting elephants in their plays . . . these animals have been less sought after' (his own play of *Around the World* had used a live elephant).

58 *As for Mr Fogg*: MS2: 'As for Mr Fogg, ~~without worries, without anxiety, without the shadow of a presumption~~'.

59 *tam-tams*: this is not misplaced terminology from another continent, but refers here to an Asian gong.

60 *Juggernaut Car*: (Sanskrit *jaganaytha*, 'master of the world') a Hindu god, a form of Krishna. His image is carried on a large wagon in an annual procession, supposedly crushing worshippers who throw themselves under it—hence a 'juggernaut'.

60 *revealed the curves of her waist*: MS2: 'revealed the undulating curves of her body'.

'*A suttee!*': (Sanskrit *sati*) suttee was particularly prevalent amongst the Brahmins of Bengal between 1680 and 1830. Sometimes it was voluntary, but cases of compulsion, escape, and rescue were also recorded. Isolated cases occurred in the Indian states at least until the 1880s.

63 *Aouda*: possibly from Auoudad, a region of Northern India, annexed by the East India Company in 1856, or from Ahu[ra Maz]da, in Zoroastrianism the only God and creator; Verne seems to adhere to the Indian practice that women had only one name, although he sometimes prefixes it with 'Mrs'.

It was reported that Verne inserted the episode involving Aouda after his wife started flirting with an Indian prince while the Vernes were staying at Piriac-sur-mer, near Nantes.

65 *apse*: throughout this scene, Verne uses Christian terminology: 'procession', 'cortège', 'temple' (the French word also means 'Protestant church'), 'religious intoning', 'priests dressed in long embroidered robes and with mitres on their heads . . . producing a funereal religious chanting', 'cross-shaped incisions'.

But there is simultaneously sexual innuendo in this scene of trying to make a hole: '. . . disappointment of the four men, interrupted in the middle of their work. . . . Passepartout was beside himself, making it difficult for the guide to hold him back. . . . vital moment.' Even Fogg experiences 'feelings'.

Just as the scene of the Long Noses is both religious and erotic, here the two innuendos combine perfectly in the Christian–sexual metaphor of the Rajah's becoming 'erect', 'a miracle', a 'resurrection' 'risen from the dead'.

70 '*The Ramayana*' . . . *Brahma*: a Sanskrit epic poem, composed *c*.300 BC; *Brahma*: the Creator in later Hindu tradition.

Yusuf Adil: (Verne: 'Uçaf Uddaul', Yusuf the Just), Yusuf (Khan) 'Adil Shah, Islamic King of Bijapur 1489–1510 and patron of the arts. A former Turkish slave, he took over Goa, but was defeated by Alfonso de Albuquerque. No trace of the passage has been found, nor of the mysterious dedicatee.

the bow of Kama, the god of love: Kama represents the enjoyment of sexual desires, one of the four aims of life in Hinduism (cf. the *Kama-Sutra*).

71 *Vicvakarman, the eternal sculptor*: Hindu creator of the universe and the god of mechanical objects and ornaments.

This erotic passage describing Aouda's charms is not fully justified by the plot. But Passepartout had been sent to buy clothes for Aouda—and it is presumably he who discovers her body while undressing her, for she later awakes in European clothes. The 'other' story of *Around the World* is undoubtedly Passepartout's many flirtations with Aouda, including telling himself he had been 'the husband of a beautiful woman', and culminating in his dawn hammering on her bedroom door. In the play, he even does Fogg's wooing for him.

73 *Benares . . . Kasi*: or Varanasi. A sacred Hindu city on the north bank of the Ganges where worshippers bathe in the sacred waters. The city encompasses Sarnath, where Buddha preached for the first time in about 530 BC.

Vishnu . . . Shiva: Vishnu is the Pervader or Sustainer, originally a solar deity, later considered the Saviour; Shiva is the Destroyer, and the god presiding over personal destinies.

74 *often a cloud of white steam masked the details*: many of the places are only half-seen from the train or not seen at all. This is hardly surprising, since sometimes it is night or the places are twenty or thirty miles away! Often, Verne seems simply to be working in his research—and revelling in the poetry of the names.

Lord Cornwallis's Tomb: Charles (1731–1805), the general commanding the British forces in the American War of Independence, whose surrender at the Battle of Yorktown (1781) ended the hostilities. Cornwallis was also Governor-General of India (1786–93 and 1805), restoring military control and laying the administrative foundations of British rule.

Golconda: previously, Verne had referred to the diamond mines of Golconda in South Central India (the earliest in the world, sacked by Aurangzeb); here he is referring to the town in Bengal of the same name; later he mentions the P. & O. ship the *Golconda*; and there is also a station called Golconda on the line that Fogg takes through the Rockies. By using the same name for many different objects, Verne may be emphasizing the uniformity of the modern world.

76 *Judge Obadiah*: Obadiah (Hebrew 'Servant of the Lord'): an exiled prophet in the Old Testament, of strongly nationalistic tendencies. He was particularly vehement towards the inhabitants of Edom, calling down a Day of Judgement and predicting that when the Jews returned from exile they would triumph over their old enemies. (Obadiah was also the name of Tristram Shandy's servant.)

The choice of name is significant because of the rarity of biblical reference in Verne's published works. Also, the central argument of Andrew Martin's *The Mask of the Prophet* (1990) is that a bearded Old Testament foreseer of doom systematically stalks the *Extraordinary Journeys*. Although Martin's thesis is not substantiated with much direct reference, it does receive interesting support here.

But also, the original title of the short masterpiece published in 1910 under Verne's name was 'Edom' (changed by the editor, M. Ganderax, to 'The Eternal Adam'). Given the importance of this posthumous short story, the continuing controversy over its authorship, and the Old Testament underpinning of the tale, this biblical cross-reference is of interest.

76 *a courtroom*: in 1872 the Indian Evidence Act was passed, which set forth the rules of evidence admissible.

Oysterpuf: possibly derived from 'the Oyster Rooms of Haymarket' (Ch. 2) + 'puff' ('increase the price in an auction by having an accomplice make false bids'—an auction scene in 'Humbug' (published in French in 1910 and in English in 1991) refers to ' "a puff, a bluff, a humbug", as the Americans say').

81 *Sir James Jeejeebhoy*: (Verne: 'Jejeebhoy') alias Sir Jamsetjee Jeejeebhoy, alias Sir Jameshedji Jijibhai (1783–1859), a rich Parsee. He travelled to China five times, had strong Hong Kong connections, and helped defeat the French in 1804, although later captured by them. He endowed, amongst other things, bridges throughout India. His knighthood was the first bestowed on an Indian.

82 *beings placed on the lowest rung of the human scale, although it is not correct to say that they are cannibals*: possibly an allusion to the murder of the Viceroy of India in the Andaman Islands on 8 February 1872.

precious salanganes, whose edible nests: salanganes are swallows of the genus *Collocalia* which provide the material for bird's-nest soup.

87 *New Holland*: the name for Australia until 1827—again showing the age of Verne's sources.

89 *Annam and Cochin China*: formerly independent regions of Vietnam. French intervention began in 1786, and Cochin China was occupied between 1859 and 1868, to be followed by the rest of Vietnam, Cambodia, and Laos.

91 *those of Uranus, which led to the discovery of Neptune*:

Neptune was discovered in 1846 on the basis of inconsistencies in the orbit of Uranus.

'*If this was an American vessel, we might easily blow up, but at least we'd be going faster!*': in 'Humbug' Verne points out that slaves were often paid to sit on the safety valves, increasing the speed but also contributing to the huge number of explosions of American steam-vessels.

93 *whipped this disobedient sea*: Xerxes had the sea whipped with rods for swallowing up his vessels.

the barometer . . . the irresponsible instrument: this scene humorously emphasizes the subjectivity inherent in scientific measurement and the egocentricity of seekers after truth. But this instrument with a will of its own, refusing to climb despite much shaking, also has a sexual undertone.

94 *Tanka boats*: from the Cantonese, meaning 'a member of the ethnic minority traditionally living on boats in Canton and Hong Kong and often employed in maritime work'.

95 *the hotel of the Club*: (Verne: 'l'*Hôtel du Club*') probably a hotel attached to the Hong Kong Club: this Club (another one!), with its traditional British values, is the sort of place where Fogg might have been at home. The original colonnaded building was demolished in 1981.

96 *Treaty of Nanking . . . war of 1842*: the first Opium War (1839–42) was the first major military clash between China and the West. By the Treaties of Nanking (1842) and the Bogue (1843), China was forced to open the ports of Canton (Guangzhou), Amoy (Xiamen), Foochow (Fuzhou), Ningpo (Ningbo), and Shanghai to British trade and residence, and to cede Hong Kong Island in perpetuity.

the Canton River: more often known nowadays as the Pearl River.

the wind-driven wheelbarrows still in use in the Celestial Empire: these ecological wheelbarrows, with their interchange between the sea and the land, are mentioned again in Japan (ch. 22) and are also prominent in *The Tribulations of a Chinese Gentleman*; they may easily have been the inspiration for Fogg's land-yacht.

97 *flower boats*: a euphemism for floating brothels.

at this age they had the privilege of wearing yellow, the imperial colour. Passepartout found this very amusing, without quite knowing why: possibly because the skin of Chinese, as Verne himself says later, is 'yellow' already, and further yellowed by age? But the significance is undoubtedly the link between humour and the unknown workings of the mind.

106 *Bunsby . . . 'Tankadère'*: the 44-year-old Verne paints a self-portrait in the 45-year-old Bunsby, as shown by the illustration. A scene in *The Tribulations of A Chinese Gentleman* shows a '*Tankadère*' (apparently a female Tanka, but possibly also her vessel) guiding her sampan across the water while singing a love-song (ch. 7).

108 *the narcotic*: this separation of Fogg and Passepartout marks the beginning of a complex sequence. Following Passepartout's intoxication in Hong Kong, the present chapter is a flash-back to Fogg, but the next two will then continue forward with him to Shanghai. Ch. 22 will take us back to Passepartout again (and will then flashback to explain how he got on board the *Carnatic*), before carrying on as far as Japan (Ch. 23), where he will 'accidentally' bump into Fogg. Ch. 24 will then have to flashback yet again to get Fogg from Shanghai to Japan.

119 *the Bay of Edo*: generally called Tokyo Bay after 1868; Edo was the former name of Tokyo, comprising the central part of the modern city and the imperial palace.

the Taikun: (hence *tycoon*) more normally known in Japan as the Shogun: the position was abolished in 1867.

Miyako: capital of Japan from 794 to 1868, now called Kyoto.

120 *Benten, from the name of a sea goddess*: also Benzaiten ('Divinity of the Reasoning Faculty'): in Japanese mythology, one of the seven gods of luck, the Buddhist patron of literature and music, of wealth, and of femininity. Generally associated with the sea; and identified with the Indian goddess Sarasvati.

infantrymen . . . armed with percussion guns: non-Samurai soldiers had only been permitted to bear arms since 1871.

blackened teeth: this was thought to make women more attractive: it was banned during the Meiji Era (1868–1912). These pages show a detailed knowledge of Japan, plus a sophisticated use of rhythm in the narration: the long sentences not only indicate Passepartout's wanderings, but the different time conceptions of East Asia, less characterized by machine-based, capitalist urgency. The following series of short clauses, in contrast, reproduces the short steps of Japanese women.

121 *as he knew that it was a sacrilege to kill cattle, strictly reserved for agricultural tasks*: until 1868, all meat eating was technically

illegal, in accordance with Buddhist teachings; but Verne's view of the status of cattle is more appropriate for Hinduism in India. Nor is it clear how the violets Passepartout spots might constitute his 'supper', nor why he changes his mind on discovering they have no scent.

124 *Barnum*: Phineas T[aylor] Barnum (1810–91), American showman, famous for his circus, The Greatest Show on Earth (1871). Between 1841 and 1868, he ran the American Museum in New York, where thousands of curiosities, freaks, and wild animals were displayed, including the 161-year-old nurse of George Washington, a mermaid, the original Siamese twins, and the midget Tom Thumb. Barnum's name was associated with the idea of 'missing links' since he exhibited every conceivable transition between the species. Many of his exhibits were fakes, with Barnum calling himself the 'Prince of Humbugs', and claiming 'there's a sucker born every minute'. Barnum is visible throughout Verne's works. 'Humbug' is the remarkable Barnum-inspired account of a hoax that revolutionizes prehistory. In *A Floating City*, Verne's *alter ego* goes to Barnum's Theatre in New York, sardonically witnessing a real fire and 'a real steam-pump worked by real firemen. Hence a "great attraction"'. Verne is systematically critical of Barnum for his excessive publicity campaigns, his vulgarity, and his mendaciousness.

126 *Tengu*: an uncanny creature with a long beak or nose and wings, glittering eyes, and a man's body, arms, and legs: a kidnapper of Buddhist priests and children; but also a benign protector of the performing arts and practitioner of supernatural skills.

the most implausible combinations . . . set-piece sprays: Verne is commenting on his own art. Creation takes on a life of its own, even exercising free-will—as Verne's railway lines do; but also the artist is shown as a public performer requiring speed and dexterity, with his overriding concern to sustain his 'perilous' work until the crescendo. The word 'combination' is revealing: Verne used the word in a famous letter to describe his exhaustion of all sublime subjects, and his consequent need to work hard at producing interest. The word 'implausible', clearly ironic here, is used several times in the novel to justify descriptions obliquely.

127 *the most incredible performances*: this paragraph is flagrantly sexual.

the 'Juggernaut Car': Verne is probably borrowing from India an idea not normally found in Japanese culture.

129 *opium intoxication in a smoking den in Yokohama*: Verne
seems to mean 'Hong Kong' here (as in Ms2), since Passepartout
has no reason to lie and the previous paragraph also erroneously
reads 'Yokohama' for 'Shanghai'.

*At a speed of twelve knots the steamer would take at most 21
days to cross the Pacific*: it would take only seventeen days for
the 4,700 miles previously quoted (Ch. 24). On the other hand,
in 21 days 6,248 miles could be covered, or about the distance
via the Sandwich Islands: is this a sign of one of Verne's sources?

134 *the North American Continent*: America features prominently
in many of the works written by Verne at this period: *Round the
Moon* (1870), *A Floating City* (1871), *A Nephew from America*
(1873), *The Mysterious Island* (1874), and 'Humbug: The
American Way of Life' (1910).

the capital of California: the capital is in fact Sacramento, as
Verne himself says in Ch. 26.

International Hotel: the grand hotel was a nineteenth-century
phenomenon, paralleling the growth of tourism. In San
Francisco the Palace Hotel was the best establishment of the
day: has Verne perhaps changed its name?

the 'forty-niners': participants in the 1849 California gold rush,
the reason for the growth of San Francisco.

135 *the local Regent Street, Boulevard des Italiens, or Broadway
. . . served on Lilliputian plates*: *A Floating City*: 'Broadway, the
local Strand or Boulevard Montmartre . . . We were solemnly
served Lilliputian stews on doll-sized plates . . . the "bar-
room" . . . where any passer-by finds iced water, biscuits, and
Cheshire cheese, all for free.'

Enfield rifles . . . robbers: the Enfield rifle helped cause the Indian Mutiny, since loading it required biting the end off the
cartridge which was lubricated in a mixture of pigs' and cows'
fat, distasteful to both Muslims and Hindus. The reference to
the Sioux and Pawnee Indians is not anachronistic, for much of
the territory east of the Rockies had only recently been settled by
a few Whites, and Indian uprisings continued as late as 1889.

A similar danger to travellers from Indians was visible in Asia,
with the danger again theatrical in style, a mere vestige of an
original natural state. There are in fact many correspondences
between Asia and America throughout the book. Both have
rivers with what Verne calls 'sub-tributaries' (in fact 'sub-sub-
sub-tributaries') and both contain towns called Golconda as
well as Dead Seas with River Jordans flowing into them. The

flying arrows and the bullet hole in Fogg's hat in India may have been borrowed from America. The plot itself exhibits strong parallels: in each half religion is subject to a sustained ridiculing, partly by means of a bold sexual imagery; in each half Fogg rescues a close companion from Indians, thereby putting his schedule at risk; in each a railway is meant to have been completed recently, with the Indians resenting the intrusion; but in each a more natural, direct, and sociable means of transport intervenes instead. In sum, a persistent metaphor equates the East Indies and the West, in accordance with the east–west equivalence fundamental to Verne's imagination.

137 *Swirls agitated the mass, flowing back and forth*: this scene equates the crowd and the angry sea: 'swirls . . . swell . . . white horses . . . billowed . . . a sea moved by a gust of wind . . . the tide'. An identical metaphor is used for Waverley Station in *Backwards to Britain*.

But the scene may also be derived from Wey's description of a set of four paintings by Hogarth, for they are presented as 'depicting the phases of an election' in terms of the 'battle between two rival candidates, the animation of their supporters . . . the speeches in the open air, the fisticuffs, and the hoorays'.

138 *Colonel Stamp W. Proctor*: Proctor is a stop on the Pacific Line west of the Great Salt Lake; a Richard Anthony Proctor (1837–88) published widely on popular science, including space and time, and became the honorary secretary of the Royal Astronomical Society in 1872.

140 *A locomotive, running on the rails of the day before, brought the rails for the following day, and moved forward on them as they were laid down*: this description and the concept itself are slightly convoluted, in accordance with the hyper-Vernian idea of a means of transport feeding on itself, raising the question of how long the process can be sustained.

141 *two undercarriages . . . carriages*: in 1872 bogeys were in use on American trains, but not on French ones. *There are no compartments inside . . . restaurant carriages, and bar carriages*: A Floating City: 'long carriages, resting at each end on a pivoting system with four wheels. The carriages are connected by gangways allowing the passengers to move from one end of the train to the other . . . [One can] buy newspapers and books . . . [There are] mobile bars and libraries.'

142 *Junction*: no trace of this station appears on modern maps. Verne is possibly making a similar joke to *BB*, ch. 18, where he

thinks he has arrived at a station called 'Ladies' Rooms', a joke itself apparently derived from Wey's Parisian asking a London cabman to go to 'Commit No Nuisance'.

145 *'Joe Smith . . . Young'*: Joseph Smith (Verne: 'Smyth'; 1805–44), founder of the Mormons. Hyrum Smith was killed by a mob at Carthage at the same time as his brother. Brigham Young (1801–77), the second president of the Mormons and the first governor of Utah, was arrested for polygamy by Federal troops on 2 October 1871. The idea of being able to found an independent territory is anachronistic in 1872—but anticipates Verne's *The Begum's Fortune* (1879), where two independent states are established in the Far West.

146 *'Abraham and other renowned Egyptians'*: Abraham was Hebrew: has Verne put a deliberate mistake in the elder's mouth?

147 *looking him straight in the eyes, hypnotizing him with his words*: words drawn from psychic phenomena, such as 'hypnotize', 'mesmerize', and 'magnetize', occur throughout the book.

   In addition to a possible influence by Poe's 'Facts in the Case of Monsieur Valdemar', which Verne's 1864 essay summarizes as a 'tale where death is suspended in a dying man by the use of magnetic sleep', one connection may be Jean-Martin Charcot (1825–93), cited by Verne in 1885. Charcot became famous for his attempt to use hypnotism to find an organic cause for hysteria, especially by employing magnets and studying traumatic events forgotten by the patients themselves. His *Lectures on the Diseases of the Nervous System* were published in 1872. One of his disciples was Pierre Janet (1859–1947), who developed the medical idea of the unconscious. Another was Sigmund Freud himself in 1885–6, his first contact with psychological theorizing; when Freud returned to Vienna after his studies in Paris, he began by using hypnosis to help neurotics recall disturbing events.

148 *Asphaltic Lake*: an old-fashioned name for the Dead Sea.

149 *To his good sense . . . that place of every delight*: this attack on organized religion forms a neat counterpoint to that of the first half of the book. Verne omits to say that polygamy was in reality only practised by a small minority of Mormons. He also avoids the official title, the Church of Jesus Christ of Latter-Day Saints, and indeed any mention of 'Christ' or 'Christian'; but his clear

target is traditional religious thinking, in particular the concept of eternity, the question of who is elected to heaven, and what goes on there (including sex). The assault is here combined with an attack on women, or at least marriage (Mormon women had been given the vote in 1870).

150 *a tunnel 14,000 feet long was bored, but it is the only one on the whole route*: Verne may possibly mean '1,400 feet' here.

MS1 stops at approximately this point, replaced by lists of points summarizing each chapter, although there are brief continuous passages for Chs. 34 and 35 (Chs. 35–7 in the published version).

156 *Some of the passengers, however, had immediately been won over by the suggestion*: this scene is announced in a semi-ironical passage in *Backwards to Britain* (ch. 18): 'The British and the Americans are the greatest mechanics on Earth; they retreat before no obstacle, and ideas enter their minds at the same time as the machinery necessary to implement them . . . they are capable of anything.'

158 *Evans Pass . . . the highest point on its route: 8,091 feet above sea level*: Thomas Cook also notes this mountain spur as the highest point reached, but calls it 'Sherman' (the name of a nearby settlement) and records it as 8,242 feet.

Julesberg, on the South Platte river: an example of Verne's self-reference.

General J. M. Dodge: G[renville] M[ellen] Dodge (1831–1916), 'chief engineer', was author of *Union Pacific Railroad* (New York, 1867), a report on lines across the Rocky Mountains.

159 *Mr Thomas C. Durant*: Thomas Clark Durant (1820–85): responsible for building the Union Pacific Railroad and organizing the Crédit mobilier of America to finance it (1864). On 4 September 1872, the Crédit mobilier was involved in a major corruption scandal. Perhaps also quoted because Durant's name is the epitome of Frenchness?

A remarkable omission in this book written for a French audience is the history of the United States, more than half of which had belonged to France only 57 years previously. Whereas French Chandernagore and Indochina receive passing mentions, such clearly French names as Platte, Missouri, Mississippi, Chicago, Fremont, Des Moines, Illinois, Nauvoo-la-Belle, and Michigan are passed over in silence. Also, the most important cities in the Midwest, St Louis and New Orleans, both largely French-speaking at this period, are not even mentioned.

159 *the first number of the 'Railway Pioneer'*: this journal is recorded in the National Union Catalog as published once only ('Platte City', Nebraska, 25 October 1866), to commemorate the 'formal opening of the Union Pacific Railroad—so far as finished'. In fact, and despite Verne's claim that it was 23 October 1867, the connection was made with the famous golden spike ceremony of 10 May 1869 at Promontory Point, north of Ogden (and the first transcontinental train reached the West Coast only on 6 September 1869). What is more, there was no bridge across the Missouri until 1872, with passengers having to ferry across at Council Bluffs.

Amphion's Lyre: Amphion built the wall around Thebes by using his lyre to charm the stones into place.

The previous sentences are the strongest praise of technology in the book, with Verne offering no apology for the destruction of the Indians' homeland. Nevertheless, some irony is attached to the futility of building railways to serve non-existent towns. In Ch. 33 there is a similar ambivalence in 'those steamers—real steel rockets, nothing but machine—which, not bothering to rise for the waves, invariably cut through them'. Elsewhere in the book, there *is* considerable criticism of technology, such as Proctor's absurd idea of using rigid trains to cross rivers. And in *The Steam House*, the completed railway from Bombay to Allahabad is apostrophized in the following terms: ' "Go! Go and tell the Viceroy of India that Nana Sahib is still alive, and that he will drown this railway, the accursed work of the invaders, in their own blood!" '

166 *Phileas Fogg was a hero*: the technique of this scene is remarkable. Faced with the threefold separation of the characters, the narrator chooses to focus on Fix and Aouda and their anxious waiting. Part of the reason may be to disguise the implausibility of Fogg being able to catch up with mounted Indians. But in any case, both threads will subsequently have to be caught up with very quickly, and welded together, before the main narration can continue.

167 *The party's tracks were still printed on the snow. But soon the imprints were erased under a new sheet*: Verne uses black-on-white imagery ('printed', 'imprints', 'erased', 'sheet') to create a text-within-the-text, simulating his multiple drafts.

172 *Mudge*: name borrowed from Thomas Mudge (1717–94), a British watchmaker who invented the lever escapement (1765) to regulate the movement of the spring-driven watch.

173 *as the bee flies—as the Americans say*: no trace of this expression has been found—it must be based on the expression 'to make a bee-line for', a phrase from 'The Gold-Bug' (1843) that Verne (mis)quotes ('a be line') in his essay on Poe. Ch. 10 of MS2 reads 'as the ~~bee~~ crow flies'.

175 *While each of the travellers . . . the whole howling pack was left behind*: the poetic effect of this passage is due to the Romantic imagery of desolation and the dead–alive duality of the living skeleton and the dying wolves. But the power also comes from the presentation of space and time. Succession and progression are emphasized, in accordance with what has undoubtedly become a general tendency in the Realist adventure novel. At the same time, the protagonists' purposeful movements contrast with an empty space, a 'deserted' 'uniform whiteness'. Because of the iterative verbs used, time seems to be hardly moving at all and, as in the best Romantic tradition, appears ethereal, non-spatial, or drugged. The impression of great urgency in slow motion comes, then, from the combination of dense events with an overall lack of movement through a desolate landscape.

176 *Chicago, already arisen from its ruins*: a fire began on 8 October 1871, destroying a third of the city.

towns with ancient names, some with streets and trams but no houses built in them as yet: *A Floating City*: 'new towns with broad streets covered with tram-lines, cities adorned with the most poetic names of ancient history'—Verne then comments that this area was the setting for *The Last of the Mohicans*, but now forms a 'civilized area', a sad thought.

White Star Line: the popular name of the Oceanic Steam Navigation Company, which took over the Aberdeen White Star Line in 1867. The SS *Oceanic* sailed for this company on her maiden voyage in 1871, making all other Atlantic lines obsolete, according to one historian.

177 *the 'Pereire' of the French Transatlantic Company*: Jacob Pereire (1800–75) was a French Jewish businessman, *député*, speculator, and director of the French Transatlantic Company. The name can be analysed as 'Père-ire' ('father-anger').

178 '*And I am Andrew Speedy of Cardiff*': there was a historic Captain (Tristram Charles Sawyer) Speedy (1836–1910), recorded in John Michael Gullick, *Captain Speedy of Carut* (Singapore: Malayan Branch of the Royal Asiatic Society, 1953).

Speedy is both 'from Cardiff' and 'American'—but this Cardiff is a formerly existing tiny hamlet near Albany, New York State. It is therefore a discreet reference to a farmer's discovery in Cardiff in 1869 of a stone giant 10 feet 4½ inches tall, to Barnum's offer of $10,000 for it, the farmer's refusal, Barnum's making of a copy of it, the subsequent demonstration that it was a fraud after all, and to Verne's reworking of the story in 'Humbug' (1910).

180 '*Four*': much humour is visible in the interchanges between Speedy and Fogg, especially their attitudes, metaphors, and speech habits. Presented under a simultaneously mechanical and animal metaphor ('sea-dog', 'a complexion of oxidized copper', 'a bomb'), Speedy himself equates passengers and freight, ship's hold and human belly. He often repeats Fogg's phrase, and speaks almost entirely without verbs. Within the scene, each interlocutor alters position several times. The humour essentially comes, then, from the two conflicting solipsisms.

180 *eastwards*: the notes summarizing this chapter in MS1 include '71st day 12 [Dec.] loxodromy'. A loxodromy is 'the curve followed by a ship when it cuts each successive meridian at the same angle', in other words a straight-line course on a map projection—similar to Fogg's habit of taking the 'shortest path'.

181 *It was Phileas Fogg, Esq.*: the themes of mutiny and the self-consuming of the vessel are central to *The Chancellor* (completed 1871, published 1874), albeit in more tragic mode.

182 *all intimacy had been lost between the two friends*: this paragraph is full of homosexual language.

187 *Queenstown . . . thus beating the fastest ships of the ocean-going companies by twelve hours*: *A Floating City*: 'Queen's-Town . . . where all the ships from America . . . drop off their important mailbags on the way past. An express, waiting with steam up, takes them to Dublin in a few hours. There, a steamer . . . takes the letters . . . to Liverpool . . . gain[ing] a day on the fastest liners.'

189 *as soon as he set foot on the soil of the United Kingdom*: at this time Ireland was part of the UK. Earlier, the narrator had asked three times why Fix didn't arrest Fogg in Ireland (Ch. 33)—but neglected to provide an answer!

motionless, sitting on a wooden bench, not angry, imperturb-
able. Whether he was resigned was impossible to say, but this
last blow hadn't been able to disturb him, at least not visibly:
MS2: 'on a wooden bench, ~~not at all impassioned~~, not angry,
cold, ~~indifferent, impassive~~, imperturbable' (the words 'at
least not visibly' are omitted). This paragraph, where Fogg has
thrown away most of his money and illusions, seems different
from the rest of the book, and may derive from Fabrice's final
encloisterment in *The Charterhouse of Parma*, 'sitting on a
wooden bench, far from all luxury, disillusioned with all luxury,
and having no serious self-reproach to make'. Verne wrote in a
letter that he reread *The Charterhouse* 'every year'.

Other parallels with Stendhal in *Around the World* include:
the sprinkling of 'etc.'; the scathing analysis of American crowd
behaviour and democracy; the ironic comment about Fogg man-
aging quite well with no books in his house; and the obsession
with figures. In *Backwards to Britain* (ch. 38), Verne quotes
Stendhal's exact measurements for St Peter's in Rome and other
monuments; and Stendhal is apparently his main source of
information about St Paul's in London.

190 *His brow wrinkled slightly*: the rest of this scene is also remarkable: Fogg is fully alone for the first time since meeting
Passepartout; both the watch-hands and Fogg's circular
perambulation point back to the chronometric circling of the
opening chapter; and we observe Fogg's consciousness via exter-
nally visible signs for the first time in the novel. The scene is also
notable for the Vernian topos of self-referential diary-writing,
here reduced to the pathologically laconic entry of recording the
date and time. Coming up to date in this way indicates both an
unusual self-scrutiny by the character and a narratorial crisis-
point (what can be narrated next?), which is invariably resolved
by dramatic outside intervention.

The extra 'depth' of the final chapters may come from a
central consciousness providing unity to the novel, in contrast
with the previously theatrical-style actions and words.

'Thief arrested three days . . . you . . . free!': (MS2 adds '~~thief~~
~~hanged~~') in contrast with his normally florid delivery, Fix here
employs telegraphic style, taking Fogg's ellipticality a degree
further and anticipating Passepartout's breathless revelation.

191 *the house*: MS1: '34 | | —xxx xxx xx | —*Saturday* 21st, 10
o'clock | —10.35 p.m. | —past | —xx xxxxxxx the passers-by |
in the street show xx | —xxxxx | —not allowed to go out | —not
at the Club |' [a line is here drawn across the whole column,

followed by '34', starting the chapter again:] 'The following day the inhabitants of Saville Row [eight words illegible] | —xxxxx of the first closed the mezzanine | but without xxx | —goes to the Club | —it is well-known to what the British | —monoman | —recourse | —Jean and burner | —Fogg at home | —keep an eye on | —Jean and Aouda | —chat | | —doesn't go out | —not Club | —sum at disposition | —xxxxxx xxxxx | —get it over with | | — | —at about 8 | —Fogg Aouda | —xx xxxxxx | —at your disposition | —xxxxx his income | —but you | —me nothing | [seven lines illegible except:] but . . . where . . . you | | | | —do you want me | —you | —you lov me | —yes | | —a Saturday evening | —come to a husband | | —Jean | —teacher | —[five lines] | —female inspirer and friend | —church | —(do) you have the resources | —make a start | —for tomorrow | —no tomorrow Sunday | —for Monday then | | | —exit cab | —at 9.30 | —Fogg Aouda | —consequences | —I love you | —I love you too | —Fix appears | —Jean | − 10.20 | —noise | —[he] cannot speak | —where | —today | —xxx xxx | —more | —today Friday | —but | —and not Monday | —a day out | —a day | —oh! by xxxx | —xxxx | − 10 minutes left | —a cab | —at a day'.

A number of points deserve comment. It is not clear what Fix is doing in this scene (his name is written in larger letters). The 'get it over with' is a stronger indication of Fogg's idea of suicide than in the published version—Hetzel generally insisted on cutting any mention of this subject. The 'do you want me | —you | —you lov me | —yes' is a fascinating insight into Verne's attempt to write a love scene: in 1863 he wrote to Hetzel: 'I am very bad at expressing tender sentiments. The very word "love" frightens me.' An interesting point is that originally a Sunday intervened, putting off the marriage by a further day: another example of a 'fantom day' creeping in everywhere, perhaps due to the influence of Poe's 'Three Sundays in a Week'. In this early draft, the whole structure of the 'false flashback' (see Introduction) does not occur, for the proposal leads directly to the discovery of the day gained.

MS2: 'The following day, the inhabitants of Saville Row were able to observe that the windows in the mezzanine floor of the house bearing the number 7 [superimposed on '4'] were half-open. On the ground floor, they were all closed. A few wise heads deduced from this that Mr Fogg had returned home again, and this was in fact correct. People could also see ~~Jean~~ Passepartout coming and going, with a sad countenance, a desperate expression.'

temp

192 *Only in the evening would he ask Mrs Aouda to be so good as to speak with him for a moment*: this paragraph is unique in clearly reporting Fogg in free indirect style.

193 *'I blame nobody'*: MS2: ' "I blame nobody but myself" '.

For the first time: MS2: 'Passepartout, having run his errands in the morning, did not go out again, and for the first time'.

the tower in Westminster: MS2: 'the Church of St Stephen's'.

195 *'the future ahead of you?'* | *'As it is fitting to do'*: MS2: ' "~~your wretched situation?~~" ' | ' "Oh, ~~wretched!~~" said Fogg.'

almost trembling. . . . Then he opened them again: MS2: 'almost trembling. Mrs Aouda was looking at him with ~~her beautiful eyes, limpid, all the Indian gentleness~~ xxxx xxxx xx. ~~He went up to the young woman, and looked at her for a long time, a very long time.~~'

the Revd Samuel Wilson: Verne's sly humour gives a Briton the name of the man who has often been argued to be the original Uncle Sam: Samuel Wilson (1766–1854), of Troy, New York, an army supplies inspector during the War of 1812 against Britain. In the 1870s the cartoonist Thomas Nast drew the figure associated with Uncle Sam today, whom Proctor resembles when he calls Fogg a 'son of John Bull' (illustration in Ch. 29).

196 *Edinburgh on 17 December*: this six-paragraph flashback opening Ch. 36 was added in the margin of MS2. Like the insertion of Ch. 5, it describes changes in public opinion—thus again anticipating the real public's reaction (although it may have been added after serialization had begun).

By having the thief arrested in Edinburgh instead of the exotic New World or the East, Verne is referring forward to *The Black Indies*, his first Scottish novel (1877). The metaphor equating the East and the West Indies is thus extended to 'the Black Indies', as Verne calls the Scottish coal-mines.

197 *for nine hours*: although 'depuis neuf heures' could also mean 'since nine o'clock', neither interpretation makes sense. Like the '24 hours' remaining at 10 p.m. off Queenstown, and Passepartout's visit to the Revd Wilson, 'about 25 hours after the travellers had arrived in London' (MS2: '24 hours'), this is a remnant from the earlier draft, when Fogg was due in at 10.35. On the other hand, the inconsistency in Passepartout's departure from the Reverend's house ten minutes before the deadline, taking 'three minutes', but then telling Fogg there are 'ten minutes left', is shared by both MS2 and the published version.

198 *'Shipping Gazette'*: the *Shipping Gazette & Lloyd's List Weekly Summary*, London, 1856–1909.

199 *Phileas Fogg in person*: MS1: '35 | —Club | —Reform | —members | —assembled | —[they] chat | —the clock | —he's lost | —last train | —~~noise~~ | —clock strikes | —the xxxxx | —31 [i.e. 8.31] | —32 | —33 | —34 | —noise | —35 | —door op. | —Fogg cold | —here I am, xxxxx | | —arrive(d) | —run over 2 dogs | —knock down 3 people | —three[?] minutes | —won! | —and xxxxxxx expla. | —And £ = | | | —what remains 1000' | —shared with Jean | —and Fix | | —what was the point | | —wife | —the happiest of men'.

The slightly cold-hearted 'knock down 3 people' (MS2: 'ten people') disappears in the published version.

200 *Passepartout*: MS2: 'Passepartout, throwing himself to his knees'.

it was in fact Friday, 20 December, only 79 days after his departure: (MS2 adds: '~~Had he got the day wrong then? Had he arrived on time? Had he, without realizing it, beaten the agreed deadline by 24 hours? And these 24 hours, had he wasted them at home, ten minutes away from the Reform Club?~~') For Fogg not to have realized what day it was, he cannot have read the newspapers since the Pacific. Hetzel in fact reminded Verne of the existence of Fogg's clock (Ch. 1). Verne wrote back admitting that 'since the clock marks the days, he would easily see that he has gained *a day*'; but pointing out that in fact 'he finds his clock stopped'.

Hetzel also tried to impose an idea of his young son's: 'Jules has had a very good idea for the ending of the *Journey Around the World* [*sic*]. . . . The gamblers will be on the look-out . . . it should be they who go and winkle Fogg out, invading his house when he returns . . . It seems to me that this [brainwave] must be used even for the serial. Think about it for an hour, and tell me which parts of the text I need to send back so that you can incorporate it.' Verne replied: '[the idea] destroys my whole ending. . . . All the emotion *you write about* exists *on his return*, during the three days before his return, for, do not forget, following my changes [presumably the addition to Ch. 36 indicated above, plus the insertion of Ch. 5], the whole of Britain makes the same mistake as Fix . . . It is at the Club that Fogg's unexpected arrival produces its full effect.'

201 *Here is the reason for the mistake.* | *. . . the day gained unconsciously*: MS1: '—And the cause of the mistake is as follows. | —

Ph Fogg had xxxxxx from east to west [*sic*], heading for the sun, and consequently reduced the days by 4 ~~degrees fo~~ minutes each time he xxxed a line in this direction. Once the trip around the world was finished, he had gained 360 times 4 minutes, or 24 hours. xxxxx xxxxx xxxxxx xxxxx. Whilst Ph Fogg saw the sun pass the meridian 81 times, his adversaries saw it pass only 80 times. Hence xxxxxx this day.'

The passage is revealing. In addition to the mixing up of east and west, Verne uses 'meridian' in the sense of 'zenith'; the words crossed out also show that there is a close connection in his mind between minutes of time and minutes of degrees; and a 'fantom day' emerges yet again, in the idea of Fogg's *81* days. Verne's original idea may have been for Fogg's journey to really take 80 days—thus making the title of the book accurate!

'now you're rich . . .': MS1: 'Aouda, Jean, and Inspector Fix, whom he was incapable of holding a grudge against [eight words]. | —Do you want me | —xxxx | —It is I who xxx xxx | —Aouda quivered briefly | Had I lost'. These lines lead directly to the draft of the passage closing the book.

'Dear Aouda': MS2: 'Dear madam' ('Chère mistress').

202 *'Mrs Aouda . . . wouldn't have been my wife, and . . .'* | *And Mr Fogg quietly shut the door*: although Fogg and Aouda had spent the night together on the *Tankadère*, with Passepartout conveniently out of the way and the crew waiting up all night (Ch. 21), this scene seems unique in the *Extraordinary Journeys* in hinting at the joys of the bedroom. Curiously, the name 'Mrs Aouda' has not here been replaced by the more logical 'Mrs Fogg'.

who—however unlikely it may seem—made him the happiest of men!: MS2: '—however unlikely ~~that is~~'.

MS1: 'And now why this journey. What was the point xxxxx xxxxxx of his journey xxx What had this gentleman brought back? xxxxx xxxxx, xxxxxx xxxxx, he had brought back a lovely wife who made him the happiest of men.'

Another draft of this passage, also in continuous prose, appears immediately after the 'Had I lost' section quoted above, but the legible parts do not differ from the lines just transcribed.

A remarkable feature of all the versions of this passage, from the original notes and these three drafts to the published book, is the consistency of the underlying message: that 'the point' of it all was 'wife' and becoming 'the happiest of men'.

A SELECTION OF OXFORD WORLD'S CLASSICS

The Oxford World's Classics Website

www.worldsclassics.co.uk

- Information about new titles
- Explore the full range of Oxford World's Classics
- Links to other literary sites and the main OUP webpage
- Imaginative competitions, with bookish prizes
- Peruse *Compass*, the Oxford World's Classics magazine
- Articles by editors
- Extracts from Introductions
- A forum for discussion and feedback on the series
- Special information for teachers and lecturers

www.worldsclassics.co.uk

American Literature

British and Irish Literature

Children's Literature

Classics and Ancient Literature

Colonial Literature

Eastern Literature

European Literature

History

Medieval Literature

Oxford English Drama

Poetry

Philosophy

Politics

Religion

The Oxford Shakespeare